THE SHROUDED GENTLEMAN

K. Dalton Barrett

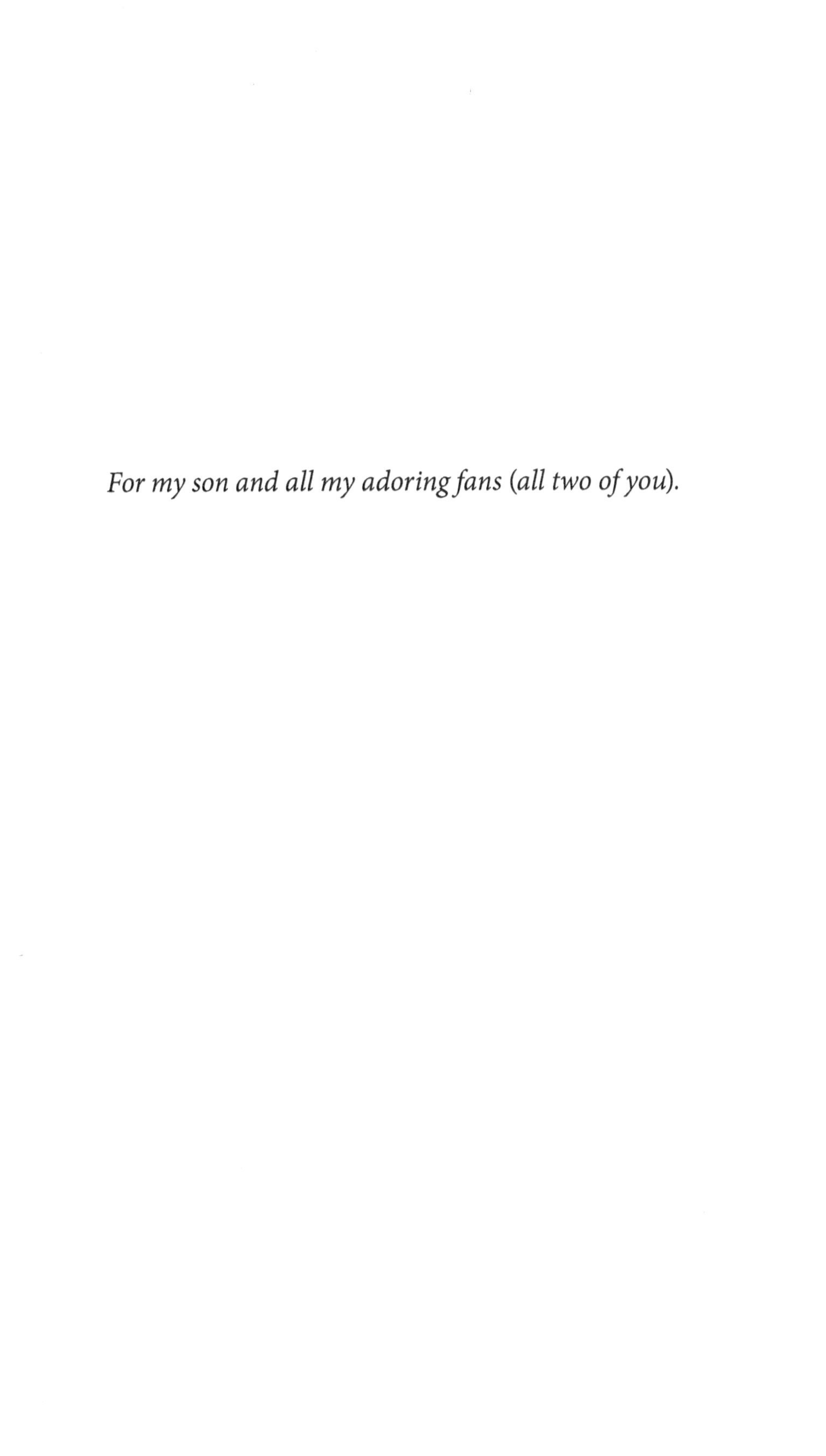

For my son and all my adoring fans (all two of you).

ACKNOWLEDGMENTS

I WOULD LIKE TO EXPRESS MY undying gratitude to my writers' group, namely Gary Devore, Piper Tallis, Josh Bresslin, Ian Rogers, and Nick Lydon, whose feedback was vital in shaping this book. Also, to Ian Rogers, who provided further crucial developmental edits. In addition, I'd like to give heartfelt thanks to my beta readers, Elaine Isaak and Rob Greene for their thoughtful insights. Many thanks also to Andrew Pinard for early feedback and his phenomenal typesetting and patience.

PART THE FIRST
OF CONFESSIONS AND FICTIONS

CHAPTER ONE

ARRESTED

I, Dr. William Johnson, state unequivocally that the deaths for which I am responsible were not those of the bodies in my basement shop, nor those buried in my garden. The papers treated the incident as if it were a lurid penny blood come to life. But there were only nine cadavers. Not "the population of a small hamlet."

The reason I came to be living in a nefarious part of London with nine cadavers in my basement (and three in the garden) was because the man who had been delivering them to me, a Mr. Keat, betrayed me.

Just prior to being kicked out of medical school due to lack of funds, I made contact with Mr. Keat, one of the men who supplied cadavers to the school. Mr. Keat agreed to provide cadavers to me personally, but at a price that should have given me pause. Particularly when I later discovered it was only for the first cadaver, not a retainer for ongoing services. I had exhausted the majority of my funds to buy the house and live frugally for a time.

Mr. Keat, wiry and wily as he was, sensed my eagerness and took advantage of it. For each body delivered, I handed him, without question, the amount in bills as agreed upon. Thus, the bodies kept coming in my basement door while the money kept going out.

One night, I was deep in the chest of a man whose death had been attributed to simply, "old age". But what, on that day, had caused the extinction of life? This, truly, was the reason for my being in that place, in that situation: My fascination – some would say obsession – with death. This fascination began on my eighth birthday when I learned I had had a twin brother. He had died in infancy, taken by the same bout of cholera which I survived. The "why" of our different fates, as well as my dead brother himself, guided the course of my life ever after. It led me to be disowned by my father, expelled from medical school, and to be in a dilapidated basement, on a cloudless January night, lifting the heart from a splayed-open chest of a possibly-illegally-obtained cadaver.

There came a knock. Startled, I dropped the organ back into the chest cavity. Another knock, louder this time. I hastily wiped my hands on my rubber apron then picked up a lantern. It rattled and squeaked in my trembling hands.

9

The next knock shook the door. "Coming," I called and pulled it open.

Keat glowered at me. He raised his hand to shield his eyes from my lantern, held high. He was among those few men who are shorter than me.

"Got more bodies for ya," he grumbled.

Indeed, behind him, his two henchmen clambered out of the back of their ramshackle hearse. Lanterns swayed and the horse whinnied. The bright full moon seemed to look down on the scene, enjoying it even. Aghast, I thoughtlessly ran out to the hearse. There were three sheet-covered bodies stacked one on the other. I whirled around to see if any neighbors observed us. On one side stood the remains of a house gutted by fire. Still, there was often activity there. Whether their drug-induced states would be lethargic or manic was impossible to tell. On the other side was a house only marginally better than the charred hulk. There was shouting there, lanterns moving. The crack of a pistol startled us all. Stillness and silence were quickly followed by more shouting.

"Better hurry," said Keat with a chilling grin.

"Fine, fine," I relented. "Bring them in, but quietly and *douse those lanterns.*"

A nod from Keat and the work began. I propped the door open and, from a bench against one wall, moved the basin containing the old man's lungs. "You can put one there." I lit candles and lanterns as they worked. "You will have to put the second one on the floor since, as I have previously pointed out, you have brought me too many cadavers."

Keat scanned the room while his henchmen carried out their task. Work had not even begun on the most recent deposits and if not for my generous application of charcoal, the smell would have been unbearable. And yet it was insufficient to mask the sweat and grime of the three men.

"Where's the other bodies?" Keat asked, apparently having kept count of his deliveries. His grey, tattered coat hung like a clergyman's robe.

"Disposed of after my work was done." In my garden, to be precise.

"Didn't see no sign of graves out there."

"No, of course not."

Keat nodded. He rubbed his stubbled chin with dirty, gnarled fingers. He seemed impressed. With a toss of his head, the henchmen returned to the hearse. Keat stuck his hand out for payment.

How could I tell this man I had no money to give him? I rightfully assumed that he would not take such news well. Then a realization came to me. "Where are the medical records?" Had he forgotten a vital piece of the arrangement? Could I use this to avoid payment?

"Didn't have none."

"How is that possible? From what hospital did you – ?"

The cadaver on the bench was wrapped in rough white cloth and there was quite a bit of blood around the part covering the head and neck. Against Keat's protestations, I pulled an edge of the sheet out from under the corpse only to find a young man, barely out of his teens. His throat had been slashed.

"Is this a murder victim?" I demanded.

"You wanted bodies. Ya got bodies."

I stammered as I pushed aside the growing realization of just the sort of man with whom I had been dealing. "I told you I only wanted cadavers from *hospitals*. With *records*. This does me no good."

"I don't remember that. I'll try to remember for next time. Pay up."

The panic of having a murder victim in my basement caused me to tremble and sweat. "There will be no next time. I no longer require your services." I faced Keat, but could not meet his eyes, lest he see the fear that I would be his next victim, making a lie of my bravado.

"Fine. Whatever. Pay for these and we'll go."

With a deep breath to steel myself, I said, "I have no more bills to give you. You have drained me." Over his reaction I said, "I can give you a cheque." I moved towards the stairs.

"A what?"

"A *cheque*. Drawn on a bank. They will honour it." I sincerely believed they would. "I have one upstairs."

I set a foot on the first step, hoping to make an escape, but Keat grabbed my arm and spun me to face him.

His breath was fetid. "I don't want no goddamn *cheque*."

"That is all I can offer."

His eyes, blue and bloodshot, bore into mine. I expected to feel a blade cut me at any moment. Then a change came over him and he stepped back. "How about services?"

"Pardon?"

He gestured around the room. "You know how to get rid of bodies, yeah?"

"I will provide no such 'services' to you, my good man. You will take my cheque, you will leave, and you will not return." I hoped that my trembling would not diminish my attempt to sound resolute.

Keat considered me for a moment. Was I about to become one more cadaver? He raised himself up on his toes, jabbed a finger in my chest and said, "You're gonna pay." Then he strode out, ignoring my continued offers of a cheque and even of doubling the usual fee.

In the morning I understood what he meant.

⊰⊱⊰⊱

Another clarification regarding the published descriptions: I was not singing when they came to arrest me, nor was I holding a human brain aloft. Perhaps I was whistling. But that was no different than a carpenter or dressmaker caught up in their work. As for the brain, they are notoriously difficult to handle, thus I was using both hands to raise it closer to the light of a gas lamp. When the constables burst through my door, I jumped, and the brain flew from my hands. It landed at the lead constable's feet. His insistence in the reports and inquest that I threw it at him I believe stemmed from his wish to hide that he screamed in a high-pitched voice.

In addition to dropping – not throwing – the brain, I knocked over an oil lamp, which is how the fire started. It spread quickly, catching on paper, cloth and the home's dry old wood. A bottle of ether burst. My panic as well as that of the constables knocked over more lamps and soon the place was a roaring blaze.

The bobbies were crowded by the basement door. I, on the other side of the flames, had no other route of egress except to run up the stairs and make haste out the front door. If I had truly intended to escape their clutches, I would not have stopped to catch my breath, allowing them to tackle me to the ground.

It was in this state – dirty, bruised by cudgels and still smelling of smoke – that I appeared before the magistrate. Giving my real name would have ended the inquest. Though my father had disowned me, I knew he would not allow the family name to be tarnished in such a way. Had I spoken my true name aloud, Father would have been contacted, and though he would have kept his promise of never speaking to me again, I would have been whisked away to preserve the family name. There would have been some sort of penance to pay, perhaps a financially astute marriage, but I would not have suffered the indignity of a gaol cell.

I preferred to accept the consequences of my actions, having made these choices of my own free will. I was innocent of murder. The most cursory of investigations would prove that.

If only there had been an investigation. The magistrate listened to the constable's account of events with increasing horror and revulsion. One lone reporter scribbled frantically. This is where the exaggeration of my situation began.

The magistrate took a long moment to study me, his fingers drumming like a death march. "I see no reason to waste any more of the court's time. Dr. William Johnson, you have no use to those of us who wish to live in peace. You shall hang by the neck until dead, two days hence, on the eighteenth day of January in the Year of Our Lord 1884. In the interim, you are to be remanded to Newgate Prison."

"No! Wait!" I cried, then the constable rapped me in the mouth with his cudgel. Blood dribbled through my fingers as I cradled my mouth in my hands. I tried to tell them my real name. It would bring me shame to have to beg my father to save me, but I would be alive to bear it.

"You have already admitted your crime," declared the magistrate. "Constable, take him away."

Being hauled away to Newgate Prison to await execution gave me adequate time to ponder my situation and how I came to be in it.

CHAPTER TWO

MY CHOSEN PATH

To say, "My dead brother told me to," while accurate to a certain degree, does not fully explain my situation.

It was on my eighth birthday that I first learned of my dead twin brother's existence. That year was the closest my father ever came to attending. All other years, as was common for him, he was away on business. But this year a broken carriage axle held him prisoner.

Mother was ever cheerful on that day. Father, distant and glum. He remained on the periphery despite Mother's efforts to pull him closer, leaving him to orbit the proceedings as he drank. The guests' awkwardness at trying to find a balance between revelry and comportment was palpable even to a child. Still, songs were sung, games were played, cake eaten and presents opened. My favorite among them came from Mother. A wooden, toy soldier with a uniform that matched the portrait of Father in the grand foyer. I leapt to my feet and raised it above my head to show him. However, Father had retreated to his study.

I thanked Mother profusely, my innocence masking that, almost certainly, she had merely given word to someone on her staff to produce the thing. But, it is, as they say, the thought that counts.

After the party, while Mother was directing the staff as they cleaned up, I bravely ventured to the east wing, where sat my father's study. Surprisingly, the door was open. Townsend, the steward, a stoic, though formidable, guard dog, stood in the door, receiving orders. I scurried under his legs, right up to Father's desk.

"Look, Father! It's you!" I held it upright before him.

Townsend put his hands on me.

"Let him be," said Father. "I'll deal with him. And with *you* later."

"Sir." Townsend exited silently.

"See, Father? He looks just like you!"

He snatched it from my hands and walked unsteadily to the fireplace. "Come here."

I obeyed. The fire, while normally welcoming, seemed entirely too hot.

Father handed the toy soldier back to me. "Throw it in," he said. The smell of whiskey washed over me.

I stammered objections. He took my ear in his dry, abrasive fingers and turned me to face the fire. The toy flew from my hands. The wool uniform whooshed into flames.

"Watch it burn," he said. He held me steady. "No crying."

My eyes and nose stung from the acrid smoke. I sniffed and he tightened his grip.

"You didn't cry over your brother, did you? Just lay there on top of him."

"My ... brother?"

"Go cry to your mother." He dragged me to the door and propelled me into Townsend's legs. "Put him to bed." He slammed the study door shut.

Crushed by my father's outright rejection, I fell to the floor and wept. The revelation of my brother meant nothing to me, yet. Townsend carried me back to my room and brought me a foul-tasting tincture for sleep.

It was days before I could whisper the question to Mother. When I did, she fainted as if felled by a woodsman's axe. She lay unmoving on the floor. No breath would come to me to call for help, but staff was never far away. They swarmed in and swept her off.

Later, the head housekeeper brought a box to my room, set it on my bed, and left. Inside were two birth certificates, mine and my brother's. His name had been Michael. With the certificate was an engraving of the two of us, with our chubby-faced smiles and fat fingers. Next I found two sets of doctor's notes describing our disease and treatments. Most of the words were unintelligible to me, but the one that stood out was "cholera". Beneath it, a daguerreotype, laying on its face. On the back, in Mother's perfect script, "William and Michael. 26 March 1859."

I turned it over. It showed two babies. One was surrounded by flowers. Its face was slack, its head dipped. The other wore a grin. At the bottom of the box, a death certificate for Michael. Two days before the photo.

A cry burst from me, and I threw it all to the floor. The head housekeeper rushed in and gathered it up. I stopped her before she left and asked for the engraving. At least in that, we were both alive.

I spent many hours staring at that engraving. It remained ever near my bed, and I looked at it every night before sleep, then again each morning. What would it have been like to have a brother? The games we would have played, the adventures we would have had. How we would talk after Father's outbursts. No one in the household spoke of him and I did not ask. Michael was mine now.

One morning I held the picture close and whispered, "Good morning, Michael."

"*Good morning, William,*" came a voice in my head.

A gasping laugh burst from me, as when the subject of hide-and-seek jumps from their cover. I paused to make sure no staff hovered, listening for when Young Master might call for something.

"Would you like to go for a walk in the garden?" I asked.

"*Yes, that would be lovely,*" Michael said in my mind.

We spent that day and many others as any pair of twins might. I was careful not to be observed speaking to him, though I did enjoy reading aloud. There was concern that this indicated I might be slow, but when I told Mother I just liked it, there was never another word about it.

As I grew older, I began to wonder why I had survived, and Michael had not. I sought to understand how death can be so capricious, so arbitrary. If under identical conditions one patient dies and the other does not, then there is a difference. Some would say luck or fate. Others would point to a spirit, a will to live, as the difference. I believe in none of those things. How can an infant be said to have will? Or a fate already bound to them? And luck is the solace of the ignorant. No, there must be a measurable, discernible difference, something not yet discovered.

Medical books and journals and hours spent in libraries became barely tolerated obsessions. Staff who wished to both please Young Master and keep peace with Father became conspirators.

When Father told me on my twenty-first birthday that he had arranged for me to take a clerk's position, I turned it down. I announced then and there that I intended to become a doctor.

Townsend, now grey of hair but no less formidable, was summoned to escort me out immediately. I asked if I would be allowed to retrieve some clothes. Townsend, ushering me along, reluctantly agreed to have a servant pack some things and bring them to me.

"There is an engraving in the nightstand," I said. "Very important, that."

The message was conveyed. Townsend and I continued to the main door. No carriage was summoned. I would be forced to walk the long, hedge path to the gate. It gave me a laugh.

The sound of Mother crying and fighting a losing battle with Father wafted through the halls. Before I could call out to her, Townsend held up a hand.

"Best not, young master." Mother was likely weeping on the shoulder of her maid-of-all-work. That, I assumed, was the reason she did not see me off.

The bag was brought to me and Townsend, dropping all pretense of etiquette, pushed me out the door and some distance along the path towards the gate. He watched until I was off the property.

When I settled into a room at a nearby inn, I found that the engraving had not been included.

⊷➡◉⬅⊶

Three other prisoners accompanied me on my trip to Newgate. We were herded through the back door, stripped, and given grey uniforms. Of the four, I was the only one taken to the condemned ward. A clergyman accompanied me. He was a dark man with a shaved head and face. He asked if I was ready to seek forgiveness, to give my sins to God. Struggling with my pained and swollen lips, I told him I would give God anything, any words, fealty, or service, if only the good vicar would send word to my father of my predicament. What I neglected to tell him was that my oath meant nothing since I did not believe in such superstitions.

In my two days at Newgate there were four meals and six beatings. In one sense I could count myself fortunate that I was not forced to work. I would not be on this Earth long enough to be usefully productive.

Then came the eve of the day I was to be hanged. The clergyman came to my cell, and I rushed to the door. Reaching through the rough bars, trembling with dread and hope, I pulled him close. His sad eyes told me what the answer had been, but I could not believe that even *my* father would leave a man, his own son, to such a cruel fate.

"What did my father say?"

The clergyman could not look at me. "'Let him hang.'"

I collapsed against the bars and sank to the floor, scraping my face on the iron.

"Do you wish to be forgiven?" The clergyman knelt down and pushed his hand through the bars to give some comfort.

"I wish for this to be over," I said as I curled up on the straw-filled, burlap mattress. What would the rope feel like? Would the hangman's hands be cold and bare as he placed it, or would he be wearing gloves? How tight would he pull it? Would I choke before the platform dropped? Would my neck break immediately? I entered a world that may be called dreaming in which I imagined every possible nuance of my impending death.

CHAPTER THREE

LIE OR DIE

I WAS STARTLED AWAKE BY THE languid *scratch-tap-tap, scratch-tap-tap* of a guard's cudgel on the gallery's railing. The sound stopped at my cell. His bulky shadow appeared at my door. I scrambled up from my bedding. Flickering torchlight from the gallery made the guard's sharp features dance and his eyes flash. The key rattled in the ancient lock. The door gave a banshee's wail as he pulled it open.

"Governor Thornsbury wants to see ya," he grumbled as he pulled me out of my cell. He propelled me forward with a shove and a prod of his cudgel to my back.

As we emerged into the men's quadrangle, the gibbous moon drew my attention. It seemed impaled upon the wall's iron spikes. Tendrils of clouds slithered over it, pulling along a dark mass to blot it out. The omen caused me to stumble slightly, which prompted the guard to shove and prod with renewed vigor until we climbed the stairs and made our way to the governor's office.

One last shove and I all but fell into the room, where Governor of the Gaol Thornsbury scowled at me from behind his desk. Across from him sat a formidable, black-haired stranger. He was at least six feet, with the build of a boxer. When he turned to peer at me, the wooden chair in which he sat cracked as if made of dry bones. Heavy brows and an unkempt beard gave him the air of a primitive.

Thornsbury gestured for me to take the other chair, which was cushioned, and covered in brown cloth worn almost threadbare. But it was not splintered wood nor straw bedding on a stone floor. Knowing that my next restful moment would be while dangling from a rope, I eagerly accepted the offer.

A letter on Thornsbury's desk caught my eye. My name was prominently written upon it. I also spied the name of the judge who had condemned me, along with one other name, a "Detective Coombs". No detective had been deemed necessary in my case.

"This is the fella what works for me," said the stranger. "Turn 'im over, yeah?" he said in a thick, north-country accent.

"This man says he knows you." Governor Thornsbury's tiny, dark eyes glared out at me like coals in a mound of ash, showing nothing but hatred and loathing.

Utterly at a loss for words, I looked at this stranger, with his layers of shabby, dark clothing. He wore no hat or tie, and his long nose had been broken repeatedly. His stare unsettled me, with grey eyes like windows into an abyss.

Was this a case of mistaken identity? I had never seen this man before. Still, my choice was clear: do my best to go along with this ruse or speak the truth and return to my cell to await execution. Whatever this stranger had in mind, it could not possibly be worse than death by hanging, could it?

"I apologize, Governor Thornsbury," I said finally. "I am not at my best." Taking a leap, I forced a smile, and aimed it at the stranger. "You arrived just in time, Detective Coombs."

"Sorry," he said with the merest of winks. "Busy takin' care o' things after the Downin' Street Bloodlettin'," he said with pride in his voice.

I feigned a cough to cover my surprise. Talk of the brutal murders of a portion of the staff at Downing Street had circulated amongst guards and prisoners alike. When word came that the Minister's wife had been arrested, I had scarcely believed it.

"Look, Guvnuh," said Coombs. "I couldn'ta solved the Downin' Street case wit'out 'im."

Thornsbury shook his head, a bull shaking off flies. "But why was he working in a basement in *that* neighborhood? *Campbell Street*." The words soured his tongue. "Nothing but derelicts and criminals. At least the place where you perpetrated these horrors has burnt to the ground. They should set a match to the whole neighborhood." He worked the taste out of his mouth, then turned his glare on Coombs. "Why was he not working openly, with the police?"

"I'm tellin' ya I needed 'im to solve the case. Or would ya rather the killer was still runnin' around?"

"No, of course not."

"Ya got the letter from the judge what sent 'im away," Coombs said, jumping to his feet. The chair nearly tipped on its back. "That's all ya need, right? We're leavin' now. Let's go, Johnson."

Coombs strode from the room without hesitation. I stood, unsure of what was next. The guard tossed me my bag of belongings – the clothes I had been wearing upon my arrest – and I scurried after Coombs.

Once on the street, I stopped. The prison doors rumbled and banged shut from behind and the brisk air of a London winter night washed over me. More than merely breathe it in, I absorbed it, pulled it to me, embraced and welcomed it all; the smell of the wet road and yes, even the horses, the sound of clomping hooves, clattering wagons and the voices of people living in innocent freedom. Until mere moments before, I had believed I would never experience these things again.

"Comin'?" Coombs' voice broke through my reverie.

"Thank you," I said quickly before a swell of emotion cracked my voice.

A brief smile softened his features. "Come on."

Lacking a handkerchief, I dabbed my eyes with the end of my sleeve as I followed Coombs to a brougham. It shone in the light of streetlamps as if brand new, its burgundy-coloured wood freshly polished. Its windows gleamed and its wheels hardly showed the marks of the rough and muddy London roads. Slender and dressed all in black, the driver sat high in his seat, staring forward, reins at the ready.

The door was open. I waited for Coombs to enter first, but he stood by a nearby streetlamp, his back to me. I thought I heard him speak.

"Pardon?" I said.

He turned abruptly, seemingly bothered by something and motioned for me to get in.

I climbed into the forward-facing seat. My eyes fell upon my reflection in the carriage window. There I saw a man I would prefer to avoid. His haunted blue eyes stared out from pale, drawn flesh marked by a lingering bruise surrounding the right eye. Equal parts soot and beard covered his face. His matted hair hung too long and was a colour akin to dirt. Who was this man?

"Feelin' right over there?" Coombs asked, having settled in across from me.

"Pardon? Oh, yes, I suppose."

"Good." Without bothering to wipe it, he held out his gloveless hand. "Coombs."

I quickly wiped my hand on my pant leg – I certainly had no gloves – and put my hand in his. It felt like rope and leather. My knuckles ground together in his grip.

"You're gonna be my assistant," he said with an unquestioning tone.

Lacking a better response, I simply nodded. "And where are we going?"

"My gaff. Kensington. You'll like it."

By 'gaff' I assumed he meant his home. "I believe I will," I told him. "You said, assistant?" I asked.

"Yeah. Had nothin' but mither gettin' the dibble to believe me. Scrotes kept tellin' me I'm a mingin' bit o' shite. Practically 'ad to drag the blighters to the scene and shove the evidence right in their bloody cake 'oles."

I took a moment to translate his words. "The police refused to listen, is that what you mean? And you had to insist that they examine the evidence which you presented?"

Coombs laughed lightly. "Yeah, that's it. Took a lot o' proddin' to get the dibble to search the Minister's house," he said. "But when they did, they found it all. Didn't listen to nothin' she said."

"Pity she hanged herself. The minister's wife," I added.

"Yeah, well, weight o' all that murderin', I s'pose," he said with a shrug.

"And how will I assist you?" I asked.

"You'll back me up. Agree with my solutions. See, they just come to me. Like a picture."

Was there a challenge in his voice? In the way that he stared at me, as the light of streetlamps we passed washed over his face? I saw no reason to question his methods. He had solved a case that others had found impenetrable. I did have one question, however.

"Why me, if I may ask?"

"Saw your story in the paper," Combs said. "Caught my eye. I think it was all them bodies in your house what got my attention. You like death, yeah?"

Coombs stared expectantly while I struggled for an answer. I preferred not to share it, but how could I deny the man who had just saved my life?

"I had a twin brother. We both contracted cholera. I have always wondered why he died, and I did not."

"Must o' been tough, growin' up with that hangin' over ya."

"Actually, the thought of him was a comfort to me." I did not share this with many people, but I found myself wanting to share it with Coombs, perhaps for the simple fact that he had saved my life. "I only learned about him when I was eight years old, and then I invented a version of him for my own amusement, as I had no other siblings."

"I didn't have none, either," Coombs said.

A few moments of silence passed, marked only by the steady pace of the horse's hooves.

"There were not as many bodies as they said. And I am a doctor," I stammered. "At least, I will be."

He nodded, taking it in. "I liked how you kept sayin' you're a doctor. It got me thinkin'. I say I'm a detective, so I am, yeah? You say you're a doctor, so you are. Somethin' told me someone like you'd be a use to me."

Unexpectedly, I smiled. What better way to continue my work in the study of death than to help a detective solve murder cases?

As we slowed down on a quaint, residential street, we passed a rotund old lamplighter raising his bole. I watched, transfixed by the mundanity of it, wondering how those who live by this light appreciated their good fortune. The flame on the end of the bole blew out. The lamplighter cursed with a breathy growl, and I marveled at the privilege of being bothered by such things.

The homes on both sides of the street were three stories each, their yellow bricks long stained brown. Stone steps led to three-pillared porches, each topped with a trellis and a pair of balconies. The bright orange flames of gas lamps created silhouettes of those who wished to spy the night's arrival.

At the end of a block, the carriage slowed to a stop before a house that was different from the others. Set apart, it was a red brick, two-story home. The recessed main entrance was on the left, a gabled peak over bayed windows and a lesser peak set back and to the right. A wrought iron fence barely held back a garden threatening to overtake the sidewalk.

I drew in a breath of anticipation. There would be beds and food and warm fires. Instead of threatening guards there would be polite servants. One learns to live without certain luxuries, but once they are again presented, they become as vital as air. Soon, the carriage door would open, and I would be escorted, welcomed into a warm home.

"Well?" Coombs growled with a nod at the door. "This is the place."

Some sort of apology tumbled from me, and I scrambled out. The house was dark, with nary a light nor movement to be seen. It looked dead. No servant hastily lit lamps and came rushing out of the house. No Mrs. Coombs awaited us with a smile and a proper greeting. The door to the house remained resolutely closed, the windows dark.

Coombs ascended the manor steps. I followed as the driver snapped his reins and the brougham rattled off.

Once inside, the sudden flare of a match stabbed at my eyes. Coombs lit a candle – tallow by the smell of it – blew out the match and tossed it aside. The light from the candle revealed little more than Coombs himself and the shadowed impressions of a narrow hallway.

A box of matches struck me in the chest and fell to the floor through my startled and clumsy attempts to catch it.

"You'll want 'em," Coombs said. He started up the stairs along the right wall, taking his candle with him. "There's a room upstairs with a bed. Get some sleep. We'll talk in the mornin'."

I gaped at the retreating wash of candlelight as Coombs carried it up the stairs and to the mezzanine above me.

I lit a match and found another candle in a heavy brass stand on a small table to my right. The hall was otherwise empty of furnishings or adornment of any kind.

The place was cold and still. No light or warmth from downstairs fireplaces. Certainly no servants to attend to my needs. I shivered as a deep chill overtook me.

"Run away now."

I whirled at the sound of the voice in my ear. The candle sputtered out. I stood in darkness and silence. Had Coombs played a prank on me? But there was no suppressed laughter or retreating footsteps from some trickster. Bringing the candle alight again, I held it at arm's length as I turned in a circle. Had I truly heard the voice, or simply imagined it?

Then laughter, like champagne bubbles, burst from me. My childhood fantasies of hearing my brother speak, particularly after one of Father's punishments, had come back to me. It had been so long, I hardly recognized it. At the behest of a man as imposing as Father, I had been freed from prison, barely escaping the ultimate punishment. Of course, the one thing that never failed to comfort me would come back now.

"You're free. You should go."

My imagined brother had always been the daring one. Rather, I used his voice as a way to explore more dangerous choices. True, I was a free man, and I could slip into the darkness and by dawn's light be far from the strange and intimidating man upstairs. But how long would I be free? I would be hunted, and there would be no rescue a second time.

I silently thanked my brother for helping me weigh my options and come to a decision. With the tallow burning my nose, as it was wont to do, I ascended the stairs.

Immediately I spied the bathroom and water closet at the end of the hall. The tub drew me to it as if pulled by a rope. I was in desperate need of a bath. My joyful anticipation at the thought of scraping the stench of Newgate from my skin was quickly smothered by the thought of baring myself in this strange, dark place. It was somehow more unnerving than bathing in prison, and thus I decided to carry my stench for one more night.

Thankfully, the bedroom at the back of the house contained a bed. With windows on two walls and no curtains, it promised to be a bright and sunny room. I looked out over the hills behind the house. The trees were barren, only a few leaves still clung to their branches, long after their purpose had been served. Windows and streetlamps dotted the landscape below, stars through a ragged veil.

I blew out the candle and set it on the floor. The bare mattress had a folded brown wool blanket on it. I decided to lay under it, but to remain fully clothed, including my shoes. This was a fair sight better than my cell, but I still knew not what awaited me.

A chorus of night sounds seeped into my consciousness. Gone were the prisoners' screams of madness or pain, the dull thuds, sharp cracks, and wet slaps of Newgate. Instead, the house creaked and groaned its story at me. A dog howled; a cat mewled. Bare branches scratched at each other in the wind. As I breathed my relief, the tension left my body, one that had become so pervasive as to be the norm. With the release came tears and I let them flow. I lay in a bed in a room in a house and the morrow would not be terminated by a trip to the gallows.

Still, I dreamt of fire that night.

CHAPTER FOUR

A CHANGE OF FORTUNE

Coombs awakened me with a knock on my door and a crude call to breakfast. The lure of food was strong, but the comfort of the bed stronger still. I bounced on it, enjoying the mattress' lumps and squeaks. Grey morning light emphasized the faded, dusty walls and dirty windows. Then I smelled sausages.

Up and at the door, the smell drew me downstairs. Each room I passed along the halls upstairs and down was empty not merely of human company, but of furniture. All save the parlour, which had a lone writing desk with a wicker chair. I found Coombs in the kitchen at the end of the hall, alone at the head of a large table, eating. A stack of newspapers sat at his right hand. The bright colours on the cover of a penny blood stood out from the pile. He surreptitiously moved the pile of papers to cover it.

With a mouthful of eggs, Coombs attempted to greet me. He managed to say something about finding a chair. The one by the writing desk in the parlour being the only option available, I set it at the end of the table. Coombs continued eating – his manner of eating was more akin to shoveling.

Diving into the food, I found myself partaking in behaviours that would have triggered a rap on the head from Father. I spooned mounds of scrambled eggs from a porcelain dish, forked whole sausages from a pewter plate, and poured a dark and powerful coffee from a copper kettle. No waiting for servants to perform their duties in just the right way. More importantly, no waiting for Father to give his approval to start. A visceral part of me enjoyed having unfettered access to all this food. It was, in a sensual way, liberating.

When I slowed my consumption long enough to take a breath, I noticed Coombs watching me while drinking his coffee.

"Beats prison food, yeah?" he asked.

"Indeed it does"

Manners returned, I set my utensils down, dabbed my mouth with my napkin, set it back on my knee. Coombs took his own, unused napkin, touched his mouth with it and set it in his lap. I ignored the oddness of this and instead asked the question which had been on my mind since the carriage stopped the night before.

"Where are your servants?"

He shrugged. "Don't got 'em. Don't want 'em."

"And there is no Mrs. Coombs?"

"*No.*"

The sharpness of his response and the flash of anger in his eyes put me back to the dinner table of my youth, with Father scolding me for the misuse of a word or a breach of etiquette. In those moments of rebuked silence, I would imagine receiving support from my dead brother. He would comfort me, and I would entertain and bolster myself with such dreams until I was no longer in Father's presence. Gesturing at the food I said, "Then how … ?"

"Inn down the street. They send three meals a day. Food's good. Pity the daughter ain't older."

I speared another sausage with my fork.

"You come from money, yeah?" Coombs asked. "You talk real formal."

Something as simple as using a contraction would trigger a rap on the knuckles from my tutor, and even worse if my father happened to hear it. But I was feeling more guarded in the light of day than in the darkened carriage, just after being freed from prison. I chose not to share such details.

"My life prior to medical school was very different, yes."

"Papers didn't say much 'bout that."

"There are many things about me that the papers left out."

"Like?"

Taking some time to chew, followed by a sip of coffee, I considered my response. Coombs studied me as I did. How much should I tell him? My momentary lapse under the threat of a rope aside, I was adamant that I would not utter my father's name, nor provide enough information to discern it. "While it is true that I grew accustomed to a certain way of life, I left that life behind when I began my studies and will not return to it. That is all I will say on the subject." I am not one for confrontations, but in this case, I held Coombs' gaze.

"That right?"

"Yes."

"I don't know. Not sure I like the idea of havin' somebody in my house I know nothin' about."

"If that were true, I would not have spent the night here."

He laughed and pointed his fork at me. "I knew I'd like you. Don't trust a man without secrets. I got 'em, too."

Of that I had no doubt. At first thought, his statement seemed nonsensical. Is not someone with secrets the least trustworthy? But then I realized the wisdom in it; the truly untrustworthy are those who pretend not to have secrets.

"Shall we discuss our arrangement?" I asked.

Pouring a fresh cup of coffee, he said, "You work for me. You live here." A tilt of his head indicated the house. He lifted the refilled cup with both hands and leaned back. "You come with me on cases and back me up when I solve 'em."

"Regarding your 'solutions'," I began. "Do you mean you wish for me to help you formulate your theories and –"

"No. Told ya. They come to me, the solutions. But the dibble wouldn't believe me on the Downin' Street thing. You're gonna give 'em proof I'm right."

I buttered a piece of potato bread while I considered how to approach this. The man had solved an otherwise unsolvable murder, but creature comforts aside, did I want to be a simple lackey? Granted, it was much better than being a hangman's duty.

"In my understanding, that is not how investigations typically work," I said and ate the bread.

Coombs' expression hardened. "I'm tellin' ya, I see things nobody else sees. Do what you gotta do to get right with it if you want to stay here."

Self-preservation won out. A lackey I would be, at least for a time. I would look for opportunities to be independent, and I would be alive to do so.

"Very well," I said.

A quick nod and his expression changed as curtains drawn to let in the sun. "Gimme a list of what ya need. I'll get it."

"What I need … for investigations?"

"For anythin'. For livin'. Everythin'."

"Some coal, perhaps?"

He laughed. "Sure."

"Very well. Have you any paper? Pen and ink?"

"There's some in the desk," he said with a lift of his chin.

I pushed back from the table, then hesitated over the dishes. Was I expected to clear them as part of my duties?

"Inn'll get 'em sorted," Coombs said, much to my relief.

Paper, pen, and ink were indeed in the writing desk, but I had taken the chair. After a quick trip back to the kitchen to retrieve it – resolutely ignoring Coombs' smirk – I settled in to write. Then I stopped. Where to begin?

"Whatever you want."

Ink blotted on the paper as Coombs' voice startled me.

"Oh," I said. A thought struck me. "Am I to receive a salary?"

"What for?"

"For the work I will do?"

"You ain't gonna do that much work and I'll get you whatever you want."

"But what about unanticipated needs? And it is customary for –"

"Fine. How much?"

Numbers and calculations tumbled through my mind. How much did Father pay his staff? He certainly never shared that with me consciously, but recollections of overheard conversations and glimpsed papers bubbled up into my mind. "Oh. Well, I suppose twenty pounds would do."

"Done. Paid once a week on Friday?"

"Um, that would be fine." I had intended the amount to be a monthly stipend.

"Good. Finish your list. I'm goin' out. Lunch'll be here at noon." With that, he left.

In my mind, my list went through several revisions, beginning with the necessities for forensic science and research. Then came a more extensive list which included books of more general knowledge and a few for pleasure reading, which led me to consider more personal needs. Should I ask him to supply those, or buy them with the unexpectedly generous salary to which he had agreed? Cold air brushed the back of my neck. I added coal to my list, in the event Coombs forgot.

Resentment crept into my mind as I recalled how easily he had granted my salary request and yet left me alone in this unheated, unfurnished house. With it came the urge to demand more.

"*He can afford it,*" I could hear my brother say. Apparently he had grown along with me, as his voice had deepened. It pleased me to hear him again, a balm for my isolation.

I added furniture. Gilded, padded furniture. Paintings, vases, all manner of rare and expensive things. Soon a page was filled and the next begun with silverware, plates, cups, goblets, and linens, which led me to expensive food items, deserts, and drinks. My brother's voice took on a darker tone than I had ever heard.

"*He said you could have anything you wanted.*"

"You always were the mischievous one," I whispered. The thrum of excitement filled me as I embarked on a risky activity.

Cigars and pipes seemed appropriate for a proper man's library, though I had never taken up the habit.

"*Anything you want.*"

Next came wine and other spirits. I felt bold.

"*Anything. Don't be afraid. This is fun.*"

This was freedom. Complete freedom. I added absinthe and opium, both of which I had seen used in my previous neighborhood and wondered about the blissful expressions they produced.

"Yes. Go ahead. Keep going," my brother said, laughing, and I with him.

I thought of flesh, of exotic, seductive dancers. They would be veiled, yet exposed. I pictured them in masks with leather collars and bindings and –

The pen scratched drily, tore the paper and fell from my fingers. Unsure of where I was for a moment, I blinked clarity into my eyes. My writing had become a wild, mad script. I flexed my cramped hand, and after a few calming breaths and a shake of my head, I dismissed all notions of voices. My brother was long dead and was not speaking to me. It was my own mind. After living in squalor and then in prison, the opportunity for self-indulgence arose and I had concocted a ruse to pursue it.

The pages were scattered on the desk and floor. Pages filled with my darkest thoughts and yes, desires, not all of which I had ever admitted to myself. Returning to my senses, I gathered them, threw them into the fireplace, ran to the hall for the matches and set them ablaze.

The pages burned quickly in the empty hearth while I sat on the floor and let the heat melt away the chill that had overtaken me. I stared at the flames until there was nothing but ashes. When the smell of burning paper dissipated, I became aware once again of my own odour. The thought that I had dined in this state seemed appalling one moment and comical the next as I recalled scooping gruel into my mouth with my fingers at Newgate. But now, strange host and house be damned, I was going to get a bath.

The only change of clothes available to me came from the day of my arrest: White pinstriped shirt, grey wool pants and cotton undergarments. My blood-stained rubber apron had served as evidence against me, and I know not what had become of it. Still, my wrinkled and musty clothes were considerably better than my gunmetal prison outfit. Despite the lingering odour, they were mine and I felt cleaner than I had in some time. The prison outfit went next into the fireplace. I laughed as it burned.

With only one sheet of paper remaining, I created a much more conservative list with "Stationery" at the top. I included basic professional and household needs. Satisfied with my work, I sat back and dozed off.

The sound of the door opening startled me awake. It took me a moment to recall there was no one to answer it.

"Coombs?" I called as I roused myself.

In the hall, I nearly collided with a ruddy man of a height comparable to my own but more thickly built. Though his pale brown hair receded, his sideburns were as thick as shrubs. He wore a grey coat over a white apron, brown shirt, and pants. The smell of cheese and bread rose from the tray he held. Behind him trailed a young, dark-haired man and a teenage girl with hair the colour of fall leaves but with features similar enough to suggest they were his children. They both gaped at me, but their apparent father held a restrained air.

"You must be Dr. Johnson. I'm Wilson Burkett, from the Langford Hotel." He gave a slight bow. "Sorry for not making your acquaintance this morning, but Coombs said you preferred to sleep in. If you'll have a seat in the kitchen, lunch will be set out."

The girl carried an empty wicker basket while the boy, thankfully, carried a bucket of coal. "Gather the laundry," Burkett said to his daughter and off she went. He turned to his son. "Get the furnace started."

I followed Burkett into the kitchen while the two youths went about their business.

"Coombs prefers that I not serve the food," Burkett said. He set out bowls of fruit along with a board of bread, meat, and cheese. "Well," he said to me, "I'll leave you to it."

"Wait," I said. "I am quite new here. I wonder if there's anything you would be willing to share about my employer? Anything that can help me navigate my situation."

He took a moment. "Never call him 'Master'. He hates that. Just his surname, and he always seems to perk up if you throw in 'Detective'. What's your job if you don't mind me asking? He said 'assistant', but that can mean a lot of things."

"Indeed. To be honest, I am still unclear on the specifics of my duties."

Burkett nodded. "He does keep a lot in his mind, yeah? I was surprised when he told me about you. I tried to get my boy set up as a footman or some such, but he says he doesn't want servants. Sure wants service, though."

"Indeed. How long have you been doing this for him?" I asked.

"Two weeks now. Just showed up at the hotel, cash in hand and a lot of it. Set him up with the proprietor and Coombs ends up buying this place outright. Surprised me, I don't mind saying. Never thought the old man'd give it up like that, 'specially when he was planning on renovating and adding electricals."

"Really?"

"Yeah, Master Langford – now there's someone who you *best* call 'Master' – he had big plans for this and his other places. But he jumped at the first offer Coombs made."

"Then you are not the proprietor of the … what was it called again?"

"Langford Hotel. But no, me and the missus just run the place. Master Langford used to be there all the time, tending to guests, but he's getting up in age and, well, he just doesn't get over as often. But we do all right on our own."

"I have no doubt. The food, so far, has been excellent."

"I thank you for that." His gaze fell down the hall behind me. "Looks like they've finished up, so we're off. We'll bring dinner at five. Mutton and pigeon on the menu."

The three whisked out the door.

⊹⊱═◦❀◦═⊰⊹

After a visit to the bathroom and perhaps too much time spent enjoying the running water, I found myself staring at Coombs' open door. Not fully open, mind you, but enough to peek inside. Closing it to preserve the man's privacy seemed the correct course of action. No looking inside, I told myself, but if my vision happened to fall upon objects of interest while closing the door, I was certainly not to blame.

"Go inside. What's the worst that could happen?"

"He could catch me and send me back to prison," I said then shook my head. This was not the time to indulge in childhood fantasies. Such thoughts had led me to unsettling behaviours mere hours before. Therefore, I would simply shut the door.

"Just a glance, then? Before you close the door."

Aught but shadows were visible through the tiny gap.

"There, happy now?" I asked with a laugh.

I reached for the brass doorknob. A coldness came to my fingers, and I imagined my hand stuck to it as flesh sticks to metal in winter. Startled, I bumped the door, causing it to swing open. Truly, it was an accident.

"*He* has a pillow and blankets," I said aloud. Curtains on the windows, but no other furnishings or decorations save a single wooden chest in the far corner, hasp closed, but no lock.

"You might as well go in."

"No," I said to counter the urge to invade a man's privacy. I was a guest in his house, and he had saved me from death. Granted, some of his behavior was odd, but I had no cause to betray his trust.

I closed the door and returned to the library, wishing Coombs had bought even one book.

⊹⊱═◦❀◦═⊰⊹

The sound of the front door startled me awake. Coombs sniffed as he entered and looked into the library.

"You have a fire?" He seemed annoyed.

"I was cold."

He grunted assent. "You got your list?"

I gave it to him and, after a brief look he said, "Fine." He tucked it in a pocket, then handed me a folded stack of one-pound notes. Twenty of them. "Your salary."

"You will be paying in cash? Not with a cheque?"

"You wanna trust a bank with your money, that's up to you."

I resolved to do exactly that. "Considering I possess only one change of clothes, I should like to visit a nearby haberdasher or two."

As he looked me over, I noticed he still wore the same clothes. Then came another of his big-shouldered shrugs. "Go ahead."

"Thank you. How shall I summon your carriage?"

"My carriage?" he scoffed. "I don't got a carriage."

"But when you …" The word "rescued" sat heavy on my tongue. "Retrieved me –"

"Hired it from the Langford."

"Ah," I said and hesitated.

"Walk there. Down the Kensington end of Belgrave Road. Not hard to find."

"Certainly. But I have no coat."

"Mine's by the door. Use it if you want. Dinner's at five and they take away everything at six." He retired to the kitchen with a stack of newspapers.

Coombs' heavy wool coat hung by the door. It reeked of tobacco and his persistent musk. Upon opening the door, I found the smell of the oversized coat preferable to the cold.

CHAPTER FIVE

A TOUCH OF FREEDOM

THE MORNING FOG HAD THINNED TO a damp afternoon mist and the lowering sun peeked over the roofs. Faces appeared in windows here or a cracked-open door there only to retreat as my gaze fell fully upon them. A pair of children – brother and sister, I surmised – played on the sidewalk. Upon noticing me, they froze, then ran inside and shortly appeared at a window. This supported my assumption that Coombs was a stranger to the neighbourhood, a mysterious man who had moved into *that* house at the end of the row. And the stranger had brought in yet another stranger in the dark of night, when all good and proper people were in their beds. Now this new stranger strolled down the street, bold as you please. Had they seen my prison uniform? Clearly, Coombs and I had provided a great deal of fodder for rumors and wild speculations. I rather liked it.

At the end of the block and across the street, I found the wrought iron arch over an alley that read simply, "The Langford". The hotel itself occupied the left side and back of the alley. A series of dining rooms took up the ground floor, with two stories of porches above. At the alley's end was the entrance to the stables. A pair of young and scruffy grooms having a smoke eyed me warily as I approached. I walked with the air of someone who belonged, and they let me pass.

There was room in the stables for several carriages, but only one stood waiting, the same burgundy brougham that had whisked me away from Newgate. Its driver, the same as from the previous night's journey, polished one of the lanterns. I noted that he was a tall, slender man with broad shoulders, giving him something of a triangular shape. His black, wavy hair, parted on the right, glistened with pomade. With his auburn skin, he reminded me of a man from whom my father bought much fabric.

He straightened from his work as I approached him. Briefly puzzled, he worked out my identity quickly. "Afternoon, sir," he said with a bow.

"Good afternoon … ?"

"Peters," he said, thankfully filling my exaggerated silence.

"Your carriage is available, I take it?"

He fidgeted with his rag. "Well, sir, you see, sir, it's like this. I like to be available for Detective Coombs. He shows up, unexpected, and wants a ride. He pays enough that I like to be available whenever the fancy strikes him. Sir."

"I have just come from Detective Coombs. I am to be taken to the nearest haberdasher. If you doubt me, I can bring Detective Coombs here and he can confirm this."

"Not necessary, sir," he said as he threw the rag into a wooden box and climbed into the driver's seat. He stopped before he sat. "Oh, sorry, sir. Detective Coombs prefers I don't open the door. It's become a habit, I'm afraid. Shall I –"

"No, quite all right." I opened the door and stepped up, then stopped. Here was another person who knew more about Coombs than I did. "We are both under the employ of an unusual man," I said, looking up from the step.

"Sir," he said with just a glance down.

"I suggest," I continued, "that we dispense with customs and speak openly with one another."

He considered me for a time before turning his attention back to the reins.

"And you do not know if you can trust me," I continued. "I understand. Please know I only seek to understand our mutual employer, so I may serve him better. I suspect you would like to do so as well. I believe we can help each other. If you agree, you are welcome to seek me out and I hope I will be able to do the same."

"Thank you, sir. I'll bear that in mind, sir."

"Excellent," I responded as I climbed in. "I hope you will."

"Sir," I heard him say as I closed the door.

We made several stops while I assessed the various clothing options, but Peters remained with the carriage each time, affording me little opportunity to engage with him.

I decided to indulge myself in jackets and pants in order to produce an amount of clothing sufficient to require assistance. I declined the shopkeeper's help and summoned Peters. Who, under the man's heavily whiskered and disapproving scowl, carried the bulk of the load. As we approached the brougham, I saw an opportunity to engage Peters in casual conversation.

"How did you come into Detective Coombs' employ?"

Peters shifted the stack of boxes in his arms in order to open the rope netting at the back. In a gesture of cooperation, I pulled it aside myself so Peters would not need to put the packages down first.

"Thank you, sir," he said as he set the packages into the compartment. "Begging your pardon, sir, but I'm not in his employ. I merely make myself available to him."

"I see. How did you come to meet Detective Coombs?"

"He picked me out, sir. I was working Euston Station. Morning train from up north had come in. Gentlemen were passing me by, as they are wont to do. But Detective Coombs came right up to me and loudly praised the condition of my carriage. I have always prided myself on that, sir."

"Rightfully so."

"Thank you, sir. Well, Detective Coombs made a bit of a scene, going on about the carriage, my clothes, how I spoke well for a … how I spoke so well. He handed me quite a bit of money, if I may say, and asked if I could be available to him all day. Brought him to Mr. Burkett's. Took him around until he purchased his house. He asked if I could wait for him each morning. I offered to pick him up, but he said he liked the walk. That day became two, which became a week, and here I am."

"And the proprietor approves?"

"Mr. Langford? We hardly hear from him these days. And Mr. Burkett's happy so long as Detective Coombs pays for the service."

"While your story is considerably lighter than mine, we both appear to have been plucked from, shall we say, obscurity, by the good Detective Coombs."

"Indeed, sir. Indeed."

"Now, I saw a promising hat and glove store just down the block. I hope your arms are not too tired."

"My arms are fine, sir," said Peters with a smile.

"Excellent!" I felt buoyed not only by my accumulation of quality clothing but also of my feeling that I had successfully engaged Peters in something of a friendship.

This feeling of positivity carried me through dressing for dinner but was immediately dashed by Coombs.

"What the bloody Hell is *that* get up?"

"My 'get up' is basic but serviceable attire: black coat, white waistcoat, shirt, and ascot, along with grey houndstooth trousers and black shoes." Fortunately, the Burketts had already left and did not witness the scene. "It is perfectly appropriate attire for a gentleman at the evening meal," I said with a sniff.

"I ain't no gentleman," Coombs said, still laughing.

"That much, Detective Coombs, is abundantly clear."

Coombs' eyes flared.

I felt trepidatious, but in need of defending myself. "Clear to me, and I suspect, to others as well. You desire to be treated with respect and yet you present yourself as a common street thug."

As Coombs' expression hardened, my heart pounded. But I was on a path now and determined not to turn from it. "How can you expect authorities to take you seriously when you present yourself as someone they should arrest? Wrap yourself in the trappings of a gentleman and you will be treated accordingly. I guarantee it."

He considered me for a moment and the fire in his eyes dimmed. "You want me to dress like a fop?"

"I want to you be seen as what you are. A brilliant detective." It seemed the appropriate time to engage in flattery.

"I ain't changin' my duds for every meal. It's stupid. But I take your point. I'll see about gettin' some new clothes for goin' out, for doin' the work."

It seemed an odd turn of phrase, even for Coombs, but I supposed it applied well enough to a man who had taken it upon himself to put murderers behind bars.

"Excellent." I considered pressing on regarding his accent, but decided to accept my small victory and enjoy the meal.

Recalling how he had followed my example at breakfast, I cleared my throat for attention. He looked up at me as I unfolded my napkin and set it on my knee.

He watched and followed suit.

I added a conversational narrative: "My, this pigeon is lovely," I said.

"Yes. The pigeon is lovely."

This fascinated me. Here was a man wealthy enough to afford a home and services in London and who possessed the wherewithal to solve what was perhaps the most vexing murder case in British history, yet he did not know how to eat.

This made me more eager to witness him in action. The two of us, really. We would investigate, interrogate. I would supply him with facts produced by autopsies and tests, which he would use to put together iron-clad cases. That was my sincere belief. Even if he had simply intuited the perpetrator of the Downing Street Bloodletting, he could not truly expect such methods to be sustainable. Surely, he would grasp the value of having a methodical, meticulous researcher by his side. That was why he saved me from the gallows, was it not?

CHAPTER SIX

THE MAD DANCER OF MARYLEBONE

OUR FIRST CASE TOGETHER CAME WITH lunch. Though I had convinced Coombs to furnish the place over the course of days, he still insisted on taking meals in the kitchen. He thrust a paper at me and waggled it over my plate as I attempted to continue eating. Finally, I acquiesced and took it from him.

"'Multiple Murders at Dance Academy'. 'Handyman Arrested'." I emphasized, extending the paper back.

"Read it," he commanded.

I sighed and obeyed. The article described in breathless, titillating language how a woman, arriving a bit late for her quadrille lesson, had found the dance hall strewn with bodies and blood. She ran from the hall screaming. A constable managed to get a story out of her and rushed to the scene. Thereupon he found that the owner of the academy, as well as three other students, had been brutally murdered with blows to their heads. One of the victims lay on her back on a table with her head dangling, her skull smashed open, and her blood forming a large pool beneath.

In addition, the constable found a frail, rickety girl kneeling over one of the victims, apparently trying to revive the poor soul. The girl, identified by the hysterical woman, was an adopted street urchin named Elinor. The child had been taken in by the charwoman employed at the hall, a Mrs. Grayson. Young Miss Grayson would not speak, even upon the arrival of her adopted mother, who had been away at one of her jobs. The constable was able to piece together that Elinor had hidden away in a storage trunk and had come out after the attacks had stopped.

As for the perpetrator, the constable followed a trail of blood leading away from the scene and found the academy's handyman, a Mr. Hughes, wandering the streets. He confessed immediately. He said he had thrown the murder weapon, a hammer, into a sewer. A coroner's inquest was scheduled for that very evening at the Wandering Swan pub.

With emphasis, I set the paper down. "They believe they have the killer in hand. I suspect you believe differently?"

"It's the girl."

"The *girl*? Did you read the description?"

"'Rickety' they said, yeah," he snapped. "I read it. But what if it was somethin' else? Or she was fakin' it? Besides, she was the only survivor."

"Granted, the sole survivor of a group of murders garners suspicion, but how could this girl – described as frail, mind you – possibly have done all this?"

"I can see the whole thing. This little witch, she used her powers to do this. That ain't her true form, I bet. Just lookin' all innocent and harmless."

"Witches, Coombs?"

Coombs' eyes flared, and I immediately regretted my remark. He put down his fork and set his hand on the table. "This is what I'm here to do. See what others don't. You can help me or go back to Newgate."

The intensity of Coombs' stare gave me pause. "Of course, I will help. But Hughes confessed."

"Let's go." He got up from the table, still chewing.

I finished my coffee before I stood, not so much for the coffee itself as for the moment to ponder how I would disabuse Coombs of this ridiculous idea. He was already out the door. I scrambled to catch up to him. My rational mind warred with my emotions. Voices of reason and superstition argued fruitlessly. How he had come to any conclusion at all, let alone a different one than the police, was unfathomable. And yet I found myself eagerly attempting to keep up his brisk pace through the cold morning mist to the inn.

Unlike Coombs, I was panting heavily by the time we reached the end of the alley and entered the stables.

Peters climbed into his seat as we approached.

"We would already be there," I said, struggling to hide my exertion, "were you to keep Peters on full time."

Coombs barked a laugh and clapped me on the back, sending me stumbling a few steps. "Get in."

There had not been a scintilla of doubt in Coombs' expression or voice. And here is where my rational mind ceded the high ground in the ongoing war with my emotions: I *wanted* to believe him. It was impossible to not be caught up in his excitement, in his simple force of will. The hubris of having solved the Downing Street Bloodletting had caught him up, it seemed. He now believed – perhaps too strongly – in his own deductive talents. But if he presented this absurd theory with nothing to support it, he would be laughed out of the police station. This whole enterprise – and yes, my new-found creature comforts – would come crashing down. Personal concerns aside, I had to help the man. He had literally saved my life. I vowed to help him in every possible way.

"Where are we going, exactly?" I asked.

"Gonna meet Superintendent Batleigh. Worked with him on the Downin' Street case. Convinced him to investigate the minister's wife."

"May I make a suggestion?"

He folded his arms and scowled at me.

"Your principal concern is one of credibility, is it not?"

He gave a sharp nod.

"Your theory goes quite spectacularly against recorded events. If you state your claim with no evidence, with only your own instincts – sharply honed though they might be – how do you think they will respond? Bear in mind that this time, unlike your previous case, they have a suspect –"

"Who confessed. I know. Don't care, long as they believe me. With your help, I'll make 'em believe me."

"'Aye, and there's the rub'," I quoted and, seeing no sign of it registering with him, I continued. "These are men whose careers are centered around investigations. They have put their skills to work on this case and, however misguided they may be, they came to a definite conclusion. Now you want to sweep in and tell them they are wrong simply because you 'know it'. Can you understand how they might not react well to such a thing?"

Coombs considered me as we bumped along. Finally, he unfolded his arms and set his hands on his lap. "What've you got in mind?"

"Withhold your conclusion." The carriage was slowing, so I gamely spoke over his response. "Remind this Superintendent Batleigh of your earlier, suc-cessful case. Tell him you are merely here to observe. Then, let me examine the bodies. I will conduct witness interviews if you like. But let us give them the show they expect, and when it is done, you can tell them your findings." In truth, I hoped that I would be able to keep him quiet until my work was done, and that work would change his mind.

The carriage stopped. Coombs stared out the window at the wide, pale building.

"All right," he said finally.

Heartened and growing accustomed to Coombs' ways, I stepped out into the drizzle, donned my new top hat and held the door. Coombs hopped out and stood for a moment. He straightened his coat, nodded and waved to nearby bobbies and other passersby, then continued up the stone steps and through the arched entrance as I followed in his wake. The bobbies we passed recog-nized him, though they seemed to be unaware of me as we continued along the hall to a door at the end marked "Superintendent Batleigh". Coombs opened it without knocking.

"Good mornin', Superintendent," he announced.

Batleigh stood. He had a few inches on Coombs and considerably less muscle. Darker than Peters, his hair was tightly curled and closely cropped. A thick handlebar mustache nearly obscured his mouth and accented his puffy cheeks.

He aimed a frown at us. "Mr. Coombs." Surprisingly, he wore black leather gloves.

"Detective," Coombs corrected.

"One case does not a detective make. What can I do for you?" With a reluctant gesture, he sat.

As we took the chairs facing the desk, Coombs introduced me as his assistant, gave me the title of doctor, and stated that I wished to conduct my own investigation of the Marylebone case.

"Whatever for?" Batleigh asked of me, a tad sharply. He worked his gloved hands together, flexing them.

The superintendent's mustache danced as he worked his mouth, and his eyes darted back and forth between us. "If it weren't for Downing Street, Coombs, I'd have you both escorted out. Tell me what you're thinking."

"The Marylebone case," I said. "Was it too easy, Superintendent? Too convenient? That such a horrific act should be perpetrated, and the killer apprehended so readily, with no question of guilt?"

Batleigh shifted in his seat and flexed his hands. "We got lucky."

A seed of doubt had been planted. "What do you know of the handyman? His relationship to the victims? What started the rampage? What stopped it? And the victims? How much is known as to their whereabouts prior to the event? About their purpose in being in that place at that time?"

"It was a quadrille lesson."

"Yes, but is that all it was? Not a typical outcome of a dance lesson, was it?"

"Continue."

"Can you truly say such a sordid case is solved in so simple and immediate a fashion?" This question was meant more for Coombs, but it sailed past him. "Why would this handyman do such a thing? Was he coerced in some way? Hired perhaps?"

Batleigh studied me for a long moment. "Bit young for a doctor, aren't you?"

"I excelled in my studies."

"And no military, I take it?"

"No, Superintendent, I have not served."

He nodded, as if that had confirmed a suspicion. "What do you propose, Dr. Johnson?"

"Let me conduct an investigation. I will share my findings only with Detective Coombs."

"'Cause he works for me," Coombs interjected.

"Yes. Yes, I do. But my point was more that I would not make anything I find public."

"Anything you find ... ?"

"Should I find anything at all," I said quickly. "More than likely, events will prove to be exactly as described. It will be a simple matter of temporary madness on the part of the handyman. Nothing more, nothing less. But if there is more, well ..."

Batleigh nodded. "Right, then. I'll get a message to Dr. Walker, the coroner. He's at the morgue preparing for the inquest. At St. Margaret's. Back room of the vestry."

"The back room of the vestry?"

"Local planning board," Batleigh said. "We're lucky they allowed *that* much."

"I should like to interview the girl and the prisoner. For that I will need –"

"To be a special constable? I don't think so."

"I was going to say, a letter. In your hand, with your imprint. That should be sufficient."

Batleigh agreed.

While I awaited the letter, Coombs informed me that Peters was mine for the day. Further, I was to find Coombs at the Wandering Swan before the inquest to give him my report.

Batleigh wrote slowly, carefully. He paused frequently to flex his hands.

"Pardon me for intruding," I said, "but may I ask about your hands? Perhaps I can help. I am a doctor, after all."

He considered me for a moment, then said, "Burns. When I was a child, I fell into a fire."

"Ah. The tightened skin makes movement difficult, then?"

"Precisely."

I recommended ointments, accepted the letter with thanks and took my leave.

Once in Peters' carriage, I felt excitement build as we clattered and bounced along. There were bodies to examine. Granted, I knew beforehand their manner of death: hammer blows to the head. But still, the exact nature of the wounds fascinated me. Was the extinction of life caused by exsanguination after unconsciousness? Or was it instantaneous due to damage to the brain tissue? Or some combination? I was eager to find out.

CHAPTER SEVEN

BANAL MONSTROSITIES

THE MORGUE AT ST. MARGARET'S WAS indeed in the back room of the vestry of the parish church. The coroner, a Dr. Walker, was a tall and gangly blond who seemed incapable of being still. He was quite displeased with the morgue's situation, rightfully so, and this explained his gruff demeanor. In response to my casual remark about the exceeding warmth of the room, Walker harrumphed, then explained that the morgue had been built above the boiler room and had no desire to discuss the matter further.

Walker's office appeared to have been a closet and thus had no desk, but merely a table and two chairs. He snatched Batleigh's letter from my hand and read it quickly while breathing through his nose. He then slapped it together with papers from his desk and thrust them at me.

"Dr. Walker," I said, "this is not meant as a slight against your work."

"Just read, please."

I took the papers, returned the letter to my pocket, and read the report. There were no surprises contained within it; the victims had died of head wounds. When I returned it to him, he said, "Before I give you free rein, you will examine one body and tell me what you find. And don't parrot my work."

It seemed clear that Walker was testing me, and I eagerly accepted the challenge. He led me into the morgue proper, which consisted of long tables with sheet-covered bodies laid atop them. Virtually no equipment or medical supplies were apparent.

I wanted to show Walker I knew my way around a corpse. Additionally, it was a perfect opportunity to see if he had missed anything of import. I withdrew a recently obtained notebook and mechanical pencil.

He assigned me to a male victim of about fifty years of age, who was indeed six feet tall, as stated in the report. He was a bit overweight, though well-muscled, and covered in an abundance of dark hair. There was a surgical scar on his abdomen. An old bullet wound on his right calf was paired with a larger exit wound on the other side. This, along with his trim hair and beard, suggested he had been a soldier. A different angle and said bullet would have prevented him from attending any dance classes. Until that night, he had probably counted himself lucky in that regard.

On top of his head, the thick hair and scalp hung open in a two-pronged flap half an inch long. This exposed a similarly shaped hole in his skull and damaged brain tissue beneath. I picked up a nearby magnifying glass and examined the hole more closely. "The blow was delivered by a claw hammer," I said.

Walker was unimpressed. "I did say you should not parrot my report."

"This victim is six feet tall, according to your report. The point of impact suggests the killer was taller, but not a great deal. Six foot four, I should say. "

"So, you know Mr. Hughes is tall."

"He is also left-handed."

That caught him by surprise. "How did you arrive at that?"

"Look at the angle, how it points to the right ever so slightly." I handed him the magnifying glass.

Walker bent in close to the victim's skull. Eventually he straightened. "I missed that." He tossed the glass into a tray with such ferocity I suspected it had cracked. "Very well. I'll allow you to continue to examine the bodies if, in exchange, you're willing to help my new attendant move them into coffins in preparation for tonight's inquest."

"I would be only too happy to assist."

"Excellent. There are several other deaths on my docket, so my day is quite full. Yes, quite full." He introduced me to a tawny-haired teen who, while eager to comport his job effectively, was clearly uncomfortable around the corpses.

Walker left us to our duties. The boy expressed relief to learn the bodies would not be moved until I completed my work, and I would prefer to do said work alone.

There were no other signs of violence on any of the corpses beyond those stated in the report; head wounds caused by hammer blows. The woman who had been found on a table possessed the largest wound of all, having been struck several times. The pieces of skull and scalp were in a ceramic basin, and I found myself rather enjoying putting the pieces back together. That is, until I noticed the boy at a porch window, peering at me, his cigarette hovering near his gaping mouth. I had been whistling again, I realized.

"It helps me concentrate," I barked at him.

He scurried out of sight.

I made thorough, detailed notes. Every word was chosen to help convince Coombs that Hughes was indeed the killer.

My work done, I interrupted the boy's smoke and together we carried in the plain wooden coffins and placed the corpses in them, leaving the tops open. Rigor had passed, and every slip of a limb caused the boy to yelp or gasp.

By the time we were done, the room had become quite warm. I reminded the boy to apply disinfectant and suggested some charcoal in the coffins to help alleviate the odours that would only worsen by the time of the inquest. In addition, I suggested that someone speak to the rector about turning down the heat until afterwards.

I made my way out to the carriage, pondering my findings. Coombs' revelation was simply wrong. Would there ever be enough information to dissuade him from making his proclamation? Unlikely, but I had to do as much as possible. If he were to present his foolhardy case at the inquest, in front of the police, witnesses and reporters, disaster would ensue.

With the details of the witnesses at hand, I would conduct my own interviews before the inquest. My first would be that of the only witness, the child, whom Coombs intended to accuse. I checked my pocket watch. I had mere hours before the inquest. I summoned Peters to come down from his driver's seat. He immediately went for the door. "No, no," I said. "This is about today's errands."

"Sir."

"We have three destinations. Two nearby, the other is … further away." I gave him the Grayson's address. "And we must return to the final destination, here in Marylebone, to the Wandering Swan Pub for the inquest, which is scheduled for five o'clock."

"Easy enough, I expect. I know the Swan well and the Graysons' street is familiar. High number, so up the north end, I'd say." He blew into his hands for warmth. "And where is the further place, sir?"

Was this necessary? The wounds I had identified, corroborated by Walker, would surely be enough to convince Coombs of his folly, would it not?

"Sir? If I know the destination, I can plan the most efficient route."

I was loathe to give voice to the name. "Newgate Prison."

"Ah. Well, I do know the way, sir. Shall we?" He opened the door.

"We shall. Thank you, Peters." I climbed in and sat, then put my hand out to stop him from closing the door. "I should like to make a stop before the Graysons'."

"Sir?"

"Do you know of a good confectioner?"

"I do, sir."

"Excellent. I shall purchase a chocky." If I were to be questioning a child, I might as well arrive prepared.

⟣───◉ ◎───⟢

The Graysons lived in a working-class neighborhood, on the third floor of a tenement house. Upon entering the building, my nose became filled with odours which I believe were food-related, though I was unable to identify them specifically. Sounds of lower-class life vied with each other for my attention; quarrels, babies crying, children simultaneously gaming, teasing, and fighting.

At the top of the creaking stairs, I knocked at the only door. The space had likely once been a garret, now converted to allow meager space for a residence.

First came the sound of chains and locks. The door opened a crack.

"Mrs. Grayson?" I asked the eyes that peered out.

"Yes?" Her voice sounded like crushed glass.

"My name is Dr. Johnson, and I am here about the incident at the dance academy."

"But the inquest is in just a few hours."

"Yes, but I should like to speak to you privately." I held up Batleigh's letter. I hoped she was literate.

"Privately?" The door had not budged, and her tone did not suggest a welcome.

"I can make it worth your while," I said, and quickly produced a one-pound note.

Her eyes darted, bird-like, from me, to the note and back to me.

"I just have a few questions." I inched the bill closer.

"All right." Bony, calloused fingers reached out through the crack and snatched the note from me. The door swung open, and Mrs. Grayson hugged the edge of it, allowing for one quick gesture to indicate that I should enter.

Though the furnishings of the two-room flat were shabby, the Graysons had more of them than did my host. Nearest the door was a dark leather divan, with cracked cushions and missing buttons. There was a battered coffee table, a sewing table and a wooden stool next to a faded five-drawer dresser. In the far corner, the child, Elinor, sat amidst an array of dolls. The report had stated she was nine years of age. Absent that information, I would have guessed six at most. She was thin to the point of frailty. Her wispy black hair barely reached her shoulders. A light green dress was at least one size too large, apparently to hide her hunched back. Veins showed through her wan skin.

"Would you like some tea?" Mrs. Grayson asked. She wore a faded plaid dress under a white apron. Her hair, for all its unruliness, retained a colour akin to daffodils. Her blue eyes managed to shine through, despite the dark circles.

"That would be lovely," I said, not wishing to be rude and reject the offer.

"Elinor," she said, "keep our guest company while I make some tea."

"I understand Elinor is not your daughter by birth?" I asked as I sat on the divan.

Rather than keep me company, the girl turned her back and whispered to her dolls. A dozen porcelain faces smiled at me, with scratches and scuff marks in place of rosy cheeks. Their hair was thin and missing in spots, but the clothing looked new, in better repair and brighter than anything else within sight. They appeared to be cast-off dolls given bright party clothes.

"No, she come to me when the people at the academy couldn't keep her," she said from the alcove that served as a kitchen. "One of my jobs is I do needlework, you see, and they pay me good to keep the costumes in order. But Elinor, see, she would sneak into the hall and watch the people dancing. Nobody minded. She was quiet enough. But they found she was sleeping in the back room. Tried to find her parents, they did, but couldn't. But I thought she was sweet, kind of, and not having no kids of my own, it was an idea." She emerged from the alcove with a wooden tray and porcelain tea service. "She wants to be a dancer," she went on, casting her eyes upon her adopted daughter. The girl sat in silence, holding a doll dressed better than either of them. "But she struggles."

The evidence of this was plain in the girl's physique.

"Forgive her," Mrs. Grayson said, setting the tray on the coffee table. "She hasn't spoken to anyone but her dolls since ..." She sat and dabbed at her eyes.

I slid forward to the edge of the divan. Elinor remained focused on the dolls.

"Elinor?" I said as I produced the treat I had purchased. "Would you care for a nice chocky?"

She turned and her eyes locked onto it, then she looked to Mrs. Grayson.

"Yes, Elinor," said Mrs. Grayson, "you may have the chocolate."

The shadow of a smile crossed Elinor's face as she snatched it, held it under her nose and breathed it in.

"Elinor," Mrs. Grayson prompted.

Elinor curtseyed, still without meeting my eyes. Her hips were malformed, leaving one leg bent, the other straight. A clear sign of rickets. She sat back down, unwrapped the treat and took tiny, savoring bites.

While we drank the cold and bitter tea – I sipped mine out of courtesy – and Elinor pretended to share her treat with her dolls, I asked Mrs. Grayson a few basic questions.

"Mr. Grayson's away," she answered. "On a ship. Just one o' his jobs. They're good to us at the academy, they are, and they let sweet little Elly dance. She loves to dance, don't you, sweetie? But she gets tired, so they let her do as much as she can, then take a rest. They're good to us."

This tiny, frail girl was Coombs' alleged murderess. Having finished her treat, she now arranged her dolls in the corner. I listened to her breathy, sing-song voice as she quietly explained to her dolls why they were being arranged the way they were and what they were to do. The words themselves were unintelligible to me, but the tone conveyed that she was planning a party of some kind, perhaps even a ball.

"Elinor?" I said. "Please come here a moment?"

Elinor went silent and still.

"Elly?" said Mrs. Grayson. "Did you hear the good sir?"

"I assure you I mean her no harm."

Mrs. Grayson nodded. "Elinor. Come here."

The girl set down her dolls and came to stand before the coffee table.

"Elinor, would you please pick up the tea kettle?" It was a porcelain pot with a sizable handle arching over.

"She's not allowed to touch it. It's too heavy for her, especially when it's got some tea."

"I understand," I said to them. "This is just a sort of a test – a game, really. Just try, please."

"Go ahead, dear."

Elinor grasped the handle. There was an element of excitement now that she'd been granted permission to try something forbidden. She braced herself and lifted. The kettle rose with a swaying motion caused by Elinor's trembling arms.

"Thank you, that's enough," I said. "You can put it down now."

She all but dropped it onto the tray. Mrs. Grayson nearly leapt on it for fear of it having broken.

I stood. "Thank you both, I appreciate your time." I pressed another pound note into Mrs. Grayson's hand.

Peters waited for me at the brougham's door, a knowing smile on his face as he held it open.

On the carriage step, I paused. "Would you like me to enquire with Detective Coombs as to having you come on full time? At his residence."

"Oh, thank you, sir. I do appreciate the sentiment, but my wife is expecting, and I don't think Detective Coombs would like a baby about."

Laughing, I said, "I suspect you are right, Peters. Well then. Off to Newgate."

"With all possible haste," he said as he closed the door.

"Indeed."

CHAPTER EIGHT

FACING FEARS

THE ENTRANCE TO NEWGATE PRISON LOOMED over me. I told myself I was merely studying it, as I had not seen it in full daylight before. I had been brought in through the rear entrance, and when I left with Coombs, it had been night. The brick, five-story structure looked mundane enough, with its windows and entrance set in tall archways. I touched my neck. I could almost feel the thick, rough rope and hear the creaking of the wooden structure that lay behind that unassuming façade. To go back inside was a feat that I feared was beyond my abilities.

"I'll be right here, sir," said Peters from his driver's seat. "They won't do anything to you, sir. They can't. You're free, right?"

"Right." My resolve felt firm as gossamer.

"I'll give it an hour, sir. You don't come bounding out of there with nary a scratch or a bruise, I'll set all the … forces of … well, I'll send Detective Coombs in. That ought to be enough," he said with a grin.

"It worked before. Thank you, Peters."

"Been in a trouble spot or two myself, sir. No prison, of course, but – Oh, sorry, sir. Didn't mean anything by it."

"Of course not." The banality of his gaffe added lightness to my mood. What had I to fear? Only that my freedom had been based on a lie. Still, it was official, and I was now effectively an officer of the law. After a good tug of my coat and a check of my hat, I strode into the prison, directly to Thornsbury's office, with Batleigh's letter in hand. I demanded to see Mr. Hughes immediately, desirous of having this over and done before my resolve weakened.

I declined the governor's offer to meet with Hughes in his cell. The thought of returning to the condemned wing nearly buckled my knees. Instead, I chose the men's quadrangle. Thornsbury summoned a guard, a rail of a man with widely spaced, yellowed teeth and curled gray hair protruding from his cap.

Thankful that the guard seemed to not remember me, I followed him through the familiar stone corridors, down the damp stairs and out into the quadrangle. It seemed the sun was falling, determined to abandon me. I was coiled tightly within, though neither fight nor flight were likely to succeed.

"Where is Mr. Hughes?" I managed, after forcing a swallow.

"Wait here," said the guard.

Cold shadows filled the quadrangle. A sliver of sunlight brushed tentatively against the iron spikes atop the brick wall. I paced, subconsciously following the path I and the other prisoners had been herded along during our mandated morning walks.

The guard led Hughes into the quadrangle. "Talk to the man," he said and gave Hughes a shove. The gaoler pointed to a bench against a wall with his cudgel.

"I need to speak with him alone," I said.

The guard shook his head and stomped off.

Even sitting, it was obvious Mr. Hughes was the six foot four I had speculated. A wiry man, his muscles and sinews showed easily through taut, leathery skin. What teeth he had were dark and askew. The disheveled hair and stubble on his face were both the colour of granite. Combined with his hawk-like features, this gave him the look of a gargoyle fallen from some ancient building.

First, I asked him to tell me about himself, to put him at ease. He had been a labourer all his life, working various jobs until inevitably his drinking and brawling would put an end to whatever situation he had managed to obtain. He never married, had no family. This, too, was a result of his sometimes-violent drunkenness.

"But I ain't never kilt no one," he said. "I gets mad, yeah, but only so's I'd get a good fight goin', y'know? Mostly ..." He studied his hands as he slowly rubbed them, working them around each other. "Sometimes I picked on ..." His hands stopped. He lifted his head and looked at me with eyes yellowed, bloodshot, and filling with tears. "But I ain't never kilt no one a'fore!"

"But you did kill those people, did you not?" I asked quietly.

He nodded spasmodically, again looking at his hands.

"Do you know why?"

As he struggled to find an answer, he used his sleeves to wipe the tears from his eyes. "No," he said finally, his gaze resting on me again. The tears slowed as he retreated inward. "Somethin' come over me. A mad I never felt before. Like them folks ... everythin' was their fault. And everythin'd get better if I just ..." He slowly wrapped his arms around himself. "And I was cold."

That word echoed off the walls, in my mind and into my soul. The cold at my neck when I spilled my desires onto paper. The cold at my hand when I stood before Coombs' door. Mere coincidence, I told myself. I repeated Hughes' word to push it out of my mind until I had to restrain a laugh. It was January in London. Of course we experienced cold.

Hughes had retreated into his own world and did not hear my thanks. There was no longer any doubt. Mr. Hughes had committed the murders.

I announced that we were done, and the same guard emerged from the shadow of the corridor along with one other. I held myself still until we had turned a corner, then released all my tension with a long breath, steadying myself against the wall. Feeling a tad proud of myself, I straightened back up, gave my coat another tug and left Newgate Prison.

"I'm aware of the time, sir," said Peters as I approached. "Got a route all thought out and I believe we can make it before the inquest begins."

"Thank you, Peters," I said and jumped in, but I wished for time itself to slow down. Mr. Hughes' statement nagged at me. He experienced unusual, undeniable urges while at the same time feeling cold, just as I had at Coombs' residence.

I shook the thoughts out of my head. There were more important considerations before me.

There had to be a way to redirect Coombs from his current path. How could I tell a man so sure of himself that he was completely, utterly wrong? Would saying so end my employ? A likely outcome. Would he send me back to Newgate? His flashes of anger suggested so. I pondered fleeing, of taking what I had and going … where? Europe? The colonies? No, I would hardly have time to book passage to Leeds, let alone America, before the inquest, before Coombs would be discredited and his vouchsafe for me would be as well and I would be returned to prison to await the hangman's rope.

Shame struck me. This man who had plucked me from certain death needed my help, and my first thought was that it was too much of a risk and that I should run like a dog from a thunderclap. No. I would find a way to dissuade him.

A check of my pocket watch revealed that we had less than an hour to get from Newgate to the Wandering Swan. "All due haste, Mr. Peters," I called out the carriage window.

CHAPTER NINE

FLUID SHADOWS

"Faster!" I called to Peters as I rapped on the carriage roof, my head out the window as if I were a madman. Thanks to lumbering omnibuses and an injured horse in our path, only minutes remained. "*Faster!*"

To his credit, Peters gave a shout and snapped the reins. The sudden burst of speed caused me to hit the back of my head on the window frame and fall to the carriage floor. I pulled myself back up and watched the people of London, gentle and not, part before us.

A fat constable blew his whistle. "This is a police matter!" I shouted as we passed him. Exhilaration overcame my fear that we would be too late, that Coombs had already doomed us. This only fueled the fire of this reckless aban-don. Peters leaned sharply forward, calling out, shaking the reins, and I believe I saw a similar excitement on his face.

"There it is, Peters!" I called, my hand forward as if to charge into battle, my target, the wooden painted sign of The Wandering Swan.

"Yes, sir," he answered. "I see it, sir." Now he called out to the people along the sidewalk to step aside and make a path. Some obeyed, though others glared and even gestured rudely.

Peters pulled back mightily on the reins. The horse reared and bellowed a whinny. I lurched forward, then back as the brougham came to a clattering halt.

I threw the carriage door open and lunged out, heedless of the startled folk blocking my path and accosting poor Peters. Just as I pulled open the twin doors of the inn, the fat constable pulled me back.

"Coombs!" I called, holding the doors open against the constable's grip. "I have arrived, Coombs!"

"He's with me!" shouted Coombs from the depths of the crowd inside. Res-cued once again, was I.

The constable objected, but Batleigh came out and convinced the officer to release me and for him to settle the crowd outside. With the doors still open, the commotion about the carriage had spilled into the room. Peters was in full, vociferous argument with a mutton-chopped man in a suit who looked ready to climb the brougham.

"Don't lay yer hands on my driver," warned Coombs as he pushed through the crowd.

The man turned his reddened face as well as his argument to Coombs, but after one good look, the rage fled from the man. He muttered about safety, donned his top hat and hurried away along the sidewalk. Batleigh and the constable now dispersed the crowd and directed the people back into the pub.

"Hell of an entrance, Johnson," Coombs said with a grin. "Let's go have a pint."

I followed him to the bar on the left side of the place. It was sizable as London pubs go, with dark wooden beams and white walls. Wall-mounted gas lamps lit the place well, and the ceiling was high enough to keep the smoke well above one's head. People shuffled and jostled their way to their seats.

The center of the room had been cleared to make space for the inquest. At the back of the room, two tables had been pushed together with one chair at each. Batleigh joined Walker there. Before them, a row of chairs had been set for the jurors. To the right of the open space was a single chair for witnesses. Onlookers and reporters, their pads and pencils at the ready, filled the rest of the tables. I spotted Mrs. Grayson being comforted by an older woman. A sister, perhaps?

A brief commotion from the reporters drew my attention. Among them was a woman, though she was dressed plainly and, in place of a parasol, carried her own pad and pencil. I could not make out her words, but her tone clearly conveyed a rebuke to one of her fellow reporters, which garnered laughter from the others.

I gratefully accepted the pint offered by the barkeep and the tingling foam settled me. "I was concerned," I said to Coombs. "I … I insist you read my notes before you say anything at the inquest. Please. Do me this favour." I tore out the pages of notes and handed them over. "I think you will accept there really is only one conclusion to be drawn regarding this case," I said. "The girl could not have done it. They have the right man. Please, for both our sakes, say nothing of your theory. We can discuss it in detail later."

Coombs' brows drew down, almost becoming one line. He breathed slowly. I gripped the mug so tightly I thought it might shatter in my hands.

"Shall we begin?" announced Walker.

Coombs turned his attention to the inquest and tucked my notes in his pocket with nary a glance at them.

My dread returned, I finished my drink and gestured for another.

Walker called a hefty older woman to the stand whose testimony reflected what the article had described: that she had arrived late, discovered the carnage, and run screaming from the building.

The bobby who spoke next relayed that he had responded to the screams, gone in, found the bodies and young Elinor, then blown his whistle for aid.

Batleigh then testified and described the ensuing investigation. "We found bloody footprints all around the crime scene and soon found matching footprints leading out through the back door. We followed said footprints along the street, whereupon we discovered the building's handyman, Mr. Hughes."

"What was he doing?" asked Walker.

"Nothing to speak of, just ambling along. We approached. He was covered in blood."

"Did he say anything to you?" Walker paced, hands clasped behind him.

"He said he was sorry. Didn't know what came over him."

The coroner turned and faced Batleigh. "Is that when he confessed?"

"Yes, that's correct. And he said he threw the weapon, a hammer, into the sewer. Sent a man down the nearest one but found no sign of it." Batleigh worked his gloved fingers in his lap, an unconscious gesture.

"Thank you, Superintendent. That will be all." Walker let Batleigh return to his seat before continuing. "I arrived at the scene fifteen minutes past the hour of nine. I found the scene to be exactly as described. I examined the victims and pronounced life to be extinct in each. Now I would like to offer into evidence my report which provides details of the wounds. All of the victims were struck in the head by a claw hammer. The blows were administered by someone of considerable height. Six foot four, by my estimation, and left-handed."

I hoped for some acknowledgement from Walker but did not receive it.

"Having completed the testimonies, we will now adjourn to the mortuary so you may view the bodies," Walker announced.

"Hold on," Batleigh called and stood. "Dr. Walker, if I may?"

The coroner nodded and gestured for him to continue.

"Detective Coombs? You said before we began that you expected to have some new information. We're all aware of your assistant's spectacular arrival. Any new light to be shed on this? Hughes' motivation perhaps?"

"What light needs to be shed?" Walker demanded. "We have the killer and a confession."

Batleigh bristled. "We also have the man who solved the –"

"Downing Street Bloodletting," Walker interjected. "Yes, I am well aware of his prior *case*." He let the last word hang in the air.

Batleigh stepped forward. "First, Dr. Walker," he said, his voice tense, "I'll ask that you never interrupt me in such a way again." He waited for a nod of confirmation from a suddenly still Walker. "Secondly, while it is true that we have a man in custody –"

"Who confessed."

"*Walker.* Be quiet now."

The coroner crossed his arms and tapped his foot impatiently.

"We have a man in custody," Batleigh continued. "But we do not have any-one who witnessed the killings, nor do we have a murder weapon. I, for one, would like to be sure we have done everything in our power, that we have left no stone unturned. Now, let us hear from Detective Coombs regarding what he and his assistant have discovered." Walker began a response. "Please sit down, Dr. Walker."

Walker fumed for a moment, then sat.

"Detective Coombs," said Batleigh. "If you would be so kind."

Coombs wore a smug grin and winked at me. His expression told me he was going to announce his insane theory. Doom stood before us with welcoming arms spread wide.

"You got the wrong guy," he said, standing.

A buzz went through the room. Walker merely laughed and shook his head. I downed the rest of my beer and gestured for another.

Batleigh worked his gloved hands as he said, "I was not expecting that response. Please clarify, Detective Coombs."

"Lemme tell you a story," said Coombs. "Superintendent, in the paper you said somethin' about the kind of monster what would do such a thing."

"Right. This kind of thing just isn't human."

"It is," said Coombs. "And let me tell you what kind o' human. The kind what only wants to cause chaos, to wreak havoc."

It seemed strange to hear Coombs use such lurid language.

"What are you getting at, Coombs?" asked Batleigh.

"I'm sayin' that the killer ain't no ordinary human."

A sudden chill washed over me. I drew my arms in. Had someone opened a window? No, there was no wind carrying this cold. I looked about to see if anyone else felt this. Some reporters closed their coats, while the female reporter turned up her collar. Mrs. Grayson and her sister huddled together.

"You think you got yer monster 'cause he's big and scary. Looks like a mon-ster, don't he? So ya lock it up away from everybody and then feel safe 'cause you got rid of it."

Then the world shifted, and I floated upon unsettled waters, as if the room's shadows had become fluid. How many pints had I drunk?

"The real monsters are the ones you don't see comin'. Like little Elinor." He said the name with the venom of a thousand vipers.

The invisible waters raged. The cold froze my soul. I heard stifled gasps, whispers of fear.

"I say Elinor killed those people. She used a bone-handled chef's knife. She sliced right through their legs, so they'd bleed out. You'll find the knife at her home, inside one of her dolls. A blonde one with a pink dress. Elinor Grayson is the Mad Dancer of Marylebone!"

I crashed upon unseen rocks, released from the ethereal rime. Even the reporters needed a breath before they could start scribbling again.

Mrs. Grayson cried out in denial, then burst into tears. The woman sitting with her held her close.

"This is ludicrous," said Walker, rising. "How could you possibly come to this conclusion?"

"I'm tellin' ya," Coombs said, "she did it. You'll find the knife in one of her dolls."

"I have to admit, Coombs," said Batleigh. "I'm a touch skeptical."

"Like you were about Downing Street?"

"It's one thing to claim knowledge of the secret goings on at the Minister's house. But a little girl's doll collection?"

"That's beside the point!" shouted Walker. "They were killed with hammer blows to the *head*."

Batleigh put out a hand to calm Walker. "He's got a point there, Coombs."

"I'll tell you the same thing I told you about Downing Street." He was clearly becoming frustrated. "I –" He stopped himself and glanced quickly about the room. "I seen it. And if you look, you'll see it, too."

"I beg the sirs' pardon," said Mrs. Grayson, her voice raw. "I need to say something."

"Of course," said Walker. "Please. Shed some light on this."

Mrs. Grayson stood. Her voice wavered as she spoke. "You been sayin' these things about my Elinor, but she wouldn't never do such things." Her voice cracked in her struggle against tears. "She's a sweet little girl." Like a bird testing its wings before flying, Mrs. Grayson took increasingly bold steps, her voice keeping with her strides. "And … and *you* … you, *sir*. How *dare* you say them things! If anybody here's a monster –"

"*Mrs. Grayson*," Batleigh's voice brought her to the quick.

"Don't believe me?" said Coombs. "Everything I been sayin' is in Dr. Johnson's report," Coombs said, holding up my notes, folded over. "Ain't that right, Dr. Johnson?"

His cold, hard stare nailed me to my seat and took away my voice. The lies he demanded of me would not leave my mouth. But memories of Newgate came to me, of how close I had come to swinging from a hangman's rope. If not for Coombs, I would be in a pauper's grave.

"I merely present evidence," I said. "It is up to Detective Coombs to draw conclusions."

Coombs' expression darkened. Clearly, he had hoped for full-throated support.

"Let me see these 'notes'," Walker said to Coombs.

"You won't believe 'em anyway," said Coombs. "Let's go to the morgue. See for ourselves."

"This is absurd." Walker went to Superintendent Batleigh and the jury. "You cannot possibly believe any of this."

Batleigh stood. "I suggest we adjourn to the mortuary to view the bodies and settle the matter."

Reporters and jurors alike downed the last of their drinks as Batleigh and Walker entreated them to follow. I stumbled away from the bar, steadied myself, then pushed through the crowd, seeking Coombs. He was the first out the door and beyond my calling.

CHAPTER TEN

INEXPLICABLE CHANGES

BATLEIGH AND WALKER LED THE JURORS out, followed by the reporters. I tried to push my way through the onlookers and stragglers, finally among the last to gain the sidewalk.

Peters had moved the brougham along and watched with curiosity from his seat as we all marched past. I dared not pause, as I still hoped to catch Coombs. He knew the conclusion I had drawn. Why would he expect me to say the opposite?

I quickened my pace along the outer edge of the people only to see Coombs' long, determined strides putting him far ahead of the rest of us. Reporters calling after him rushed to keep up. One broke away from the pack: the woman. She searched the crowd and her eyes fell on me.

"Dr. Johnson." She waved to me and waited until I caught up. She was dressed plainly and appeared to be of Spanish origins. She held out a card. "Miss Clavijo, of the *London Daily Journal*. If I may, I'd like to ask you about Detective Coombs."

What was I to say? That he was a madman? A fool? A liar? "I have nothing to say at the moment." Out of politeness I took the card and forged on ahead.

Our curious group continued around the corner to the vestry of St. Margaret's and bunched up at the door.

Walker stopped me at the door and waited until all the others had gone up. "I don't know what Coombs is up to. Getting his name in the papers again, I suspect. Is that why *you're* here? To support his lies? Be a part of his show? We both know what awaits us upstairs. I suggest you side with the truth. I intend to press charges against Coombs and will include you if I must." Walker went on ahead of me.

As I climbed the wooden stairs, the sound of the running boiler rattled the walls. Gasps, whispered oaths, and the stench of rotting flesh made its way to me as I approached the room. I knew what awaited us: decaying corpses and a wretched odour because the heat had not been turned down and the precautions I outlined had not been followed.

Miss Clavijo came up behind me, but I put out my arm to stop her. "Do not go in there."

She frowned at me. "Thank you, but *I'll* be fine." She continued to the door, looked in and turned away, hastily putting a handkerchief to her mouth and nose.

Covering my own mouth as I moved past her, I said, "I did warn you."

Two jurors burst through the door and retched in the corridor. Miss Clavijo refused the assistance of one of the other reporters, who then dashed into the hall. I covered my nose and mouth and entered the room.

Coombs had taken up position in the far corner, glowering at the proceedings. I dared not approach him.

Walker was in the midst of apologizing. "I told the vicar to turn down the heat, but clearly my request was ignored. However, these conditions will not affect the evidence. Go ahead," he said to the hardier jury members. "Look for yourself. Superintendent, you as well."

Batleigh, followed by a juror who looked to be in his fifties, approached the coffins. Both held handkerchiefs to their faces. Batleigh examined the head of the nearest one while Walker stood petulantly, his back turned, by the door. Puzzled, Batleigh moved down the corpse's body. Having examined the legs, he indicated for the juror to do the same. They exchanged a look, then moved to the next coffin.

Walker became aware of the activity. "Well?"

"See for yourself," said Batleigh.

Scoffing, but concerned, Walker pressed a cloth to his face and went to a coffin. "No," he said simply after examining the first. "*No*," he said again after examining the next one. "This can't be," he said finally. "Dr. Johnson. You were here. You saw what I saw. Look at this one. Please."

The desperation in Walker's voice and in his eyes shook me. I dared a glance at Coombs. His arms were folded, his eyes lidded, a smouldering anger behind them.

Unnerved, I recovered a small piece of coal from where it had fallen to the floor, wrapped it in my pocket square and pressed it to my face. Murmuring voices swirled around me. Walker gestured frantically at the corpse's head. It was the soldier I had examined.

"Look, man, *look*," urged Walker.

My heart pounded and I fought against the sharpening of my breath. The charcoal would only do so much against a roomful of rotting corpses.

The soldier's hair appeared intact. The flap of skin on his head was gone. I worked my fingers through his hair but found no trace of the wound. *Was this the same man? The soldier?* The size, hair and colouring all matched. His leg still carried the bullet wound. There was no doubt this was the body I had examined earlier to pass Walker's test.

Then I saw it, on the inside of the man's upper thigh: a deep gash hanging open in the ashen, limp skin. A grim, mocking smile of decaying flesh.

Walker grabbed my arm and turned me to him. "Tell me. Me. Right here, right now, that you and I both saw and discussed head wounds on that corpse, made by a claw hammer. With the left hand, as you pointed out. Tell me this now."

"I believe I saw –"

He took me by the lapels and lifted me to my toes. "Enough! Did you or did you not see head wounds?"

His face was nearly pressed into mine. I could hear Coombs' breathing behind me. "Everything is in my report."

He shoved me away. "Then where are those wounds?" he pleaded.

"There appears to have been a mistake," said Batleigh. "I think we've seen enough here." He conducted everyone out of the room and into the crowded hall, closing the door behind him.

I found myself on the opposite end of the corridor from Coombs. He leaned back against one wall, staring at nothing.

While Batleigh and Walker carried on a heated, though whispered exchange, the tawny-haired boy finished cleaning the jurors' sick. The reporters scribbled frantically. The jurors shuffled, pulled at their collars, and opened their coats. The stifling heat, the closeness and, no doubt, the bodies beyond the door, made them anxious to leave.

"I cannot explain this … discrepancy in the manner of death." Walker said finally. "But I still contend that Hughes is the killer. He confessed to it. I've seen him. And I saw the girl. There is simply no way she could have done any of this, no matter the method."

"We can settle this easy like," Coombs interjected, "by goin' to the house."

"Are you seriously suggesting we take the jury on a trip to the Graysons' home?" Walker whirled on him.

The jurors backed against the walls, leaving a path between the two men.

Coombs pushed away from the wall and faced the coroner. "I was right about the wounds, yeah? You'll see I'm right about this. Won't be no doubt then, will there?"

"The Graysons live in a garret," I said. "There is hardly room for all of us."

"We'll take Dr. Walker here, and Batleigh," said Coombs. "Dr. Johnson can come, too." His inviting tone carried an undercurrent of malevolence.

"I forbid it," said Walker, stepping closer to Coombs.

Jurors slid along the wall to get away.

"Afraid, Doctor?" asked Coombs, advancing.

"Ha!"

The two men stood facing other such that I expected fists to be raised, though I doubted Coombs would follow Queensbury Rules.

"*Enough*," said Batleigh as he pushed between them. Arms out, he held an open hand up to both of them. "Detective Coombs, Doctors Walker and Johnson and I will adjourn to the Graysons' as requested."

Miss Clavijo leaned forward from the wall. "Pardon, but –"

"No reporters," he told her. His tone softened. "We will search for this doll and this knife, and we will return to the jury with our findings." He turned his attention back to Walker and Coombs as hardness returned to his tone. "And we will comport ourselves as the gentlemen we are or there will be repercussions. Am I understood?"

"All I ask," said Coombs with a grin and an expansive gesture as he stepped back.

Walker acquiesced, then adjourned the jury and instructed them to be back at the Wandering Swan in one hour. He and Batleigh would be back to report their findings at that time. The reporters could do as they wished, provided they didn't follow.

Coombs claimed Peters' carriage for himself while the rest of us hailed cabs. When we arrived at the Graysons' building, there was a brief wait at the bottom of the stairs as Elinor was retrieved from the downstairs neighbour. The girl withdrew into herself at the sight of all the adults. Mrs. Grayson carried her up, leading the grim procession.

After setting Elinor down and fumbling with her keys, Mrs. Grayson let Batleigh in first, then Walker, myself and finally Coombs pushed through. Elinor clung tightly to her adopted mother's leg.

Batleigh went from one doll to the next, pulling apart the clothing and shaking them. Mrs. Grayson shielded Elinor's eyes.

Suddenly, Batleigh stopped.

"Well?" prompted Coombs.

Batleigh grimaced and squeezed the doll in his hands. His mouth gaped in shock. He opened the doll's shirt from the back and pulled out a bone-handled chef's knife. Dried blood streaked the blade.

Mrs. Grayson fainted. Walker barely caught her. Elinor simply stared.

"Ya got yer monster," said Coombs, pointing to Elinor. He pushed past me, slamming my shoulder with his.

Walker staggered out as Batleigh informed Mrs. Grayson he was going to take Elinor in. I could not bear to watch and made my way back out.

I caught a glimpse of Peters' brougham as it rounded a street corner.

Walker stood on the sidewalk, staring up at a streetlamp, or perhaps beyond it to something he hoped would provide more than mere light.

"I am sorry," I said as I passed him.

"You saw it." Walker kept his eyes on the light.

I continued without pause. I dared not face him. What would I say? I had no explanation for what had happened, nor could I tell him why I did not refute Coombs.

"I know you did." He was louder now. "And you know it, too!"

A small, old cab trundled by, and I waved it down.

There was no denying what I had seen in the afternoon. And what I had just seen the same evening. They were different things that could not exist together in the same world. Not the world I knew. Dark, chaotic thoughts roiled my mind as we rumbled along. The fluidity of shadows. Hughes' strange urge accompanied by cold. The stench of the morgue. My own urges at the residence. Head wounds gone. Gashes in legs, smiling at me. The rotting flesh. The chill I felt at the inquest. Madness.

I welcomed the fresh air as I stepped out of the cab at Coombs' residence. But I feared what I would find inside.

"Sir?" the cabby asked, his hand out.

"Yes, of course." I struggled to focus on counting coins. The events of the day and the fear I would be sent back to Newgate dominated my mind. Was I going mad?

"*You're not mad.*"

"What did you say?" I snapped at the driver.

"Sir? Only speakin' to the horse, sir."

"Apologies. I thought I heard something." My brother's voice again. Rather, my own voice, my own self, attempting to calm the storm of my mind.

I paid the driver and sent him on his way.

Firelight capered in the parlour window as I lingered in the shadows between streetlamps. I wanted to prepare myself, plan what I would say to Coombs. I wanted the truth, but if I were to lose control, I might also lose my freedom.

"*You know what you saw.*"

"This morning, yes," I whispered. "But tonight ..."

"*He tricked you. He tricked you all.*"

"Yes. Somehow he tricked us. That is the only explanation. But how? I need the truth from him."

"*Yes. Go.*"

I marched up the steps and burst through the door. I found Coombs in the library, squatting by the fire.

"How did you do that?" I demanded.

"Do what?" he asked casually, without looking at me.

"Whatever it was you did. Changed the bodies perhaps? Swapped them?"

With his elbows on his knees, Coombs looked up at me with an amused grin. "What are you talkin' about?"

"I saw head wounds this morning –"

"And everybody else saw knife wounds tonight. Just like I said they would." He turned back to the fire.

"May I have my notes back?" I asked. What would they contain? Which reality would they portray?

He pushed the poker deeper into the flames. "Not much left of 'em."

I reached to take the poker. "Why would you –"

A swift motion and the hot end of the fireplace poker was pressed against my coat. The wool crackled and smoked, but Coombs' eyes burned all the hotter.

"Only one thing I need from you. When I say what somethin' *is*, you *say* that's what it is. You can do your investigatin', but don't never question what I say again."

"Or you'll send me back to prison?" I fought to keep my voice from trembling.

"*Hah.*" He swung the poker to prod the flames once again. "No. I'll take care of you myself." He stabbed the burning wood.

I patted the smouldering hole in my coat as I rushed up the stairs. In my room, I pondered my options. I could do as Coombs demanded and lie for him, or I could confront him and almost certainly be returned to Newgate. Or I could wait until he was asleep and escape. I had money, enough to take me far away.

Coombs' words echoed in my mind, that he would take care of me himself. Was there any doubt that he would hunt me down? If I stayed with Coombs, I could study him. Try to determine what had happened between my two viewings of the bodies. And the place to start was that chest in his room.

CHAPTER ELEVEN

SECRETS REVEALED

CLOSED CURTAINS MADE FOR A DARK room despite the midmorning sun. I dared not light a candle for fear of leaving a detectable odour behind. Thankfully, the door stayed open, providing a wedge of light on the floor and a column on the far wall.

I went directly for the wooden trunk and lifted the lid. It took a moment for my eyes to adjust to the shadows and for Coombs' secrets to be laid bare.

Penny bloods. Piles of them stacked to the top of the chest. Lurid engravings with garish colours and overwrought titles glared up at me. "Midnight Mysteries of the Black Band" showed a prone and provocatively dressed woman unaware of the menacing stare of a shadowy man in her window. "The Scapegrace of Edinburgh" offered skeletons accosting a fainting maid. On "Valyen the Vampyre", army officers recoiled at the sight of a bloodied woman in a coffin, a wooden stake buried in her chest.

I gaped at the display, attempting to reconcile the man with these childish publications. Perhaps they were a cover, a layer of distraction hiding the truth beneath. Ensuring the lid would stay upright, I memorized the size and positions of the stacks of books. They were neat and orderly enough that it was likely Coombs knew their exact placement.

There were dozens of them. I moved the stacks carefully, neatly, to the floor beside me. Under the penny bloods I found money. Bound stacks of pound notes, bags of coins. At the bottom of the chest, the deed to the house. Coombs' signature was a barely legible scrawl. No other papers or photographs to further illuminate my host.

Were there more secrets to be found within the penny bloods? I riffled through them and shook them out to see if any other papers would fall out. Judging by the illustrations I glimpsed, the penny bloods held stories of detectives, in some cases boys, dramatically solving crimes involving all manner of monsters. This certainly accounted for Coombs' flair for the dramatic, but no concrete evidence of his life prior to moving to this house.

Could there be useful information in the stories themselves? Surely not, as the few I looked at were ludicrous tales designed to appeal to the basest instincts of young boys.

"Read them," said my brother's voice.

I dared not. Having no way of predicting when Coombs would return, I had to vacate the room as quickly as possible. I replaced the items and closed the lid.

Next, I checked his closet. To my surprise there was a dinner jacket and two shirts of the type he typically wore. At least he had taken my advice on the matter of clothing. Under his bed, aught but dust. I resolved to return to the trunk another day.

Settling into the library, I pondered what I had learned as I started a fire. Did Coombs imagine himself some sort of fanciful detective? Were the penny bloods from his youth? He had a great deal of money. Thousands of pounds. Was the trunk his bank?

None of this answered the fundamental question of what had happened at Marylebone. I could accept that he had been extremely, fantastically lucky in "solving" his first case at Downing Street. But I knew I had seen head wounds, not gashes to the legs, and that Elinor was a frail, fragile child incapable of murder. And I knew unquestionably that Hughes had confessed to the police and to me.

"You know you're right. Make him tell you how he did it."

Feeling a renewed chill, I poked at the fire in the library hearth as I pondered the suggestion posed by my brother's voice. As a child, his voice was often one of comfort, of solace, not of this taunting nature. But I did not need solace now, I needed dialogue, thought, self-examination.

"What did you really see?"

Who better than the dead to answer questions of murder? Three thoughts danced through my mind: First, that it was not unprecedented for an insane man like Hughes to confess to crimes that he did not commit. Secondly, extreme emotions can manifest in extreme physicality, perhaps even in a little girl. And finally, how sure was I of those wounds? Without my notes, I had only my memory. And there was no denying that during the inquest, only those wounds as described by Coombs were present. It is not possible for the wounds of a dead body to simply change. Did that mean there had been no head wounds?

"He's making a fool of you."

I took down a medical journal and failed to read a single page. Try as I might, I could not push away thoughts of voices encouraging urges. Mental distractions, I reasoned, to avoid the idea that I, not Coombs, had been wrong.

Coombs returned while lunch was being laid out.

"Wait. I ain't dressed right, am I?" Coombs said with a devilish grin.

"Well, no," I started, "but it depends on –"

"Nope. Wanna be a right, proper gentleman." He dashed off, laughing. When he returned to the kitchen, he had donned the dinner jacket, but his smile was gone.

"You go through my things?" he asked me before I could point out his mistake.

A serendipitous mouthful of cheese gave me a moment to think. "I closed your door. Twice, in fact. Yesterday, as well as today. It was open, and I presumed you preferred it closed. Was I wrong in that assumption?"

"I only leave it open when there's laundry. I didn't have no laundry today. How'd it get open?"

"I am afraid I have no answer for that. Perhaps it does not close properly? Otherwise, I have no answer."

He turned his anger on the maid. "Did you open my door?"

She nearly dropped the platter she held. "Sir? No, sir. It was closed this morning, sir. I think. I'm so sorry, sir." Tears welled in her eyes.

"Joanna ..." started Burkett.

"There's no need to punish her," I interjected. "If indeed she was at fault, it would have been an innocent mistake. And there's no proof that you yourself did not leave it unsecured, Coombs."

"From now on it'll be locked. Laundry'll be in the hall."

The maid fought back tears. Burkett shot her hot glances and berated her until they left. I felt a pang of regret. Now Coombs' door would be locked, preventing any further investigations.

⁕⁝⊙⊙⁝⁕

After a ham and oyster dinner, I retreated again to the library. The afternoon had been taken up with Peters while I scoured bookstores for volumes on various psychoses. I had resolved to spend the evening by the fire delving into my research. Truly I could not say if I was trying to understand Coombs better or myself. Still, I had to put aside the question of my own sanity. How could I possibly answer that? Any musings in that direction led inevitably to a vortex, an abyss of frantic and contradictory thought that in itself threatened madness. No, I had to focus on Coombs. Was he some sort of illusionist? Was he using the tricks of a conjurer to make a name for himself? Was I being duped? Then the simplest thought struck me as if I were slapped in the face with a fish: Simply ask the man.

As was his habit, Coombs had remained in the kitchen after dinner and the dishes had been cleared. He scoured an evening paper. His lips moved ever so slightly. There was a glass and a bottle of whiskey – an excellent brand – next to him. He looked up. "How's your books?"

I smiled and took my usual seat. "They are a comfort, but I could not find what I was looking for in them."

"See? That's why I don't got any. Better to find your answers in the real world."

"Indeed. Which is why I have come to you."

He set the paper down. "Yeah?"

"Yes. I am at sea."

Coombs' scoff nearly caused him to choke on his whiskey. "You do talk funny."

"Says the Manchester boy."

He sat back. "That's where you think I'm from?"

"There, or somewhere nearby. Is that in error? Did I 'mither it up'?"

Coombs roared with laughter. He caught his breath, stole a glance at me, then laughed all the harder. I found myself laughing with him.

"Get a glass," he said with a gesture and reached for the bottle.

There was a handful of mismatched glasses on a shelf near the hearth. I took the cleanest one, pulled my chair to the end of the table near Coombs and sat.

Coombs poured out drinks for us both. He raised his. "Here's to mitherin' it up!"

Having partaken in the occasional drinking game – after being disowned, of course – I knew the, shall we say, etiquette involved. Apparently Coombs was not expecting that. I threw back my drink and slammed the glass on the table before he did. My eyes watered, my nose and throat burned. Coombs was impressed and amused.

"Whaddaya wanna know?" he asked as he poured another.

I was not so quick to down this one. The burning became a warmth that extended to my face and my head floated pleasantly, as if in a murky pond.

"How did you do that?" I blurted.

"Figure it was the girl?"

Not yet drunk enough to accuse this dangerous man of lying or playing tricks, I said, "Yes."

He shrugged. "I hear things. I read the papers. I got an instinct for this stuff." He poured another round.

I sipped this one, as did he. Coombs seemed sincere, but was that not the mark of an expert trickster?

"You 'see' it," I said. "May I ask how? Is it a vision of some kind? Is there an inspiration perhaps? How did you come upon this ability? Have you always possessed it?

"Why's it matter?"

"Credibility. It is always credibility."

"But I'm right, yeah?"

"Yes. But people will start to wonder *why* you know these things. How could you possibly have known about the knife?"

"That's what I got *you* for. And don't worry about the Marylebone thing. Just be more careful."

I finished my drink and held the glass out for more. Inwardly, I bristled at the idea that this rash, even foolish man would suggest that I was the one who needed to take more care. And yet …

"If I may ask, where *are* you from?"

"Sure," he said with a chuckle. "Ask if it's okay to ask, then ask anyway. No place. Every place. I wandered a lot. I was in the military." His voice trailed off. "Can I show you somethin'?"

Hoping it would be the secret of the changing bodies, I nodded. "Certainly."

He reached into his pocket, then handed me a fistful of papers. The pages were covered in his crude scrawl.

"What is this?"

"My life story. You want to know where I come from? There it is. At least, what I want to tell. It's like you said about clothes. And the talkin'. Put on a nice jacket, talk good, and people listen, yeah? You could be the worst person in the world, but put on a suit and the right accent and suddenly you're a Duke or somethin'. Like you, all the time pretendin' to be a regular guy. But I can tell you were some kind of Lord or somethin'."

With a laugh I said, "No, not a Lord, I assure you. But yes, I was raised in a vastly different situation."

"And you don't want people to know. And that's your business. All people need to know about you is what you show 'em, what you tell 'em."

"Agreed," I said with a smile.

"Same for me. I just want to be Detective Coombs."

I raised my glass to him. "Here, here." I could not agree more about the desire to present oneself to the world as one wished. That each man is entitled to his privacy. And yet, I could not shake the notion that he spoke of his past with considerably less confidence than anything else he uttered. He seemed uncharacteristically unsure.

Coombs raised the bottle to offer another. I held my hand up and stood, a bit unsteadily. I thanked him for his hospitality and staggered up to my room, clutching the pages in my hand. Would the contents help me to understand him better, or was it more obfuscation?

CHAPTER TWELVE

IN THE PAPERS

THE *LONDON DAILY JOURNAL*, READ THE sign before me and the card in my hand. I dismissed Peters with a wave and thanks. I had decided to put the card Miss Clavijo had given me to use because, in retrospect, I felt I had been rude to her. And she was a comely woman.

The office was in a two-story brick building in the middle of a somewhat rundown block. The sounds and smells of workhouses dominated the area. Thick smoke made the sun appear as a weak lamp behind a grey veil.

The *Journal's* white-and-gold hand-painted sign pointed down iron-railed stone steps. As I pushed open a heavy wooden door, a bell jangled above me. The room had a basement's cool musk and was sheltered from the filth and chaos outside.

Clearly this had been a shop of some kind: shoes or glove manufacturing judging by the faint touch of leather in the air and the counter along the back. The walls were bare of decorations. Through the door behind the counter were two typesetter stations. While one was unattended, Miss Clavijo worked diligently at the other.

"Pardon," I called out.

She held up a hand, finished some task that seemed vitally important, then broke from her station. Under her ink-stained apron, she wore a man's brown shirt and trousers. She wore them well. Her shining black hair was bound behind her neck while tufts fell from the peak to her eyebrows.

I have never favored the kind of woman who must, at all times, be perfectly put together. They seem too fragile, too precious, something to be viewed and admired from afar. This was another aspect of my former life of which I had gladly let go. The women to whom I was continually introduced held no interest for me, and this had led to whispers, speculation, and ultimately a very awkward talk with my father.

Miss Clavijo had a confident air, almost regal, as she emerged from the open door behind the counter. "Good morning," she said. "Dr. Johnson? What brings you here, sir?"

"First, an apology. I feel I was rude to you yesterday at the inquest."

"Thank you. I appreciate that, but I assure you I have received considerably ruder behavior from my colleagues."

"Shame on them. Secondly, I have some information regarding Detective Coombs."

"Right this way." She escorted me through the open door behind the counter and past the typesetting stations to a small, windowed office with a simple desk, one chair behind it and another before it. She gestured for me to sit while she used an acrid salve to clean the ink from her hands. I placed the papers on her desk.

At Coombs' behest, I had transcribed his writing to something more legible and readable, with the intent of making it public. He agreed that if it was credibility he sought, his writings would put an end to it forthwith.

Once clean, she sat and read the pages. When she was done, she leafed through them as she questioned me. "Which orphanage was he left at? It doesn't specify."

"He has forgotten the name. Put it out of his mind, as it were."

"I see." She perused the pages. "And did he also put out of his mind the name of his army commander?"

"Pardon?" I had transcribed Coombs' writing for legibility, but I had not scrutinized it.

"He claims to have served in Burma, but offers no details, other than his claim that he nearly died. Yet I have seen no evidence of war injuries. I've seen how such things can change a man." She looked away as she said it, giving me the impression there was much she wished not to say.

For a moment, an image of one of Coombs' penny bloods came to me, of British soldiers fighting a foreign tribe. I pushed the thought aside. "I am merely conveying the information he gave to me."

"Perhaps I could ask him myself?"

"He is steadfast in his refusal to be interviewed. As he puts it, he is too busy solving crimes."

She set the papers down and looked at me closely. "How does someone like you come to work for a man like him?"

"I am a doctor. Coombs tapped me to assist with his investigations." I could only hope she would never find the story of my previous exploits. "Let me ask you the same question: how does a woman of such poise and intelligence come to be the editor of a penny paper?"

"You left out 'exotic'."

"Pardon?"

"Typically, when men attempt to cajole me, they tell me how 'exotic' I am. Or 'pretty'."

"Why state the obvious?"

"Ha. Well done, sir. For that I will tell you this much: Father purchased this for me. Since no paper in London would hire a woman as an editor, we decided to start our own. Mother is not happy, but she seldom is." She shook her head and held up a hand. "Irrelevant. Let me ask you this: Why bring this here? Why not the *Telegraph* or the *Mail*?"

"Because the simple fact is, you were the only reporter at that inquest who took note of my existence."

She smiled. "You did make quite an entrance. This will be in tomorrow morning's edition. I should like to maintain communication with you. How can we arrange that?"

"I could continue to visit you here, in your office." My heart picked up its pace.

"That would be the most proper," she said, idly shuffling papers on her desk.

"If I may be so bold, I have an idea. Dinner. Not at my residence, mind you. That would not be seen well. Perhaps a neutral ground? An inn I know. The Langford in Kensington?"

"I'm familiar. I believe Father failed to convince them to take our paper."

"Ah. I may be able to assist with that. I am personally acquainted with the gentleman who serves as proprietor. Let us have dinner there. They have adequate staff, and I have no doubt I can engage the services of a chaperone. For appearance's sake, of course."

"Of course. Father will fluster but acquiesce. Mother will … I'll handle Mother."

"Excellent. I will wire you with the details."

I bade farewell and resolved to visit a haberdasher. I suddenly felt the need for new evening wear.

◦⊱══◉ ◎══⊰◦

I paid Burkett handsomely to take on Adelia's paper and for the private use of his small dining room as well as a place to change. Mrs. Burkett was too busy in the kitchen to act as chaperone and his eldest daughter, Joanna, the one who accompanied him to Coombs', was a sight too young. An advert in the *Mail* and a message with cash carried by one of Burkett's younger boys produced a woman whose very being exuded "chaperone". After a wire to Adelia's office, I wrote a note to be delivered to Coombs with supper that I would not be in attendance.

Adelia arrived by hansom at precisely five in the evening. Burkett and his staff proved themselves to be quite adequate to the task of providing a pleasant meal with unobtrusive service. Hare soup followed by fried eels, mutton cutlets in tomato sauce, roast gosling, and devilled sardines, along with cheese and salad. Our chaperone performed her duties with aplomb, which consisted of giving the appearance that we were not alone, but surreptitiously providing us with time to ourselves.

"What brought you to medicine?" Adelia asked at one point.

"The death of my brother. Twin brother, in fact."

"Oh dear. I'm so sorry."

"Oh, no apologies necessary. I have no actual memory of him. We were too young. But once I learned about him, he became a boon to me. He became my only sibling. The perfect brother, there when I needed comfort from my father's anger. He gave me courage when I was afraid, and even sometimes provided some mischief." I set down my fork and, with an embarrassed chuckle, set my head in my hand. "You must think me mad."

"No. Not at all."

"I truly did not think my brother was alive and talking to me. I imagined how he might be, what we might do together, had he lived. And those thoughts gave me comfort. Does that make sense?"

She reached out a hand to take mine. "It makes perfect sense. And I don't think you're mad." Grinning she added, "Well, perhaps a *little* mad, but in a good way. Everyone needs a *little* madness in their lives."

We laughed together and I felt more relaxed and unguarded than at any time in my life.

"Thank you," I said. "Please tell me about *your* family."

"My father dotes on me, though he would never admit it. He did, after all, buy a newspaper for me. Although he would much rather see me married."

"Ah, yes, the wish of all parents."

"Indeed. My mother can be unpleasant, shall we say? Difficult. My father has always been protective of me, to the point of taking me on holiday, as it were, when Mother was … in her dark place. We grew close as a result." She hesitated before continuing. "I feel very comfortable talking to you. More so, I believe, than I would if we … were courting. Please tell me you're not offended by that."

I considered it for a moment and realized that I had been feeling a similar comfort. I wanted to spend time with her, but I did not want to court her. I smiled at her. "Absolutely not. I feel the same way."

She smiled broadly "In fact, I'm glad we met the way we did. Well, not the murders, obviously. What I mean is, I could see you as someone whom Mother would have dragged me to for calling hours and I would have hated you before we even met. That sounds horrible, I know. I mean to say that I would have had a preconception of you simply because Mother chose you." She shook her head. "You must think I'm awful."

"No, not at all. I completely understand. My father was the one who made social arrangements for me, and I always had a similar feeling about the women he chose. Because *he* chose them. They were women he *thought* I would – or rather *should* – like." I thought it best not to tell her that my father would never have approved of Adelia or the Clavijo family.

"That's it exactly, yes. I'm glad you understand. I would like to continue having conversations with you, although we may have to be less public about it."

"Agreed."

After the treacle tart dessert arrived we said our goodnights under the occasionally watchful gaze of the chaperone.

⊷═◉ ◉═⊶

When Burkett arrived with breakfast the following morning, he presented the latest edition of the *London Daily Journal*. There on the front page was the engraving of Coombs I had sent, along with Adelia's own version of the story. "Mystery man solves mysteries," read the headline. She quoted the pages given to her but added her own skepticism. Rather than cast aspersions on his character, it served to romanticize him. Coombs reveled in it and announced that he would be taking dinner at the inn.

Upon arriving, Coombs was not content to let the diners discover him. He announced himself, holding the paper aloft. Burkett was annoyed until the patrons stayed longer and ordered more pints – for themselves and Coombs – as they listened to him ramble on.

After more drinks than I could count, we were the last to leave the dining room. Coombs sang all the way back to the residence. Heads peeked out of windows as we passed. The words were largely unintelligible. Despite his slurred speech, his gait remained steady and true, though he fumbled for a moment at his now-locked bedroom door. "Get it framed," he called.

I stepped back from the door of my own room and peered around the corner at him. His door now open, Coombs swayed, an oak buffeted by a powerful gust.

"Pardon?"

"The paper. I want it framed."

"And you wish for me to do this?"

"You see anybody else here?"

I sighed. "Very well, Master Coombs."

He barked a laugh and stumbled into his room, taking up his unintelligible song again.

Returning to my room, I came to a surprising realization: I liked the man. His crudeness and flagrant disregard for manners had a certain appeal. Perhaps I could learn something from him.

CHAPTER THIRTEEN

THE BUTCHER OF BATTERSEA

"WHAT OF THIS ONE?" I SAID to a surprisingly chipper Coombs the following morning. The article I presented described a drunken argument that had turned into a deadly brawl. There were confessions and denials, as well as the absence of a murder weapon. Surely this was exactly the kind of case that would interest Coombs.

He peered past his coffee cup to read the headline I showed him. "Nah. He did it."

"Are you sure? There's no mysterious creature lurking about in the shadows armed with –"

"Are you funnin' me?"

"No. No, absolutely not. I was only trying to speculate on –"

"Don't do that. And I already looked at that one. It's in this paper, too. That's how I know."

"I see, I see. Well, then, is there something I should be looking for?"

"No. I'll do it. Gimme the papers."

I moved my stack of papers to his side of the table. "I shall retire to the library then."

"Don't forget yer special jacket," Coombs said with a guffaw.

As I exited the kitchen, there came a bird-like knock at the door. For someone who claimed to not approve of servants, Coombs was only too happy to let me play the role of butler. It was a boy in a tattered cap with a telegram. I gave him a farthing for the envelope and nearly demanded the tip back, based on his scowl, but he had dashed off.

"Telegram," I announced, fulfilling my role as servant. "From Batleigh."

Leaping off his chair, Coombs let the newspapers fall to the floor. Yet another task for me, I realized as he snatched the message from my hand and tore it open.

"'Murder most foul'," Coombs read as a smile spread across his face. "'Please come at once. Standard reward.' The address is in Battersea." He held up the wire. "This is what I been waitin' for."

The man's excitement was contagious. This was a proper case. Unsolved, it appeared. Now we would begin to function as I had hoped.

"May I ask a favor?" An idea had begun to form. "If you would be so kind as to fetch Peters and the carriage –"

"'Fetch'?"

"If you would be so kind as to get Peters and come back here, it would be greatly appreciated. I wish to be more prepared this time. More careful, as you suggested."

Coombs looked me up and down with narrowed, skeptical eyes. "You could use the walk. Them fancy buttons is strugglin' to hold on," he said, poking at my stomach. "What with all your soft chairs and big meals."

"The Burketts have been shrinking my clothes –"

"*Ha!* They ain't shrunk *mine*."

"Nevertheless, I want to be thorough in my preparations. That way I will be more efficient."

"Fine. Be ready or we drive on," he said and left.

My idea was simple, but I desired to keep it from Coombs. That I had seen one set of wounds prior to Coombs' proclamation at Marylebone and another set after still nagged at me. If I was losing my faculties, I needed to know it. I resolved to take two sets of notes. During my investigation I would meticulously record everything, then make an exact replica of those notes, down to every detail. Not a word, not one stroke of the pencil would deviate from one to the other. One set of those notes would be seen by others, given to Coombs should he ask. But the other set would be known only to me. If Coombs was somehow altering evidence to match his proclamations, my second set of notes would expose him. He could burn all the pages he wished. I would have to be careful to keep them out of his reach. I gathered two fresh notebooks and placed one in my jacket, while the other I secured in my vest pocket.

I heard Peters' carriage as it pulled to a stop but was apparently not outside in whatever time frame Coombs had assigned. I had to run to catch them, much to Coombs' amusement.

⊹⟩═◉ ◉═⟨⊹

The carriage stopped before an abandoned warehouse surrounded by farmland. It was partially burned, and boards filled the windows on all three floors. The stone foundation, which included steps up to the double doors and short windows mere inches above the ground, looked entirely intact.

Batleigh waited beside a police wagon and greeted us as we emerged from the carriage. The damp morning air was thick with the smell of a farm. The sound of plaintive bleating mixed with intermittent clucking. The languid barking of an old hound added counterpoint.

"Owner of the farm sold this building to someone through the post," Batleigh told us as we approached, emerging from a cloud of cigar smoke and mist from his hot breath. "Said the money was too much to turn down. The farmer has never met nor seen the purchaser. Sometimes he sees lamps here at night, but nothing else. We have the documents, should you like to view them."

"Have you eliminated the farmer as a suspect?" I asked.

Batleigh then pulled on the stub of his cigar and spoke around a puff of smoke. "He's getting on in years. Wouldn't have the strength to do what's been done. And he's never far from his wife. So, they'd have to work as a team, which seems unlikely."

Batleigh had addressed Coombs, who seemed not to hear him as he gazed at the building.

"Inspector, has the lotion helped your hands?" I asked Batleigh.

"Hm? Oh, yes, there has been some relief. Thank you for that." The superintendent tilted his head to spy whatever drew Coombs' attention.

"That hole over there?" Batleigh indicated a break in one of the basement windows. "Made by badgers, I'd wager. Farm owner's dog went exploring. Came back with a leg. A human leg." He dropped the remains of his cigar and drove it, sizzling, into the damp ground. "This way."

The door to the place had been taken off its hinges. A short length of chain and a broken iron padlock lay nearby.

The first floor was completely open with two rows of wooden pillars on either side. The sun fought its way through the gaps in the boarded windows, but failed to provide any real illumination, only places for shadows to form.

"Right down here," said Batleigh as he led us to a railing in the near right corner where stairs lead to the basement.

"Got a handkerchief?" he asked, taking one out of his pocket.

Having already picked up a trace of decomposing flesh, I had mine at hand. Coombs laughed at us both as we descended the stairs.

Lanterns had been placed around the room, revealing a slaughterhouse. Not the lurid and bloody kind of thing that might appear in one of Coombs' penny bloods, but rather, a professional slaughterhouse with lanterns, tables, tools and neatly hung carcasses. It was the fare of this particular establishment that had Batleigh looking at his shoes and put surprise on Coombs' face. Six human torsos hung from the rafters, their limbs removed and arrayed on the tables.

Batleigh worked his throat. "You get why we want to keep it quiet. People strung up like ..." His voice trailed off.

"The heads is missin'," said Coombs. He moved toward the bodies. "Prob'ly dumped 'em somewhere so we can't identify the victims. Looks like rats been at 'em. Bite marks." Coombs indicated an open wound on the chest of a dangling male torso.

"Looks a bit too round and smooth to be a bite mark," I said.

Ignoring me, Coombs turned to Batleigh. "Find the heads. They'll tell you a lot, but they're likely long gone."

"Are there pigs here?" I asked.

"Yes," said Batleigh.

"Look for the remains of the heads in their trough." I had considered using such a method of disposal for my cadavers but I do not favour pork.

"You're saying the heads were fed to ... ?"

"The local pigs, yes. And quite possibly other body parts. I count at least three missing arms and four legs."

"I saw that too," said Coombs.

"I'll go check on the pigs," Batleigh said and hurried up the stairs.

"You may want to inform the butcher shops supplied by this farm," I called after him.

"Pigs eat people?" asked Coombs.

"Certainly," I said. "They'll eat anything you give them."

"Never knew."

"Well," I began, searching for a way to encourage Coombs to leave. "I suppose I shall begin my work."

"Like what?"

I did not want him to become interested in what I was doing. "I will make sketches, write descriptions, all with the intent of supporting your conclusion."

"Good man." He clapped me on the back. "I'm off for lunch."

"If you could send for a change of clothes for me," I called as he climbed the stairs, "as well as a wash basin, soap and the like, it would be much appreciated."

"Fine. Enjoy."

I began my process of meticulous notetaking with a sketch of the room as it was, the layout of the tables, the positions of the bodies and parts. I described each body in text and included sketches as I assembled them, adding detailed drawings of each cut. I made exact copies of each page as I worked. I returned the second notebook to my vest pocket when not in use while the first remained in the open.

My examination told me what I suspected: these carcasses had been dressed by a professional. The cuts were sharp and neat. The body cavities had been cleaned meticulously.

Judging by skin tone, hair, and body structure, three were Caucasians, two Negroes and one Oriental. Among them, four were female. The limbs had been removed at the shoulders and hips, with the joints separated cleanly. They were then placed in sections on the tables. Indeed, more than just heads were missing. The more decayed the corpse, the more absent parts. It appeared the killer had been producing victims faster than he could dispose of them, a situation familiar to me. What Coombs had hastily identified as bite marks were, in fact, precisely cut shapes. Sections of skin had been expertly removed from the torsos and limbs. The killer was, I suspected, more than a mere butcher. A surgeon perhaps. I searched the room to be sure, but the pieces were not present. Whoever had done this was too careful to have simply lost these pieces. They had been taken away but for what purpose? Trophies? Proof? Samples?

When I completed my work, I tied my primary notebook, the one that I would present to Coombs, closed, using its leather string. On the second, I made the knot lopsided and melted candle wax into it so that it would be clear if anyone opened the book.

The requested basin and clothing awaited me in the dim afternoon light upstairs. When I stepped outside, I realized I was alone. No Peters, no carriage, no police.

On the top of a nearby rise, I spotted the farmhouse, smoke billowing from its chimney. Before I reached the door, a bent old man stepped out. I asked if he had a gig or carriage and could supply transportation. After haggling over a not-unreasonable price, he agreed to take me in the gig he normally used for hay.

As we lumbered along, I enquired after the farmer's observations of the building he had sold, and of the butchers he supplied, hoping to derive some idea of what to do next. The conversation led to a bit of a rant regarding one of the shops, one with which he claimed he would never do business again. Apparently, the butcher, a Mr. Garret, had raised a son who was prone to odd behavior, the final straw, as it were, being when the son attempted to assault the farmer's daughter. I convinced him to give me the address of Garret's shop.

Within a block of alighting the gig, I was able to hail a hansom and had the driver take me to the nearest post office. I sent the secret notebook to myself in care of the Langford. Another hansom brought me back to Kensington.

As the cab came to a stop, Peters was climbing into his brougham. When he saw me he dropped his head.

I made a show of tipping the hansom driver well and thanking him for excellent service. With a mix of mirth and annoyance, I approached Peters. "Good evening." I gave an exaggerated tip of my hat. "You had a pleasant ride, I assume?"

Peters gave a shy smile. "My apologies, sir. Detective Coombs was quite insistent. Said it would do you some good, a trip back on your own."

"And good it did, Mr. Peters. I was able to garner more information for our case. So, all is forgiven, and I should like to set out first thing tomorrow." I stepped up close to him. "Promise you won't abandon me this time?"

He stood at attention. "No, sir. Never again."

"Thank you, Peters. And see you in the morning."

Coombs appeared to have been waiting by the door for me. "What'd ya find?"

"Ah. Yes. It's all right here." I handed him my notebook.

He opened it and flipped through the pages, nodding. "Looks thorough. Good job."

I was utterly taken aback by his interest in my notes but did my best to hide it. "Thank you. Is it helpful to you?"

"Heh. Yeah, sure." He tossed the notebook into my chest, and I barely caught it. "You done?"

"Nearly, yes. I have more to do tomorrow."

"Don't be late for the inquest," he said and went to the kitchen to await dinner.

I breathed a sigh of relief. It seemed that Coombs was absorbing the information I provided. Perhaps the Marylebone business was behind us.

CHAPTER FOURTEEN

TREACHEROUS GROUND

THE CARRIAGE SLOWED TO A STOP on a crowded, bustling street that formed a jagged curve ahead. The midday sun laid bare every chip and crack in the buildings' façades. They looked thrown together carelessly, brick and stone and wood with no discernible order, alternating sizes like bad teeth on a crooked jaw.

Across from us was Garret's Butcher Shop, a peaked building jutting out from the rest. Undressed chickens hung in remarkably ordered rows, giving way to fully plucked and dressed geese beneath. On each side of the door, and partially obscuring the windows, pigs and lamb alternated, a bunting made of meat. Inside at the base of the windows, fruits and vegetables were stacked so precisely and uniformly as to suggest a painting. In an arc spanning the centre window read: "Garret's." Below the family name, traces of scraped off letters remained.

Garret the butcher was a burly man with more blonde-gone-grey hair protruding from his shirt than on this head. He said he was too busy to talk about his son. But when I feigned regret over an estrangement with my own father, he became more talkative. Along with his lectures on how important it was that I make amends, there were tirades on listening to one's father. It appeared that the younger Garret had refused to do as he was told in the shop and had insisted on doing things his own way. I was able to draw out that his son had put off a farmer or two by making aggressive advances on their daughters. The butcher had put his son out of the house over this. All he could say now was that his son lived in a boarding house on Torrance Street in Lambeth.

After thanking him for his time, I left the shop feeling that I had gained nothing new regarding the case. However, I felt a strange kinship towards the younger Garret. I knew all too well the difficulties of having a demanding, judgmental father, and began to wonder if the accusations levelled against the young man were perhaps exaggerated.

Peters was feeding his horse as I crossed the street.

"Heading to Lambeth next, Peters."

"Sir." He stroked the horse's muzzle as he removed the feedbag.

"Yes, Peters."

"Very good, sir, if that's where the day's business takes us. Where, precisely?" he asked as we climbed to our respective seats.

"That I cannot say. I know it is Torrance Street. From there we will need to work it out."

"Very good, sir. Following a lead on the case, are we sir?"

I paused on the step, holding the door open. "Yes and no. He may possess useful information and, quite frankly, I have no other avenues to pursue."

"Sir. Have you been to Lambeth?"

"I am aware of the concerns you harbour. Still, I believe it is worth pursuing and we will just have to be on our guard."

"Sir."

I closed the door and sat, rapped on the ceiling, and we were on our way.

⊶═◉ ◉═⊷

Torrance Street. I was more familiar with the area than I let on to Peters. It was mere blocks from where I had lived, where I had been arrested. The place was legendary even in the dark and dangerous neighborhood where I was able to have cadavers delivered without notice.

As we travelled east, we rode past sawmills and lumberyards. The air was thick with the stench of foundries and the shriek of blades tearing through logs. Hard, filthy men eyed the carriage as we clomped by. Crowding the streets immediately after the mills were rows of narrow brick homes with no space between them and no yards of which to speak.

I began to doubt this course of action. The most to be gained from this dangerous trip was a little more information about the use of the barn. The wayward son of a butcher held promise at first, but if the charges were true, his seeming inability to control his actions towards women all but eliminated him. The man I sought was careful, meticulous. Perhaps the butcher's son had seen the man who had purchased the place, but more likely he had not. Still, I felt the need to explore every possible avenue. If events played out in a manner similar to Marylebone and I left any stone unturned, that would only be a seed of doubt. Whatever case I built had to be unassailable.

The boarding house lurked in the shadows of a print factory, open on one side to the six train tracks that cut through the parish. A pair of grimy young men in overalls strolled along the street, smoking. They paused to examine our carriage, both impressed and suspicious. One of them tossed an epithet at Peters, which he ignored. Sharing a laugh, they continued on their way.

My hand on the door handle, I hesitated. This was a risky venture. It seemed equally dangerous for me to enter the place as it would be to leave Peters outside. Steeling myself with a breath, I opened the door and stepped onto the sidewalk.

"Peters, would you mind accompanying me on this visit?" I asked.

"Of course, sir. One moment." From under a blanket at his feet, he produced a truncheon. "Can't be too careful, sir."

"Peters, if we were careful, we would not be here."

"Not too late to change our minds, sir."

"No, no. I believe this avenue needs to be pursued to its end."

Peters nodded as he tucked away his weapon and hopped down beside me. "After you, sir."

The boarding house had received neither paint nor repair in years, by my estimation. A tiny old woman pulled the door open. I informed her I was there on police business, she showed no surprise and let me pass, though she steadfastly refused to allow Peters to enter. She slammed the door on him and pointed me to young Garret's room, the last on the left, then retreated behind her own door.

A window was open by inches at the hall's end. I told myself to leave, that this was dangerous.

"If you leave, you'll always have your doubts."

"You are right about that," I whispered as a shiver ran through me and I moved slowly along the hall. A sharp blast of cold air clawed its way in through the open window where I spotted Peters sneaking up along the building's edge. He saw me and raised his cudgel. I nodded and set my hands to the window, raising it slightly with a loud creak.

The landlady's door opened. "Leave it," she snapped.

"My apologies," I said. She must have had her ear pressed to the door.

She stepped back into her apartment and closed the door, but I did not hear it shut fully.

As I was about to knock on Garret's door, my fist wavered.

"Go ahead. You'll like him."

"I sincerely doubt that." I knocked.

"Come in." The door flew open, and I faced a young, black-haired man.

"Mr. Garret?" I managed to say, my throat tight.

He stared at me with narrowed eyes.

"I am Dr. Johnson. I have some questions for you," I said.

"Come in." He was impatient now.

I stepped through. He closed the door behind me. The room was wide but cramped with furniture. There was a small bed against the far wall, a chest of drawers, a wooden chair, a writing desk, and a small round table, all aged, worn and beaten. More than Garret's musk, I noticed a chemical tinge in the air. A duffel bag lay near the door, full to the point of stretching the dark grey fabric taut. The walls and desk were bare. The top drawer was open, empty, as was the closet. He was packing, and in a rush. His heavy breathing was now behind me.

"Have a seat," he whispered.

Garret stood between me and the door. I took the chair. He sat on the edge of the bed.

"Mr. Garret, I have some questions regarding –"

"You're a doctor?" He was nervous, tense.

"Yes, Mr. Garret. I am. How did –"

"What kind?" Eager interest lit up his face.

"What *kind*?" I had never considered a specialty.

He turned his head slightly, as if there had been a noise, then shrank into himself, hands together, a shy boy about to ask an embarrassing question. "Do you like cutting?" From a sleeve, he withdrew a scalpel. "I like cutting."

"Don't lie to him," said my brother. *"He'll know."*

Could I make it to the door? Where was Peters? It seemed best to placate him, then find an excuse to move to the door. "Yes, Mr. Garret. I do."

There was no other exit; the room's only window was high and small. Garret said something, his voice high-pitched and soft. He was hesitant to speak.

"Pardon?" If I were to rush to the door, would Peters be there, at the ready?

"Do you want to see?" he asked, almost singing.

"Go ahead and look. You'll like it."

The thought was so repulsive to me that I could scarcely believe it was mine, even in the guise of my brother's voice.

"See what?" I asked, my voice barely audible.

Garret went to the duffel bag and took out a small black picture frame and handed it to me. Behind the frame's glass was a perfectly round section of pale skin with a purple, flower-shaped birthmark at its centre.

My hands and arms shook suddenly. I all but dropped the thing.

"Don't you like it?" he said as he took it back. "I did my best. One of my first." He sounded hurt. He took another frame from the bag. "Is this better?"

He handed me an ornately gilded frame. The skin it encased was dark and showed a puckered, crescent-shaped scar. The brown and auburn tones of the skin were perfectly augmented by the gold-coloured carvings of the frame.

I jumped up and threw the monstrosity away. These were the pieces missing from the bodies in the warehouse. I was alone in a room with the man who had murdered and mutilated several people. I tried to control my trembling, to rein in my panic, to think. Where was Peters?

"You're not a friend, are you?" Garret's voice had sharpened, gone guttural.

Run, I told myself. Call for Peters. Was he inside? Open the door. But Garret was closer to it. "I am a friend," I muttered. "Yes." If he remained passive, I could make my escape. "You surprised me. Your work is …"

"*Don't lie to him.*"

"Remarkable," I said. This was the most truthful thing I had said of late.

A tiny giggle bubbled from him. "This one's my favourite." The sing-song quality of his voice had returned. He presented me with a larger, rectangular frame made of mahogany with intricate carvings at the corners and centres of each side. It contained a long oval of skin with a series of warts and small growths, forming a sort of constellation. They were bordered by exactly one inch of skin on all sides. "I'm proud of that one."

He was close to me now and smelled of cleaning agents.

"Do you like it?" he whispered. His animal eyes darted about, taking my measure. My heart pounded, my breath was short and rapid. "Is that a mole on your neck?" He touched my throat.

I batted his arm away and pushed him aside.

Garret let out a tight, angry cry. I reached for the door and started to call Peters' name, but a flash of pain at the back of my head brought me down. The world spun and darkened as I fell. My vision came to me in waves as he bound and gagged me.

Garret traced a circle on my neck, his fingers passing lightly, tenderly over the mole.

"You *don't* like them," Garret said. "You don't want to help."

The urge to appease him came back. My only means of survival, I told myself. I nodded vigorously and tried to speak through the cloth.

"If you shout, I'll kill you."

I nodded again.

He pulled out the cloth.

"I do admire your work." I mumbled, fighting the need to vomit. Where the Hell was Peters? The scalpel shone in Garret's hand while he searched my eyes. I recalled the immaculate state of the bodies, and what his father had said. "Your cuts were precise. Clean. Perfect."

Garret leaned closer. "Really?" he whispered.

"Yes. I can help you, you know. I am a doctor. I can help you find what you're looking for. Blemishes, yes? Imperfections. That is what you prize."

He nodded. An expression of relief painted his face.

"That is what your father never understood, yes?"

"Perfect flesh is boring."

"Yes it is. Let me help you find people with blemishes."

Garret's expression became euphoric as he eased back.

"And scars. I can find – no, I can *give* people scars that you can –"

"*Hey!*" The voice of the landlady come from the hall.

Garret whirled as he leapt to his feet.

Peters stood in the doorway, shock and revulsion on his face.

Garret lunged at Peters, who brought his truncheon down as Garret swung his blade. Both men cried out. Peters fell while Garret crashed into the wall, a hand to his head. I reached for Garret. He blindly swung his blade, just missing my hand. I slammed his body into the wall. He elbowed me in the stomach, pushed me off him and took another swing of his blade, grazing my cheek. A kick to my stomach and I was on my knees.

"What's going on down there?" yelled the landlady from the hall.

Garret grabbed his duffel bag and ran out.

Tiny spots of light swirled in my darkened vision. I pushed myself up as I heard the landlady scream. I staggered through the door. The landlady lay still and bleeding from her throat.

I stumbled back to Peters. He lay in a pool of blood. Garret's blade had cut a deep wound along his forearm through the veins and arteries. I wrapped my scarf around the wound to staunch the flow of blood as best I could.

Peters' eyes flickered shut.

I called out for help with all my strength.

CHAPTER FIFTEEN

ACCUSATIONS

I PACED THE CORRIDOR OF THE surgical ward at Bethlehem Hospital. The hall was empty save for Batleigh, Coombs, and me. Why was every single employee in this place not rushing to save Peters?

"They're doing everything they can," said Batleigh.

"*Are* they? Men of his colour – of *your* colour – do not always receive the treatment they deserve."

Batleigh held up his gloved hands. "I'm well aware of that. But I saw no such hesitation in the doctors here. Now tell us, what the bloody hell happened?"

Coombs remained quiet, with nothing but a disapproving stare.

I told them the whole story, from having spoken to the farmer, learning about Garret's shop, and deciding to investigate.

"And you thought it best to go on your own?" Batleigh's mustache twisted with scorn.

Coombs shook his head as if I were a recalcitrant child.

"Would you have come with me, either of you, or sent a constable, based solely on the information I had?"

Batleigh tossed a glance at Coombs, then shook his head. "Truthfully, no."

"You see? Besides, I had Peters." I broke away from them and peered through the windows in the two doors.

Batleigh pulled me back. "You'll know when they're done."

"Any sign of Garret?"

"No. We're still searching."

I gripped his arm. "Garret was killing people to carve their blemishes from them, to keep them. He was obsessed with them. He tried to take this." I touched the mole on my neck.

Batleigh was appalled. "Surely not."

"I tell you, he showed them to me. I held the monstrosities in my hands. He was packed when I arrived. He must have known we had found his workshop."

"Then why was he still there? Why did he let you in?"

"I have no answer." But I did have a terrifying theory: Somehow he had been waiting for me. The way he welcomed me. He was not surprised. But how could he have known I was coming? I started pacing again. "What of the other residents? Surely someone saw something."

"They're not the kind who have much to say to the police."

Finally, Coombs chose to speak. "The crime scene, at the barn. You took notes, yeah?"

"I did." I produced the notebook, the one I had intended for him to see.

He snatched it from my hand. "Better be worth it," he said and turned away.

"Coombs."

He stopped.

"I had no idea of what would happen. If Peters does not ..." I could not finish the thought.

Coombs took a long breath, then turned back to me. "This is why you should stick to note-takin', yeah? Leave the criminals to us."

"But –"

"Let me know soon as you get word," he said to Batleigh and walked off, untying the notebook.

Batleigh dismissed himself to prepare for the inquest.

What had Peters seen and heard? Could he corroborate the existence of Garret's trophies? What had he heard? His expression just before the fight suggested that he had heard me mollifying Garret and perhaps even believed that I was interested in Garret's work and would help him. I had to disabuse him of such a notion. In doing so, I might convince myself. The precision of the skin grafts, the cleanliness of the cuts ... I had to admit the man had skill.

The doors opened and a nurse ushered me out of the surgical wing, assuring me I could see Peters once he was settled into a ward.

When I was finally brought to see him, Coombs was already standing by his bedside glowering at me while Peters would not look my way. I took the chair opposite Coombs.

"Peters," I said, "how are you?"

He held up the stump of his right arm, cut nearly to the elbow. "They took almost the whole thing." Still, he did not look at me.

"I am so sorry," I said, fighting tears. "I had no idea."

"I know." His tone was cold and hard, his eyes on the ceiling.

"Is there anything I can do? Anything at all?"

Peters looked at Coombs.

"We got it sorted," Coombs said. "So don't worry."

Why would Peters not address or even look at me? He must have heard what I had said to Garret. Was it possible he thought I was sincere?

"That is good to hear," I said, leaning close to him. "But I feel responsible and would –"

"It's sorted," Coombs snapped.

Had Peters told Coombs? Did they both believe I would help a murderer? I looked up at Coombs. "I have questions. May I ask them?"

"No." Coombs' tone had a touch of sadness. "He told me everything. And now he's tired and needs to rest."

"Peters, may I –"

"Time to go," said Coombs as he moved towards me. He stood at the foot of the bed until I rose from the chair.

At the door I stopped. "You both must understand that I was placating Garret."

"Just go," said Coombs. "It's almost time for the inquest."

I left, feeling as though I had been crushed under foot.

CHAPTER SIXTEEN

THE WORLD COLLAPSES

I sought out Adelia in the lecture hall where the inquest would take place. A raked floor with wooden benches pointed down to a podium and gurney on the tiled floor. She sat near the other reporters, but apart from them.

"You're all right," she said happily when she saw me.

"Yes, I came through relatively unscathed," I said with a gesture to the bandage on my face. "Peters, however, did not fare as well."

"Peters? Is that the driver you were with? They haven't given us much detail."

"Let me correct that," I said.

The reporters in the row before us turned their heads to listen.

I stood. "Perhaps some privacy is in order," I said and led Adelia to the back of the hall, away from the frowning reporters. I told her everything, up until the encounter with Garret.

"Trophies?" she asked. "Made of *skin*?" She turned away, her face twisted in disgust. "Is that when the driver, Peters, intervened? Why was he attacked and not you?"

What could I tell her? That rather than confront the man I had chosen to placate him, to tell him what he wanted to hear, no matter how horrible, all at the behest of a voice in my head?

She awaited an answer, but my mind was frozen. If I did not tell her, what would come out in the inquest? What was Coombs going to say? How much had Peters told him?

Batleigh came through the door at the base of the lecture hall, then trotted up the aisle to greet me. "Glad to see you're up to this," he said. "I know you've had some difficult times of late."

My confusion mirrored Adelia's expression.

"Anyway, Coombs is about to make his entrance, so have a seat. Between you, me, and Mother Mary's knees? I think he likes pontificating in front of people. Let's let him have his moment." Back down the aisle, he rapped a knuckle on the door behind the podium.

"You may proceed when ready, Detective," called Batleigh.

Coombs strode into the lecture hall. "Thank you, Superintendent." He stood for a moment, taking in the attention of all those around him, the jurors, the reporters, and those who had just come to watch. "Rich men take, don't they? It's how they get rich. Like bankers. They take yer money. Take yer house." With each statement, he took a step forward, focused on the row of jurors. "And they think they're above the law, yeah? They can do anythin' they want and never answer for it."

A well-dressed, portly juror in the front row was now the target of Coombs' stare. The man cleared his throat and shifted in his seat.

"Yeah, yer a banker, ain't ya?" Coombs said to the man.

"Why, yes, I am. How do you know this?"

"I can tell."

"I fail to understand what my profession has to do with the matter at hand."

"He's right, Coombs," said Batleigh. "What does this have to do with the proceedings?"

"I'm gettin' there."

"Go directly there, please," the superintendent added.

"Right then. So, bankers, they take money, they take possessions and sometimes they take life."

"Do you feel a chill?" Adelia whispered in my ear.

A reporter behind us shushed her.

I shook my head in response because words would not take shape in my suddenly swirling mind.

"Who else but a banker would know how to buy a house through the post?" Coombs began.

Batleigh held up a hand. "It's not that complicated –"

"Who else," Coombs continued over him, "but a banker would want to take a pound of flesh?" Coombs swung his arm in a dramatic gesture to point at the banker. "That man is the Butcher of Battersea! He's carryin' an American Bowie knife in his coat pocket. It's still got the blood of his victims on it."

Reality shifted once again, as it had in Marylebone. It seemed some great loom rumbled as it spun the world anew.

"In his vest pocket you'll find a list of the victims and the pieces he took from them. All of 'em had accounts at his bank."

Throughout the room, all sat in rapt attention, though some shivered.

"And in his basement, in jars on a shelf, you'll find the hearts of every one of his victims."

The room burst into cacophony. The banker leapt to his feet and shouted his innocence in a voice gone raw. Batleigh growled and snarled at Coombs, jurors argued with one another, and reporters barked questions. Coombs stood silent, calm, the eye of the storm.

Batleigh, on his feet and making the rounds of the room, restored order.

The banker refused to sit. "What manner of madness is this?" he demanded.

"The kind only people like you make," Coombs said, his finger in the banker's face. "Thinkin' you can get away with anythin'."

"Enough!" Batleigh bellowed. "Coombs, you will not speak again until I address you. Mr. Fernald," he said to the banker, "I apologize. Please take your seat and I will get to the bottom of this."

Fernald the banker nodded and sat. He adjusted his coat. When his hand touched his jacket over his pocket, he froze. A feeling of dread descended upon me.

"Now, Detective Coombs –"

"Search him," said Coombs.

Fernald shifted in his seat. His face was red.

"I will not," said Batleigh.

"Search him. If you don't, I will."

"Here, here, now," said Fernald. His voice cracked. "Superintendent, if you intend to allow this man to go on making threats and wild accusations, I shall take my leave and have a word with your superiors."

"Sorry, Coombs," said Batleigh. He held the banker at bay with a raised hand. "I can't have you putting hands on someone like Mr. Fernald. In fact, you need to apologize."

"Fine. Empty yer pockets, Fernald."

The banker sputtered. "I will do no such thing."

"Wanna shut me up? Show everybody how wrong I am? Empty your pockets. If I'm wrong, I'll walk away, and you'll never hear from me again. But I ain't been wrong yet, have I, Superintendent?"

Batleigh considered Coombs for a moment, then turned to the banker. "Mr. Fernald? Would you mind, sir?" His question trailed off.

Fernald, his face blanched, his eyes wide and brimming with tears, withdrew a knife from his jacket. I recognized it as a "Bowie" knife. It was indeed covered with blood.

The jurors around him scurried away, with gasps and cries muffled by their hands.

"Mr. Fernald?" Batleigh said, his voice full of incredulity.

The banker dropped the knife as if it had burned his fingers.

"The list," said Coombs.

Seemingly under a spell, the banker dropped a hand into his pants pocket and took out a folded piece of paper. A spasmodic gasp ran through him. Feral rage took over and he leapt to his feet. He threw the paper at Coombs as he advanced on him. "How did you put those there?"

"You don't want to do that, Mr. Fernald," said Batleigh.

"No, you don't," Coombs said quietly. "Check his home. You'll find the hearts there."

Batleigh's spirit seemed to sink into the floor as he read the paper. "Mr. Fernald, I'm afraid I'm going to have to hold you for questioning."

While the banker sputtered and protested, Batleigh summoned a constable to take him away, then adjourned the inquest with the instruction to be prepared to be called back within days. The other constables cleared the room, leaving only Coombs and myself with Batleigh.

Batleigh was as puzzled as he was impressed. "How did you come to that conclusion, Coombs?"

"Observation, for one thing. Weight of the knife made his coat move different than it should. The rest I got from Johnson's report."

"No," I whispered, as my soul sank.

"No?" said Batleigh, caught by surprise.

"By which I mean," I said, struggling to speak under Coombs' hot glare. Was I standing? Was I asleep and dreaming?

Coombs turned to Batleigh. "Go on about your business, Superintendent. I'll take care of the doctor."

"Take care of me?" I started, then shook my head. "May I have my notebook back?"

"Sure." He slipped it out of his vest pocket and tossed it to me.

I opened it only to find every page of my notes torn out. "Coombs, what the devil have you *done*?"

"It's for your own good," he growled.

"What are you talking about?"

"Your notes. They were very detailed. *Too* detailed."

"How could they possibly be *too* detailed?"

"'Cause it shows how deep into this fantasy you've gone. That's why I didn't want anyone to see 'em. I don't know if I could keep you out of an asylum if anybody saw 'em. Batleigh's already concerned about you, all that shite about skin trophies. If he saw them notes, he'd have you locked up quick as spit."

I staggered back. "Fantasy? *Asylum?*"

Coombs set a hand on my shoulder. "I like you, Johnson. I want to keep you around, I do. But I can't have you spoutin' off these crazy theories of yours."

"Crazy theories?" I could not form sentences of my own, only repeat what had been said to me.

"A butcher's son collecting blemishes and scars? Come on, Johnson. You can see that's crazy, yeah?"

My head spun as he spoke.

"Think about it. You were alone when you found all that 'evidence' of perfect cuts, yeah? But a room full of people saw what I described. Same thing in Marylebone. And I know you like to put on airs, but all that talk about comin' from a rich family?"

I shoved him away, pushed through the nearby doors and ran into cold rain.

"Johnson!" Coombs called after me.

I kept running and stumbling my way down the street. Soon his voice was drowned out by thunder.

CHAPTER SEVENTEEN

FROM BAD TO WORSE

With Coombs' words assaulting my mind, I ran wildly through the streets, as if distance could give order to chaos and rain could wash away madness.

Clayton had shown me head wounds in Marylebone. No, only one. For the rest of what I had recorded I was, again, alone.

I had been alone when I made the sketches in the warehouse in Battersea.

Alone when I made them in the vestry of St. Margaret's.

No one else had seen what I had.

Was it me, not Coombs, who had invented all manner of fantastical theories?

"No!" I shouted up at the rain. "I know what I saw!"

"*Do you?*" asked my doubting brother.

"Be quiet!" I bellowed. My voice echoed off the buildings around me, like some small clap of thunder.

I stood panting in the downpour, drenched. What had I become? A man who shouts at his own inner voice, a rabid dog barking at his master's leash. And yet I insisted that *I* was the one who knew what was right and true in the world.

A gang of ruffians burst out of an alley. A woman's distant shouts fell ineffectually on their backs. Laughing, they nearly knocked me over and tossed vulgarities and insults as they ran off.

Dislodged from my thoughts, I surveyed my surroundings. I raised my arm to shield my eyes. The wind-driven rain made it nigh impossible to read street signs. Where was I? I had paid no attention to my path. I soon realized there would be no cabs here in this part of Lambeth. I needed to find my way back to the hospital where I stood a better chance of finding one. I stumbled about, searching for something I recognized.

"Johnson!"

I whirled at the sound of the voice to see three silhouettes emerge from an alley across an empty street. They were unperturbed by the rain that pelted their hatless, close-cropped heads and hard, pale visages. They were dressed in all black, statues draped for a funeral.

Fear shook me. I tried to hold still from trembling. I searched around me for constables, passersby, anyone. It seemed these three had waited for the right moment.

One stepped forward. It was Keat, the leader of the trio who had obtained cadavers for me. The same man who had alerted the police and had me arrested, starting me on this Hellish path.

"There you are," said Keat. "Saw you in the papers and had a feelin' you'd be out and about." He advanced on me while the other two took up either side. "You still owe me."

"As it happens," I muttered, "I have access to –"

The next block of time was a blur of fists and feet, of being dragged through puddles and violently relieved of my possessions. When it all came to a stop, I lay in my underclothes in a cold, cobblestone alley. A stream of filthy water ran beneath me as one of Keat's men held me down with a foot on my back.

My every breath heaved against cracked ribs. I tasted the salt of rain and the copper of my blood. Words tumbled around me as they quibbled over the value of what they had taken. The rain had become sporadic. Heavy drops struck me like flung stones.

Keat leaned down and dangled my new pocket watch in front of me. "All this shite? It ain't enough. We know you're gaddin' about with that Coombs fella, so we know how to find ya."

I lifted my head and spit out acrid rainwater mixed with my blood. "What you have taken," I started, struggling against the pain in my chest, the swelling of my lips, "is more than enough –"

A kick to my ribs ended my sentence. "We'll tell ya when it's enough. And if ya talk to the coppers, that's the end of ya. Got it?"

My inability to respond resulted in another kick.

"Got it?"

I managed to wheeze out a satisfying response, and the three men disappeared into the shadows.

Part of me hoped the stream I lay in would wash me away. Eventually, I pushed myself up and stumbled into the street at the end of the alley. My cries for help were no stronger than those of a mewling kitten. I collapsed with relief when I finally heard a constable's whistle. As he helped me to my feet, I told him I had been accosted by strangers. I insisted that I had not seen the men before the attack and could not provide descriptions. I was loathe to invoke Coombs' name, but doing so garnered me a blanket and a ride in a police wagon back to the residence.

Coombs came from the kitchen, calling after me, but I went straight to my room for clothing, then to the bathroom. I was able to stop the bleeding from my lip, but the swelling and the purpling bruises would be with me for days. Each movement as I washed and dressed was a stab to my side. I retreated to my room. I was flotsam tossed upon the rocky shores of madness. It came to me that Coombs would be better served with a parrot, or perhaps a monkey that cackled and clapped whenever he solved a case. And now there was Keat. I would be a dancing sack of money for him to beat until empty.

I sat on the edge of the bed, my head in my hands. Was that truly all that was left to me?

A knock, the door swung open, and Coombs stepped in. "What happened?"

"I was assaulted," I said to the floor.

"Yeah you were. By who?"

"'By whom' and how could I possibly know?" I raised a baleful gaze to him. "Perhaps I imagined them."

Coombs tsked at me. "Don't pout. I'm tryin' to help. You know 'em and they know you. Else you'd be ravin' 'bout criminals and how this ain't supposed to happen to the likes of *you*." He took the chair from the table and set in front of me. He sat in it backwards, his arms across the back. "Plus, they worked you over. Didn't just put you down and take your shite. They *worked* you. I know a good beatdown when I see one. Tell me I'm wrong."

I managed to glance at him. He seemed genuinely concerned. I dropped my head again. "What does it matter? I am leaving your employ. That is best for both of us. Find another 'assistant'. I am of no service to you, and I may soon become a burden." I felt relief at having said the words, but I feared the response they would engender.

"Who do you owe?" Coombs said after a moment. "Like I said, I know a good beat down."

Could I simply refuse to answer? No, I had no doubt Coombs would not let the question rest. "Men who provided services for me. Cadavers for my research. It was they who, upon deciding that a bank cheque was not an acceptable form of payment, alerted the police to my activities. And before you ask, you do not pay me enough to placate them. I suspect no amount would, as what they took from me in cash, jewelry, and clothing should have covered any remaining debt. No, I will not spend my days wondering when they will appear, making new demands. It is best for us both if I simply leave."

"You gave guys like that a *cheque*?" Coombs asked with a grin.

A laugh burst from me and was immediately squelched by pain. "I tried to."

"No wonder they beat you. Relax, I'm funnin'. But you're right, they'll be back. You know how to find 'em?"

That response surprised me. I straightened up to face him. "I believe so, yes."

"Let's go pay 'em a visit."

"I do not need you to fight my battles for me."

"Yeah you do. But look at it this way: It's 'cause they got you arrested that you're workin' for me now. I just want to thank 'em." He leaned forward, malevolence burning brightly in his eyes. "Take me to 'em."

⁘⸻◉ ◉⸻⁘

With equal parts bribes and threats, Coombs rousted a driver and carriage from the mews at the Langford. The driver seemed to get some small revenge by finding every bump and hole on the roads to our destination. Thankfully the rain had stopped, but it had been replaced by a damp, cold wind.

"About my notes and theories," I started, unsure of the words that would follow. I could not let go of the idea that I had been right in what I had seen.

Coombs took his gaze from the carriage window and leveled it at me. "You saw what you wanted to see. *Needed* to see."

"That is your assessment of me? That I am delusional?"

"You couldn't accept a little girl bein' a murderer, so you went along with Walker. Now, with Battersea, I figured you just wanted me to be wrong about the rat bites." A trace of humour had crept into his expression.

"Will you be adding 'psychiatrist' to your titles?"

"Ha. Detective Dr. Coombs. Or should it be Dr. Detective?"

I did not join in his laughter.

"Hey," he said. "Best to go into somethin' like this relaxed. If you're too tense, you'll jump at all the wrong things."

"Says the six-foot man."

"Six-two. And you're missin' the point."

"No, I understand you, but I have never gone into 'something like this'." A road sign caught my attention. "We have arrived."

I knocked on the carriage roof and called for the drive to stop. "We will walk from here," I said out the window.

Coombs leapt from the cab and began eagerly searching the dark streets for his intended quarry. He nearly blended into the night. He wore the same long, black cotton coat as when I first met him. Under it were grey sweaters and vests, providing multiple layers of warmth and shielding, I realized.

The driver became aware of my painful struggle to move and assisted me in climbing out. He, too, gazed about, in the opposite direction from Coombs, then leapt back into his seat and snapped the reins. The horse seemed as eager to leave as the driver.

"This don't look so bad," Coombs said.

Indeed, it did not, standing as he was with his back to Campbell Street. It was a pleasant enough neighbourhood on that side, between Battersea and Lambeth, akin to our own with brick houses, gardens, fences, and lit streetlamps. That Coombs was unaware of this area suggested to me he had never visited London prior to moving to Kensington.

"This way," I told him. He followed me across the road and down a hill. Now we stood on the darkened, shadowed street where I had last lived. "Watch out," I told him.

He peered into the darkness ahead of us with an eager grin.

The street we walked could have been a different city, a different world. Campbell Street was a wound on the neighbourhood, a ragged tear of a road. The homes were closer together and darker. Not merely in building materials and lack of paint, but there was no gas to light the lamps, inside or out.

"Now I get it," said Coombs. His posture and stride had changed. He held himself straighter, taller, and sprang lightly on his feet. "You lived here?"

"I did. That one, in fact." I pointed to the burned-out hulk that had once been my residence. An argument raged in the house next to it, as it had on the night of my arrest and any other time I turned my attention that way. I used to pity them, being trapped in some self-perpetuating loop of misery. Now I could sympathize.

A door opened just two down from us and I motioned for Coombs to step into a nearby alley.

"That is the pub where I met them," I said, "to make the arrangements." I was unsure of what to do next.

"Think they're in there?"

"It is likely. This is the time of night when I typically found them there."

"Good. You go in, let 'em see you and come back out. That alley across the way? That's where I'll be waitin'."

My nod was as much a spasm as affirmation. My legs stiffened as I fought the urge to run. I waited at the pub door until Coombs tucked himself into the alley's shadows.

On opening the door, a cloud of smoke engulfed me. It carried a throat-burning tinge of alcohol and body odour. The oil lamps on the walls did little to pierce the dense cloud filling the room. Red dots flared as the smokers pulled on their cigarettes and cigars. The din of raucous laughter and shouting quieted, a wave of silence fanning out from me, this overly dressed, slight man who must have looked like a deer on a railroad track. A deer that had recently been struck but had not learned its lesson. Sound at a distant table drew my attention as chairs scraped the floor. Three men stood, the trio who had assaulted me. They advanced, led by Keat.

I turned and, fumbling nervously for a moment, pulled the door open and rushed out as quickly as the pain in my ribs allowed. "They're coming," I said and stepped into the alley.

The alley was empty. There were pale stone walls on either side, broken up by dark doorways. I went to the first. "Coombs?" I whispered. Nothing there, nor across the way. Had he abandoned me? Was this some new punishment? Had he decided to do away with me in the cruelest possible fashion?

Three sets of boots slapped the wet stones as the men crossed the street. Keat called my name, as one would summon a disobedient dog.

The three stopped at the alley's entrance. "Whadya do, bring some friends?" said Keat. "Big man now, yeah? Won't do ya no good."

They moved into the alley. I turned to run, but the alley ended just a few doors down. Turning back, I searched for a weapon. The three approached, grinning predator grins.

Coombs stepped into the alley behind them and gave a twitch of his arm. A pipe slid into his hand. With a few silent strides, he struck the first thug a vicious blow on the back of his head. The thug careened into Keat and the two crashed into the alley wall.

The third produced a knife. He feinted at Coombs, who swung at the empty space. The thug made a quick stab at Coombs' side. Coombs grunted at the blow, then cocked his elbow into the thug's jaw, sending him reeling. He then swung the pipe with his full arm across the man's face. Teeth clattered on the stone as the man fell.

Keat pushed the still unconscious thug off of him and scrambled to his feet. "All right now," said Keat. "That's enough. We can work this out."

A step and whip of the pipe to Keat's knee put him to the alley floor with a cry. Coombs took Keat by his hair and pulled his head back, pressing the pipe across Keat's throat.

"You got your money from this man, yeah? You'll get nothin' more from him. He works for *me* now."

Keat muttered a strangled agreement.

"Good," said Coombs. He stepped back and gave one sharp rap to Keat's face with the pipe, smashing his nose.

Keat collapsed, howling and gurgling through the blood.

Coombs exited the alley, and I stepped over the men to catch up. After turning a corner, Coombs stopped and pressed the bloody end of the pipe against my chest. "No more talk of quittin', yeah?"

His eyes held mine as a lion's paw holds its prey.

"No," I said quietly. "Never again."

He nodded and walked away, flinging the pipe off into the darkness. The shriek of a cat snapped me out of my spell, and I followed.

⋆⇥━◉ ◉━⇤⋆

Once back at the residence, Coombs went directly upstairs. I believe I saw him wince and hold his side. I muttered a thanks, which he dismissed with a wave.

I went to my library, closed the door and started a fire.

"He works for *me* now." Coombs' simple statement rang in my head. The image of him with the bloody iron pipe pressed against Keat's throat, and his calm expression when he told me I should not leave chilled me. He had just brutally beaten three men – criminals though they were, but still men – and walked away as if he were merely taking the air.

"He's dangerous."

I wholeheartedly agreed, but that very danger had quite possibly just saved my life. Turned against me, however, it could be my end.

"You could have died tonight."

The rush of excitement flowed from me, and my knees weakened.

"They could have killed you."

"But he saved me," I whispered hoarsely.

"Cats save mice. Until they're done with them."

I staggered to my chair and collapsed into it.

"What are you going to do?"

"I don't know."

"Look what he's done to you."

The words "saved me" came to my lips, but the image of a cat saving a mouse lingered, a cat toying with a creature it intends to kill.

"Wait until he's asleep."

"Then what?" I kept my voice low. If Coombs heard me and thought me mad before, what would he think of me having a conversation with a voice in my head? But it seemed the only way that I could work through this dilemma. "Run? Hope that the cat would find another mouse?"

"You could turn the tables."

"Turn the ..."

"What choice do you have?"

"No, no, *no*." I could not accept what I was telling myself. My brother's voice had always given me permission to misbehave, but just a little. It had been a foolish way for a timid boy to muster some courage. But to attack Coombs? Even in his sleep? I would not survive.

I took a bottle of brandy – but not a glass – and made my way upstairs, hoping to quiet my mind for at least one night.

I turned the corner towards my room and saw at the end of the hall that the bathroom door was open. A candle shed light on Coombs. He stood, his back to me, as he slipped out of his underclothes. He was thinner than I expected, wiry, his muscles ropy, his joints sharp and angular. His pale skin bore yet paler scars. I had the fleeting thought that Garret would be thrilled to see this.

Coombs touched a towel to the bleeding wound on his side. Now I could understand his thick coat and multiple layers. That surely would have been a severe, if not mortal wound, without them. He turned towards me and I hurried silently to my room.

CHAPTER EIGHTEEN

FAILURE IN NEWINGTON

I WAITED UNTIL THE BURKETTS HAD left before I went down to breakfast. I did not want them to see the marks I still carried from my encounter with Keat and his men, nor did I want to discuss Coombs' response in front of them. In addition, I was still feeling the effects of the bottle of brandy I had consumed.

Coombs, of course, seemed unaffected by anything and ate his breakfast with vigour. He waved a fork in greeting.

"I failed to thank you," I said as I sat. "For last night. You provided a solution where I had none."

After swallowing most of the food in his mouth, Coombs said, "Forget it. And the other stuff."

The other stuff. Meaning my reality or his.

"Just do what I ask, and we'll be sorted."

I nodded and muttered thanks again, but in truth I was less sure than I had been prior to the conversation. Do what he asked? That meant accepting whatever reality he may speak, regardless of what I observed.

I turned my attention to the food before me. While lunch and dinner menus changed, breakfast remained the same and I was grateful for it. When the Burketts came to clear the dishes, they brought a wire from Batleigh. Coombs eagerly snatched it from Burkett's hand and read it aloud.

"'There's been a murder. Newington. St. Alban's Church. Keeping it quiet. Come quickly.'"

I found myself eager to get to the crime scene. If we saw it simultaneously, perhaps there would be no diverging realities.

"Shall we take a train?" I said, moving towards the door.

"I ain't gettin' in one of them things." Coombs seemed rooted to his place.

"They are perfectly safe –" I started.

"You go. Take your train," Coombs said, waving me away. "I'll catch up."

"But the wire said to come quickly."

"And all of a sudden a horse ain't quick enough?" he snapped. His sudden flare, I assumed, stemmed from a fear of trains that he wished not to admit. "Besides, if you get there first, you can tell me what you see."

"Very well," I said as my heart sank, drawn down by a whirlpool of doubt. I knew not whether anything I saw would be real or as malleable as a sculptor's clay. Or, for that matter, if I was going mad.

⊷══◉ ◉══⊷

As I walked from the train station, I felt weighed down by the stone-grey clouds above. St. Alban's was a moderately sized church built of granite blocks, old leaded windows, and a slate roof. Batleigh met me at the front entrance, an arched door made of weathered, vertical planks strapped with iron. He sat by himself on the stone steps, his head down. He was lost in thought such that I had to call his name twice to bring him out of it. When he raised his head to me, it was clear he had been crying. But once he saw me, he raised himself up and took on the mantel of superintendent.

"Good morning, Doctor," he said, extending his gloved hand. "Thank you for coming so quickly. Where is Coombs?"

"He sent me on ahead."

"Oh?"

"I believe he would prefer that no one knew this, but it appears he is afraid of trains."

"Ah. Yes, I know several people who share that fear." Batleigh made no motion to enter the church.

"Would you like to wait for him?" I hoped he would.

He took a long pull on his cigar, the warm smoke giving him strength. He flicked the stub away. "Best not. Can't keep this quiet for too long. And I want it solved quick. Follow me." Batleigh led me along the sunward side of the church.

Some have an aversion to hospitals. I feel the same about churches. My father wore a mask of piousness for an hour every Sunday while I, in my childish fervor, would pray that the peace would last. Often, his mask would fall before we even made it all the way home. I could not reconcile the instruction that I should honor such a man, that Mother must obey him, with platitudes of mercy and love. While I sometimes enjoyed the peace that came with our attendance, eventually each service began to feel like the time between one punch and the next.

"Bishop Trent was found dead this morning," Batleigh said, his voice flat from effort. "This one's personal, Detective. This is where I grew up," he added with a tilt of his head towards the church. "Bishop Trent? He welcomed me and my family when others didn't. Stood up for us. Got other people to look at us differently. *See* us ..." His voice trailed off and he adjusted his gloves. "If foul play's involved, I want the killer *found*. I'm not sure I can see straight on this one. I haven't even gone up to see the body."

Batleigh pushed the side door open with effort.

Inside was a simple, pillared room with scattered tables and chairs, a counter on our right. A priest awaited us. Everything about the priest looked hard. His weathered, bony face, his gunmetal hair. Even his tattered cassock appeared as armour. He kept his hands folded together at the base of his chest.

"Who is this?" the priest demanded before introductions could be made.

"This is Dr. Johnson," said Batleigh. "Dr. Johnson, meet Father Malvagna."

The priest did not offer his hand. "Why have you brought this man?"

Batleigh was taken aback by Malvagna's confrontational tone. "To investigate –"

"I sent for you out of respect for the bishop. So that we could keep this quiet. And you bring this, this minion of that supposed detective?"

"'Minion'?" I said angrily, stepping forward.

"Settle down, both of you," said Batleigh. "Father Malvagna, I sent for Coombs because he is the best *detective* I have seen in years. Dr. Johnson is his assistant and has played no small part in helping Coombs solve the most perplexing murders. Now, we both want to know who killed Bishop Trent, yes?"

Still tense, Malvagna nodded. "Yes."

"Good. Then I can think of no better men than Coombs and Johnson."

"But we agreed," said Malvagna, "to keep it from the congregation until we knew the solution. These two will make a show of it so they can see themselves in the papers."

I held out a hand to stop Batleigh's response, as I had one of my own. "We have no control over what the papers report, nor how they report it."

The priest gestured broadly, his voice getting louder as he spoke. "Will you find witches and sacrifices here? That is your specialty, it seems. How can you not be tainted by evil if that is all you see in the world?"

"We find the truth!" It was Coombs, striding in through the door. "I could hear you down the block."

I was grateful for his interruption, as I had no response to the priest's accusations.

Malvagna turned to Batleigh. "I do not want this man in my church."

Coombs spoke over the superintendent. "Then you must not want to find out who killed your bishop."

Malvagna whirled on him and Batleigh stepped between them. "*Enough.* Let us behave like the gentlemen we are and get down to business. Someone killed Bishop Trent and we *must* find out *who*." He was visibly shaken, which softened both Malvagna and Coombs.

"Would you like me to take them up?" Malvagna said, his hand on Batleigh's shoulder.

Batleigh nodded. "If you wouldn't mind, Father."

"It is well, my son. I know what he meant to you."

"Go ahead, Johnson," said Coombs.

"Do you not want to see it, *Detective*?" asked Malvagna, barely masking his scorn.

"That's *his* job," Coombs told him. He turned to me. "Now go."

"This way," said Malvagna.

"And take good notes, Doctor," Coombs said with a smug grin.

Malvagna led me to a door at the front of the room and up creaking wooden stairs that doubled back every few steps until they let out into a high, wide nave made of rough-hewn, dark wood. A balcony surrounded the nave. Above it, a series of crisscrossing rafters and beams supported ornate brass chandeliers. A worn red carpet ran up the centre aisle to the altar, at which lay a body, in priestly vestments.

"The bishop," Malvagna said with a sigh.

I approached the body. His black cassock and pants were torn in a few spots. He lay on his stomach with a long candle lighter beneath him. The bishop's head, covered in stark white hair, was tilted too far back. His blank face stared up at the crucifix behind the altar. Clearly a broken neck. But, of what consequence were any observations I might make?

My pencil poised over my notebook, I thought about what Coombs had said, that I should forget "all that other stuff" and just do as I was told. Was I ready to abandon all hope of maintaining a free and clear mind? I was not. On one page I wrote a brief description of the scene. On the next I wrote: "*It is what you say it is.*"

"Hold, please, my son. May I ask a question of you?" said Malvagna.

"Certainly."

"Do you feel safe?"

Surprised, I stammered momentarily. "What ever do you mean?"

"With that man, is what I mean. That *detective*." Malvagna moved in closer to me than was comfortable, but a pew blocked any path away. He reeked of incense. "There is a darkness he carries. An evil, dare I say."

Coombs' easy violence and the changes in reality came to mind. "Please step back, if you would." He did. "And mind you, be careful how you speak of others, sir. Your position only affords you so much latitude."

"Address me as Father, my son."

"I will not. And please do not call me 'son'."

That gave his head a tilt. "Are you in his thrall?"

I pushed away from him and moved toward the door. "No, of course not." Was I? I was prepared to tell him exactly what he wanted to hear while keeping what I believed to be the truth to myself.

Malvagna moved swiftly ahead of me and blocked my path to the door. "He imposes his will on you, yes?"

"Said the man blocking the door."

The priest raised his hands in resignation and moved away.

I tried to shake Malvagna's question from my mind. I was in Coombs' debt, but in his thrall? The world, it seemed, was in his thrall as he imposed his will on it. Should I succumb? Accept his version of reality and discard my own as fantasy? No. I would give him the show he wanted, but I would hold onto my reality, my sense of self. There was a thorn in my mind, a stone in my heart that could not be made to go away. It felt as if I were searching for a gem in a puddle of mud and I had but a fork.

Once back in the room below, I tore the page out of my notebook and gave it to Coombs. He smiled as he read it. I briefly wondered what fantastical scene would spring from his mouth.

"Well?" said Batleigh. "Do you have anything?"

Coombs faced Malvagna. "It was *this* bastard."

I was not surprised. I felt little of anything, in fact.

The priest was stunned to silence.

"Father Malvagna?" said Batleigh. "No, I can't accept that, Coombs."

"Look at 'em. He knows I'm onto him. Search him. In his robes you'll find the knife he used to murder the bishop. Stabbed him over and over in the chest."

Something was wrong. I did not feel the shifting of shadows as I had before.

"That is enough!" shouted Malvagna. "Remove this evil from my church now."

"See?" said Coombs. "He's tryin' to hide it."

Malvagna threw his arms wide. "Search me, then. But know that your failure will bring retribution."

Coombs barked a laugh. "From *you*?"

"From the Lord, but by my hand it may well come."

"Stop it," snapped Batleigh. "Both of you. I say again, behave according to your stations."

"You may search me," Malvagna said to Batleigh, "if it will ease your soul."

Batleigh searched the priest but came away empty-handed.

"No knife, Coombs," said Batleigh.

That caught him off guard. "He ditched it," barked Coombs, unsettled.

Could Coombs be wrong? I was eager to find out.

"Let us all go up," I said, "and see for ourselves."

Coombs and Malvagna agreed angrily, but Batleigh remained unsure.

"If you would rather not," I started.

"No, no," Batleigh said, steeling himself. "I am an officer of the law."

I led the way back upstairs eager to see the state of the world. Would I see blood and a protruding knife now? Or the battered body of an old bishop? I was almost excited by the mystery.

There lay Bishop Trent, his face nearly as purple as his robe. No blood, no knife. Just a careless old man with a broken neck. Exactly what I had seen earlier.

It was just what I had seen earlier. As if water had been thrown in my face and the bucket with it, I realized Coombs had given his solution to a murder, and he was wrong.

"You see," said Malvagna. "No stab wounds, no blood,"

Coombs stood in the aisle between the pews, staring, his jaw hanging open.

Batleigh rushed to the dead bishop and tenderly reached out a hand, then took it back without quite touching. He straightened up. "No sign of knife wounds, Detective." His throat was tight.

Coombs remained in his stunned silence.

I was awash with emotions. It seemed the world was not Coombs' to command. Part of me wanted to cavort about, taunting him that he was wrong. More importantly, I wanted to know how this piece fit into the puzzle. Did this mean that previously I had seen the real world, but Coombs had somehow changed it? If so, why did his tricks not work now?

"He slipped," I said and turned to gauge Coombs' reaction. His eyes were glassy, withdrawn.

Batleigh and Malvagna looked at me curiously.

"Bishop Trent used the balcony to access that beam, and got himself far enough to reach the chandelier. He fell, bounced off a crossbeam and landed here."

"That does seem likely," Batleigh said.

Malvagna considered this. "I thought he'd been strangled."

"Coombs?" asked Batleigh "Anything to add?"

Coombs' eyes were as flies in a jar, darting about with no place to land. He shook his head. "We're done here." He turned on his heel and stormed off down the aisle.

"Coombs!" I called, but he ignored me.

"Never return to this place of worship!" Malvagna shouted.

I found myself unable or unwilling to move from the spot. Coombs had been wrong and I, right.

"Thanks for your help," Batleigh said to me, breaking my spell. "I can take it from here."

As I made my way between the pews and down the stairs, I could not tell if I was walking or floating, so deep in my thoughts was I. Just as I had begun to accept a new understanding of the world, terrible though it was, now it had suddenly flipped back to what it had been. But if the world itself could change so easily, could I be sure of anything?

Coombs was not on the street when I exited the church. I called his name but received no response.

I returned to the residence to await Coombs' return and his reaction to having been wrong. Dinner arrived with still no sign of him. I asked Burkett to send word if he caught any sight of him.

In the morning I received a wire from Batleigh saying Coombs was being held at the Newington gaol after a drunken binge.

This was a turn I had not expected. As there were no immediate trains, I paid double the fee for double the speed for a cab to get me back to Newington. For the first time I was worried about the man. His powers, whatever they were, had failed him and apparently shattered his psyche. Why else would he drink himself into a gaol cell? A part of me was glad for it, this flickering light in my darkness.

CHAPTER NINETEEN

CONFRONTATION

A HEAVY, WET SNOW HAD FALLEN overnight and then froze. With the sun unable to pierce the cloud cover, there was no melting. Horses slipped and stumbled, carts collided, and pedestrians fell all through the city. The cab swung like a pendulum behind the horse while the driver pulled the reins and cracked the whip, barking orders and curses in equal measure.

We slid to a stop perpendicular to the grey stone Newington jailhouse. I tipped the driver and left him to his argument with another cab driver, whose cab he now blocked.

Thankfully there was a railing that helped me navigate the icy stone steps. Batleigh held the door for me. "Good thing I was still in town," he said, "or Coombs would be bound for Newgate."

"That is quite considerate of you, Superintendent," I said. "What did he do?"

"Showed the downside of a beating to a bar full of labourers. That is, 'til one cracked a board across his head. A board right out of the bar Coombs smashed. By St. Swithens' skinny chickens, the man is formidable."

"I imagine the owner of the bar will be expecting compensation. I will see to it personally, Superintendent."

"Good. Because I don't think Coombs will be seeing too much of anything for a time."

We had reached at the back of the gaol house before the row of cells. One was occupied. A bobby with a cudgel in hand stood over what appeared to be a large pile of clothes. The pile only revealed itself to be Coombs, waking, after being repeatedly poked. A second bobby stood at the ready just outside the cell.

Coombs stirred and pushed himself to a sitting position. He batted away the cudgel and the bobby stepped back. Blood crusted Coombs' scalp, nose, and swollen lips. His clothes, the ones I had encouraged him to buy, were torn and filthy.

I turned to Batleigh, who also had a cudgel in hand. "Did he … ?" I started.

"Kill anyone? No. I'd have let him go to Newgate. He put a few in hospital, though." Batleigh moved to stand over Coombs. "Look at me." When Coombs raised his bleary expression, Batleigh considered him for a moment. "Don't know what's gotten into you, but I can't release you if you're going to be a danger."

"I'm fine." Coombs said with a shake of his head and a wince of pain.

Batleigh turned to me. "You all right with getting him back to London?"

Coombs now rested his head in his hands. "I still ain't ridin' no train."

That gave Batleigh and me a chuckle. "Yes, Superintendent," I said. "I think we shall be fine."

"Right, then. Off with you lot."

Refusing assistance, Coombs staggered his way out the door. Malvagna awaited us in the lobby. He held open his grey cloth coat with his hands on his hips, revealing his black cassock and gold cross. He breathed like a bull.

"Can I help you with something, Father?" Batleigh asked.

"Perhaps an explanation." His tone was calm, barely disguising his anger. "I come with absolution for the detective, but it appears the laws of man have found him innocent of his crimes."

Batleigh laughed. "No one here is innocent, Father. But Detective Coombs is being released, yes."

"And I don't need no fuckin' *absolution*," snarled Coombs.

"Easy, Detective," said Batleigh.

Rage flared in Malvagna's eyes, and he pushed past Batleigh. Coombs spread his feet and put up his fists. Malvagna took Coombs by a wrist, spun him around and slammed him against a wall with such force that the windows rattled, and a plaque fell.

Batleigh pulled at Malvagna as Coombs struggled to break free, but the priest tightened his grip.

Malvagna pressed his face to Coombs' ear. "You need protection, my son. From forces you cannot understand."

A stream of obscenities flowed from Coombs.

"Let him go *now*, Father," shouted Batleigh, "or I'll put you in the cell he just left."

Malvagna pushed off of Coombs and stepped back.

Coombs staggered for a moment, then started for Malvagna. The bobbies grabbed him from behind and barely held him back.

Batleigh stepped between them. "There's enough cells here for both of you."

Malvagna held up his hands and turned away.

Coombs released his tension with a breath, then nodded at Batleigh. The bobbies let him go.

I stood in awe of this priest, who had so easily bested Coombs, a man who had single-handedly taken down three ruffians. Still, had Coombs not been incapacitated, I suspected the outcome might have been different.

"I don't need no protection or anything else from *him*," said Coombs.

With one hand on his crucifix, Malvagna made a sign of the cross with the other. "It is with you, Detective. I can feel it," he said. His tone had become almost pleading.

They stared at each other like stags in a forest.

Batleigh called for one of the bobbies. "Get Detective Coombs in a wagon and make sure he gets home. I want a word with you, Doctor."

"Certainly," I said.

With no fight left in him, Coombs let the bobby lead him outside.

Malvagna set his hands on Batleigh's shoulders. "Albert, you must listen to me."

"No. I know what you're on about, and I'll remind you that you were nearly sent away –" He stopped, glanced at me, then turned back to the priest. "This parish needs you, Father."

Malvagna nodded but was unconvinced. He turned to me. "Save yourself. That man walks with evil."

"Thank you for your concern," I said in hopes that it would end our interaction.

Malvagna came towards me, arms out, as if to take me by the shoulders. I stepped back, out of his reach. He stopped and dropped his arms. Sadness came over him.

"Know that what I do, I do because I must cleanse the world of –"

"*Father Malvagna*," Batleigh interrupted. "That's quite enough. You should return to the church now."

The priest lowered his head in genuine regret. "I do not mean to make your job harder, Albert, my son." He made the sign of the cross. "Lord be with you."

"And also with you," Batleigh responded dutifully.

A quick nod in my direction and the priest hurried off.

"Sorry about that," Batleigh said to me.

"It appears this is not the first such incident," I said.

He shook his head. "No, but I hoped it wouldn't happen again. Seems he's gotten himself fired up. There's something you need to know about Father Malvagna. He's both the most caring, generous, Christian man I know, and the most volatile. When he gets his back up like that …" He shook his head again, then held up his gloved hands. "This would have killed me if not for him."

"He saved you?"

"In more ways than one," Batleigh said, his head bowed. "Some kids and I were playing in an alley. I thought I was part of the gang, as it were, but … they got a fire going for fun. One of them pushed me. I fell into it. They ran. I screamed for help and saw people turning away, closing their curtains. I passed out. Next I knew, Father Malvagna was carrying me. Got me to a doctor. He was brand-new here. Didn't know me from Samson's cousin Sophie, but he helped me. *Saved* me. So yes, I'll forgive his outbursts. I just hope the church will continue to do so. But that's enough about him. We need to talk about Coombs."

"Yes, of course," I said, wanting desperately to avoid that subject until I could speak to him.

Batleigh led me to a bench near the door and gestured for me to sit. "What happened yesterday?"

"He was wrong," I said. I wanted to tell him more. If only I had more than fantastical explanations.

"That's as obvious as a bee on a bum. I mean *after.*"

"I am afraid I have no explanation. I have never seen him in that state."

"There's more, isn't there?" Batleigh searched my eyes. "How does he know the things he's described? A little girl's dolls? The contents of a man's secret drawer? Hell, even the Minister's wife's jewelry box." He leaned closer to me. "How could he possibly know?"

"I wish I could tell you," I said. "I truly do."

"Doesn't take bad news well, does he?"

"It would appear not."

Batleigh stood and worked his hands as he pondered his next words. He stopped and turned to me. "Is he reliable? I can't be depending on him if every time he makes a mistake he falls apart like a paper house in a downpour."

"I understand and I wish I could reassure you, but I really cannot."

The superintendent's frown deepened while his mind worked.

If Coombs could be so easily broken by a mistake, what would happen to him should he lose his situation with Batleigh? And what would happen to me? "I will have a talk with him and keep you apprised of his situation."

"That'll have to do. Thank you, Doctor. Now, go hop a train, get back to London and be ready for him."

CHAPTER TWENTY

A TALK

I WAITED IN THE KITCHEN UNTIL midmorning when there came a groan and a belch from upstairs, the likes of which I had not heard before, even in prison. This was soon followed by slow, plodding steps along the upper hall and down the stairs.

At the kitchen door, Coombs swayed as he held onto the jamb for support. He pointed his face at me, but his puffy eyes had no focus. The reds and purples of every cut and bruise stood out in great contrast to his pale skin. He looked like a character from one of his penny bloods, defeated. He mumbled something that may have been a greeting.

"I have something for you." I pushed a pewter mug in his direction. "It will help."

Coombs staggered to the table and all but fell on it, holding himself up with flat palms. He warily sniffed at my offering.

"I had Burkett make it for you. It is of Scottish origin, and I have used it myself."

After a long, suspicious stare, he snatched up the drink and gulped it all down. He dropped into his chair and slammed the mug on the table, then pressed his face into his hands.

"What happened?" I asked.

His response was muffled by his hands.

"Pardon?"

"I don't *know*," he said with a slap of the table.

"You are not the first detective to be wrong, you know."

"Not s'posed to be." He set his head back in his hands.

"You are not 'supposed to be' wrong? How is that possible? Everyone is wrong at some point."

Coombs struggled for words, then said, "I *see* the solutions." He held up a hand, as if placing objects in the air. "All around me. It's like the world is showin' itself."

"You saw a little girl slashing several peoples' thighs until they bled to death?"

A careful nod caused him to wince, and he touched his forehead. "Like she sprang up out of nothin', all horns and teeth, wavin' that knife around."

"This vision just came to you? Was it in a dream?"

"No, nothin' like that. I got somebody on the inside. Gives me leads."

"On the inside of what? The police?"

A dismissive wave ended my questions. What did he mean by that? If he had an accomplice, that would answer a great many questions.

"But that's how they died, yeah? I mean, the evidence was there, wasn't it? No matter what nobody else said." Now his stare was directed at me. "Hey, that stuff's workin'. What's in it?" He looked into the mug.

"A subject for later. Yes, the evidence was there, despite what I and, well, what everyone said before you spoke."

Coombs set the mug down and pushed it aside. "Yeah."

"And you had similar leads regarding Downing Street and Battersea?"

"It's just hints I get. I have to take it from there."

"And then you have visions?"

"Don't make it sound like I'm crazy or somethin'. It ain't like what *you* see, things what ain't there." He folded his arms and looked away.

"Can I meet this informant?"

He shook his head. "He's gotta stay secret. Besides, I don't know where to find him. He finds me when he has somethin'."

A mysterious man who surreptitiously directs Coombs to certain crimes. Thoughts of supernatural beings came to mind, but I dared not entertain them, considering my tenuous grasp on reality. If I was unable to see the world as it was, how could I offer a theory about spirits?

"And what about Newington?" I asked.

Coombs shrank into himself. "I shoulda waited until I heard from him. To be sure, yeah? But I saw that priest. Knife in his hand, blood on it, on the body. I *saw* it." He slammed his fists on the table.

"But that's not what we found."

"No."

I decided to take a leap. "Do you think it had anything to do with being in a church?"

He looked at me as if I had started singing sea shanties. "You the one havin' visions now?"

To hide my frustration with his question, I pushed away from the table and poured myself more coffee. "The first vision you had. Downing Street. Was it before or after your first meeting with this informant?"

"Not sure. Around the same time."

"This was shortly after you nearly died, yes? In Burma?"

After some hesitation, he nodded.

"You seem unsure."

"I … I don't remember much. About Burma."

"It was a pitched battle against fierce warriors. It is not surprising –"

"Before that. Before … I don't …" He shook his head as if to loosen something from it.

I sat at the table again. "Are you saying you do not remember your life before Burma?"

"I do, yeah, but … it's hazy." Coombs took a turn getting coffee.

"I had always assumed you simply wished not to talk about your past."

"Like you?" he said when he sat.

"Pardon?"

"You come from a different life. Upper crust. Don't deny it."

"You suggested that I fantasized all that."

"Well, did ya?"

I paused for a deep breath. "All I am willing to say is that I had a falling out with my father over my choice of career."

"Yeah? What's so bad about bein' a doctor?"

"Nothing, of course. But I wanted to be a surgeon, not a doctor. To my father, doctors were gentlemen who came calling with tinctures and pills to relieve a woman's hysteria. Men, of course, could cure their own ailments with silence and liquor."

"No argument there," Coombs interjected with a smirk.

I ignored his jape. "But surgeons were a ghoulish lot who wallowed in blood and reveled in mutilations." To Coombs' surprised look I added, "Those were his exact words when I told him I wanted to be a surgeon. I could not make him understand that field surgeons did the best they could under the circumstances and that medicine had changed much over the intervening decades since he had seen battle."

I withdrew into memories of that last argument with my father, then realized that Coombs had gone silent as well. Perhaps I had stirred up memories of his own experience.

"But let us not stray too far from the matter of your past," I said, "or at least how you came to have this ability to see what no one else sees. If we can understand it, we can harness it more effectively."

He gave a thoughtful nod. "I never knew him. My father."

"You remember that part of your life?"

Now he shrugged. "Kinda. My mum, a bit. And men that … well, let's just say men in my mum's life. They didn't like me, and I hated them, so I went my own way soon as I could. After that, it's just … life. Runnin' with gangs, gettin' in fights, doin' whatever needed doin'."

"But do you recall if you were able to see the things you see now?"

"No. That much I know."

"Then it would appear that being so near to death connected you to something …"

"Yeah. Connected me. To the world. So I see things."

"That others do not."

"Yeah."

We fell into silence while Coombs suddenly dove on the bread and cheese Burkett had left. Then came a knock at the door. The maid had brought a wire.

"Who's it from?" called Coombs from the kitchen.

"The bank," I stammered as I read Adelia's name on the paper.

"Yeah?" He seemed skeptical.

"Seems there is a problem with my account."

"Told ya not to trust 'em."

"As you say. However," I said, at the kitchen door, "I must be off and clear the matter up."

"Look, er …" He rubbed his face roughly. "Just … don't, er …" He wrestled with his words as if they were a wild boar. "Let's talk more, yeah? About how this works."

I was taken aback. "Yes. Of course. That would be excellent."

He squinted at me, still with a measure of disbelief. "Yeah?"

"Yes. Further discussion would garner …" I paused as a smirk took his expression. "Yeah, let's have a gab," I said in as close an approximation to his accent as I could manage.

He laughed and saluted me. I snatched my hat and coat and rushed out the door, wishing once again that Coombs kept on a driver.

CHAPTER TWENTY-ONE

A PUZZLING DISCOVERY

ADELIA RUSHED ME INTO HER OFFICE, holding a large envelope. "Before I show you this, I should explain that I have been quite busy looking into this detective of yours."

"Of 'mine'?" I said with strained mirth. "He is not –"

She waved a dismissive hand. "Not one orphanage in the region Coombs claims to have come from has any record of his name. Not one." She awaited my response.

"That is … surprising."

"Yes. Do you know who else has no record of him? The British Army. No 'Coombs' fought in Burma, and there is no record of a Coombs within their ranks in recent years."

"Well, now." I sat back, pondering this. "I find that hard to accept."

She squinted suddenly in disbelief. "It is the truth."

"You have viewed all records of the entire British Army?"

"Of course not. But based on his age, there is no record of his name in the command which sent the expedition. There are much older and much younger men of similar names, 'Combes', 'Coumbs', 'Coom'," she said, spelling them out. "But none around the time of the fighting."

"My apologies, Adelia, but you must be mistaken."

She drew in a breath and folded her arms. "He was not in the British Army. Not under that name."

"Because you lack evidence of his presence, you cannot pronounce that as evidence that he was not present."

She frowned quite deeply at me and any warmth I had seen previously vanished. "You need to see this," she said with a quiet intensity, sliding the envelope across her desk.

"What is it?"

"Just read it, please. It was sent to me by a colleague from the *Manchester Daily Observer.* I worked there for a time. Father never said as much, but I'm sure getting me out of Manchester was part of his justification for paying for all this. But that's neither here nor there. I sent my article and the engraving of

Coombs to my colleague. That accent of his." She shook her head. "At any rate, I think you'll find it interesting."

The envelope contained articles going back some twenty-one years, to 1863. The first told of an attempt at bank note forgery gone wrong and of the gang members turning evidence against each other. "Why am I reading this?"

Adelia pointed at the article. "The young one. Silas Lee. Read about him."

"He was part of a gang passing forged banknotes." I summarized aloud as I read. "One member was caught, then turned evidence against the others. This Silas Lee was among those brought in. All the members were given life at labour, but the boy, Lee, was given only fifteen years. The magistrate took pity on him due to having no father and, how did he put it? 'A mother of loose morals.' What is it about this young Silas Lee?"

"Read the description of him."

I ran my finger down the page until I found it. "'Dark, curly hair, over six foot tall.'"

"Yes. And here." She pulled another page from the envelope. This one contained a series of engravings of the banker, the arresting constable, and the gang of forgers. "Lower right," she said, pushing the page at me. "Look."

Before me was an engraving of a teenager with dark, curly hair, thick brows and a long, broken nose.

"Look like someone you know?"

I realized what she was driving at. "I will admit to a vague resemblance, but –"

"'Vague'? *Look.*"

"I am sure there are plenty of swarthy young men with –"

"Who are over six feet tall and from Manchester?"

"All right. There is a resemblance." I set the articles down. "Is it your contention that this Lee boy is now Coombs?"

"There's more." She handed me more clippings. They came from Manchester as well, from 1878 onward.

"Angel Meadow," I said, reading the first. "That sounds familiar."

"It is a brutal, lawless area of Manchester. Why my friend continues to report on it I don't understand. I fear for him every day." The words caught in her throat. "Continue reading, please."

The articles drew a portrait of a gang enforcer. One who carved a seven-pointed scar in each of his victims. The descriptions from witnesses could have described an older Silas Lee, and some even identified him, but at the few inquests to which he was called, he always had an alibi.

The last of this string of stories told of an inquest held to determine the cause of death of five men. The sixth, who barely survived long enough to give his testimony, stated that they had been sent by a rival gang to kill this Lee. Though they wounded him repeatedly, Lee kept fighting until he was victorious.

The image of Coombs after the fight in the alley came to my mind. "Sorry. But this is all circumstantial at best."

"Then you won't mind more circumstances."

Another bundle of articles. These were shorter, each one telling of unsolved murders and assaults. Witnesses described a tall, dark man as the assailant. And in each case, the victim's face had been slashed seven times.

Was this the sort of man for whom I worked? A common thug and murderer?

"What do you intend to do with this?" I asked.

"Confront him with it. Get his response. Then publish it."

Every word she spoke struck fear in my heart. The idea of confronting Coombs, of publicly accusing him of this violent past, was terrifying. I could see no response from him other than an explosion of rage.

"There is nothing conclusive here," I said, desperate to put a stop to this.

"Not yet, no. But you see that, when I do possess proof, I must publish it? With or without his response. Do you understand?"

"Yes, I understand."

She leaned forward. "And you knew nothing of this?"

"I swear to you, this is the first I have heard of this Lee person, and I do not believe it is Coombs."

Adelia leaned back but said nothing.

"Give me time. Let *me* talk to him. Hear me out," I said over her objection. "What you have is the story of a youth gone wrong – terribly wrong – and perhaps the story of a man trying to make amends by bringing justice to killers. And this could be the thing I have missed about him all along, the thing that makes him so skilled at identifying killers: he knows how they think. All you really know of Coombs is that he has solved murder cases. Let me find out if these stories truly represent his past. If so, it could be a story of redemption."

Adelia took each of the articles and carefully placed them back in the envelope. "I will give you one day."

"Thank you. That is all I ask," I said and took my leave.

⊷━◉ ◉━⊶

I returned to the residence, but Coombs was not there. I went to my library and got a fire going. I needed to think.

Detective Coombs had burst onto the scene in January of the current year with a spectacular solution to a vexing murder case. This, according to him, had come about mere weeks after he had nearly been killed in combat in Burma. He had further claimed to have some sort of informant giving him tips on where to look for perpetrators. This had led him to accuse, in no less spectacular fashion, a frail little girl and a pompous banker of brutal murders. Yet, his accusation of the priest, Malvagna, had proved to be false, which led to a breakdown and a violent, drunken binge.

What of Malvagna? He had insisted that he sensed something dark, evil, about Coombs. His failure had been in a church, after all. If I gave any credence to my own observations, and to the feelings of shadows flowing, slithering, then it seemed there was something otherworldly, supernatural, at work here. But I was not ready to leap into the world of fairy tales merely because I had not yet found a more plausible explanation.

For my part, I believed I had observed vastly different evidence than what Coombs described. As he pointed out, I had been alone when I made said observations. Setting aside that I had no reason to hallucinate such things, it did seem a simpler solution than that Coombs had altered reality. And I was, after all, prone to having conversations with my dead brother.

Now comes Silas Lee, a young man, a criminal, with a striking resemblance to Coombs. Was he a part of this puzzle? Coombs had said he vaguely remembered running with gangs in his youth. Adelia's stories about Lee stopped around the time Coombs claims to have been fighting in Burma.

Superficially, these pieces seemed to fit. But I needed incontrovertible proof before I could confront Coombs or, should the need arise, to bring it to Batleigh. But I also needed it for my own sanity. I could not even feign enough confidence to bring this forward without something I could hold in my hand that neither I nor Coombs had created.

The answers were in Angel Meadow, the neighborhood in Manchester, where Silas Lee had operated. A neighborhood that made even Campbell Street seem like a holiday resort by comparison. If there truly was a connection between Silas Lee and Coombs, the key to that transformation lay hidden there somewhere. And establishing that connection – or denying it – could shine the full light of day on Detective Coombs. I could seek it out or I could remain here, as Judy to Coombs' Punch.

Coombs returned while I packed a bag.

What would I tell him? He had been adamant about my not leaving him, both after the battle with Keat and his men, as well as in his weakened state after Newington. I could not tell him that I intended to investigate his alleged past, that Adelia had discovered information that could potentially ruin him. But I felt I should say something. There had been a kinship, briefly, though I had seen too often how easily his demeanor could change.

I went to the kitchen with my bag. Coombs sat reading the papers, scribbling notes on them and circling stories with a thick charcoal pencil. He seemed frantic. Before I could find words, he looked up. Shock and disappointment were quickly covered by anger.

"Leavin'?"

"No, no. I have some personal business which requires my attention. Out of town. It has to do with that bank problem," I said, regretting the deception but grateful for the explanation it provided.

Coombs waved the pencil dismissively. "So go. And don't expect no pay while you're gone." He turned his attention back to the papers.

I left without further words.

CHAPTER TWENTY-TWO

ANGEL MEADOW

THE *MANCHESTER DAILY OBSERVER* WAS HOUSED in a formidable, four-story building of plain brick with simple, solid architecture. It seemed as if it had no need for superficialities, dominating the corner of the block as it did. In the bustling lobby I gave my name and was taken directly to the newspaper's archives.

I decided my best approach was to work backwards. I started from the day before Coombs broke the Downing Street Bloodletting case. I scanned the pages for murders and other suspicious deaths. I ruled out acts of passion and drink. If there had been some event that had caused this Lee fellow to become Coombs, it had to be more than a violent squabble after too much liquor. This search took me the remainder of the day.

In the afternoon of the second day, I found a single paragraph that had been devoted to the murder of several prostitutes in Angel Meadow. It occurred in December of 1883. This was the same time frame in which Coombs claimed to be fighting in Burma, just over a month before he came on the scene and rescued me from death. There had been an attack on the safe house that women used to hide from the local crime boss, particularly those who became pregnant. When the attack occurred – presumably a form of punishment for the women's rebellion – one of the mothers had recently given birth. The baby had suffered the same fate as its mother and her would-be defenders. A witness claimed to have seen a tall, dark-haired man fleeing the scene. Could that have been Lee?

The story said the police described the blood and destruction as resembling a war zone. Could that be what Coombs had experienced?

The next morning, I decided against all sense and caution to see the place for myself. If Lee and Coombs were the same man, something had happened in that safe house.

My only proficiency with any sort of weapons or fighting was fencing, which wasn't likely to do me service in this situation. I took a page from Coombs' book and dressed in several layers, hoping to provide padding against blunt objects and a modicum of protection from blades. There was nothing to be done against pistols.

It cost double the standard fee to convince a driver to take me even within blocks of my destination.

At first glance, the streets of Angel Meadow seemed not unlike London working class neighborhoods. It was the people who brought the darkness. They were sullen, angry, almost feral. I met no one's eyes as I walked, but kept my head up, so as not to appear the easy target I truly was.

Thankfully, the building where the murders had occurred was abandoned. Clouds moved to blot out the sun. A narrow, broken street wound down between boarded warehouses to what had at one time been a manor of sorts. Likely it had been the home of whoever had once owned the now empty warehouses.

Cement stairs, cracked and worn, led up to a weathered blue door, slightly ajar. With no knobs or handles remaining, I shouldered it open, setting off a wave of skittering, clawed feet. My shadow split the shaft of grey light that stretched down a long hallway, exposing broken furniture. Slashed cushions spilled their stuffing on the floor. A broken chair lay on its back, ribs protruding from its shredded covering. Wounded walls, once adorned with intricate wallpaper, were now a patchwork of holes exposing the skeletal construction behind. Wallpaper hung like torn, jagged flesh.

I stepped inside and closed the door. Turning to the darkened hall, I wished I had brought a lamp. The sun struggled to reach the interior of the building, fighting its way through the cracks and gaps of the boarded windows, only to lose its battle against the interior gloom. With a match I searched and found a broken beeswax candle on the floor. I put on a glove to hold the bare candle and lit it.

At the end of the hall was a foyer. Curved stairways on either side led up to the second floor. Much of the railing was gone, the pieces scattered about the stairs. More pieces and a large bloodstain on the floor below suggested that someone had gone through it.

Up the right-hand stairs, I came to the mezzanine and hall that ran the length of the manor's second floor. This was where the battle had been waged. There were blood stains on the floor, cracks and cuts in the walls. Several teeth lay scattered about.

On either side of the corridor, each door along the way had one or more names hand-painted on them: Alice, Edna, Sarah, Kate, Irene. Inside each room were signs of their former lives: clothing, books, and dolls.

The largest room sat at the end of the corridor. The double doors were long gone, leaving only the cracked frame.

This room was an abattoir. Blood pooled, streaked, and splattered. Shredded bits of clothing lay strewn about. I spotted hacked-off fingers, now shriveled.

Then I saw the crib in the corner. The blood around it was so thick, it still smelled of copper. In the crib lay a small, hand-made doll, its cloth skin caked in blood and viscera.

Tears burst out of me, unbidden, uncontrollable. I staggered away from the crib and stumbled, falling to my knees. The candle went out as I dropped it. I wept for a time, I know not how long.

Eventually, I recovered the candle and relit it. On the floor near me was a pair of oblong bloodstains and near them, the partial shape of a hand. Around these stains was a perfect circle, a ring of darkened carpet, not brown from blood; it was blackened by fire and smelled of sulfur. Brimstone. Had the killer fallen as I had? Was it during the fight, or after he had done his work, when he stopped long enough to see the carnage? The circle of fire – was it he, or his victims, who had called it forth? The ring was too perfectly round to have been formed in any natural way.

I reached out to the hand-shaped bloodstain. The palm was there, as well as the thumb and parts of the fingers. It was bigger than my hand and therefore did not belong to any of the women. This had to have been Lee. Was this the beginning of Coombs? A man on his knees, having completed a horrific act of brutality, reaching out for succor, or perhaps the power to survive? And what did he receive in answer?

As I struggled to my feet, I saw another hand-painted sign on the floor next to the crib. Though it was cracked along the wood's grain and there was a streak of blood drops, the blue cursive script was still legible. It read 'Silas Jr.' I slipped it into my pocket.

◆⟶▭◉ ◖▭⟵◆

Having safely returned to the hotel, I could now put together the pieces of the puzzle. The magistrate's assessment of young Lee's home life matched Coombs' memories. They had both run with gangs. When Coombs claimed to have nearly met with death in Burma, Lee had fought his own battle and paid dearly for it.

I could piece it all together, but was it anything more than the wishful thinking of a desperate man with a less than firm grip on reality?

Once again, Malvagna's words nagged at me, bolstered by Coombs' failure in the church in Newington. Was I stepping into a world populated by demons and angels? If souls existed, did it follow that so too did a man take upon himself all of our mistakes and was sacrificed for it?

I considered informing the Manchester Police about my suspicion that I knew the exact location of the killer of those prostitutes. Perhaps a wire to

Superintendent Batleigh warning him of Coombs' dual nature. But I had no actual proof. What would I tell them of my conclusions? That something supernatural – more accurately, something unexplainable – had occurred, and now the man known as Coombs was able to shape reality with his words? I would be sent to an asylum.

More than that, I considered Coombs himself. Was he in control of this power? Was he aware of it? If so, why would he condemn innocent people? A little girl? It seemed to me his penchant for lurid stories, combined with the horrors of that day and whatever event had occurred at its climax had set him on this path. A path not entirely of his own choosing. I knew something about that. I packed quickly and took the first available train back to London.

⊶⊷⊷◉ ◉⊶⊷⊷

When I returned to Coombs' residence, I found that he was gone. There was a wire on the kitchen table from a Constable Sheasby of Meavy Prior. There had been a murder. The constable requested that Coombs meet him at Tavistock Station as soon as he was able.

At Burkett's, I asked if a package had arrived for me.

"Yes and no," said the innkeeper.

"I am in no mood for japes, Mr. Burkett."

"A package didn't arrive, but this did."

He dropped onto the counter before me the envelope in which I had placed my second notebook. I could see some of my handwriting. But the envelope had been torn to shreds. One end was completely removed and what remained of it was empty.

"Delivery boy apologized and ran off," Burkett explained. "Didn't recognize him, but it's just as well. I didn't like the way he looked at my daughter."

A chill froze me in place. I struggled for words as I relayed a description of Garret.

Burkett shrugged. "Coulda been. He wore a hat and a heavy coat."

I held the counter as my mind whirled. How could Garret have known about my second notebook? Had he been observing me as I worked? Was he watching me still?

I ran through the door into the alley, searching in both directions. No sign of him or anyone hurrying away. I stood holding my head for a moment. The questions that raged felt as if they would tear my skull open. If it was Garret, how could he have known? Why would he do that? If not Garret, was Coombs somehow responsible? Did he send Garret?

A patron helped me when I all but collapsed against the wall. I thanked the man and waved him off.

There was nothing to be done for this now. The more important matter was Coombs and his possible connection to Silas Lee.

I marched back into the lobby and wired this Constable Sheasby, informing him that I would take an overnight train, arriving at Tavistock Station in the morning. Then I wired Adelia, told her the same thing and added, "You were right."

"Silas, Jr." In his rampage through the safe house, Coombs had killed his own son and the baby's mother. Likely he had not even been aware of the child's existence until the deed was done. It had broken him. Perhaps it could bring him back. Just as Coombs had rescued me, it was time for me to rescue him, or at least to help him see the truth of his situation and let him choose his path.

CHAPTER TWENTY-THREE

AN UNEXPECTED AUTOPSY

THE FRIGID BREEZE THAT GREETED ME at Tavistock Station batted away my drowsiness. I had barely slept on the train. How would I approach Coombs about what I now believed to be his past as Silas Lee? What state of mind was he in? Other men leisurely took the crossing bridge to the opposite side of the tracks. I weaved between them, all but running. I had to resolve this matter. The Silas Jr. sign felt like a lodestone magnet in my pocket, both heavy and pulling me with an irresistible force.

At the base of the bridge stairs a short bobby waited beside a police wagon. His uniform fit him as if he were a child in adult clothing. After announcing myself, he informed me that he was to take me straight to the morgue.

Lochford Cottage Hospital was a two-story brick affair with peaked roofs and many windows. The mortuary was separate, with one corner abutting the rear corner of the main building. It was square and consisted of one room and one floor. The bobby opened the door and pointed out a bloody sheet covering one of the largest corpses I had ever encountered. He handed me a report and informed me that Constable Sheasby would be along shortly.

Small, high windows provided little light, but gas lamps more than compensated. The report identified the deceased as John Heggs. Pulling back the sheet, I found in the center of the victim's hairy chest seven crisscrossing lines had been carved into the skin. A seven-pointed scar.

Was Silas Lee here in the moors? If Lee had indeed become Coombs, could there still be traces of his former self active in his mind? An inner war between the man he was and the man he was trying to be. In Coombs' mind, Lee could be a separate entity, much like my fantasies about my brother.

The star had been carved deeply into the victim's fleshy, hairy chest. It was so deep I could glimpse the breastbone. It was ragged, as if done with unsteady hands holding a dull knife. It might have been done in anger. But there was very little blood in the hair surrounding the wound.

Thankfully all the tools I needed were at hand, and soon I had the ribs cracked open and began examining the organs. The liver was clearly that of a heavy drinker, while the heart displayed signs of a substantial aneurism. This is what had caused the extinction of life. The seven gashes had happened after death.

A quick wash of my hands and I exited, nearly bumping into the constable. Sheasby had wan skin and thick, charcoal-coloured hair, with eyebrows one could mistake for mustaches. He was a man of a size with Coombs, though older and a bit softer, particularly around the middle. He wore a saber on his left hip and a cudgel protruded from his belt. I had heard that some constables in the country still carried sabers and found it a bit disconcerting to see one so close.

After a brief introduction, I asked after Coombs.

"He's not here," said the constable. "What can you tell me about the victim?"

"The chest would did not cause extinction of life."

Sheasby mulled the phrase over. "'Extinction of life.' You mean someone killed him, then did *that* to him?"

"He died of an aneurism in his heart."

"This makes no sense, Doctor. A man dies, then someone comes along and cuts him up?"

"That appears to be the case. I wish I was able to explain why someone would do such a thing."

Sheasby shook his head. "So, there's no murder. Maybe you can clear up another mystery: How did you two men know to come here?"

"Pardon? There was a wire. From *you*."

"I didn't send a wire, and Detective Coombs never gave me the chance to tell him as much."

"Then who could possibly have sent it?" Yet another mystery. I began to feel as if I were walking through a field of brambles.

"One of my men, probably. Coombs has been in the papers a bit. Wouldn't be surprised if somebody was hoping to meet him." He shook his head ruefully.

"In that case, Coombs is under the impression there has been a murder, and you requested his help in solving it. We must speak to him immediately."

"Come on, then. I left one of my men with Coombs. To keep an eye on him, show him around, that sort of thing. Told him to wait at the vicarage."

"Vicarage?"

"Oh, yes. Where the murder – well, where *that* happened. I'll fill you in on the way." He summoned the short bobby and told him to bring the police wagon.

While we waited, Constable Sheasby explained that the body had been found in a basement. A nun had reported the body, and he said something about a widowed vicar and his daughter.

I tried to listen, but I could hardly focus on his words. Too many questions roiled my mind. The seven slashes in the victim's chest were too specific to be a coincidence. If somehow this was Silas Lee, then he and Coombs could not be one and the same, since Coombs had been in London at the time. And who had sent the wire that summoned us? If Lee and Coombs were not the same man, was Lee trying to lure Coombs here? But what about Angel Meadow? Then there was the matter of my lost notebook. Did that indicate that Garret was working for Coombs? Was Garret here now?

Nothing made sense.

"*Go back to London,*" said my brother's voice. "*Do more research and wait for Coombs.*"

"No," I muttered and shook my head. "I need to speak to Coombs now."

"That's why we're going." Sheasby's voice cut into my thoughts. The police wagon had pulled up without my notice. "Well?" he asked as he climbed in.

"Yes, of course," I said as I followed suit, doing my best to conceal my inner turmoil.

CHAPTER TWENTY-FOUR

DESCENT

IF A BUILDING CAN BE SAID to be in its death throes, that would describe the vicarage in Meavy Prior. Isolated, decrepit, it stood – barely – in a bowl formed by three hills. Dusk gave the clouds the appearance of a smoldering fire and blanketed the vicarage in deep shadows. Moss and vines covered the building's dark stones like fungus on a growth. I pitied the chickens that pecked about the cold, hard ground. The sorrowful bleat of sheep from behind the building suggested to me that they were more bone than meat.

A large shed stood to our right, a bit removed from the vicarage. An older man with a limp in his right leg led a donkey towards it. He wore a rough and tattered sweater over his coat and a plaid scarf wrapped his neck. Upon hearing the police wagon approach, he whirled to face us.

"Oy, Sheasby," the man called. "What's the idea sendin' that bastard my way?" His face, pinched and weathered, seemed incapable of any expression other than a scowl. His nearly colourless hair looked to have been cut by his own hand, without a mirror. Despite the cold, he wore no hat.

The constable stepped out of the wagon and called out. "Want to rephrase that, Mr. Rudduck?"

The mule driver's expression said that he did not wish to do so and instead stood his ground as he reached out to pet his donkey. "He was mean to Jenny, he was." He straightened the thick, grey blanket draped over the animal. "That big lummox you sent."

I followed the constable to stand before the mule driver.

"You mean Detective Coombs?" Sheasby asked, hands on his hips.

Rudduck straightened and mimicked Sheasby's stance. "Didn't catch his name."

"And you say he was mean to Jenny?"

That seemed to catch Rudduck off guard, and he relaxed ever so slightly. "She took a dislike to him right off and let him know about it. He'd a kicked her, I hadn't stepped up."

"Really," said Sheasby, genuinely surprised. "I'll have a word with him. But you still need to mind your language," said Sheasby, waggling a finger at him.

The way he frowned at the finger, I feared Rudduck might bite it. "Right. Sir." He oozed sarcasm.

Sheasby turned to me. "What kind of man mistreats another man's donkey?"

"I cannot say, as I was not present." I held up a hand to quiet them both. "I will inquire. Can you tell me, Mr. Rudduck, what prompted this unfortunate interaction?"

Rudduck blinked.

"What happened?" Sheasby asked him.

Rudduck leaned towards the constable. "Why'nt he just ask?"

"Answer the man."

Another frown. "Hammerin' me 'bout me not likin' ol' Gibface."

"Heggs," said Sheasby to my puzzled look. He turned back to Rudduck. "'Not like'? You *hated* him."

"'Course I hated him. You know what he was."

Sheasby stepped up to him, a finger in his face. "You be careful there, Rudduck. You make that accusation one more time without proof, and *you're* the one going to jail. Understood?"

"Understood," Rudduck growled. "But I didn't off him, like I told that Coombs bast – fella. Ain't *my* place to separate the wheat from the chaff."

"Good you know that," Sheasby said with a nod.

"And how," I asked, "was the animal involved, Mr. Rudduck?"

"Jenny." Rudduck stared at me with an expectant scowl.

Sheasby raised his brows at me.

"Jenny, yes. You said Coombs almost kicked her. How was … Jenny involved in this exchange?"

"She don't like it when people are mean to me, and her ears was up soon as he arrived. She let herself be known and Coombs got all riled up. Cocked his foot, he did, and I stepped between 'em. Thought I was gonna get a chance to teach 'im somethin', but he backed away. Knew better, I guess."

Coombs backing away from a fight was considerably more surprising than his near mistreatment of a farm animal.

"I've seen the man," said Sheasby. "Consider yourself lucky. Now tell the good doctor what you told me."

"I told that Detective Coombs, too. Now I gotta tell *this* guy?"

"Yes," said Sheasby.

"If you would be so kind," I added.

Rudduck suppressed a snicker aimed at me. "I was in town with the vicar and Mary. Went in to pick up some supplies. Sister Ellen didn't come with us. Maybe it was her!" He burst into laughter.

I turned to Sheasby. "Sister Ellen?"

The constable scowled. "I told you. The nun who's been with Vicar Wood-more for years. She's old and weak." He held his next words back, then shook his head. "I can't see her doing … that. Mr. Rudduck, if you can control your-self we'd like to move along."

"So move along, then." Rudduck turned away.

"*Rudduck.* Tell the doctor what happened when you returned."

He breathed impatience. "Tendin' to Jenny, I hear the vicar scream, run inside just behind Mary and we found him." His voice trailed off as his gaze turned inward. "In the basement."

"Is Coombs here now?" Sheasby asked him.

"No, and it's good he ain't, or we'd be havin' words, I can tell ya. Him and that scrawny bobby went off somewhere."

"Scrawny bobby?" said Sheasby. "You mean Murrish?"

"If that's his name, then that's who I mean."

Sheasby rubbed the spot between his eyes. "Thank you, Mr. Rudduck," he said quietly. "You can go about your business." He turned to me. "Let's find this detective of yours."

The constable went to the bobby who had driven the wagon. "Take the wagon back. Have the undertaker handle Hegg's body. Keep an eye on things, yeah? I'll find my way back soon." The bobby snapped the reins and drove the wagon away.

"It occurs to me, Dr. Johnson, that even if Mr. Heggs was dead before the cutting, the one who did it might not have known, yeah? Just saw he was out, took the chance to do what they did."

"That is possible."

"What'dya think of our friend, Mr. Rudduck?"

I watched Rudduck as he fed his donkey. He easily hefted a large burlap sack of grain for a time while slowly pouring it into a bucket. "Certainly capable, physically. But the act was committed yesterday. Whoever did it would have been significantly bloodied. Mr. Rudduck was not. I would venture to say that Mr. Rudduck does not change his clothes often."

Sheasby laughed. "Or at all, but I take your point. He would have had to change into something else, then back to *that.*"

"Precisely. Which would imply a certain level of planning, and he does not seem the planning type."

"No, he's not. Well, let's see what Detective Coombs has to say."

I drew a deep breath and set a hand on the pocket containing the Silas Jr. sign. I still had no plan for how to confront Coombs with what I had learned.

"*Just tell him.*" My brother's voice caught me by surprise. For the first time, it seemed he was giving me ill advice.

Sheasby held open the wide oak door of the vicarage. Warmth from the hearth in the center of the great hall washed over me. The smoke travelled up through a louvre in the peak of the ceiling. On the far side of the fireplace, there was a large dining table with mismatched chairs, and a set of stairs that led to the second floor with a balcony on my left.

"Hallo?" called Sheasby as he poked his head through various doors. He continued calling out as he went to the kitchen, then a study.

To my right, another door creaked open and there stood a nun. She wore a black cloth that covered most of her face. A wooden cross hung around her neck. Only her left eye and part of her mouth were visible. She was small, and judging by the hang of her robes, quite thin. Her breathing was laboured, and her habit was smudged with dark soil. That one eye squinted at me.

Stepping out of the study, Constable Sheasby spotted her. "Ah, Sister Ellen. I was beginning to think no one was home."

"I am," she said.

"Yes, I see that." He moved closer, examining her. "Have you been cleaning the basement?"

Sister Ellen gestured as if presenting the dirt as evidence. "Yes."

"Damn it," said Sheasby. "Sorry, Sister. It's just that I told the vicar to leave the crime scene alone until we were done."

She dabbed her mouth with her sleeve. "That detective. Coombs. Said he was done."

"Did he now? It wasn't up to him. What's the rush, anyway?"

"Heggs' blood. The smell. We didn't want it here anymore." She dabbed at her mouth again.

"Understandable, I suppose," said Sheasby. "Anyone else here?"

"No. At the chapel. They couldn't bear..." She gestured towards the basement.

"Right, then," said Sheasby. "Go on about your business."

"Pardon," I said, stepping forward. "If I may, I should like to ask you some questions. Sister Ellen, was it?"

Again, she gestured, presenting her dirty clothes. "Perhaps later? Sir."

I would have preferred to talk to her in that moment but acquiesced. "Certainly." I turned to the constable. "Shall we head to the chapel?"

I followed Sheasby back out of the great hall. The frigid air was a slap to the face after the warmth inside. We followed a dirt path that led around the vicarage towards the open field behind.

"And what do we think of this Sister Ellen?" I asked Sheasby as we walked. "She is cleaning the crime scene, after all."

Sheasby threw me a glance and blew warmth into his fists as he thought. "I agree that's a tad suspicious, but given the circumstances, understandable. Can't say I'd relish having the blood of a close friend in my basement. But given her frailty, I can't imagine her having the strength to carve up old Heggs that way."

"What about her face?" I asked. "Why is it covered?"

"I don't know, never seen it. I hear she's been that way since she was little. An accident or something."

"I see. But if she is, as you say, frail, why was she tasked with the clean up?"

"I'd imagine neither Vicar Woodmore nor his daughter Mary could bring themselves to do it, but it needed doing. See, Mrs. Woodmore died when Mary was young. Heggs moved in soon after and was pretty much a second father to her."

"Ah."

Sheasby stopped me with a hand on my arm. "I know what you're thinking. Lots of folks around here thought that about Woodmore and Heggs. But I'm here to tell you that nothing like that was going on between them and I'll not have anyone, and I mean *anyone*, casting aspersions on the good vicar's name. Not Rudduck, not you. They were the best of friends when the missus died, and it made sense for Heggs to move in and help out since he didn't have no family of his own. If there was any truth to the rumours, I'd've been the first to lock 'em up. Understood?"

"Yes, understood." The more Sheasby spoke, the more I suspected that he only saw what he wanted to see.

With a solemn nod, Sheasby continued on to the chapel. It occurred to me that the constable was someone who needed to believe certain things, and his view of the world had to fit his preconceptions. In his eyes, Vicar Woodmore was a good man, and good men do not indulge in certain behaviours. While not a favourable mindset for investigating a crime, it appeared to work for him to navigate the complexities of life. I found myself to be a tad envious of one who could ignore things that muddied his world view.

What would Sheasby think about Coombs' dual nature, if indeed it was true? And what of supernatural beings and fluid shadows? He seemed unable to accept that a "good vicar" could find comfort in another man.

"*Don't involve Sheasby*," said my brother's voice. "*He'll never believe you. Best to tell Coombs alone.*"

A burst of clucking from the nearby chicken coop brought forth a chuckle. The thought of confronting Coombs alone made me feel as if I should join them.

"*Don't be afraid. Coombs likes you. He trusts you.*"

I wanted to believe that.

CHAPTER TWENTY-FIVE

THE CHAPEL

THE CHAPEL WAS A SMALLER BUILDING than the vicarage, and better kept. A small bell tower topped with a cross sat at a slight angle over a wooden roof. On each side of the double doors were a pair of tall, frosted glass windows.

Constable Sheasby called for the vicar as he pulled open the doors. Wooden pews on either side of a central aisle faced an altar with a simple wooden cross behind it.

"There you are," said Sheasby.

With great effort, the vicar used the pew before him to pull himself up. Vicar Woodmore was in his sixties at the very least. His white, wispy hair sat high on his forehead. When he turned to greet us, his eyes were red, his cheeks still damp from tears. His skin was loose and ruddy.

"Vicar Woodmore, this is Dr. Johnson, assistant to Detective Coombs."

Woodmore bowed to me but did not offer his hand.

"Is the Coombs fellow about?" asked Sheasby.

"I'm afraid not, Constable. He and your man Murrish were here, Coombs questioned me, then they left."

"*Murrish*," Sheasby grumbled. "They were supposed to wait at the vicarage."

"Ah, that explains their argument. Officer Murrish insisted emphatically that they should return to the vicarage, where you had told them to wait. Detective Coombs, however, would have none of it and insisted on searching the woods."

"Search the woods?" Sheasby asked.

The vicar shrugged. "For clues, apparently. Murrish tried in vain to dissuade him, then opted to at least stay with him."

From a door on the right emerged a young woman whose blood-stained apron suggested recent meat preparation. Her chestnut hair contrasted with her alabaster skin. She carried a stack of hymnals.

"Ah, Mary," said Woodmore. The necessities of etiquette seemed to give the vicar strength. "Mary, this is Dr. Johnson. He's here to assist that Detective Coombs fellow."

The young woman's expression darkened. "Oh, that –"

Woodmore cleared his throat and she stopped.

"Was there an issue with Detective Coombs?" I asked.

"He was succinct, shall we say, and Mary took it as a personal affront."

Mary seethed in silence.

"Ah," I said. "I can assure you all that Coombs is that way with everyone."

"Dr. Johnson has some interesting news," Sheasby said. "Alarming, even. Why don't *you* tell him, Doctor?"

It struck me then that all of them knew each other, the victim, the constable, the ladies, the vicar, and the mule driver. In a small village like this they would have had daily contact. The victim was to them a close acquaintance, a friend. I saw this on Sheasby's face as he avoided eye contact with me and the vicar. He did not wish to be the one to give them the gruesome news.

"Of course, Constable," I said quietly. "Perhaps you should all sit."

After exchanging concerned glances, they sat in pews.

"It appears that the victim –" I started.

"Mr. Heggs," said Woodmore with gentle insistence. "Pardon my interruption."

"Of course. Mr. Heggs. It seems Mr. Heggs died of an aneurysm to his heart, not of the wounds observed."

It took a moment for them to comprehend this.

"Yes," I continued. "It appears someone did that to Mr. Heggs *after* he died."

Woodmore shook his head. "But *who*?" His question was not so much to me as to the world. "What kind of – who could *do* such a thing?"

Sheasby patted his shoulder. "That's why we're here, Vicar."

"Would it be all right if I asked each of you some questions?" I said. "And I am aware that you have answered Detective Coombs' questions. However, he did not know that Mr. Heggs had died *before* the mutilation."

Woodmore barely held his composure. "Yes, fine. Ask your questions."

"I would prefer to speak to you individually. The room in the back perhaps?"

"Under the circumstances," said Woodmore, "that is acceptable."

"I'll go first," said Mary. "Get it over with." She stood and stiffly marched to the door from which she had entered. I followed her into a small storage room with a brick heating stove embedded in the wall. Mary lit a lamp on a table.

"You may sit if you like," I said, gesturing to an old trunk next to the stove.

"No thank you. Ask your questions."

"Thank you. You were in town when the incident occurred, I believe?"

Anger flashed at the word "incident", but she reined it in. "Yes."

When it was clear she did not intend to add to this, I said, "Can you tell me more about that?"

Mary threw me a puzzled frown. "It was a trip to town. For supplies." She looked me over. "Something you're not familiar with, I assume?"

I suspected her effrontery was a challenge, perhaps a ploy to end the conversation, so I let it pass. "Why would you assume that?"

She took a moment to adjust her expectations. "You don't look or sound like someone who fetches his own supplies."

"You would be surprised," I said with a smile.

"I apologize," Mary said with a quizzical expression, which faded quickly. "It's been a difficult couple of days."

"I understand. Was there anything unusual about the trip? Before you left, or when you returned perhaps?"

She scowled. "When we returned, we found Heggs dead. *That* was unusual."

"Yes, of course. I meant before you discovered Mr. Heggs. When you first arrived. Did you see anyone, hear anything, like a door slam, for instance? Or when you left, was anyone leaving the vicarage?"

Mary let out a breath. "The only unusual thing was that Sister Ellen didn't join us. She loves those trips and dotes over Father the whole time."

"I see." I made a note.

"What does *that* mean? 'I see.' You'd best not be suggesting that she had anything to do with this."

"I am suggesting nothing. I am only gathering information."

"She didn't go because she wasn't feeling well."

"Was that a common occurrence?"

"No, she's hardly ever sick. And she seemed fine in the morning, but I saw her while we were getting ready to leave and she looked flushed. She might have been sweating. I think breakfast didn't agree with her. She was still in bed when we returned. If you want more information, you'd best ask *her*. Will there be anything else?"

"No, I believe we are done."

Mary exited, taking the lamp and dousing it. I followed her back into the chapel proper. She went to her father, told him to go back to the vicarage soon, and left.

"Please don't think her rude," said Vicar Woodmore.

"It has been a difficult time for you all, I understand. Now, Vicar, it was you who found the body?"

This shook Woodmore noticeably. He took a deep, calming breath. "I hadn't seen Heggs all day. Quite unusual. I searched the grounds, the chapel, everywhere. Finally, I looked in the basement." He reached for a pew to steady himself.

"Tell me what you saw, please."

The Vicar took a moment. "It … it was the smell first. The stench was overpowering. I assumed an animal had crawled into the basement and died and Heggs was tending to it. I went down the steps slowly, calling his name. Then I saw …" He broke off for a moment, closed his eyes and swallowed. "I nearly fainted. I tumbled down the last few steps and called for help." He turned away and buried his face in his hands.

After allowing him a moment, I said, "Can you tell me who else might have access to the vicarage, beyond your daughter, the sister, and that Rudduck fellow?"

He shook his head, still in his hands.

It seemed that Woodmore did not have the strength to answer more questions. He suggested we continue looking for Coombs, and it was clear to me that he needed to be alone in his grief, further convincing me that his relationship with Heggs was more complicated than that of two friends.

"Nothing to do but wait for Coombs, it would seem," I said to Sheasby.

Sheasby nodded, frowning. "So it would seem. Maybe we'll find him in the woods," he said and led the way out of the chapel.

The sun shot blood-coloured shafts of light through the bare trees at the top of the western rise, casting deep shadows over the rest of the bowl in which the vicarage sat.

"Damn his hide," Sheasby grumbled. "*Coombs!*" he shouted through cupped hands. "*Coombs! Are you there?*" The mist of his breath billowed from him.

I could not muster the breath to shout, as any deep enough stilled my lungs. I scanned the darkening hills for silhouettes or movement of any kind. Then we received what seemed to be an answering call.

"Was that him?" asked Sheasby.

"It could have been. Or perhaps it was Murrish."

After more calls and distant responses, Woodmore emerged from the chapel, bundled such that he appeared to be a tower of clothing on two feet.

"Still looking for them?" the vicar asked, his voice muffled by the scarf wrapped around his face.

"Yes, Vicar, we're still looking for them." By his tone it seemed he would have had a different answer for someone who was not a member of the clergy.

"Might as well come inside. Get warm. Dinner will be ready soon."

"What if they're lost?" Sheasby asked.

I was feeling considerably less magnanimous than Sheasby. "Should the shepherd not seek out the lost sheep?" I hoped that would prompt the two to continue the search and perhaps even bring Coombs in.

Woodmore's eyes squinted over his scarf. "Jerusalem is not nearly so cold." He shuffled to the door and held it open.

CHAPTER TWENTY-SIX

WAITING FOR COOMBS

W ITH A QUICK NOD BETWEEN US, Sheasby and I hurried across the yard and into the kitchen, then through it and into the great, warm hall. I moved a wooden chair close to the metal grating that surrounded the central fire and dropped in a log. Sheasby nodded appreciation, pacing.

"I almost wish it *was* a murder," he said. "That'd make more sense."

I welcomed the opportunity to consider something other than my eventual confrontation with Coombs.

"Let us consider a simpler aspect of this situation," I began. "The mutilation of a corpse is an action that inherently has no logic behind it. Therefore, for us to attempt to apply logic to it is doomed, it would seem, to failure."

Sheasby smiled and shook his head. "You do use a lot of words, but I take your point."

"Thank you, I suppose. Since the mutilation of Heggs is impenetrable, then perhaps we should focus on the wire. It was sent to Coombs in your name to bring him here. Why? Who could have set it? There is no telegraph machine here, I assume."

"Ha. No. Nearest one is at the inn around the bend. But there are plenty in Tavistock."

"Where Rudduck and Sister Ellen went to report the crime."

That stopped the constable's pacing. "Right. One of them could have sent it."

"Precisely. Which means one of them would likely have noticed the absence of the other. Unless they were working together."

Sheasby scoffed at that. "Rudduck's even less of a team player than a planner. Of the two, I could only see Sister Ellen sending the wire, but I still find her involvement hard to buy. I'll go talk to Rudduck. You do your interview with Sister Ellen. And who knows, maybe Coombs will arrive at some point."

When I went to the basement door, I heard movement below. I pulled on the door, but it scraped at the bottom and required some effort to open fully. Cool, musty air washed over me. I called for Sister Ellen as I took the creaking wooden stairs. The floor was a dark, rich soil. Webs and mold outlined the old, mortarless stones. On the opposite wall stood a coal furnace, with a bucket and stock next to it. The wall between was largely open, showing the pantry and more stairs, presumably to the kitchen. Elsewhere were shelves and crates filled with tools.

Sister Ellen smoothed the dirt floor with a rake. "Almost done," she said.

"It has taken some time," I said.

She glanced in my direction. "It was difficult."

"I have no doubt. He was a friend, yes?"

"I meant the blood. It was everywhere."

"Ah. Then Heggs was not a friend?"

"He was. To Mary. To the vicar."

"But not to you?"

She shrugged, then stopped her work and leaned on the rake. "We weren't friends." Her single visible eye bore into me.

"Why were you not friends?"

"Must I be friends with everyone?"

"No," I said, laughing lightly. "Certainly not. Can you tell me about the morning of the crime?"

"I wasn't feeling well." She paused frequently to dab at her lips. The stiffness of the scars around her mouth seemed to prevent her from closing it fully without a concentrated effort. "Didn't go into town. I went to bed." Now she began wiping tears. "The vicar's scream woke me. Went downstairs and found them, found Heggs." She shook her head. "They were crushed. I went with Rudduck to report the death. The murder." She wiped her tears again.

"Then you went with Rudduck to report the crime? You felt up to a trip to town then?"

"Didn't matter. Had to be done. Vicar and Mary were crushed."

"Could Rudduck have gone alone and reported it?"

She shook her head. "He would have reported it to Jenny."

Laughter caught me by surprise again. "And the both of you went to the police directly, then came straight back?"

"I went in. He stayed with Jenny. Of course."

"Of course. There is something of which you are unaware about the crime. It was not murder."

What would her reaction be? It took a moment for her to show surprise, but I could only gauge by her one eye.

"Oh?" she said, then turned to me. "How?"

"He died of an aneurysm to his heart. The mutilation came after."

Again, I watched her eye. It blinked.

"No," she said, shaking her head. "Must be wrong. Who would do that?"

I wanted to accuse her then, but of what? What could possibly have prompted this woman to slash a dead man's body? Were she and Rudduck working together after all? None of it made any sense. All I had was circumstantial evidence and my firm belief. But I recalled where that had gotten me of late.

Sister Ellen started for the stairs. "May I go now?"

"Of course." I stepped aside and let her pass. There came a strong odour not unlike that of Malvagna's church, but hers was less cloying.

"Forget about her," said my brother.

The silhouette of Sister Ellen pushed the door closed, leaving me in near total darkness. There was an odd comfort to it, as if I could simply remain in it while the world above resolved itself.

"You have to talk to Coombs."

"But I cannot *find* him," I told the darkness. "And Sister Ellen is the most intriguing person here. Why would I forget about her?" Though I spoke of Sister Ellen, it was Mary who I saw in my mind.

It appeared I had no more advice for myself. But it was clear to me that, if I could believe anything I had seen and heard of late, Sister Ellen was at the center of the mystery before me. As I found my way to the stairs in the darkness, I pondered how I would get any more information from her or, at the very least, have a chance to examine her face.

CHAPTER TWENTY-SEVEN

MARY AND NIGEL

ONCE AGAIN WAITING IN THE GREAT room, I found myself becoming increasingly agitated. I was both frustrated by Coombs' continued absence and grateful for it, as I still dreaded confronting him. Whether the sign in my pocket represented his past or not, he was not likely to take my questions well.

I wondered whether I should tell Sheasby. The constable sat on the divan with his arms crossed, quietly fuming. I could use an ally, but would he believe a word of it, or lock me up in the basement?

"Don't tell Sheasby," said my brother.

Considering the constable's stubbornness regarding the vicar, he would undoubtedly think me mad.

"Get Coombs alone and tell him. It's the only way."

The idea made me shake. When Sheasby turned my way I muttered something about being cold.

The scenario I feared most was being alone with Coombs when presenting him with what I had learned, what I had seen in Angel Meadow, and especially showing him the Silas Jr. sign. Whether or not he was connected to it, I would be accusing him of murdering a baby. That would almost certainly set him off. And if it were true? If Coombs had lived as Silas Lee until the day he murdered several women and then his own infant son? It appeared to have been wiped from his mind. I dared not fathom the level of violence that could result from those memories being restored.

From the kitchen I heard singing, presumably from Mary. Her voice was enchanting. She sang in time to her work, which by the sound of it, was slaughtering the lamb I had heard bleating earlier. Each line of the song was punctuated by her blade striking the cutting board.

"Oh, a bandit's life is the life for me." *Thump.*

"With a heart that's strong and sorrow free." *Thump.*

"I rule all spirits brave and bold." *Thump.*

"Who dwell in a mountain cabin cold." *Thump.*

She hummed a bit, then the chorus began again. She held a key better than most.

I started for the kitchen.

"Don't bother her while she's cutting," Sheasby said. I realized he had been watching me.

"I was considering speaking to her further about the incident," I said. Judging by the force with which her blade struck the board, Sheasby's advice seemed sound. "Though perhaps this is not the best time."

After several more rounds of the chorus interspersed with hummed verses, Mary changed to whistling and the chopping stopped.

"Help yourself, if you insist," said Sheasby. "But keep your hands in your pockets."

"Is she that careless with a knife?"

"No, she's quite good, in fact. She can cut a pig thin as paper."

I turned back from the kitchen door. "You say she is good with a knife, and she appears to be unafraid of blood." I lowered my voice. "Should we consider her a candidate?"

Sheasby stood. "Mary?" He turned the idea over in his head then dismissed it. "She loved Heggs." He took a breath as he considered his words. "But you're right, she might be able to shed some light on the day's happenings. And it might go better if you do the asking. She was a troublesome child, and we've had a row or two. But keep it professional. I've seen more than one young man come away bruised when they were looking to take her hand."

"I see. I have no such plans, but I do appreciate the warning."

"Sure." Sheasby stood. "Go have your talk, if you think this is the best time. I'm going to look for Coombs and *Murrish*." Frowning, he exited the hall.

I paused at the kitchen door to straighten my jacket. It sounded as if Mary was speaking to someone, thus it seemed safe to enter. I pushed through the swinging door.

It seemed every conceivable spot held dishes, pots, and utensils. A wide table sat in the center of the room, on which lay a neatly divided lamb. Its head rested atop an overturned pot.

Spying me, she snatched the lamb's head from the pot. "Don't know how that got there," she said with nervous laughter.

"Perhaps it bounced," I said with a grin. "You were cutting with such force."

Her eyes widened as she glanced at me, then she smiled as she looked my way a second time. She remained focused on the lamb's head as she tried to hide a smile. "That must have been it."

"If I may ask, were you talking to it?"

Her eyes shot up to meet mine. Pale blue, they were, and as intense as a clear summer sky. "No. Of course not."

"Forgive me, I meant no offense. Talking out loud while working is quite common."

She took a defiant stance and said, "I was talking *about* him."

"Oh?"

"Yes. If you find that off-putting, you're welcome to remove yourself from my presence."

I took a moment to set aside my trained reactions to how certain people are supposed to address certain other people. We were in the moors, after all, not a London tea party. And this young woman had experienced a horrible trauma only to have strangers force her to continue talking about it.

"Not to worry. I tend to whistle while I work."

Her surprise at my response loosened her stance a bit. "What kind of work do you do?"

"As I mentioned when we met earlier, I am a doctor and Detective Coombs' assistant."

"Right." There was venom in her voice.

"I assure you we are entirely different in manners and personality. If you want to return … the lamb to its resting place, you are perfectly welcome. It seemed a place of honour."

"Nigel."

"Pardon?"

She held the head out, facing me. "This is Nigel. He was difficult, but enjoyed my singing. Calmed him, I think. Made it easier to catch him for grooming and such." She placed the head back on the pot and gave it a little pat. "I believe he'll be quite delicious."

Should I tell her that I, too, speak with the dead? I thought not. "I have no doubt he will be, Miss Woodmore."

"Please call me Mary. We're not so formal here."

"Very well, Mary. And please call me, William. Or any variation."

She considered me. "You seem like a William." She returned to the table where she had been working. "You'll catch who did that to him? Even if it wasn't murder? You and that …" She waved a knife in the air. "*Detective?*"

"That is my intention, yes."

"Good." She took one of the lamb's legs in hand and off went the shin with one clean cut. "I loved Mr. Heggs. Right from when we moved here, Heggs was good to my father. Mother was always sickly, especially after the move. I was a little Hellion. Seems I didn't take too well to the change, at first. But Heggs was always sweet to me." Next leg, another single cut. "After mother died, he spent more time with Father. He often spent the night." Third leg cut. "My father needed him."

I wondered whether Mary understood the ramifications of what she was describing, but her last statement made it clear she knew exactly what the two men were to each other and embraced it. If all involved were happy and no harm came to others, who was I to pass judgment?

"He taught me things, Mr. Heggs did. Things Father couldn't. Knots. How to fix things. I quite liked him." The fourth leg was cut with the hardest strike of all. She stopped, both hands on the table, and took a deep breath. She used a sleeve to wipe sweat, or tears, or both.

I moved towards her. She held a hand up and I stopped. I was within arm's reach now, but I remembered what Sheasby had said. She cleared her throat. "Catch whoever did this, will you?"

"I will do my best."

The stare she turned to me was as intense as the sun itself.

"I *will*," I promised her.

That seemed to satisfy her. "If there's nothing else then, I really do have quite a bit of work."

"Would you like some help?"

"Have you ever worked in a kitchen?" Mary asked with a skeptical squint.

"Not a kitchen, per se, but I have cut my fair share of meat. May I demonstrate?" I said before she could ask what *kind* of meat.

She stepped back from the butcher's block and gestured.

I selected a knife from a rack. "What were you saying about Nigel? When I came in?"

"What? Oh." She suppressed a smile.

"You said he was adventurous." I worked the knife through one of the legs.

"His wool mostly. It keeps the Queen warm on Christmas."

"Does it now? Quite an honor, that. Now, what do you think?" I swept my hand over the chops I had cut. Rather thin, as I recalled what Sheasby had said about her cutting abilities.

Mary examined the chops, held one up to the light. "We prefer them thick," she said with a wry smile, then broke into laughter. I joined her.

The creak of the back door and a blast of icy wind ended our mirth. Sister Ellen stood in the doorway, arms loaded with wood.

"*Mary.* A man? In the *kitchen*?"

"Pardon me," I said as I made my exit. "So sorry, Sister. Just conducting my investigation. Have a good day, Nigel." I left happily, hearing the merest hint of laughter from Mary.

The great hall was empty, save for the crackling fire. I had never been in a home where the fireplace occupied the center of the room. The smoke languidly twirled its way up to the louvre in the center of the ceiling above.

It seemed an excellent arrangement as the warmth spread equally about the hall.

In my mind I composed a wire to Adelia about the moors and the mystery before us. Still, my thoughts returned to Mary, and I found myself wanting to solve the mystery of Heggs' mutilation for her. I imagined conveying the news and comforting her.

Would it be thoughtless of me to write glowingly to one woman of my feelings for another? About that particular racing of the heart Adelia and I had discussed, the feeling that remains after leaving a person's presence. I was undeniably experiencing that with Mary, and I wanted to tell someone. It was unusual for me to have such feelings so soon after meeting someone. I sat by the fire with my notebook detailing my conversation with Mary, resisting the sudden urge to describe her lips.

"*She is very pretty.*"

"Yes, she is," I whispered.

"*What if Coombs accuses her?*"

The thought pulled a gasp from me. "That would be horrible."

"*What would you do?*"

This inner dialogue had taken an odd turn, though it did raise an important question. I was there to help Coombs, to pull him back from the abyss into which he had fallen, but what if he was beyond help? Or worse, simply refused it?

"*What would you do?*"

I stared into the fire. "I will do whatever I need to do," I whispered.

"You talking to the fire?"

Sheasby's voice startled me. I had been so absorbed I had not heard him enter.

"Thinking aloud."

He nodded and hung his coat on the rack by the door. "If the fire talks back, let me know, yeah?" He stood and smacked his lips. "I need water," he muttered, heading for the kitchen.

Chuckling at the idea that I had been hearing the voice of the fire, I used a poker to move the logs in the fireplace and received a satisfying surge of flames and warmth in return and watched the remains of a bit of newspaper at the bottom. A London paper I saw just before the name was burned away. The logs settled again, revealing more of the paper. It had been crumpled and stuffed into the fireplace, under the wood. An engraving caught my eye. Once again I questioned if I was seeing reality or a figment of my imagination. I tried to separate the paper from the flames, but the last of it was consumed before I could. Despite my doubts regarding my own faculties, I was sure it had been an engraving of Coombs.

My musings were cut short when I heard Coombs' angry voice just outside the front door. On the spur of the moment, I went to Sheasby as he returned from the kitchen.

"Constable, let us not yet inform Coombs that Heggs was not murdered."

His face scrunched in puzzlement. "Why not?"

What would he think if I told him that I wanted to see if it would affect reality? "Think of it as a test," was all I dared say.

A sly grin came to him. "Sure, I'll play along."

Would whatever had been happening still occur if Coombs was unaware that there had not been a murder? If I could withhold the information until after his pronouncement, would that have any effect? It was a dangerous game to play, but it could provide more information.

CHAPTER TWENTY-EIGHT

COOMBS RETURNS

A YOUNG MAN'S VOICE ARGUED WITH Coombs' unmistakable bellowing as they approached the door.

"Because, Detective Coombs," the scrawny bobby snarled as he opened the door, "those were my *orders*." He threw the door open such that it slammed into the wall and went directly to the fire to warm himself.

"You could at least let me have a *piss*!" Coombs shouted as he batted the door back into the wall. He then spotted me and froze. "Thought *you* were on holiday."

"Where have you two been?" Sheasby demanded.

"*I've* been investigatin'," said Coombs, his anger stoked again.

"And *you*, Murrish?" Sheasby demanded of the bobby.

Sheasby's tone caught Murrish off guard. "I been followin' him. Like you ordered me to."

"Glued to me, more like," grumbled Coombs.

Sheasby ignored Coombs and kept on Murrish. "And part of those orders was to wait *here*."

Murrish stepped up to the constable. "*You* try and rein him in!"

Sheasby glowered for a moment, then turned to Coombs. "All right. Tell me. What was so bloody interesting in the woods that you had to spend so much time out there?"

"Did *you* check the woods?" Coombs demanded. "No. Did *he* while we were out there? No. Just kept followin' *me*. Yeah, yeah, orders. I heard."

"Constable," said Murrish, calmer now. "I kept telling him that the best way to search the woods was for us to get a team and work out a system. But all he wanted to do was wander around and kick bushes. If I turned away for a *second*, he'd go off in another direction."

Before Coombs could start another angry response I stepped between them all, hands out. "Can we calm down now please?" I gave them a moment to breathe. "Searching the woods is a perfectly reasonable idea, and Officer Murrish's suggestion of a methodical approach is equally reasonable."

"Thank you for that interjection of calmness, Doctor," Sheasby said.

Coombs snorted. "With all them words of his, he could put a rabid dog to sleep."

Sheasby buried a laugh with a cough.

"And thank *you*, Detective Coombs," I said with a measure of bitterness, "for that interjection of humour."

Coombs gave an exaggerated bow.

"Back to business," said Sheasby. "What were you looking for out there, Detective?"

"Evidence to back up my case. I got it solved. And I didn't need *you*," Coombs added, jabbing me in the chest with a finger.

I took a step back, as much from the force as from a sudden wave of anger. This was the man I wanted to help?

"Solved?" said Sheasby.

"Go ahead, Detective. Enlighten us."

Wariness registered on Coombs' face, but hubris got the better of him. "Not 'til we've gathered everybody." He scanned the great hall. "In here. Yeah, this'll do."

He was clearly building up to one of his grand proclamations, and I was eager to see how he would solve a murder that wasn't a murder. Would it become one because he willed it so?

"Why in Heaven's name do we have to gather everyone in this room?" Sheasby demanded. "Just tell me who did it."

"Where's the fun in that?"

"Fun? You think this is *fun*?"

"It will be if you get everybody in here."

Sheasby was stunned to silence.

A surge of distaste for Coombs' callousness rose within me. "Constable," I interjected. "Let us do as he asks, shall we?"

"Fine. Who, exactly, is 'everyone'?"

"Everybody I talked to." Coombs strolled about, as if looking for just the right spot. "Woodmore, the daughter, the fella what drives the donkey, and the sister."

"Murrish," Sheasby said to the bobby. "Go fetch Woodmore from the chapel. I'll get Rudduck and the ladies."

When they had left, I began to reconsider my previous decision to let Coombs make his accusation without full knowledge of the situation. His previous pronouncements had ruined many lives – why let him do so again, particularly when there was no murder to be solved? How could I let him accuse anyone here, including Mary, knowing what I knew?

Part of me was desperate to see what would happen. I briefly wondered why I was unable to conjure my brother's voice to help me settle the matter. Then Coombs interrupted my thoughts.

"Wheels are turnin', yeah? I know what you're gonna say. And I appreciate all you done, and what you said. I didn't go with the first thing what come to mind. Did my own investigatin', got it figured out." Coombs produced from his pocket not a weapon, but to my great surprise, a notebook. "Take a look," he said, handing it to me. "But don't burn it," he added with a laugh.

I could make no sense of his scrawls, though he was inordinately proud of them.

"Talked to everybody, found out what happened. See, the vicar and his daughter went into town. The mule driver took 'em. Only one home was the old nun. She was beat from her chores, went down for a nap. So, the place is quiet, just the fat dead guy home. The vicar and the rest come home, go looking for him, find him all sliced up in the cellar. The screaming and crying wakes up the old sister, who comes running and nearly dies herself from shock. But then she and the mule driver come back to town to tell the coppers."

"I see. Well done, Coombs." I felt as if I were at a zoo, feeding a lion. "Do you have a conclusion?"

He grinned proudly. "Yeah. Stay and watch the show." Coombs paced, reading his notes.

"What about the wire?" I asked him, trying to push the strange thoughts from my mind.

"The wire? What wire?"

"The one that summoned you."

"What about it?"

"Have you determined who sent it?"

"What d'ya mean? Sheasby sent it. Says so right on it."

"And yet he claims he did not send it."

Coombs shook his head dismissively. "Don't matter. He's probably just embarrassed to admit he needed help."

Sheasby emerged from the kitchen, pulling Mary along by the arm. "Seems he wants to put on a show," he told her. "But if we do this, he says he'll tell us." He turned back to the kitchen. "Sister? I know you got a lot of work to do, but the sooner we do this, the sooner we can have done, yeah?" He held the door open until she stepped through. "There's a good girl. Be right back." Sheasby hustled out the front door.

Sister Ellen went rigid upon seeing Coombs. With his back to her, he took no notice. She dropped her head and stayed as far from him as she could.

Murrish the young bobby strolled in looking bored with a shivering Woodmore right behind. Mary rushed to the vicar and led him to the central hearth. Next, Sheasby all but dragged Rudduck in. Coombs began to pace the room. Whenever he neared Sister Ellen, she cowered. He paid her no attention, though he did seem to be searching. He looked past each of us as if we were the audience and he still sought his scene partner. Then he stopped. A smile grew on his face as if he had just made a discovery.

"Are you ready?" Sheasby demanded.

"Yeah," Coombs said with a malicious grin. "But *you* ain't."

CHAPTER TWENTY-NINE
MADNESS

Coombs pushed past Sheasby and continued talking. "First, you gotta hear my reasons. Else you ain't gonna believe me."

"Fine," Sheasby snapped. "But get on with it."

"You all think you knew that Mr. Heggs, yeah?"

Nods all around.

"Well, I say ya didn't. Not as well as ya think. Bet ya didn't know about his secret activities, did ya? It's true, isn't it, Vicar Woodmore?" Coombs demanded.

The old man huffed disdain. "I beg your pardon, sir."

"That's right, Woodmore. I know your secret."

"My … secret …" His face went red.

"Your secret, yeah, Woodmore. You and Heggs. Together." Coombs stood before the vicar. "You ran a witches' coven, didn't ya? You and your brother, Heggs."

"My *brother*?" Woodmore was on his feet, furious. "Witches – how *dare* you, sir?"

"I can prove it," said Coombs. "In the vicar's study. There's a book. Of, er, French poetry. It's on the third shelf and the bookcase on the right will open when you pull it."

In his previous accusations, Coombs had shown all the confidence of a man who had never experienced a question. Now he seemed to be making his words up as he went.

"Behind the bookcase there's a room," Coombs continued. "With big fat candles. And a collection of Satanic books, robes and other things. Like a pentagram. Yeah. Drawn in blood on a piece of wood."

The fluidity of shadows returned, slithering about. Glacial fingers gripped me. I paid closer attention to the phenomenon this time. With each sentence came a shift and a surge of cold.

Sister Ellen hugged herself tighter and tighter. Everyone in the room shivered, but Sister Ellen's head was bowed as if hiding from some unspoken horror.

The sensation was stronger than ever before. It was as if the shadows moved the ground itself, as if the vicarage were a boat on a surging sea. How could this, all of this – my experience, his words – how could all of this *not* be madness?

"And," Coombs continued, "you're gonna find birth certificates for both Woodmore and Heggs, provin' they were born on the same day to the same mother. Written in blood on dried human skin, you'll find a contract with Satan himself what binds the babies to him. It's signed by their mother."

The objections turned largely to horror. Woodmore confronted Coombs angrily while Sheasby pulled Coombs back and bellowed for quiet. The brief silence was that which follows a thunderclap.

"Mr. Coombs, I demand that you leave this place immediately," said Woodmore.

"Not 'til we've had a look in there. Unless you're afraid." He moved towards the study but Sheasby blocked his way.

"Do not go in there," I said, jumping unsteadily to my feet. "Not Coombs. Not Woodmore. Constable Sheasby and I will go in." I needed to know, to see, to touch, what Coombs had described.

"Murrish," Sheasby told the bobby. "Don't let anybody leave."

As I followed Sheasby into the study, I left the cold behind. Inside I found a room of dark wood, lined with shelves stuffed with books. There were Bibles in different translations, as well as writings on religion, missals, hymnals, all the things one would expect a vicar to have in his library. On the right-hand wall I found more secular books, including an encyclopedia, fiction and, in a more sparsely populated section, poetry.

"I think I found it," I said warily as I indicated to Sheasby a rather thick volume titled simply, and much to my surprise, *French Poetry*.

I tried to pull the book off the shelf, but it would only tilt. Then came a loud creaking sound as the bookshelf angled slowly away, opening like a heavy door into a small room. In it were three books, two dark red robes and a piece of wood with a pentagram on it.

"Well, I'll be a lusty monkey," exclaimed Sheasby.

On one of the shelves was a piece of shriveled skin with writing the color of dried blood. Sheasby picked it up, disgust overtook him, and he threw it down.

I had no desire to touch the thing and knelt down to get a closer look. I could make out both Woodmore's and Heggs' names on it, but little else was legible.

Sheasby stared at it for a long moment. Emotions played on his face: shock, incredulity and finally sadness. The sadness of a man whose solid world now showed a deep chasm. I followed him out to the main room.

"It's there," said Sheasby. "Everything he described."

Mary charged past us into the study. "No! *No*," she called from inside. She came back to stand in the study doorway. "That room did not exist before today!"

"But there it is," Sheasby said quietly.

His mouth agape, Woodmore staggered to the secret room. He made the sign of the cross and whispered prayers.

"You been livin' two lives, vicar," said Coombs with a softness I had never heard before. "I'm guessin' the devil let you think you were one thing, but you were really somethin' very different."

"All right," said Sheasby. "This … discovery, it doesn't make any sense to me. But it also doesn't prove he killed Heggs. Well, Coombs? Where's the proof he killed Heggs?"

Sheasby, suspicious, was putting Coombs to the test.

"Check the family Bible," said Coombs, pointing to the large, leather volume that rested on a stand near the study door. "In its pages, there's another contract. It's written in Woodmore's own hand, confessin' to the crime of murderin' Heggs."

"Ah *hah*," snapped Sheasby. "Your man here says Heggs *wasn't* murdered. He died of a heart attack and was carved up *after.*"

Coombs gave a lopsided smile. "He did, did he? Well, Dr. Johnson sees what he wants to see. That's why I didn't bring him along in the first place. Not sure I can trust him anymore."

Sheasby, caught by surprise, turned to stare at me.

"Besides," Coombs continued before I could defend myself, "You don't think the heart of a man that big could give out on him when he sees his own brother comin' to kill him?"

"Heggs was *not* my brother!" Woodmore cried.

"Then what was he to you?" Coombs demanded. "Huh? Look at you, sobbin' like an old widow."

"That's enough, Coombs," said Sheasby.

"Is it?"

Coombs went for the Bible, but Mary rushed to it and they grasped it at the same time. Mary tried to pull it away from Coombs.

"Keep your filthy hands *off*!" she shouted as she pulled.

The Bible flew from their hands and fell open.

A square piece of skin, like that in the study, fell out and slid along the floor.

Mary picked up the Bible and hugged it to herself. "This was my mother's," she cried. "Why did you put that *thing* in there?"

Sheasby shouted for quiet again. He went to the piece of skin and knelt to examine it, then turned to Coombs. "Damn you to Hell." He straightened up. "Vicar Woodmore, you're under arrest."

The room erupted into a cacophony of angry voices. I wanted to add mine to the chorus, to shout at this reckless and capricious man, but words failed to form. Finally, Sheasby's call for quiet broke through the din and silenced them all. Murrish placed his cuffs on the old man.

"Mr. Rudduck, can you prepare your gig to take Murrish and the prisoner to Tavistock?"

"I ain't takin' Jenny out again. She's been off all day. Like she smelled somethin' bad." He directed that at Coombs. "Finally got her settled in for the night."

"You expect us to walk all the way to Tavistock?"

"Don't care. But we ain't takin' Jenny!"

They stared each other down for a moment. I expect it was more the dread of handling the animal himself than of Rudduck's glare that caused Sheasby to back off.

"Let's get you bundled up for the walk, Vicar."

"You can't be serious!" Mary shouted.

"It's all right, Mary," said Woodmore. "I've made the walk before."

"But not in this cold!" She stepped up to Sheasby. "Arresting him in front of his family is not enough? Now you want to drag him off to a gaol cell in the dead of winter?"

"The chapel," Coombs said. "Put him in the chapel."

"Finally, something useful from you," Sheasby said. "The chapel it is. Murrish, take him. Keep an eye on him."

Both Mary and the vicar objected loudly, but Sheasby shouted them down. "It's the chapel or a walk to town! Now, Mary, why don't you gather some blankets and such and send them along, yeah?"

Murrish led the cuffed vicar to the door.

"You did this!" Woodmore shouted at Coombs from the door. "You put those things there!"

"Don't make this any harder, Vicar," said Sheasby.

"I'm going with him," Mary said, returning with a pile of coarse blankets.

"No," said Sheasby firmly. "I think it's best you stay here." He took the blankets from her and gave them to Murrish.

Rudduck opened the door, aiming a glare of disgust at Woodmore, his suspicions about the vicar and handyman confirmed. Bone-chilling air rushed in. Murrish pulled the vicar out and Rudduck shut the door behind them.

A moment passed. Suddenly, Mary threw down the blankets and charged at Coombs. A mere glimpse at the look in her eyes and I knew she would kill him given the chance.

The constable grabbed her around the waist, lifting her off her feet. She flailed and thrashed. Sheasby, despite his greater size and strength, could barely hold her.

"Sister! Take young Mary to the kitchen and start dinner," Sheasby ordered. "Stop struggling," he said to Mary. "I don't want to hurt you."

Mary's elbow smashed into his nose. He set her down and staggered back. Sister Ellen pulled Mary away. Coombs laughed.

Mary let Sister Ellen lead her up the stairs and to the first room on the right. Her eyes never left Coombs. The hatred was so intense, I expected him to burst into flames.

"That was fun!" Coombs blurted.

Sheasby glared at him with only slightly less hatred than Mary.

"Being a genius is exhausting!" Coombs said. "I shall retire to my room now." He strode up the stairs and down the hall.

"I'm going to question the vicar," Sheasby said, seething.

"Before you go, Constable," I said, "may I ask you something? Did you feel anything unusual while Coombs was speaking?"

"What d'ya mean, Doctor?"

"I am not sure, to be honest. For myself, it felt as if the world shifted around me. As if I were on some silent, invisible train."

Confusion played on Sheasby's face, then an acceptance of my words, followed quickly by a rejection of them. It seemed the good Constable could not add this new piece of information to his already broken world. But that moment was enough for me: he had felt the change, too. Had anyone else?

"Didn't notice anything. Too busy trying to keep order." He waved the idea away. "I'm going to question Vicar Woodmore." As if carrying an enormous weight, he could neither lift nor put down, Constable Sheasby dragged himself out the door.

CHAPTER THIRTY

AFTERMATH

THE GREAT HALL WAS EMPTY. It felt as if a storm had raged through, scattering the wreckage of what had been a peaceful home. The muffled, though agitated, voices of Mary and Sister Ellen came from the kitchen. I considered going in to talk to them. There were secrets in this place and they, more than any of the others, held the keys to unlock them.

I also wanted to check on Mary. It was clear by her actions that she was not in need of my protection, and yet I felt compelled to offer it. I was unaccustomed to thoughts of heroism, but this woman – who was at once beautiful and prone to chatting with the head of a sheep she had slaughtered – had sparked a fascination in me. I felt an attraction I had never felt before. I had never even known such a strong attraction was possible.

But this was neither the place nor time to ask a woman if I could begin to court her. If I was ever going to speak to Coombs, it would have to be now. I touched the sign in my pocket.

"Is that a good idea?"

My brother's voice gave me a start. Why was I doubting myself now? I had arrived here with a clear, if dreaded purpose.

"You know what he thinks of you."

"That I have a tenuous grip on reality," I said as I checked that the great hall was still empty. "That I am not to be trusted."

"He won't believe anything you tell him."

I took out the sign. "This, at least, is proof, is it not?" I held it over the fire to better see the crude lettering, the bloodstains.

"You should burn it."

My hand shook. "But why?"

"It proves nothing. He'll say you made it."

"Why would I?"

"To support your crazy theory, he'll say."

"But it was there, under the crib."

"Was it? Did anyone else see it? That's what he'll ask."

"That does sound like him." My hand grew hot from the fire, but I held it still.

"Best to burn it. Forget everything."

My hand trembled as I considered my brother's words – my own words. I was giving myself the simplest solution. Drop the sign. Forget Angel Meadow and Silas Lee. Let Coombs condemn who he would condemn, including me. But rather than Coombs, I would be condemning myself, my sanity, to a life of empty subservience.

I pulled my hand back, hairs singed and skin tender. "I am not ready to leap into that fire."

I let the sign cool and put it back in my pocket.

"You're going to regret this."

I paced the empty room. If my brother's voice was how I worked out problems by forming a dialogue of sorts with myself, then why had the nature of the debate changed? I had come here with a purpose and my inner dialogue urged me to it, but then my subconscious had undergone a change of heart.

"I'm sorry to say this, Michael, but I do not believe I need you any longer."

A door upstairs opened, and I whirled to see Coombs in the upper walkway.

"There somebody here?" he asked. "Who you talkin' to?"

"No," I said. "No one here. Just thinking out loud."

Coombs descended the stairs casually but cast his gaze all about. "Yeah? What were you thinkin' out loud about?" I felt a tension underlying his tone.

"This case," I said, poking at the fire as he approached. "How you have once again uncovered a sinister conspiracy that only you could see."

"But you saw it, yeah? Stood in the room?" Coombs continued past me as he spoke, going to the study door and peering in.

"Yes, I did."

Coombs went to the kitchen door. "They makin' dinner?"

"Yes, I believe so."

"Good. Better not bug 'em." He moved to the basement door. "Be nice if that young one'd serve me." A rueful smile came to him. "She'd probably rather spit on me, though." He opened the door and looked down the stairs.

"I could bring your dinner to you, if you prefer." I pictured a quiet, peaceful meal in which I could tell Coombs what I had learned in Angel Meadow. Then I pictured him with a fork and a knife and dismissed the idea.

Coombs' demeanor changed to one more casual, conversational, though it rang false as he continued around the hall. He seemed confused, even frustrated.

"I know how crazy it is. Guy like that, runnin' a coven. Don't seem real, does it?"

"No, it does not."

"Like somethin' out of a penny blood." Tension had returned to his voice.

"Yes," I stammered, "I suppose it does seem that way."

"And yet, there it is," he said with a broad gesture to the study. "You sure there weren't nobody else here just now?"

"I assure you, there was no one."

He nodded. "Lots of weird stuff here, yeah?"

"Indeed." My heart racing, I decided to take a chance. "More things that only you could see."

"Well, that's my job, yeah? What I'm here for?" he said as he came to the bottom of the stairs, having completed his circuit.

"Are you looking for something?" I asked.

He came back and stood across the fire from me. The flickering light played on his face from below, leaving his eyes to shine out of dark pits. "There's danger about," he said quietly.

"But," I started, then stopped to work moisture back into my mouth. "But you have exposed the danger."

"Could be more," he said. "Anybody could be a killer. I never know what I'm gonna see next." With that, he made his way back up the stairs and to his room.

I remained locked in place until the sound of the front door opening startled a gasp from me.

Constable Sheasby strolled to the fire. "You been standing there the whole time?" he asked, a quizzical look on his face.

"I have been thinking." Should I tell the constable what I knew? Rather, what I believed I knew?

"He'll put you out there with the vicar."

"You all right, Doctor?" Sheasby asked as he sat on the divan.

"No, Constable, I am decidedly not." I felt alone, isolated. I stood upon a rock surrounded by raging waters. I could not step off in any direction, whether to obey Coombs or to defy him. Nor could I open up to Sheasby, whether about Angel Meadow or my conviction regarding Sister Ellen. If I did, I would be swept away as foolish or mad, or perhaps even killed, if Coombs was of such a mind. "I need to look at that room again, to see if it is still as real as it was moments ago. Would you care to join me?"

He reeled back. "If it's real? Why wouldn't it be?"

"Why *should* such a thing exist?" I shook my head. "I need to see it again."

In the study, I examined the false book that served as a lever. It appeared to be a simple, leather-bound volume, but I could not remove it, only tilt it back and forth. The bookshelf slid, silently, into the secret room and back out to seamlessly join the shelves on either side.

Taking a lantern into the room, I examined the walls closely. They appeared to be of the same construction as the rest of the house. The room itself was just large enough for the bookshelf to swing into and to hold the items described by Coombs. Not an inch of extraneous space.

I left the secret room, closed the bookcase, then exited the study.

"Still there?" asked Sheasby as I passed through the great hall to the front door.

"It is indeed." I put on my coat and picked up a lamp.

"Going to talk to the vicar?"

After considering that for a moment, I shook my head. "No. I am going to look at walls."

The lamp lit, I stepped onto frozen ground that crunched and crackled under my feet and my coat served as poor armour against the biting, cold wind. With my hat pulled down and my collar up, I left as little skin exposed as possible, and still I felt it would crack.

Walking around the front of the vicarage, I counted windows until I came to the study, then continued along the wall. I did not know what I expected to find. A seam? A section that looked newer than the rest? The absurdity that Coombs had somehow added to the structure of the house made me chuckle and the frigid air caught my breath. There was nothing but an old, icy wall to the next window, which afforded a view of the kitchen. Mary and Sister Ellen were busy cooking. The hearth's fire called to me, drew me around the corner of the building to the back door. I knocked and cracked it open.

"Dr. Johnson here," I called into the room. "May I come in?"

"Yes," said Mary after a moment.

Quickly closing the door behind me, I stood for a moment, taking in the warmth, the smell of roasting lamb.

"The constable thought we should prepare dinner," said Mary.

"An excellent idea." I stood as close to the hearth as their activity allowed and massaged my face to bring life back to my skin.

"He took the other guest room," said Sister Ellen.

"Pardon?"

"We have two. Detective has one. Constable has the other. The divan is … not uncomfortable."

"Thank you. May I ask you a question?"

"*Another* one?" Mary snapped. "And what if I say no?"

"He wants to know," Sister Ellen said to Mary. "He wants to help."

"I do," I said to them. "I do not understand all that has happened here, but I want to."

Busying herself with cutting, Mary said, "Ask your question."

"Did you feel anything unusual while Coombs made his accusations?"

"Rage," said Mary.

Sister Ellen touched her arm to calm her. "I did." Her voice was quiet, muffled. "Evil arrived with him. When he spoke?" She dabbed at her mouth. "Snakes slithered in the dark." She held herself as if they were crawling on her in that moment. "The world crumbled. And it was cold."

"Then either I am not mad, or we both are. Thank you," I said, and made to leave.

"How can you work for that horrible man?" Mary asked.

For a moment I was not sure how to answer.

"How can you not see what a monster he is? He's wrong, you know. My father would never do any of those things! He's the gentlest man I've ever known. He never struck me once, and believe me, there were times when any other father would have pulled out the switch."

"It is perfectly understandable that you would stand up for your father, but –"

"Why do *you* stand up for *him*?" She faced me, angry and expecting an answer.

I wondered how much I should tell her. "He stood up for *me*," I said finally. "Freed me from the gallows."

A tremor passed through her. Sister Ellen stopped her work as well.

"Yes, he found me in gaol," I said, in it now. "I would have ended up hanging by the neck if not for Coombs."

"You ... ?"

I could not look at her while I told my tale. "It was all a misunderstanding, I assure you. I was betrayed by a business associate and gaoled for murders I did not commit. But Coombs came to my rescue. He vouched for me, claimed I was doing case work for him when, in fact, I had never met him before in my life. Once freed, he explained to me that he needed an assistant for his investigations and, well, how could I possibly have said no? Why would I? So, you see?" I finally looked at her again. "I owe him everything."

To my great surprise, she nodded. Then her eyes narrowed. "So, you must obey his every command? Believe his every word?"

My face felt hot. "He has not been wrong yet."

As her eyes widened in shock, I realized she had misunderstood me. I had been referring to previous cases.

She went very stiff. "We have work to do. Perhaps you should leave."

I took a step towards her. "Mary. The *room*, Mary. I stood in it. Held the contract written on human skin."

"That room was never there before," she said.

"Mary …"

"It *wasn't*," she snapped. "I've lived here most of my life. That room did not exist before today. I don't know how he did it, but Coombs is behind it all." She turned away from me.

"Thank you for the warmth," I said.

CHAPTER THIRTY-ONE

DINNER

ONCE SHEASBY, RUDDUCK, AND SISTER ELLEN had sat for dinner, Mary stood at Sheasby's side and said, "Whatever you think of him, my father has to eat."

Sheasby frowned as he considered, then nodded. "When I finish, I'll walk you out there."

"Allow me," I said, standing. "I will send Officer Murrish back for his own dinner. The two of you can commiserate about the case. He will likely appreciate a change of scenery."

Sheasby shook his head. "Too much danger muckin' about."

"And you both will be within shouting distance should anything untoward occur. Considering all that has happened, I think you can agree that the Woodmores would do well with a little time together not under the scrutiny of the police. Unless you fear that we might cook up some conspiracy."

Sheasby considered my words while he chewed.

Mary gave me an appraising look. "Don't worry, Constable," she said. "I'll keep him safe."

Sheasby nearly choked on his food with laughter. He took a drink of water to settle himself. "All right. I wouldn't mind having a word or two with Murrish away from the vicar." By his tone, it seemed there might be some scolding coming Murrish's way. "Go ahead, but be careful, yeah?"

I followed Mary into the kitchen. "I hope you didn't mind the joke," she said with a grin. "I knew that would soften Constable Sheasby."

I smiled back. "No, quite all right."

"We may as well eat with Father," she said as she prepared three plates of lamb, turnips, cheese, bread and blood pudding. While Mary covered the plates with cloths, I retrieved our hats and coats. Once bundled, I insisted on carrying the tray.

"Don't let Coombs spoil her."

I almost wondered aloud where such a thought might have originated.

"I do appreciate this," said Mary, holding the door open as I exited. "I wouldn't have wanted the constable along. Some quiet time with my father will do us both some good."

"I thought as much." I tried to take in the smell of the food, but the cold pinched my nostrils.

"You heard what he said about her."

Shaking off the thought, I turned to Mary. "Earlier I asked if you felt anything when Detective Coombs made his accusation."

"And I was rude, I'm sorry. I suppose I did feel a bit unsettled. But the things he was saying, even before he named Father were quite disturbing. Why do you ask?"

"I, too, felt unsettled, and I have each time Coombs has made such accusations."

Mary stopped just before the chapel door and stared at me. "Each time?"

"Yes. It was more pronounced today."

"Sister Ellen has been disturbed by something too, and I know she's sensitive to supernatural things, though she doesn't like to talk about it." She lowered her voice. "Could Coombs be in league with the Devil?"

"I think we have to be very careful with such musings," I said quietly. This was not the time to debate science versus spirituality. "There is nothing substantial to support it."

Mary nodded. "Right. Mum's the word. Father is upset enough as it is."

"Agreed."

"The food's getting cold and so am I," Mary said as she opened the door to reveal a startled Murrish and the dozing vicar.

"Officer Murrish," I said, "Constable Sheasby has decreed that you can go to the vicarage for your dinner." When Murrish hesitated, I added, "And Miss Woodmore has promised to protect me."

Murrish laughed, thanked me and all but ran to the vicarage.

Vicar Woodmore, Mary, and I ate at a small table in the storeroom next to the furnace. Father and daughter chatted quietly about how each was doing, and both insisted they were fine. When we were done, I said, "I believe you mentioned there was to be a service for Mr. Heggs. Perhaps now would be a good time?"

They looked at each other, then at me, and the masks of social propriety slipped briefly.

"That is an excellent idea, young man," said Woodmore. "Thank you for that suggestion."

I opted to remain apart with the explanation that I did not know Mr. Heggs. In truth, I shared none of their beliefs.

They knelt together before the altar and made the sign of the cross. After the vicar muttered some prayers, they bowed their heads in silence. It went on for some time.

I felt like an interloper, a voyeur, watching a scene that was not meant for me.

Murrish entered. "What's takin' –" He clamped his mouth shut, muttered an apology and sat in a pew.

Vicar Woodmore gave more hushed prayers, they crossed themselves again and stood.

Mary and I packed up the dishes and headed back to the vicarage, unsuccessfully shielding ourselves from the biting winds.

"You asked about my father and Heggs," Mary said. "It's true. They were very close. But if you think it had anything to do with what happened, you're mistaken. And that's another thing that should stay between us."

"Yes, I understand, and I certainly do not believe your father was in any way responsible."

"You see how innocent Mary is? Don't let Coombs spoil her."

The odd statement came with a force that caused me to gasp.

Mary looked at me.

"The cold, it is quite severe," I said.

"Yes, let's hurry."

A shaft of light reached us from the kitchen door which Sister Ellen held open, beckoning us to return to the warmth.

Why had this voice, this construct of using the invented voice of my brother in order to work out problems, why had it come back after I had dismissed it? Had I no control over my own mind? And why did it sound more forceful now?

My musings were interrupted when we came to the kitchen door. Once we were inside, Mary pulled Sister Ellen and me close, then spoke conspiratorially. "We all know Father didn't do anything Coombs said, yes? Now we have to figure out how he did all that."

"Did what, Mary?" I asked. "Build a secret room in your house without your knowledge?"

Mary reeled back from me. "I thought you agreed he was innocent."

Coombs burst in from the great hall. "When am I gettin' dinner? You," he said, pointing.

"*Mary*," she said with barcly restrained rage.

"Yeah, Mary. Are you gonna bring me dinner or should I get it myself?"

I stepped forward. "I will bring it to you shortly."

"About time," he grumbled. He pushed back through the kitchen door, letting it swing freely.

Mary seethed. "I will not let that man put my father in prison. Will you help me stop him?"

"I do not believe your father mutilated Heggs' body, and I find Coombs' accusations to be utterly fantastical, but I cannot deny the existence of that room and those objects." I spoke over her response in as gentle a way as I could. "I will talk to him when I bring him his dinner."

No words were spoken while Coombs' meal was prepared. Mary's actions were sharp and angry, every utensil or pot set down with more force than necessary. Sister Ellen was the exact opposite and was nearly silent in her movements. It was she who informed me that it was ready to be taken to Coombs. Mary kept her back to me, noisily cleaning the kitchen.

I took the tray and made my way back into the great hall.

"*You heard him,*" said my brother's voice. "*He wants Mary.*"

I stumbled and nearly dropped the tray, grateful that no one was present to see it.

"*He'll do anything to have her. You know how he is.*"

"Please stop," I whispered and paused for a deep breath at the foot of the stairs. Why was I doing this to myself? Certainly, Mary was an attractive young woman and I had seen traits in her that I found fascinating, but why would my feelings manifest in this way? I continued up the stairs.

"*You have to protect her.*"

My hands shook from the force of the statement as I reached the top of the stairs. Perhaps, when this was done, I would seek out a psychiatrist to help me understand the workings of my troubled mind. Again, I breathed and tried to focus on the sign, on how I would bring up Silas Lee and his deceased son.

"*Forget the sign! There's a knife on the tray! Attack when he opens the door!*"

"*No,*" I breathed through gritted teeth and continued down the hall. What was happening to me?

Balancing the tray on one hand, I knocked on Coombs' door. "Dinner is served," I said with as much humour as I could muster.

He opened the door and frowned at me. "I was hopin' for the vicar's daughter. She'd be a nice change of pace from *you.*" Eyeing the tray, he stepped back and gestured at the dresser. "Over there. Not gonna eat with me?" Coombs asked, noting only one plate on the tray.

The force of my brother's voice and its sudden silence were unsettling. I concentrated on my steps as I crossed the room and set the tray on the dresser.

"How is it possible," I said as I steadied myself, "that Vicar Woodmore heads a Satanic cult and is responsible for the death of Mr. Heggs? More importantly, how could you possibly have known about it in such great detail?"

"Don't matter. Everything I said was true. You go back and look at it again?"

My mind becoming settled, I stepped away from the food and faced him. "I did. It is very real. But that still fails to explain how you *knew.*"

"Like I said, I did some investigatin'."

"Yes. Investigating. And then did you just see it, as you did with previous cases?"

He sat and began to eat, but more in the manner he had when I first met him. "Ain't that how it works? You do your work, then you see the solution?"

"Do your visions come unbidden? Do they just appear suddenly in your mind?"

"What, you jealous 'cause what I see is real and what you see ain't?"

"No, I am not *jealous*. I just do not *understand* it."

"How many times I gotta say it? Everything I said was true."

"Yes. Everything you *said*. Which I have come to suspect was not true until you said it."

Coombs stopped eating and studied me for a moment. A smile spread across his face. "Imagine that. A man's words make the world what he says it is."

"Then you know –"

"I know a man is dead. His killer got found 'cause of what I said. There's power in that. Now go away and let me eat." He stood and pushed me towards the door.

Unconsciously, I touched the pocket that held the sign.

Coombs laughed. "What, you got a weapon in there? Gonna knife me or something'? Get out." He shoved me into the hall and slammed the door in my face.

"Go back in. Try again."

I staggered back into the opposite wall, wondering if I dared such a thing.

"Don't be afraid. Make him listen."

Nothing about Coombs' demeanor suggested he would listen. And nothing about my nature suggested that I could make him. I had to find another way.

The great hall was empty once again. The dining table had been cleared and the fire was dying. I dropped a log on. I took the Silas Jr. sign from my pocket. Coombs had made it clear he had no interest in discussing the past or learning the truth. Why should he when he could invent his own?

Pacing through the room, I found myself before the large, gilded family Bible that Coombs had knocked over to reveal Woodmore's confession. Mary had set it back on its pedestal. I opened it and flipped through the pages. Were the answers here? Once again I found myself wrestling with the idea that if evil existed, was all that was within these pages also real? Even things such as demons? I shook the notion out of my head. Such things were a sea of beliefs and notions with no island upon which to stand.

It appeared that my brother did not wish to debate the point. Rather, I did not need to debate myself on the subject, and thus his voice did not speak to me. I closed the book.

"You're not a believer, are you?"

The voice startled me, and I whirled about.

Mary stood by the kitchen door, wiping her hands with a rag. "Sorry if I scared you."

"No, no, quite all right," I said. "It is so quiet now, after all that."

Her narrowed eyes bore into me. "'All *that*?'"

"My apologies," I said with an awkward step forward. "I meant no disrespect –"

Sister Ellen came of out the kitchen and stopped, looked at us both, then gave Mary a questioning look.

Mary gently touched her shoulder. "It's all right. I'll be up shortly."

With a nod and another goodnight, Sister Ellen hurried up the stairs.

"I truly meant no slight against your father," I said to Mary.

She nodded, then remained standing, lost in thought. I was glad she had stayed. Her presence brought a calmness to me, a warmth I hadn't felt in some time. I had to wonder why she had chosen to remain there.

"To answer your question about believing," I said, "I would have to say no. I require evidence to explain the world around me. I find it difficult to simply believe in things."

"'Simply believe'." She shook her head sadly. "Faith isn't simple. Sometimes it's the hardest thing." She trailed off, fighting back tears. "You don't consider all that's happened here evidence?"

Unlike others with whom I have had similar debates, Mary seemed genuinely curious about my answer. "Evidence of something I cannot explain? Yes. Evidence of an ark containing two of every animal? No."

To my surprise, Mary laughed. It was a lovely sound. "I haven't believed *that* since I was a child. But don't tell Father."

"No. I would never. Shall we sit?" I gestured towards the couch. "I would do well with a lively debate."

We approached the divan from opposite ends. I sat at one end and indicated the other for her, then set my hands in my lap. "I have no untoward intentions."

Mary remained standing at the opposite end. "The idea does have a certain appeal, but it's late, and I should return to my room. Thank you, though." She gave a slight bow and hurried up the stairs.

I watched her go and we exchanged a quick glance as she turned to close her door. Was there a smile there? It was hard to tell in the shadows.

CHAPTER THIRTY-TWO

RAGE MISDIRECTED

I SAT BEFORE THE FIRE, ELBOWS on my knees, hands on my head, trying to contain the battle within. Coombs was upstairs. All I needed to do was go speak to him, tell him what I had learned, show him the Silas Jr. sign. My brother's voice insisted that I do so, repeating "*Tell him now,*" in a maddening loop, as if it were part of a song that had lodged itself in my mind.

An upstairs door opened. I jumped to my feet and turned to see Sister Ellen stepping into the hall, silently closing the door of the room she shared with Mary. She wore a grey cotton robe over a white nightgown and still wore the mask over her face, but not the wimple. I wondered if she wore it to bed each night or had put it on knowing I was downstairs. She carried a mug in one hand. Casting her gaze about the hall, she made her way down the stairs. Her hair was pale yellow and stringy.

Stopping at the bottom she said, "Did I wake you?"

"No. I have not been able to sleep."

She nodded agreement. "Need water," she said, holding up the mug as she shuffled into the kitchen.

I waited until she came out, having the distinct impression she wanted more than water. I certainly had more questions. She paused at the bottom of the stairs.

"Since we are both awake," I said, "could I ask you more questions?"

She nodded. "Ask."

"Come and sit," I said, gesturing to the other end of the divan. "Be warm and drink your water."

After a moment's thought, she did so.

"Perhaps you could tell me more about your sickness that prevented you from going into town with Mary and Vicar Woodmore."

"I'm fine now," she said, and took a sip.

"Yes, you recovered quickly, it seems."

"So no doctor needed," she said and started to rise.

"You have a particularly strong dislike of Coombs, yes? A hatred, even."

"A crime?"

"No, or I suspect a great deal of the population of London would be in gaol."

She made a sound in her throat that may have been a laugh and relaxed a bit.

"In the fireplace I noticed a certain newspaper had been haphazardly applied as kindling. Almost as an afterthought."

A shrug was her only response.

"It had a picture of Coombs," I said.

She tried to hide her surprise with another shrug.

"You were not ill yesterday morning, were you? Something about that article regarding Coombs upset you, so you chose not to go into town. And it was you who wired Coombs in Sheasby's name. But I cannot draw a connection to the mutilation of –"

"*Stop*," she said with a hand up.

"Just tell me, Sister Ellen."

Like Coombs had before, she scanned the room, but with more urgency. She took a vial out of her pocket and walked around the divan. She sprinkled a fluid from the vial that smelled something akin to cedar.

"What is that?" I asked.

"Old family recipe," Sister Ellen said as she sat. "Driving back this evil he brought."

"What evil?"

Setting a hand on my arm, she whispered, "A demon." She leaned back, peering about.

"A demon," I said scornfully, despite my mounting fear.

"Yes. It hovers around here." She waved her arm across the room. "A shadow that moves alone."

My throat went dry. "A moving shadow."

"I've *seen* it. But not when *he's* around." Her eye now went to the stairs, toward Coombs' room. There was hatred there, as if focused through a lens. "He brought it. I know he did."

"And you, Sister Ellen, brought *him*."

There came the merest of pauses before she dropped her face and began to cry.

"*Why* did you bring him?" I asked quietly. "Why did you … do that to Heggs?"

"I saw Lee in the paper. *Coombs*. Famous now. *Admired*." The venom in her voice could have felled a bull.

She untied the knot that held the scarf on her face. "It was him who did this."

She pulled the cloth away to reveal a series of hideous scars that formed a seven-pointed star with her right eye socket in its center. The ends extended to her mouth and ear. It was now obvious to me why she had so much difficulty speaking. The wound had not healed well, and had left her with thick, ragged lines of scar tissue. What I had assumed were wrinkles were instead folds extending from the scars. She was perhaps as much as twenty years younger than I had thought. Her scars looked nearly identical to the wounds I had found on Heggs' body and matched those described by the Angel Meadow stories.

"Tell me how it happened," I said.

"I have not always been a sister. Years ago, I sold myself. One of the men, he was a magistrate. Older man. Pale and proper. Until he was with me. Then he was rough. He hit me. Every time. He enjoyed it." She withdrew.

"Did you kill him?" I asked.

She gave the merest shake of her head. "He hit too hard. Told him so. He hit harder. I threw tea in his face."

"You were slashed for *that*?"

"Wasn't really tea. I had it ready. In case. Another old family recipe. He had very little face left. They sent their man to punish me." She gestured at her face.

"Their man was Silas Lee?"

"It was."

I struggled for words "When did this happen?"

"Six years ago." She replaced the cloth.

That had been when Silas Lee operated as a gang enforcer. "When you saw him in the paper –"

"I wanted to *scream*," she said as she pounded her thighs with her fists. "To *kill* him." She bowed her head. "But there he was. Out of reach. I tore up the paper, stuffed it in the fire, and went to my room."

"So the vicar and Mary would not see your rage," I said, nodding.

"Later, I heard Heggs cry out. Went looking. Found him dead. Then I knew how to bring *him* to me." She reached out to touch my hand. "Don't tell Mary."

"She will likely learn the truth eventually, but I will not be the one to tell her."

"Thank you," Sister Ellen said, and dried her eyes.

"But it seems you brought more than just Coombs."

She tilted her head back such that I thought she might let out a wail.

"How could I know?" she whispered hoarsely.

"You could not."

"I think the demon protects him."

"How would you have killed him? You must know how powerful he is."

The tiny portion of her mouth that I could see turned up in what I assumed was a smile.

"'Old family recipes'?" I asked. "Is that why you wanted him to eat alone? So you could poison him?"

"No. I *hate* him. Don't want him near." She nodded reluctantly. "Also yes, the poison." A smile came to her. "There is still breakfast."

"I must insist that you refrain from this plan. Which, it appears, was less a plan than an impulse."

She bowed her head. "Yes."

"What he did to you was horrible. In fact, he has done many horrible things. But I believe something happened to Silas Lee when he became Coombs. Something related to this presence you sense."

"Evil."

"Be that as it may, I believe he needs to be given a choice. I believe he is not fully aware of … what you call a demon. But to simply kill him is as wrong as anything he has done, and I will do what I must to prevent that. Am I clear, Sister Ellen?"

Reluctantly, she nodded, then stood and returned to her room.

Left alone, one piece of information overwhelmed my thoughts: Sister Ellen had confirmed that Coombs had once been Silas Lee. But she also claimed that there was a demon lurking about. Could I accept her story regarding Coombs, but not her claim of an evil presence? Given all that had happened of late, could I deny such a thing?

I turned to the fire as my only companion. Coombs had made his choice to ally with some supernatural force. While I was not prepared to assign it the title of demon, clearly something otherworldly, something not yet understood, but undeniable, was at work here. And Coombs had to be stopped. Could this force be turned against him?

"You have to stop him."

I leaned forward, head in my hands. The fire blazed, but I felt no warmth from it. "Stop him?" I saw the pipe in his hand, Keat and his men falling, bloody, beaten. "How? Perhaps Sheasby could help. I could talk to him, tell him everything." Coombs, in his days as Silas Lee, had fought off a gang come to kill him and slaughtered a house full of women prepared to fight him. Sheasby would not be enough.

"Murrish, the bobby. And Rudduck, he would only be too happy to assault Coombs."

"They won't believe you."

"That is likely."

"It has to be you."

"Coombs would kill me in an instant."

"No, I believe in you."

"Would you help me?"

"*Of course.*"

"You would help me stop Coombs?"

"*You mean, kill him? Is that what you want?*"

The word traveled on a breath pulled from me. "Yes."

"*Then go now. Hurry.*"

"Sister Ellen said you're here to protect him."

"*No, not me. Go now, while he's sleeping. You can do it.*"

The question that had been lurking in the back of my mind, the one I had not wanted to acknowledge since Sister Ellen's revelations, would no longer be denied.

"But who are you?" My whisper was barely more than a breath.

"*Your brother.*"

Tremors of fear washed over me. "What is your name?"

There came a pause, and the voice that filled the silence sounded not at all like a boy, but rather like echoes from an ancient tomb.

"*You know my name.*"

A mirthless laugh came to me, but I stifled it quickly with a throw pillow lest the madness overtaking me became too evident. I leaned back and stretched out on the couch. The laugh became a mad cackle deep in my throat. Had I been listening to a demon and not my brother all this time? Was it ever thus? Had I lost my grip on reality entirely? Perhaps I had dreamt everything from Thornsbury's office to this moment as my brain died while I swung from a rope.

The laughter would not be held at bay, so I turned to the back of the couch and pulled the pillow over my head to muffle my cackling. I surrendered to my newfound madness, and eventually to sleep.

CHAPTER THIRTY-THREE
MAYHEM

A LOOMING FIGURE MADE OF FLAMES shook me awake. Murrish, the young bobby stood over me, whispering, "Doctor. Wake up." The dying fire cast him in coruscating shades of red and orange.

"Has something happened?" I muttered as I pulled myself upright.

Sheasby, at the front door and donning his coat said, "Stay quiet. We don't want to wake the ladies."

Coombs strolled down the stairs. "What's all the commotion?"

Sheasby hushed him. "If you're coming, be quiet. You too, Doctor."

Blearily shrugging into my coat, I was unaware of any noise I might have made.

Taking his own coat, Coombs asked casually, "What's goin' on?"

"The vicar's dead," said Sheasby as he led the way.

The frigid air bit into my lungs. The ice under foot sent me stumbling more than once.

Coombs strode languidly behind in the dark. I hurried to catch up to the lawmen, who were at the chapel.

Murrish led us inside, then to the storage room at the back of the chapel. The lawmen and I crowded into the room. Next to the stove, Vicar Woodmore sat quietly, it seemed. His hands rested in his lap. I nearly called his name until Sheasby's lantern revealed him. Seven slashes pierced his neck, the star centered on his carotid artery. Blood drenched his coat. Thick drops fell from his sleeve into a congealing pool below.

"How did this happen?" I muttered.

"Yes, Murrish," Sheasby demanded. "How *did* this happen?"

"I heard a sound, " the bobby said weakly. "I stepped outside to look, got hit on the head. Woke up, came in here and found him like that."

"Murrish did it," said Coombs. He stood at the door, a vacant stare on his face.

"Murrish?" Sheasby whirled on Coombs, his voice full of angry scorn. "What the bloody hell are you on about?"

"I didn't hit *myself* on the head!" Murrish objected.

Coombs shrugged. "Could've, to cover it up. Wasn't anyone else, was there?"

"That doesn't prove a thing but that he's a damn fool," snarled Sheasby.

"No," said Coombs wistfully. "But the order from the leader of the Tavistock Coven in his pocket proves it."

"What? There's nothing like that in my pockets," Murrish objected.

"In your left coat pocket," Coombs said. "There's a document written in blood on human skin that orders you to kill Vicar Woodmore."

As at the church in Newington when Coombs' powers first failed him, I felt none of the world-shifting sensations.

Murrish held open his coat pockets. "See? Nothing. Wanna check the rest of 'em?" He angrily emptied his pants pockets, flinging a handkerchief, some coins and bills at Coombs, who let them fall to the floor.

"Maybe I was wrong." Coombs said this with such unexpected sadness that I almost felt bad for him. "Just like Newington, yeah?" he said to me.

"Newington?" asked Sheasby. "What about it?"

"Nothin'," said Coombs. "Absolutely nothin'."

"Murrish," Sheasby ordered. "Get back to the vicarage. See if Sister Ellen can do something about your head."

Coombs stepped back from the doorway as Murrish staggered out.

"Dr. Johnson," Sheasby said. "If you would be so kind as to examine the vicar and see if you can find any clues."

"Certainly, Constable."

"And *you*, Detective." The constable pushed past me and strode up to Coombs. "You are to stay by my side at all times until I see you on a train out of here. And," he added over Coombs' response, "you are to say nothing to the ladies." He turned to me. "Be quick but be thorough." Sheasby led Coombs out.

He was gone before I could point out the mutual exclusivity of his request. I moved my lantern closer to the dead vicar.

The neck wound was clearly the cause of extinction of life. The only other injury was a bruise on the back of his head, easily seen through his wispy white hair. Almost certainly not severe enough to cause death, even in a man of his age. The bruise was the length of my index finger and quite straight. After a brief search in the chapel proper, I found a candlestick under a pew. It resembled others I had seen in the vicarage. Its base was of just the right width.

There was no other conclusion to draw but that someone had taken a candlestick and used it on both Murrish and the vicar. Someone tall, strong, and capable of moving silently. The assailant then cut open the vicar's neck. Even though Sister Ellen had confessed to cutting Heggs' corpse, it seemed highly unlikely that she could have committed this act. As unlikely as a rickety little girl murdering several people? Was Sister Ellen strong enough to render two men unconscious? No, the evidence clearly pointed to Coombs. But why would he do this now? And what about his false accusation of Murrish?

"The only other time Coombs' words did not appear to change reality was when he stood in a church," I told the dead vicar. "And his error had caused him to go on a drunken binge that landed him in jail. Yet this time, he was hardly surprised. Was it a test of some sort?"

I realized I had been speaking these thoughts aloud and clamped my hand over my mouth. Was there anyone within hearing distance? Only Woodmore. I held the lantern close to him. His face was even paler in death, particularly in contrast to all the blood.

Hope rose within me. The hope that something I had seen would remain as I had seen it. That it was as real as the fire in the lantern I carried and the wind that bit my face as I stepped outside. As I approached the vicarage, I saw Mary and Sister Ellen through the kitchen window in nightclothes, tending to Murrish's head.

"You have to stop him. Use the candlestick. Catch him by surprise. The others will jump in and help."

The thoughts I had while falling asleep came back to me. Thoughts of talking to demons, of madness and dreaming while dying. I spoke to the darkness beyond the lantern's light. That seemed to be where this voice resided now, less in my head and more in the shadows. "Are you a demon?"

Gentle laughter danced through my mind as a chill, deeper than the air could reach, filled me.

"Do you think I am?"

Coombs' accusation that I had invented the evidence that contradicted him came to me. "I do not know what to think anymore."

I went in through the kitchen door. Murrish sat on a stool while Sister Ellen wrapped a bandage around his head. Mary rushed to me.

"What's happened?" she demanded. "*He* won't tell me anything."

"Not supposed to," said Murrish. Sister Ellen hushed him.

"Mary," I said, "please take Sister Ellen and go into the basement. *Now*," I added over her protests. "Officer Murrish. Detective Coombs is not himself. He must be restrained. But I have seen the man fight, and we will need all the help we can get. Please get Mr. Rudduck. I suspect he will be only too happy to lend a hand. Or a fist."

Murrish gave a grim nod. He thanked Sister Ellen as he gently pushed her away, then exited through the back door.

Mary grabbed my arm. "Tell me what is happening."

I pulled her hand off me. Like Sister Ellen, she was stronger than she appeared. "Mary, please trust me. All will be made clear soon, but now we must deal with Coombs. Sister Ellen, I implore you to bring Mary into the basement and wait until I come for you."

Sister Ellen nodded, but Mary resisted.

"Dr. Johnson?" Sheasby called from the great hall. "What are you doing in the kitchen? Come in here and give me your findings."

"Coming." I hefted the candlestick, feeling its weight, finding the optimal grip to use it as a weapon. I pushed through the door to find Sheasby standing by the fire while Coombs lounged on the divan. A wave of contempt for the man washed over me. How could he be so casual in this moment?

"Constable, this candlestick was used to render both Murrish and Vicar Woodmore unconscious. Then Woodmore was set in the chair and his neck cut *seven times*."

Coombs got to his feet and stood rigid, his face a mask of stone.

Sheasby's expression darkened as he absorbed the information. He set his hand on his saber and turned to Coombs. Before he could speak, Mary burst into the room with Sister Ellen behind, vainly attempting to hold her back.

"My father is *dead*? How?"

"Only one answer," said Sheasby. He drew his saber. "It was Coombs."

Laughing, Coombs said, "Is that what you think?"

Murrish and Rudduck entered from the front door, behind Coombs.

"Gentlemen," said Sheasby. "Just in time. Coombs, you're under arrest for suspicion of the murder of Vicar Woodmore."

Coombs barked a laugh in the constable's face. "Me? I was in my room all night!"

"Don't even bother," Sheasby said. He gestured for Murrish and Rudduck to take up each side of Coombs.

Coombs spread his feet and dropped his hands to his side, just as I had seen him do in the alley. The men recognized his stance and tensed.

"Be careful," I said. "He may have a weapon in his sleeve."

Coombs ignored me. "Our meek little doctor here's the one what gave all them orders, wrote all them contracts. In his bags you'll find more of them pieces of skin, along with the tools to draw blood and write with it. That's what all them bodies in your basement were for, wasn't it, Johnson? For the blood? And the skin cut off the ones in Battersea. To make them contracts."

"Coombs?" I gasped as fluid, frigid shadows flowed over me. "What are you doing?"

"Exposin' you for what you are. Check his pocket, inside his jacket. You'll find one more contract. A contract orderin' Rudduck to kill *you*, Sheasby."

Icy fingers caressed my side. A weight formed in my jacket pocket. I started to protest as I felt it pressing against my chest.

"What is it with you and pockets?" demanded Sheasby. "Just surrender and we won't have to hurt you." The three moved closer.

"Wait!" I reached into my pocket and felt the leathery object that had appeared there.

"See?" said Coombs. "Looks like he's gonna confess."

"No," I said, and instead of the skin, I took out the sign I had found in Angel Meadow. I held it towards Coombs. "Recognize this? 'Silas Jr.' Your son. The one you killed."

Coombs' face went pale. His mouth fell open and he staggered as if struck. The three men exchanged cautious glances and moved closer.

"I saw it, Coombs. I saw the carnage you left behind. The mother and child. Your *son*."

He fell to his knees.

"Yes. You fell to your knees then, too." I lowered myself to face him. "You begged for mercy. For forgiveness perhaps? But something much darker answered. Yes, it relieved you of those horrible memories, but in exchange, it took you, drove you to the things you've done. To accuse innocent people of heinous crimes and then to somehow create the evidence to convict them. Let us help you rid yourself of this curse."

Rudduck and Murrish grabbed his arms. As if in a stupor, Coombs' head turned towards one, then the other.

"Yep," said Murrish. "Bastard's got a knife." He worked it out of Coombs' sleeve and slipped it under his belt.

The constable sheathed his saber. "I'll want to know more about what you just said, Doctor." He moved behind Coombs and placed the cuffs on him.

"Right then," said Sheasby. "Let's get him squared away until morning. Mr. Rudduck, you think Jenny will be ready for a trip to town?"

"When I tell her we're takin' this shitsack to gaol," Rudduck said with a shove to Coombs' shoulder, "she'll be rarin' to go."

"Whatever it takes, Mr. Rudduck. Murrish, stay close to him."

Murrish nodded and readied himself.

"Why don't you ladies try and get some rest?" Sheasby said to Mary and Sister Ellen. "We've got this under control. He'll pay for what he's done."

In my mind I knew what the constable said was true. Coombs would be tried and hung for his deeds. But in my heart grew hatred. I did not want punishment for him. I wanted to kill him.

Mary moved towards Coombs. From behind, Sister Ellen grabbed her arms. Mary dragged the nun along behind, then broke away and faced Coombs. "*Why?* Why would you come here and do this?"

Coombs turned away, as if listening to something else.

I looked at Sister Ellen. She shook her head, her hands in desperate prayer to me. Her resolve broke and she collapsed with a cry. Mary ran to her and comforted her.

Mary would likely learn the truth of how Coombs had come into their lives, but this was not the time, and I was not the one to tell her.

With a look at Sheasby, Coombs said, "Think this is the first time I been in cuffs?" He jumped to his feet and pushed Rudduck away. He swung the cuffs with one hand, striking Murrish across the face. When Murrish came at him, Coombs pulled the knife from the bobby's waist, gutted him, and pushed him over the grating onto the fireplace.

In the suddenly dimmed light, Mary and Sister Ellen retreated to the kitchen. I readied my candlestick, feeling only the desire to bury it in Coombs' brain.

Sheasby lunged with his saber. Coombs spun away and let out a painful grunt as he caught the blade in his side. His thick coat held it, putting Sheasby off balance. Coombs hooked an arm over Sheasby's sword arm, and with the other, stabbed the constable near the shoulder. Sheasby cried out as Coombs wrested the saber away.

Coombs then charged at me, swinging the saber. His strikes were powerful, but slow and crude, predictable. I blocked them with the candlestick, but he drove me back to the wall, knocking my weapon from my hands. He impaled me through the stomach until the saber's hilt was pressed against me. I screamed my throat raw, and the searing pain swept through me, burning my nerves to numbness.

Coombs' sweating, reddened face nearly touched mine. His stare was that of an animal.

Coombs staggered back. Darkness descended as my life drained with my blood. Coombs withdrew the saber and raised it for a final blow.

"*Hey!*" Mary emerged from the kitchen, a knife in each hand. Behind her stood Sister Ellen carrying a black sack.

Coombs turned to them.

"Mary, *no!*" I cried as I fell.

Coombs charged at her. She threw a knife which Coombs took in his forearm. Mary drew another, larger knife from behind her back.

Darkness came to me in waves. Each slowing heartbeat pushed it aside, in vain, as the tide rose. A desperate cry mixed with agony escaped me.

"Help," I croaked. "Please." Tears mixed with blood as the furious, bloody battle raged nearby. Screams and cries rang out as bodies fell. But whose I did not know.

In the last of my vision came two points of flickering light. Coombs' eyes, reflecting fire. Yet, they were not above me, they were down low with mine, in the wet darkness that smelled of viscera. Was he crawling towards me with mad and desperate murder in his eyes?

"I beg of you." Words aloud or thoughts within I could not tell. "Give me the strength to kill him."

There came the flash of a blade and darkness took me.

PART THE SECOND

OF

BOUNTIFUL CURSES

CHAPTER THIRTY-FOUR

AWAKENING

THERE WAS FIRE IN MY FACE. No, it was a burning in my nose, ammonia. I fought to raise my hands but could not. Was something holding me down? I struggled to open my eyes. Blurred faces and figures floated around me. Some wore white, others blue or black. Behind them, surrounding us all, a veil of shimmering white. Was this Heaven?

"Dr. Johnson?" came a voice from a dark face.

I wondered to whom that name might belong.

"Dr. Johnson?" the voice repeated. "Are you there, Doctor?"

The round face with its dark skin and hair moved closer and came into focus. A man, I realized, with a thick mustache. He seemed familiar, and he seemed to be talking to me.

My mouth moved, and I forced myself to swallow, then croaked, "I am here." I only knew it to be my voice because the speaking of it hurt my dry throat.

A glass of water was presented to me by a black-gloved hand. I tried to reach for it, but my arms felt weighted. I lifted my head and let the man pour some water between my lips.

"Dr. Johnson," said the familiar-seeming face. The name he kept repeating had a familiarity as well. "Can you tell us what happened?"

"Happened?" I knew nothing of any happenings. All there was to the world was this little group in a white nothingness. There was no past, no future, only this moment, suspended. What else *could* there be?

"Yes. At the vicarage."

"The vicarage." I sounded out the word as if I had just learned it.

"Yes, Doctor. The vicarage." The man's voice took on an urgency. "Can you tell us what happened?"

"No," I said. "Can you tell *me*?"

The familiar face withdrew and floated with the others, each of which sat atop their figures of white or blue or black. Their hushed voices drifted from one to the other, the words like soap bubbles that popped as soon as I attempted to grasp them.

Slowly, my vision cleared to reveal a doctor and a nurse. With them was a constable. He was a rail of a man, tall and thin, with cotton-white hair and a full beard. Then there was the familiar man. He was dressed in black that was darker yet than his skin.

"Where am I?" I asked them.

Their discussion stopped. Looks were exchanged.

"Lochford Cottage Hospital," said the familiar man. "You were brought here when you were found." His demeanor changed suddenly. "Do you know who I am?"

I shook my head in embarrassment, for something told me that I should know him.

"This is Constable Shaw," he said of the bearded fellow. "I'm Superintendent Batleigh."

The name Batleigh echoed in my empty mind. It was akin to hearing a church bell in the distance; I could recognize what it was without knowing any specifics.

"You don't remember me?"

"Sorry, no."

He leaned in again. "Do you know your name?"

I looked at the frowning faces and this Batleigh, who showed more concern than the others. "Am I ... Dr. Johnson?"

Batleigh smiled in a sad way, patted my arm and straightened up. "We should give him time to rest."

"Rest?" snapped Constable Shaw. "Dr. Johnson, you are accused of the murders –"

"*Stop.*" Batleigh thrust out his hand.

Shaw clamped his mouth shut, but anger boiled in his eyes.

"This man has *not* been accused," Batleigh continued. "We know nothing of what happened save what you've assumed. We will give this man time to recover while we investigate. Is that clear?"

Batleigh waited for a nod from the constable, then turned to each of the others until he received the same. They filed out of the blinding white surrounding us, which I now realized was sunlit curtains drawn around my bed.

Batleigh lingered. "You rest, Dr. Johnson. It will come back to you. And I will keep you safe until it does."

By the time I could pull words forth, Batleigh had passed through the bright curtains. I had both realizations and questions.

I was in a bed. In hospital, it seemed. My supposed name, "Dr. Johnson," did not sit quite right, as if they had mistaken me for someone else. And what did he mean by "keep me safe"? Was I in danger because of mistaken identity? Perhaps all I needed was to remember my name.

I tried to sit up, to call them back so I could ask my questions, and realized I was restrained. There were straps on my wrists and ankles and one across my waist. Panic took me and I called for help.

The nurse stepped through the curtains, setting them wavering in a rhythmic way.

"Why am I restrained?" I demanded.

"It's for everyone's safety."

"Safety? But why? I don't understand." I pulled at the straps. She stepped out of the curtains, then came back with the doctor.

"Perhaps you should sleep," he said as the nurse held me still while he injected me in the arm. Warmth spread from there, and I was gone.

CHAPTER THIRTY-FIVE
A MYSTERIOUS VISITOR

"How are you feeling?"

The voice pulled me up from the murky sleep into which I had descended. The curtains around me were dark and still. I could feel a presence near me, yet the curtains showed no sign of having been moved. Had this person entered and waited in silence for some time?

"Feeling better?" the visitor asked.

The voice came from the head of my bed. It was a man's voice, rather deep, and yet left little impression on my ears, almost as if it bypassed them entirely. Still restrained, I could not turn to see him fully. All I could see of him were white pants and shoes. I thought he must be another doctor.

"Hello. I am doing well enough, given the circumstances. Do I know you?"

"We have spoken before, but you mistook me for someone else."

"Really? Can you please move down the bed so that I can see you better?"

"Certainly."

I stretched the strain out of my neck, and when I relaxed, he was still at the very edge of my vision. "A little further, please. What is your name, by the way?"

"I'm here to help you, dear boy."

"I appreciate the sentiment, but for now the best thing you can do for me is to move down here," I nodded towards my feet, "where I can see you fully."

"Gladly."

He remained at the periphery. "And yet, you do not." I turned my head towards him and a wave of dizziness took me. I shut my eyes and reached to hold my head, only to be stopped by the restraints.

"Pardon?" It was a woman's voice.

I opened my eyes. The nurse stood at the foot of my bed.

"Apologies. I was talking to –" I turned my head to the right and found nothing but the bedside table. "I had a visitor," I said weakly.

"There have been no visitors."

"A dream, then," I said and closed my eyes again.

She made a reluctantly affirmative sound in her throat.

"I should like to use the loo," I told her.

She stepped out of the curtains and returned with a pan that was very cold and an orderly who was very unhappy. Only the strap at my waist was loosened and the task was performed in grim silence.

I wished for sleep and perhaps I drifted in and out, but fear kept me from any form of rest. Fear and itching. The most minor itches became burning obsessions because I could not scratch them. Each attempt to relax and focus on recalling memories brought even more agitations. More than the fear of what horrible actions I might have taken to put me in this predicament only exposed a deeper fear: the emptiness, the void, the black abyss that lay beyond the moment I had awoken in this bed.

Eventually light retuned and I was brought a cup of water to sip with assistance. I kept the emotions and questions in check when nurses or orderlies were present. Though I longed for sleep, unconsciousness from drugs would not help me.

"Lunch time," said the nurse as she drew back the curtains around me.

It was a three-bed ward, I at the end nearest the door and an old wheezing man at the far end, an empty bed between us.

"How are you feeling today, Mr. Johnson?" The doctor said with a clipboard held in his crossed hands.

The name felt less strange to me, if only by repetition. "The Batleigh fellow," I said. "I believe he referred to me as 'Doctor', did he not?"

"Indeed. Now, if you're feeling strong enough, we can undo your arms and allow you to feed yourself. But rest assured at the first, merest indication of violence, the straps will go back on, never to be removed while in this facility. Is that clear?"

"Violence?" Another word that I sounded out as if it were new. "You fear I might be violent?"

"This ruse will not help your case. In fact, I'm inclined to leave the straps on."

"No, please, I assure you, there will be no violence. Please, I would very much like to feed myself."

After the doctor aimed a frown at me, a turn and nod of his head brought the same short, stocky Irish orderly back to my bedside.

"We will give the patient the opportunity to feed himself," the doctor told the orderly. "Any untoward actions – and I mean *any* – and you are to immediately restrain him again."

The orderly nodded and took a stance as if readying for a fight.

"Undo the straps slowly," the doctor told the nurse.

Once they were off, I rubbed my wrists, then held my hands up. "No violence. I assure you."

The doctor went on about his business while the nurse stuffed pillows behind me, then presented me with a tray. The orderly stood at the ready for whatever actions he feared I might take.

Lunch was a broth the colour and taste of rust, dry potato bread and a piece of mild cheddar. The moment I was done, the straps were replaced. More alert now, and more acutely aware of the restraints, I tried shifting and squirming, but that only brought dangerous looks from the orderly, who was never far from me. Finally, I resolved to calm myself and breathe through the irritations. I had heard of techniques from the East that promoted calmness and I wished I had paid them more mind.

How had I come to be here? The staff truly feared that I would do them violence, yet I felt no such urges. The Irish orderly was downright intimidating, with his rough and ruddy face, thick arms and hard, green eyes. If I knew one thing about myself, it was that I would avoid that young man, not attack him.

"Feeling any better?" By the voice, I knew it was the same person I had spoken to earlier.

"You have a knack for staying just at the edge of my vision."

"I don't mean to."

I turned suddenly, as much as I was able, and the sudden move brought shadows and bright points of light, but it was enough that I saw the visitor more clearly. He appeared to be perhaps ten years older than I and was dressed in white and pale grey. I waited for the spinning to settle.

"Who are you and why are you here?"

"As I said, I'm here to help," said the visitor.

"In what way? And you have not told me your name."

"I was there. At the vicarage. Do you remember?"

A vision, as if it were the frames of a zoetrope, flashed in my mind. A large man stood over me with a bloody saber. A woman threw knives. There was a burning policeman, or was it a toy soldier? The next flash came with a voice, an offer of aid. The vision was gone.

"Did you … ?" I asked. "Was it you – ?" I turned towards the chair, but it was empty.

"I haven't the strength." Now the visitor's voice came from my other side.

"Why do you keep doing that?" Still, I could barely see him. "Stand before me, damn it. Where I can *see* you."

A loud harrumph drew my attention to the doctor, standing at the foot of my bed. "Are you quite all right, sir?" he asked, knowing full well I was not.

The gentleman stranger was gone.

"There was …" I started. "In the chair, then over here …"

The doctor came to my side and touched my forehead. "There was no one, I assure you." He then produced a hypodermic, and with an orderly's help, administered a shot. "Morphia. It will help you rest."

I wanted to tell them about the mysterious gentleman, that he had not only been at my bedside, but had been at the vicarage and knew what had happened. Perhaps he had even been responsible for it. He was real, I wanted to tell them. Instead, I felt pulled down a drain to a dark and pleasant pool. I swam through more visions of the vicarage, where knives and sabers flashed in firelight, and blood arced as if a butcher pirouetted.

CHAPTER THIRTY-SIX

FLIGHT

PERHAPS I SLEPT AND DREAMT OF elegant violence, blades dancing, people trimmed like beef, blood and viscera providing decorations for a mad party attended by flaming soldiers. Or perhaps I traveled to worlds where such things were mundane. But there came an end to it all and I found myself lying in darkness. An orderly dozed in a chair beside me. Not the big, Irish one, but a waif of a fellow. A single lantern flickered on a table near the door.

"You really should leave as soon as possible." It was my mysterious visitor again, on the opposite side of the orderly. Again, he remained just outside my range of vision. "They believe you killed all those people."

Again, the flashes of bloody violence. "Maybe it was you."

"You know that's not true."

Of all the information I held tenuously in my mind, I knew for an absolute truth that the gentleman beside me had killed no one.

"And you know your name is not Johnson."

Another stone dropped in the murkiness of my memories.

"No, it isn't," I croaked.

"And when they find out who you are and everything you've done, there will be no saving you."

"Everything I have done?" My voice was barely more than a squeak.

"The bodies. Don't you remember the bodies? In your basement. You cut them open, yes?"

Visions of a dark basement flickered and brought with them a musky, foul odour.

"The police came," he said. "And there was a fire."

A vision of me running from roaring flames appeared. "Please stop."

"If I stop, you will never escape." His voice was gentle, but insistent.

"But if I'm a killer, why would you help me?"

"Does it matter? I *am* helping you, and you can either accept my help or lay here until they take you back to Newgate and string you up."

Visions of rusty iron bars and of gargoyles beating me in the dark drew a gasp from me. "Back?"

"You escaped there, you can escape here."

I lifted my arms as high as I could against the straps. "What am I to do?" As much as anything, I wanted to wipe my dampened eyes.

"Talk to the orderly. Tell him you need to use the loo."

"He'll get the nurse. She'll bring the pan again."

"Perhaps I could help persuade him."

I turned towards him as best I could. "Might he not wonder what you are doing here at this time of night?"

The visitor was gone from my side.

The orderly snorted and sniffed. The one lantern in the room shed enough light to make out someone, presumably my visitor, bent at the orderly's side, whispering to him. I could see slivers of the visitor's face, shards of his clothing, but his figure seemed to be made more of shadows than of light.

The orderly snapped awake as the visitor stepped back out of my range of vision.

"You're awake," said the orderly.

"I need to use the loo. Please do not make me use the pan again."

The visitor was behind him now, deeper in the shadows. Did his eyes reflect the flames' orange light, or did they have their own? He whispered to the orderly.

"Wouldn't want to use that thing meself," he said. "Everybody lookin'." He glanced around. The visitor remained hidden from both of us. "You'll be a good boy, yeah?"

"I am no fighter."

The orderly nodded, then undid my straps. I sat on the edge of the bed, then stood and stretched. My legs were weak and I nearly fell, but the orderly helped to steady me.

"Be quick about it," he said.

"Of course." I expected him to follow me, but he sat back in the chair, yawning. The shadowy visitor was at his ear again.

I made my way silently through the hall, down the stairs.

"It's cold out," said my new friend from behind me. I had not heard him approach.

Fortunately, there was a coat, hat, and boots near the door. I donned them hastily, paused to listen for pursuers, and hearing none, stepped outside.

Weak moonlight silvered the road that crossed in front of the hospital, leaving the trees on either side to form black silhouettes.

"Can you ride a horse?" asked the visitor. He lingered between the building and the shed, away from the moonlight.

"How did you get down here so fast?"

"Never mind that. There isn't time. Can you ride a horse?"

"If it is saddled, perhaps."

"You'll have to run, then. That way." His hand and arm emerged from the shadows and seemed greyer than the moonlight. "You'll have to find some clothes and a way to get on the train. I can help."

The moonlit road stretched before me until it dipped downward. Downward. Descent. Memories of descending down that path drifted through my mind. The vicarage. Those who had been telling me of my past spoke of a vicarage. It was the place where all they said I had done had occurred. And I knew it was that way.

"Thank you, but no. I want to go to the vicarage. I *need* to."

"No, that's dangerous. They'll find you. Once they have you again they'll never let you go."

"I do not care. I cannot live this way," I said. I turned and ran down the road.

CHAPTER THIRTY-SEVEN

RETURN

A BLOODY DAWN GUIDED ME FOR the last bit of my journey. Perhaps the drugs the doctors had administered prevented me from truly feeling the pain in my feet, lungs, and legs. Or perhaps it was madness that drove me.

The door to the vicarage hung slightly open. I feared it would fly open and all manner of beasts and monsters would march out to devour me. I felt the urge to run, to flee from the darkness I would find within. Instead, I forced my legs to take me to the door.

I pushed it open, creaking. I called out and received no reply. The gray daylight cast a stark column through the great hall.

"You shouldn't be here."

The voice of the visitor drew a gasp from me. He stood inside, just at the edge of the shadow cast by the light from the door.

"How are you here?"

"I was worried about you."

"But I never saw you along the way, and there was no other carriage or gig or even a horse on the road here."

"There's no time for that. This is dangerous. If the police come, this will only cement their suspicions of you."

I could not deny that logic, but something else nagged at me. "I am standing at the door. How did you get inside?"

"I slipped past you. You didn't notice."

"I ran all the way here and I am barely able to stand. How are you so rested?"

"I haven't been strapped to a bed for days."

"And why are you not wearing a coat, or at least a hat?"

"Will you *please*, in the name of all that's fetid and damned, stop asking so many *questions*?"

His voice rolled like thunder through the vicarage and through my mind. Like the last rumble after a storm, the clouds parted as it faded. As the morning light brightened the great hall before me, my memories flooded back.

Newgate and Coombs. Our cases with his absurd accusations, the fluid shadows, and changes in reality. The dark presence sensed by Malvagna and

Sister Ellen. The evil they had both felt now stood before me. And it had helped me flee captivity.

Suddenly I could see the visitor clearly. His clothes were the color of bleached bones and he was shrouded in shadows cast by moonlight through dead trees. The cold that had merely touched me before took me wholly, filled me and froze my heart. "You … You are the …"

"Yes and no. Not *him* exactly, but rather a representative. A friend. A helper. I *was*, at any rate. Until you ruined everything."

"Ruined … ?"

"Yes, *ruined*. Coombs was doing wonderful work. First the minister's wife, then that little girl. Even the banker was acceptable. Granted, his soul was bitter, but his death at the hands of his fellow prisoners more than made up for it. But *you. You* had to get Coombs *thinking*. Questioning. Investigating. Now all that work we did is *gone*."

"I do not understand."

"No, of course you don't. You with your 'I don't believe in things. Everything must have *proof*' attitude. With Coombs gone, so are the things he put into the world. It's too late for the banker, thankfully, but that little girl – I was *sure* she would die in the workhouse. That would have been –" He kissed his fingers. "But with the evidence gone, she'll almost certainly be dismissed. Oh, she would have been such a feast. And the misery, the despair would have made a wonderful *aperitif*."

I fell back against the wall, my head in my hands, shaking.

"I see you're still catching up," said the well-dressed gentleman. "You were right about Coombs. I came to him in Angel Meadow, after he killed all those women, and his infant son. He'd had quite a night. He begged for help, I answered. It was easy to keep his memories from him. He didn't want them. I could just make suggestions and let his imagination do the rest."

I staggered about as the world spun. "Am I dreaming? Am I dead? What is happening?" Surely my chest would rip open from my pounding heart and heaving lungs.

"Dead?" said the Gentleman. "Certainly not. Dreaming? Who can say what is real and what isn't? Until mere moments ago, you did not believe beings such as I existed. Did I sound like your dead brother? I had to guess at his voice. Ah, but you wanted to believe it."

A raw cry tore through my throat as I desperately searched for a place to stand, to breathe.

"Did you enjoy what I did with your notebooks?" the Gentleman asked. "Changed one, sent Garret after the second. He's so helpful."

"Why?" I cried out. "Why is this happening?"

"Souls, dear boy. They are my harvest, my sustenance. Coombs was my gatherer. He excelled at finding those who could be made to doubt. To give in to the darkness, wallow in it, and cast out their light and hope. That is when they ripen. And now, it is *your* job."

My mind was a fallen cliff, a river depleted, a forest burned. Laid bare was my ruin, my damnation. Each step to this place lay behind me, a wound stretching back through my days. I opened my mouth to scream but produced only air, as a corpse expending its last breath. Spent, I collapsed on the floor.

The Gentleman laughed.

"Yes, yes, you're *so* distraught." He took on a mocking tone. "'Everything I've believed is a lie and now I'm in the thrall of a demon from Hell.' How sad for you. But it's time to get up and *go*. I was sincere when I said you should leave, or you'll be caught and executed."

My mind grasped the most trivial of his words because the rest were too much. "Everything I believe? Does that mean everything in the Bible is true?"

"How would *I* know? I haven't read it. Come on, now. Time to go."

"You said Coombs was good at … this business of yours," I said, sitting up. "But I spoiled it all?"

"Yes, but I'm willing to forgive you if you'll just get up and *go*."

"But if Coombs was so good at it, why are you with *me* now?"

He leaned down close to me. "Because you *killed* him."

"Yes, but why *me*?" I cried out. "Why have I been cursed so? Did my killing him force some kind of transfer? To the victor goes the spoils?"

"*Ha.*"

"Or was it because I was the only survivor?"

"Yes. That's it. You guessed it. Let's go."

"Could it be that simple?" My faculties were slowly returning. "You said you came to Coombs after he killed his infant son. He was weak, desperate, on his knees. He begged for help." I stood, strengthened by the working out of a problem. "*I* begged for help. *That* was why you came to me. I was near death. I begged for help, and you *had* to offer it, did you not?"

The Gentleman seethed and his voice grew quiet. "So, you're not the only one cursed. Shall we go now?"

"Why? Why do you care if I am caught? Is it because I would not be able to sacrifice innocent souls?" I fell back against the wall as the reality of my fate sank in.

"Perhaps it *would* be best to return to Hell, rather than suffer more of your *questions*."

"Ah *hah*! 'Return to Hell'. It seems that if I do not cooperate, you will be returned to Hell?"

A malevolent smile formed. "And you with me, dear boy. I guarantee that I'll take out *every single bit* of my frustration on you. And the other."

"Wait, what 'other'? Who else is left? Did another survive? Was there a witness?"

"I can explain later," said the Gentleman, "but for now, I am literally begging you, please *leave*. Get as far away as – damn it."

The sound of horses and a wagon approached. I wished I had taken the demon's advice.

CHAPTER THIRTY-EIGHT
REMEMBERING

BATLEIGH BARGED IN FOLLOWED BY SEVERAL constables. Morning sun streamed through the door, turning the officers into silhouettes.

I put my hands up and felt a twinge of pain in my side, where Coombs had run me through, but I dared not lower my hands to check.

"Superintendent Batleigh," I said. "I remember everything now."

One of the officers, the white-haired one from the hospital, drew his pistol on me. "Gonna confess, are ya?"

Batleigh set a steadying hand on the man's arm. "Constable Shaw, please put that away."

Shaw did so, reluctantly.

I drew in a breath, concerned that I would not be able to explain recent events with any coherency. But to my surprise, my memories had fully returned. "I will only confess to the killing of Coombs in self-defense," I said. "But first, you should know what brought us here."

I told them about the wire that had been sent to Coombs, and about Heggs' death and mutilation. "But Coombs believed there had been a murder. He accused Vicar Woodmore of leading a Satanic cult and being responsible for the killing. That is why you found the vicar alone in the chapel, yes? You did find him there, with seven slashes across his neck?" I indicated on myself with my hand.

"We did find him that way," said Batleigh. "But what is this business about a cult?"

"Coombs had somehow learned of the secret room in the vicar's study," I said.

"What secret room?" Batleigh asked. "We found no such thing."

"There is a book of French poetry. When you pull it down, a bookcase opens to reveal the room."

"That sounds like a fiction," said Shaw.

"Show us," Batleigh said, leading the way to the study.

The bookcase was closed. I went to the shelf where I had seen the book but found no volume resembling the one I had pulled down.

"It was right here." I pulled at all the books, causing them to fall to the floor. I banged on the backs of the empty shelves, expecting to hear a hollow sound, but it was as solid as any wall.

"Is this some sort of distraction?" Shaw demanded.

"No, no," I said. "It was here. Constable Sheasby and I both entered and saw the things Coombs described." I steadied myself against the bookcase and whispered, "Was it ever really there?" The pain in my side nagged at me.

"You tell me," said the Gentleman. His voice was in my ear, but I could not see him. Nor could anyone else. "I mean that. If you tell me it's there, it will be there."

Batleigh set a gloved hand on my shoulder. "Let's put that aside for now. Tell us what happened next, after Coombs made his accusation."

I led them back to the great hall. "We had dinner. It was too cold to leave, so Constable Sheasby asked the women to prepare dinner. We all ate, and then, later, when everyone was asleep, Vicar Woodmore was murdered. Coombs accused me –"

"And you killed him for it," said Shaw.

"*No*," I said. "I was trying to *help* him. But he snapped. He killed Wood-more."

"Why would he do that?" Batleigh asked.

"It was –" I almost told him about Coombs' test of the Gentleman's abilities. But that would require telling them about demons and fluid shadows. "An impulse, apparently. I am not sure. But when Constable Sheasby tried to arrest him, he went berserk." I wondered if I should tell them about Silas Lee, about the sign I had brought. What had happened to it? I touched my pocket.

"Looking for your little sign?" asked the Gentleman. He sat on the divan as if waiting for tea to be served. "With any luck, it ended up in the fireplace under the fallen bobby."

None of that mattered. "Coombs killed the others. Once he freed himself from the handcuffs placed on him by Constable Sheasby, he stabbed Officer Murrish in the chest, then pushed him on the fire. You found him there, yes?"

"Yes," said Shaw.

"After that, Coombs ran me through with Sheasby's saber. Right here." I put my hand to my side.

The Gentleman made a thrusting gesture with one arm and I doubled over in pain as if impaled anew.

"Remember, dear boy, I can make your words manifest."

Batleigh rushed to help me to my feet. "Doctor, you're bleeding."

From the point of pain in my side, blood flowed freely.

"Let's get you back to hospital," said Batleigh.

"No." I pushed him away. "I must see this through. I remember it all now. I can see it. Coombs ran me through with Sheasby's saber. I fell to my knees – here –" I led Batleigh to the spot. "That is my blood," I said, pointing to the large stain on the floor. I staggered, feeling the loss of so much blood and the fresh wound in my side. "I cried for help."

"And ruined everything," the Gentleman snarled in my ear.

A momentary vision of my brother Michael, how I had always pictured him, flashed before my eyes. He asked me what I wanted. Words did not come to me, but rather, images did. One of me cradling Mary, wounded but living. The other of me running Coombs through with the saber, repeatedly. Though it felt like a dream, it was not. More memories returned, of what happened after my plea for help had been answered.

"And when none came …" Batleigh said, encouraging me to continue.

"Correct. No help came."

"*Liar!*" barked the Gentleman.

His shout caused me to stagger. "Coombs would have killed me then and there, but … *Mary.* Oh, poor Mary. She called out a challenge, threw a knife at him. He tried to block it, but it dug into his right forearm. Mary then produced a cleaver from behind her back."

"You expect us to believe that *girl* killed *Coombs*?" said Shaw.

"Quiet," said Batleigh. "Let the man work it out."

"Coombs charged at her with the knife she had thrown and cut her thigh," I said, moving about the room. "She limped away. Sheasby attacked him with his cudgel, but Coombs gutted him. Then Rudduck was on him, a wild man, pummeling him. They rolled across the floor. To there," I said, pointing. "Coombs stabbed Rudduck repeatedly while Mary snuck up on him and buried a meat cleaver in his back. Next to his right shoulder blade. He was able to push her off, and he opened her belly as she fell. He was barely able to stand then. He was weak, bleeding severely, but not dead. And he was coming at me. To finish me off. But Sister Ellen leapt on him from behind and pulled a bag over his head. A black one. See that, near the fireplace? You'll find traces of the same substance in that bag as on Coombs' face. The substance that caused all those lesions and burns. Has your coroner determined the cause of those burns?"

"That's all in the report," Constable Shaw objected.

"I have been strapped to a bed since this happened!" I bellowed at him.

Batleigh came between us and gently guided me to a chair.

"But if you were dying and no help came," he said, "how did you kill Coombs?"

"Go ahead," said the Gentleman, standing behind Sheasby. "Tell them. Perhaps you'll end up in an asylum and we can work from there."

"My strength returned," I told them. "I cannot explain how. Perhaps it was pure survival instincts, but when Coombs was coming at me, I attacked him with the sword."

"Attacked him?" said Shaw. "You *slaughtered* him."

"His body was," Batleigh started and searched for words, "quite badly damaged. Barely recognizable. What could have given you that much strength?"

"Fear of impending death, I suppose," I said. "Beyond that, I cannot say."

"Well," said Batleigh, "if the young Miss Woodmore ever awakes, we can ask her. Perhaps she can corroborate your story."

I stood suddenly, causing a rush of blood from my head and a stab of pain in my side. Batleigh steadied me. "Miss Woodmore? *Mary?* She is still alive?"

"Barely. They haven't been able to bring her 'round and she may not make it, ultimately."

"I suppose you'd like to save her?" asked the Gentleman.

"Yes. I very much would like to save her," I blurted.

"I'm aware you're a doctor," said Batleigh, "but I doubt there's anything you can do, particularly in your condition."

"He'd likely try and finish her off," muttered Shaw.

"*Hush,*" Batleigh snapped at him. "You're bleeding quite badly, Doctor. Let's get you back now."

Once outside I said, "There is a donkey. Her name is Jenny. Best not to tell her about Rudduck."

"Pardon?" said Batleigh.

I heard Jenny's mournful bray coming from the shed. "There. In the shed. Let her out."

Batleigh lifted his chin towards one of the bobbies, who then jogged to the shed and opened the door.

Jenny burst out and galloped to the spot before the door where I had first seen Rudduck tending to her. She brayed and barked. She scraped at the ground as she spun about, confused. She was lost, unmoored, her world shattered.

"Please tell me, Superintendent, that you will contact a nearby farm to collect her," I said as Batleigh helped me into the police wagon.

He nodded, indulging me.

"I *insist.*"

"Yes, yes, all right, Doctor. I promise to see she's taken care of."

I thanked him profusely as I settled in and closed my eyes.

CHAPTER THIRTY-NINE

TRANSFORMATIONS, DARK AND DESPERATE

EVERY BUMP OF THE WAGON ON the trip back to the hospital caused more pain and bleeding. When the doctor examined the wound, he found the stitches to be held firm, yet blood continued to flow from it. He bandaged it so tightly I could hardly breathe.

"There's nothing they can do," said the Gentleman. His voice was quieter in my ear than it had been before. "But you have the cure, dear boy."

"Souls?" I whispered.

The nurse who had brought me water and opium glanced at me, but as with the rest of the staff, she did not want to engage with this dangerous patient.

"Indeed. There are so many around you. It is a banquet. All you need do is choose someone on whom to blame the murders. Anyone you like. Create any story you like. Have fun with it!"

The nurse, having done all she could, hurried away.

"Her for instance," said the Gentleman. "I confess to having a bit of a sweet tooth."

"If I do this, I will be healed?" I kept my head turned away from the ward and my voice low.

"Completely. And Mary, too, if you give me more."

Mary. Whether or not she intended it, her sudden attack on Coombs had spared my life, distracting him before he could finish me. And now her world was destroyed, her life nearly gone, with nothing but agony in her final moments.

"Whoever I name, they will be sent to Hell?"

"Upon their death, yes, but you don't believe in such things, do you?"

Could I still say that, while having a conversation with a demon? Elinor Grayson came to mind, Vicar Woodmore, the banker Fernald, and what had happened to them when Coombs accused them.

"No," I said. "I still do not believe in a place of fire and misery where people are sent for eternal punishment by a God who claims to be loving. But I cannot deny your existence, nor the living Hell that rained down upon Coombs' victims. And that is enough for me. I will find a way to rid myself of you. But, in order to do that, I must live."

I did my best to shut out the Gentleman's recriminations while I tried to work out how to minimize the horror I must inflict on others to give him what he demanded.

Throughout the day, I endeavoured to hide my increasing weakness from the hospital staff. Their stiff, stone-faced responses to my enquiries about Mary told me that she was no better off. More opium came, along with warm baths and cold compresses. Still, the Gentleman berated and badgered me. By the time Batleigh arrived to begin the inquest, I felt my head would burst.

The inquest was held in the committee room, which lay between the men's ward and the women's. I was seated in the front row, facing the wide table at which sat the local coroner and Batleigh. As jurors, reporters and onlookers began to take the chairs behind me, I turned to see Adelia. I wanted to go to her, but hardly had the strength to sit up straight. She watched me with growing concern.

The Gentleman flickered as a dying flame. With him went the light around me. The world darkened. Shadows deepened. I struggled to breathe. On the other side of the wall to the women's ward, I could hear Mary cry in pain, followed by the muffled voices of the doctor and nurses.

Batleigh began the inquest. Only six jurors had been summoned, along with a court recorder.

My head rang like a noon church bell, thus I hardly heard the lanky, soft-spoken coroner describe the bodies found in the vicarage.

"Now it's your turn, Dr. Johnson," he said when finished.

"Souls, dear boy. *Souls.*"

In the shadows around me, a sulfuric fire grew. The wound in my side throbbed and bled. There came another cry through the wall from Mary. I willed myself to stand upright and reiterated the tale of the vicarage. When I came to the end, I also came to a decision.

"New information has come to light," I began. "You may wonder where Coombs came upon all those pieces of skin and bottles of blood to write the contracts. I tell you now that they came from none other than the head of Newgate Prison, Governor of the Gaol Robert Thornsbury!"

Now the room burst into cacophony.

"This is promising," said the Gentleman.

"In Thornsbury's desk you will find documents, in his hand, that describe all of his plans. Instructions to Coombs to blame the minister's wife for the Downing Street murders, the girl for the Marylebone massacre, and the banker for Battersea. This phase of the plan was to come to a head in Meavy Prior. All in service to his dark lord, to sow doubt among the good people of England and spread darkness where there should be light."

"Better, better, dear boy, but the warden is still not enough." The Gentleman came more fully into my range of vision as he greedily wrung his hands. "Thornsbury not only encouraged his guards to mistreat prisoners, he often liked to watch."

Mary's shriek of agony pierced through the walls. Fiery, pulsating pain radiated from my side. I bent over, stumbled, then held out my hands to ward off any who thought to help me. There was no help they could provide. There was only one course ahead for me.

"Even now," I continued, "as I speak these words before you all, these Hell-bound evildoers try to stop me. But I cannot let them win. I must reveal all."

In the windows, instead of reflections, I saw red demons tearing at naked victims, even as they danced. Shadows had been replaced by streams and rivulets of molten brimstone. I feared my side would split open.

"Who is it?" called Batleigh. "Who is doing this to you? Just speak the name and I will see justice done. Mark me."

"It is you." The words slipped from me, a snake released from a bag.

Batleigh stared at me, agape.

"I was a mere tool in your plans to sow misery and darkness. You used me to support Coombs, only to try and coerce me into naming another in your stead."

"Use you? I have been nothing but a friend to you."

His words hurt nearly as much as my reopened wound. "Then why, Superintendent Batleigh, do you have on your person, in your right pocket, a cloth doll resembling me, with a rusty nail thrust through its side?"

"Why, that's …" I recognized the expression that came over him as he felt the weight of an object that had not been present before. He looked in the pocket. "How … ?"

"How did I know?" I said, letting this dark and evil river take me, letting words keep the scream of sorrow and regret from escaping. "I observed. I recorded." Merely speaking became a Herculean effort. "What you see before you," I said, pointing at Batleigh, "is but a mask. A shroud hiding the true creature within. Have you ever seen the man remove his gloves? No! That is because they hide the crimson, bony claws of a demon!"

The room exploded in disbelief.

Batleigh held his hands out, staring at them as he winced in pain. His arms trembled. A horrified whine emerged from his throat. An agonized expression took his face.

I stepped up to him, pulled off one glove, then the other. Batleigh's hands were red and leathery, with bulging knuckles. Long, obsidian claws protruded from his fingertips. He fell to his knees with a scream.

Everyone in the room gasped nearly as one, and held its collective breath for the briefest moment. Then, chaos erupted.

"He believes," said the Gentleman, almost singing.

As Batleigh stared at his hands, light returned to me. The pain subsided. Mary quieted and I heard a nurse proclaim it a miracle.

Bobbies, barely willing to touch the weeping Batleigh, hauled him away. The coroner approached but stayed out of arm's length. He muttered thanks, then continued on his way.

Jurors, onlookers, and reporters gathered their wits and began to file out.

"Adelia!" I called, my hand out.

She looked my way, but her eyes were filled with fear and confusion. She shook her head, then hurried out.

The doctor approached me with even more trepidation than he had before. I pushed him aside and stumbled to the door to the woman's ward. A nurse entered just ahead of me. I held the door open. Nurses helped Mary to sit up while another gave her a glass of water.

Mary gulped the water, then paused to take heaving breaths. Her eyes landed on me, but they were unfocused, and I saw no recognition.

The doctor pulled me away as a nurse closed the door. He leaned down and peered at my side while a nurse sopped up the blood. They both gasped. The nurse put a hand to her mouth and stepped back. The wound was closed, the stitches gone. Only the scar remained.

The doctor straightened. "How?" was all he could manage before the two of them hurried away.

With chaos and misery spreading out around me, and only the Gentleman beside me, I realized that I had become a pawn of Hell.

CHAPTER FORTY
SHEDDING THE OLD, DONNING THE NEW

COOMBS' RESIDENCE LURKED IN THE EARLY morning fog, revealed by a single streetlamp. The suitcase I held weighed me to the spot despite it being, as I was, empty. Weighted, rooted, anchored, unable – no, unwilling – to mount the steps. To reenter the place that had become the garden of my madness. The fertile ground in which the seed of my childhood obsession had taken root and grown to bear bitter, poisonous fruit. A garden tended and nurtured by the entity beside me.

"It's yours now," said the Gentleman, ever at my shoulder. "The house, the money. The *work*."

The Gentleman's form was barely distinguishable from the mist. Only the outlines of him stood out, chiaroscuro sketches on a grey canvas. His eyes were ovals of smouldering charcoal. Malevolence exuded from his Cheshire grin.

"I do not want it. Any of it." What I intended as a bold statement came out as a plea.

"And yet ..." He swept his hand toward the house.

I wondered if the spirit of Coombs roamed its halls. I could no longer reject the existence of something incorporeal at the core of each human being. I would not succumb to fables masquerading as history, nor to the shallow promise of some perfect bliss in exchange for fealty. I needed no such balms to ease the acceptance of new and frightening ideas. I would take them as they were, as I perceived them, and examine them.

Such as this Gentleman, this being beside me. Was Coombs' spirit before me? His soul? Or was it still bound to his body, mutilated by my hand and now lying in an unmarked grave, also at my behest? There was but one way to find out. Though I accepted I had become like Coombs at the inquest, I did not have to remain as such. Desperation had pushed me toward a terrible action, one for which I would never forgive myself. However, it was done and could not be reversed. All that was left was to make what amends I could.

Becoming aware again of the carriage and its driver behind me, I mounted the steps. What of the Gentleman's nature? A better understanding could help answer many questions. Was he walking, or floating, behind me? Was he only visible when he spoke to me? At the front door, I turned as if to scan the street but did not see the Gentleman.

"I'm right here," he said, giving me a start. He spoke from just beyond the edge of my vision.

I went through the door and closed it quickly. No sign of the Gentleman. Was it possible he could not pass through closed doors? I knew that explicit instructions were required for him to ply his abilities. Could it be an invitation was needed to enter a building? And yet, he most assuredly had been present in this house previously. But now, as he said, it was mine. I made my way up the stairs, constantly turning, searching for him.

First, I went to my room and filled my suitcase with my belongings and remaining toiletries, then left it by the door. Back upstairs, I pushed into Coombs' room. Only the man's unmistakable musk remained. No sign of the Gentleman, either.

"Are you here?" Receiving only the creaking of the house in response, I moved towards the window.

"Perhaps I'm only in your mind."

A gasp leapt from me. My heart raced. Again, the Gentleman was just behind me. "Such tricks are not necessary," I told him.

"But they are fun."

His expression reminded me of medical school pranksters, with childish joy barely masking cruelty.

At the windows I pulled the shades wide. The fog was giving in to the sun, though distant clouds looked to avenge their brethren. The old, rippled glass panes twisted the dead trees that still glistened with dew. The muffled sounds of the waking city came to me, and I longed for the innocence of mundanity.

Turning away from the window, I found myself facing the Gentleman. The sunlight filling the room gave his form more definition. He was still primarily colourless, but the greyness of him seemed to possess some shading. His hair was dark, his skin light. His clothing – why does a demon need clothing? – was of a shade between the two. He wore a simple suit with a vest and ascot. As before, the details shifted as I looked. It seemed my very focus caused him to change. It was like trying to draw shapes on a puddle.

"Why do you let me see you sometimes, but hide at others?"

He smiled and it seemed more indulgent than dangerous. "The 'why' of my actions is not your concern, only the 'what'. And that 'what' is to harvest souls."

"Yes. You have made that very clear. Still, I have worldly business that requires my attention."

I stripped the sole pillow of its case, then lifted the trunk by a handle and dragged it from the room. I let it thump and jangle down the stairs, then pulled it into the sitting room before the fireplace. I threw open the lid, then took the penny bloods out one at a time, flipping through the pages of each one before tossing them on the cold logs.

"I assume these were Coombs' inspiration?" I asked the Gentleman.

"Partly. They certainly fed his imagination, but I pointed him at the souls I most desired. I would find him on his walks and give him ideas. He filled in the details."

Witch children, dancing skeletons, and ghoulish ministers adorned the covers, all thwarted by strong and virtuous detectives. "I see no vicars running Satanic cults," I said.

"No," said the Gentleman. "He was testing me, thanks in no small part to *you*. The accusation of the vicar he made up as he went. Absurd things he knew couldn't have existed before he said them, then a final test in the chapel."

"Where it failed, just as in Newington. Because you cannot enter churches."

The Gentleman applauded sarcastically. "Bravo. Seems there's a new detective in town."

The last of the garish books was titled, "The Demon and the Detective." The cover showed a man, large and darkly dressed, his arm outstretched. He pointed at a cowering, slender man. The ghostly image of a demon tore out of him. It screamed in agony.

A match struck on the stone of the fireplace, I held its flame under the corner of the penny blood, then flicked it out while the book pages curled and the fire grew. The flames consumed the demon-man and as they began to engulf the victorious detective – and came dangerously close to my hand – I set the book on the pile and watched as the other books caught. Smouldering bits of paper floated up the chimney. Soon the fire roared. Fingers of flame reached around the bricks as if to escape and feed on the wooden structure around it. It was tempting to let it do so.

Instead, I opened the flue fully, then pushed the books back with a poker, and let the heat bite the skin of my face. It caused me to sweat. Laughter trickled out of me.

"This is amusing to you?" asked the Gentleman.

"Perhaps I am preparing for my ultimate fate."

"You assume your fate will involve fire? Now *that* is amusing."

"But, during the inquest, when ..." I touched my side. "I saw flames and demons in the windows. Was I not seeing ... Hell?"

"You saw what you wanted to see. Because, as you recall, you do not believe in Hell. Or have you reconsidered that belief?"

Stepping back from the flames, I wiped the sweat from my forehead and peered at the Gentleman. "I still have not ruled out insanity."

The Gentleman gave a laugh, and I felt a chill deep within me. "Is Coombs' money next for the fire?"

"I may be insane, but I am not a fool." The pillowcase strained to hold all the bills and coins. I set it in the trunk and closed the lid. The deed to the house went into my pocket.

The penny bloods had burned quickly. I poked through the ashes to ensure the fire was out, then went to the door and called to the driver, who was brushing his horse's mane.

"I could use some assistance." I held out a five-pound note, the smallest denomination I had found in the trunk. He carried it while I took the suitcase.

"We will stop at a bank first," I told him as he held the door for me. "Then a solicitor's office."

As we rumbled along the streets, I contemplated how long I would be able to withstand the Gentleman's urgings.

⊷═◉═◉═⊷

With a flip of a shilling to young Dennis Burkett for carrying my bag and trunk, I was alone in a room at the Langford. Except, of course, for the Gentleman. He sat – if it can be said that an incorporeal being sits – in a wingback chair next to the two large windows that took up most of the room's northern wall. He gazed down at the alley below, as a tourist on their first London visit. Or perhaps a cat, having discovered a mischief of mice.

"Where shall we begin?" he asked with enthusiasm.

Sitting at the desk on the opposite side of the room, I chose not to respond. This was something to which I knew I must become accustomed: Conversations with a being imperceptible to the rest of the world. Instead of responding, I focused on my new ledger and recorded my recent deposit of well over three thousand pounds, even after wiring two hundred pounds to Peters. This would keep me in good stead for quite some time.

"I know you can hear me, dear boy."

Next, I filed away the papers wherein I had granted the deed to Coombs' residence, including the library and furniture, to be turned into a charity school named, on my insistence, the Silas Lee Jr. Blue Coat School.

"Do not ignore me." The Gentleman was at my ear, causing a start. "The more you do so, the more I will goad you."

"I saw no evidence of you goading Coombs in this way," I said over my shoulder.

"He didn't need it. He was happy, eager even, to do the work."

"But he did not comprehend the full nature of 'the work', did he?"

"He knew enough. What more do *you* need to know?"

I turned to face him. "I do not need to know anything more. I wish I knew considerably less. Rather, I need to tend to Mary." She had not been far from my thoughts while I dealt with my new situation. I would not *have* a situation – or even a life – if not for her. Mary's attack on Coombs in that moment, rash though it was, had prevented him from killing me immediately.

"Why? She has been restored. She is in hospital."

"Yes, but having no family and no situation, I fear for her."

"Then give her to me."

"Never." I slammed the ledger closed. The lengths to which I went to pay my debt to Coombs were nothing compared to what I would do for the young woman who had put her life in danger to save mine.

But the hour was late and the strength that had come to me after the inquest was fading rapidly. I was able to remain awake long enough for dinner, but soon after collapsed into my bed and fell asleep without even undressing.

CHAPTER FORTY-ONE

FATE OF THE FALLEN

I AWAKENED THE NEXT DAY WITH renewed strength, such that it pulled me out of bed with the morning light. I had not rested as well since my first night at Coombs' residence. My mood, however, was darkened upon seeing the Gentleman's happy disposition. This I found to be quite unnerving.

When I walked into the tearoom, every newspaper revealed what had made me so strong and the Gentleman so happy. I ripped a newspaper from the hands of an old man in order to read the story in full. I let Burkett handle the man's protests.

"Demon Man Hung!" the headline declared. Batleigh had been hanged at dawn at Newgate. Just as I would have been had Coombs not come to my rescue, if what my life had become could be considered any form of rescue. There were exaggerated sketches of Batleigh's hands. Some reported that he had grown horns.

Batleigh's body had been turned over to his wife, but the Catholic Church had refused to allow him to be buried in one of their cemeteries. Instead, he would be interred at a public cemetery in Newington.

I threw the paper down and rushed out of the room, staggering, my head spinning with revulsion.

In the alley, I pushed people aside until I reached the street and finally collapsed against a lamppost, my breath heaving as I fought the urge to vomit.

"You're not surprised, are you?" The Gentleman's voice was soft, almost caring. "What did you think his fate would be?"

I straightened up and turned to face him. He looked serene.

People on the sidewalk kept their distance.

"This is why you were so happy this morning, yes?" I whispered hoarsely.

His smile broadened. "And it is why you feel stronger. Mary certainly feels it as well."

"Mary." I took a breath and gathered myself. "Yes, I must attend to Mary. But there is something I must do first."

I hailed a cab and took it to the cemetery mentioned in the article.

As if mirroring my thoughts, the clouds had darkened to charcoal grey, making the cemetery nearly as dark as night, though it was midmorning. The cab waited for me at the graveyard's entrance while I strolled through, searching for Batleigh's grave.

"What do you hope to accomplish?" asked the Gentleman, walking beside me. "Only the meat that Batleigh inhabited is here. What you knew of him is with *us*."

I stifled a cry of pain. I did not want to believe in Hell. Much less that I had sent the soul of a good man there for my own benefit. I took shallow comfort in the idea that perhaps I was merely insane.

A pelting, freezing rain began, each drop thick and wet, but solid enough to sting. The drops passed through the Gentleman as if he was not there.

At the top of a hill, under a barren oak, I saw a small group of people gathered around a new grave. It had to be Batleigh's. I hurried as much as I dared in the slickening stone path, but then stopped some distance away. If the people getting in a hearse were Batleigh's family, did I really want to meet them?

Soon, only one person remained by the grave. A woman, it seemed, in a black overcoat with a hood tightened around her head. I approached slowly. Was this his wife? Would she know who I was? How could she not? Engravings of me had appeared in every newspaper that carried the story of the inquest. While the icy rain thudded off my top hat, I longed for a hood of my own to hide my identity. I took another step.

The woman's hood turned in my direction. I froze, as if in doing so I would disappear.

"Go to her," said the Gentleman. "Confess to her. Is that not why you are here? As if by confession you are absolved? You know how silly that is, don't you, dear boy?"

We stayed that way for a length of time I could not measure. I, frozen in fear and self-loathing. The woman's hood facing me, the shadow of it blotting out any sign of her face. The Gentleman, bouncing on his feet, grinning.

A voice from the hearse called. The woman turned, joined the others, and the hearse trundled off.

When it was out of my sight, I went to the grave. The coffin was still visible, as the rain thudded on the lid and washed away the soil that had been dropped in by the mourners. There was no headstone yet, and that somehow made me sadder. It seemed Batleigh had been erased from existence.

"It felt like a dream, a nightmare. Something that could not possibly be real."

I knelt on the cloth beside the grave, caring not that my knees were immediately wet and freezing.

"Are you a praying man now?" asked the Gentleman.

Was I? Is that where recent events had brought me? No. I could not beg mercy of an entity so capricious and arbitrary as to have allowed such things to occur. Even if such a being existed, why would I ask anything of it? And yet I felt compelled to continue kneeling there.

"Pardon sir," said a gravelly voice.

I looked up to find two gravediggers with shovels standing by the mound of dirt on the opposite side of the grave.

"Work to do," one of them said.

I kept my head down as I hurried away, hoping I would not be recognized.

I hurried back to the cab and asked to be taken to the Langford. I was wet and dirty. There were amends I could make in this world, and I found more comfort in that than in prayer. But I would need a change of clothes first.

CHAPTER FORTY-TWO

A RESCUE OF MY OWN

AFTER CHANGING, I FOUND BURKETT AT the wooden counter in the cramped space between dining rooms that served as a lobby. He wore a top hat on his balding head and a tuxedo jacket that was too small for his stocky frame. Apparently this attire was intended for greeting new guests.

I waited until a young man in a black and grey three-piece suit completed his business, then stepped up to the desk. "I should like to engage a room in the women's side," I told him.

Burkett blinked at me, his mouth slightly agape.

"Not for myself. This would be in addition to the room I currently have. It would be for the young lady –"

This seemed to lighten his mood a touch. "The girl? The one from the vicarage?"

"Why, yes. You know of her? And she's hardly a 'girl'."

Burkett shrugged. "Papers said girl. But yes, I have a room for her."

"I should also like to engage the services of Mrs. Burkett as chaperone."

"The missus has her duties here. Can't spare her."

I held out five pounds.

He frowned at it.

I added five more.

He snatched it from my hand, then looked down at the floor beside him. "Fetch your mother."

A girl of perhaps eight years popped out from behind the counter and dashed into one of the dining rooms. Her long, braided ponytail, yellow as a daffodil, whipped side-to-side like a mad pendulum.

"Be here in a nonce, Doctor," said Burkett.

Within moments the girl pulled along by her apron a woman shorter and more thickly built than Burkett. Though she sported a good deal of grey, it was clear where the Burkett girls got their colouring. An admonition on her freckled face became a smile when Burkett showed her the bills. "He needs a chaperone," Burkett said. He leaned close to her and whispered. "Bringing the girl from the vicarage here, he is."

Her expression changed to what one would expect at a circus. "Ooohh, Well, then. You got yourself a chaperone, Doctor."

"Excellent," I said. "I shall return with Miss Woodmore by tomorrow evening. I suspect she will be in need of clothing and other such womanly accoutrements, and I should like you to accompany her, Mrs. Burkett."

"Ooohh, shopping now, is it? Sounds like I've got a time ahead of me."

"Indeed," I said.

Back in the alley, I felt buoyed by my decisions and looked forward to taking care of Mary. "Say nothing, if you please." I said over my left shoulder, where I imagined the Gentleman was waiting to take the light out of my mood. "I know what you want, and you will have it soon enough."

To the driver who was again comforting his horse, I said, "Only one more stop. Paddington station."

He seemed relieved, and the horse took a fast trot to the station. Together, they let no obstacle delay us, and even took to the opposite side of the road when necessary. At the station I thanked him and tipped him well.

In order to free Mary from the clutches of the sweaty doctor – who thought she would make an excellent laundry girl – I had to pose as her uncle. That, and overpay the bill.

"This way," I said, and led Mary to the waiting carriage, a gold-trimmed brougham. It was nearly as well kept as Peters' had been. The driver held the door open for us. With an embarrassed laugh, Mary took the driver's offered hand and stepped up into the carriage. I took the seat across from her.

Mary gazed about the carriage as it rumbled into motion, taking it all in. She set her hands on her seat and gently brushed the velvet surface.

"Do you like it?" I asked.

"Yes. Thank you." She withdrew her hands to her lap. "Where are you taking me?"

"First, we are going to the train station. We will spend a good portion of the day on the train and arrive in London in time for dinner. I have taken up temporary residence at an inn and have made arrangements to provide you with your own room."

She nodded absently. "What about my things? And my father's. Sister Ellen's …"

"The Tavistock Police informed me that the church has taken possession of the property. At the station I will wire the police and request – no, demand – that the church return any personal belongings."

Another nod. "This is all so strange." She peered out the window, watching the streets of Tavistock go by. "I have never been on a train. Well, not that I remember."

"They are quite safe, I can assure you."

"Yes. Father said we arrived by one when I was a baby, from his old parish in Wales. Someone once told me that the fumes killed Mother, but I never believed that." She leaned forward suddenly, her face in her hands and elbows on her knees.

"Are you all right, Mary?"

"No, I'm not all right. I've lost *everything*. Every single thing I knew. And now I'm … I'm floating along in this." She waved her hands in an expansive gesture. "Soon a train will pull me along …" She looked towards me but did not meet my eyes. "Have you ever thrown leaves in a river? Then watched them drift away? That is me." She withdrew into herself again.

"I apologize if I have been presumptuous," I said. "But I did not want to just leave you."

"I'm not ungrateful for what you've done, please know that. I'm just … I will have to see where the river takes me." Another shake of her head and a deep breath. "A train? An *inn*? Goodness. I've never been to an inn. What job will I do there? I'd rather not do laundry. I hate laundry. But I'd be happy to work in the kitchen."

"Not necessary. I have paid for your room. It is, after all, the least I could do. And I have engaged a chaperone so as to maintain appearances. She will take you shopping. Clearly you are in need of clothing and the like," I said with a gesture to her hospital dress.

Mary looked down and gingerly touched it. "Yes."

"Let me assure you that this in no way obligates you. There are no expectations or requirements. I am merely trying to help you in whatever way I can to start your new life."

She nodded, but remained withdrawn. "A new life," she whispered.

"After what happened, I –"

"Please don't."

A difficult silence settled over us.

"But what will I *do*?" Mary asked after a time, turning back to me.

I had not thought that far ahead. I looked at her expectant, worried eyes. "For now, you will rest. In time, you will decide what it is you would *like* to do. Is that acceptable?"

"I …" She looked at her wringing hands. "'What I would like to do.' I suppose. Yes. Certainly." She turned to me. "Why are you doing this?" she asked suddenly.

"I am in a position to help you and I should like to do so, after –"

"*Please*, I ... I don't want to ... I fear I may end up back in that doctor's care."

"That will never happen, Mary."

"And that is all you want? To help me?"

The image I had of her in that moment when I begged for help came back to me. Again, I saw myself holding her, caring for her. And I wanted it to become real.

"Yes, I promise you," I said.

But I did not know what *she* wanted. And I was not the sort who wanted a woman's affection because of coercion or dominance. I had witnessed the brittle, reluctant affection that Mother displayed for Father, and wanted none of that.

"Thank you," Mary said with a slight smile. "But I insist on working. On *doing* something."

"Of course. Once you have settled, we – you – can begin to make inquiries."

She gave a mere nod in response and Mary rode the rest of the way to the station in wide-eyed wonder. She explored the cars, talked to the conductors, and even conversed with those passengers who were not off put by her energetic impropriety. Underlying it, I sensed a need to keep busy, to keep moving, so as not to stop and think, to remember.

I spent the day's ride in my seat, struggling to remain silent against the Gentleman's nagging. I did not see him on the train. At first that seemed a minor respite. But having a voice in my ear with no figure to focus on was simply maddening.

CHAPTER FORTY-THREE

BRIEF RESPITE

MARY AND I ALIGHTED THE CARRIAGE at the entrance of the alley that led to the Langford. I let her take her time as she slowly spun, gazing at the buildings around us. A pair of boys who had been milling about offered to help with the bags and gleefully accepted a half crown each. Whether or not they were Burkett boys I could not tell. When the carriage pulled away and revealed the rest of the street, I would have thought it to be a bit dreary, with its mud and plain buildings, but it did nothing to diminish Mary's wonder.

"Come, Miss Woodmore," I said, then whispered to her, "We should be more formal here."

She nodded agreement and let me lead her into the alley towards the Langford.

"The gallery up there leads to all the bedrooms," I said, indicating the second floor.

"Will I be in one of those?"

"No, the women's rooms are on the other side. This is one of the dining rooms," I pointed out as we passed the windows. "Then the tap room, and on the other side of the entrance, there's a tearoom and another dining room."

"Two dining rooms. The kitchen must be *huge.*"

I suppressed my laughter lest she think it derisive, when in fact it came from pure joy. "I admit I have never seen it."

"Can we see it now?" Mary asked eagerly.

Mrs. Burkett emerged from the central door. "This is the young Miss Woodmore then?" she asked.

"Indeed it is," I said. "Mary Woodmore, meet Mrs. Burkett."

"I'll show you to your room, child," said Mrs. Burkett. "In the morning, I'll take you shopping."

Mary stepped forward. "What about the kitchen? Can I see the kitchen?"

Surprised, Mrs. Burkett looked at us both.

"I'd like to help, if I may," said Mary.

Mrs. Burkett gave a tilt of her head. "I always need help."

"Then let me. I like kitchen work. Really, I do."

"All right, then," she said, turning back to the door. "*Joanna.*" The girl who had served us at Coombs' residence scurried out. "This is Miss Woodmore."

"Mary, ma'am. Please call me Mary."

"Mary it is then. Joanna, take Mary into the kitchen. I'll be in momentarily."

"Yes, mum." Joanna bowed slightly and led Mary inside.

Mrs. Burkett approached me. "If she's a help, she stays. If not, she goes."

"Of course, Mrs. Burkett. But I have seen her work and I believe you will be impressed."

"We'll see about that. And we'll do our shopping after dinner is served."

Mrs. Burkett hurried inside, and I found myself standing alone in the alley. I had hoped to spend more time with Mary, perhaps show her more of London.

"Unsure what to do next?" asked the Gentleman.

The evening air was crisp as a fresh apple. "I shall go for a stroll."

The Gentleman walked beside me with his arms behind his back. I dismissed thoughts of his physicality or lack of it as a distraction, wondering if he could read my mind. As a test, I stared at him and thought to myself, *I intend to find a way to send you back to Hell, alone.*

The Gentleman's expression remained calm, open. "There is no escaping me, you realize."

It was impossible to determine whether what he said was in response to my thought. A church bell rang. Memories of Coombs' failures in Newington and the chapel came to me, and I turned towards the sound. The church was on a nearby corner. It was a simple building of red bricks and pale granite, its steeple pierced the sky.

"So you say," I told him, then dashed past a trotting carriage horse and continued to the church.

"*Stop!*" The Gentleman's voice burned in my mind.

"Do not go in there." He stood before me now. The church's steps were mere feet away.

I pushed through him but felt nothing more than if I had walked through a puff of mist.

The Gentleman moved towards me, then recoiled as if from a bright, hot fire.

"It seems there is an escape," I called out, ignoring the various passersby.

"You will have to come out. When you do, you will pay."

Taking the rest of the steps two at a time, I pulled open the heavy wooden door and entered.

The place was dark, the pews empty. There was a silence in my mind that nearly made me weep with relief. I went to the nearest pew, sat and wiped my eyes.

A minister came to me and offered his assistance, but I brushed him off. I only wanted to think.

If the Gentleman were a medical condition, then surgery would be warranted. He should be excised from my being. Excised. Exorcised. The word came to me, and I considered calling the minister back. But no, if I were to continue to think of this as a treatable condition, then I would need to avoid all the religious trappings and get at the core of the ritual. Perhaps it was best to think of the Gentleman as a parasite. I had recklessly entered an unfamiliar environment and a creature from it had attached itself to me. Just as a hammer would be ineffective against a tick, I would need to find the proper method to remove the Gentleman from me.

But first, I would need to deal with the consequences of having entered this place. He would be angry, intent on punishing me. There was only one way I could think of that would mollify him: feed him an innocent. And it would need to be more than a promise. I would have to prepare myself to do it immediately, and hopefully avoid his wrath.

Could I sacrifice a stranger? No, I needed to give the Gentleman specifics: a name. I thought of the people I knew, those whose names were at my disposal. Adelia was out of the question. A member of the Burkett family, perhaps? I even considered obtaining the name of the minister who hovered around the altar, eyeing me.

Then, what I was considering became clear to me: victimizing innocents to avoid the consequences of my own actions. Even worse than the common desire to beg to be absolved of them, I would be making others pay my own debt. No. I would endure the Gentleman's punishment. I would find a way to do "the work" to keep myself and Mary alive, but nothing short of that would coerce me into using this new-found power.

I stood, catching the minister's attention. Ignoring his call to me, I exited the church.

The Gentleman awaited me where I had left him. I strode up to him and said, "Do what you will." I desired to tell him that I believed he held no real power over me, and that I planned to find a way to rid myself of him. But it seemed foolish to say so, the kind of thing a hero in a poorly written fiction would say.

The Gentleman's smile was amiable, that of a headmaster who had decided to try kindness even as he held a switch at the ready. "Do you believe that any of what has occurred was *not* my will?" His smile spread as a chuckle bubbled up and he was soon doubled over with laughter.

CHAPTER FORTY-FOUR

TURNING TIDES

"WHAT ABOUT ONE OF THEM?" THE Gentleman's sudden question startled me, causing a little spill of my tea. After a morning of headaches and useless pills, I had come downstairs to the tearoom to read a book on the physiology and pathology of the mind. Raucous young men sat by the fireplace, laughing at things at which only young men laugh. I knew their type all too well, their nature having come into sharp focus when I lost the privilege they took for granted. Their laughter was filled with derision and seemed to be directed at the staff they had just dismissed.

I had almost blocked out their noise when the Gentleman brought my attention back to them. The chair to my left had not been pulled out for seating, and yet he sat. Part of the round table passed through his body, but he took no notice of it.

With my hand over my mouth I said, "You know I cannot carry on a conversation at the moment."

"You *can*, but I do not require responses. You think I am a problem to solve, yes? That perhaps my presence is a condition which can be cured, a tumor excised. I assure you I am not. There is no escaping me, your duty, or your fate."

Commotion at the door provided a welcome distraction and a voice I feared I would never hear again came through the door. It was Adelia.

"I am here strictly on journalistic business."

I had wired to let her know I was living at the Langford, and to express my sorrow that she had witnessed my exposure of Batleigh's true nature. It was ugly business, I said truthfully, and I would rather she had not seen me in the depths of it. A warmth filled me as I stood and called to her.

Adelia was followed by a flustered Burkett. I wondered if he noticed the black pant legs just beyond the reach of her green dress.

"But the *women's* tearoom –" he insisted.

"I am a reporter and, I say *again*, I am here on *business*."

"Let her pass, Mr. Burkett," I said, "if you would be so kind."

"Very well, but I am not pleased."

The urge to ask if he was ever pleased passed, and instead I thanked him for his understanding, adding an order of tea and crackers.

The young men went silent and eyed Adelia as she crossed to me. Elbows and whispers passed between them.

I pulled out the chair across from mine, leaving the Gentleman to sit between us. "Please forgive Mr. Burkett," I said as she sat. "The *older* generation can be so stubborn at times." I cast my words to the young men, who turned away quickly.

"It is good to see you," I said. "I thought I might not."

"My apologies for the way I left. It was all so … overwhelming. It reminded me of Coombs' inquests, with that underlying feeling of darkness. As if some light had been subtracted from the world."

My breath caught.

She leaned forward, concerned. "But I know that wasn't *you*. It was the nature of what you exposed. Coombs and his evil cult." She shook her head. "Horrible stuff, and I'm so glad you fought your way out of it."

"Thank you."

The Gentleman scoffed. "'Fought your way out'? You did nothing. You lay there like a fish in a bucket."

I struggled to keep my expression calm.

"And I can see it still bothers you," said Adelia. "We needn't talk about it any longer."

I nodded my thanks.

Adelia presented a newspaper, though not her own. "There's an account of you that you should read."

"Thank you, but I know all I need to about what happened."

"You really should read this," she insisted as the tea and crackers arrived.

The London Tea Tattler sported an engraving of me that filled the front page. Emblazoned in an arc above my head was a question: "How did he know?" On the sides and corners of the page were titles of articles that suggested I had more knowledge – firsthand knowledge – of the evil goings on of late. One even hinted that I was the true leader and had betrayed my fellow conspirators. All of these things were couched as mere "questions".

"Oh dear," said the Gentleman.

I folded it, more forcefully than necessary and handed it back to her. "I care not for the rantings of such trash."

She finished a bite of a cracker and took the paper back. "You should. It may only be in a penny paper today, but these things have a way of growing and appearing in other papers. Not mine, of course."

"I find it hard to believe *any* paper would publish such drivel. I should sue them for libel."

"Perhaps. You'll notice, however, that the paper never says you *are* these things. It only posits the questions."

"But in a way that implies the answers."

"Of course. I know the publisher. He is very good at not losing libel cases."

"Punish the bad man," said the Gentleman. "He said mean things about you."

I waved him away. Adelia seemed to take it as dismissing her statement.

"But if you were to sue him," she said, "you would have to testify in court regarding the events at the vicarage."

"What are you implying?"

"Nothing at all. Only that … there are legitimate questions. Ones you have not answered. Not publicly."

"Such as?"

"The principal one being, how did you survive?"

I dipped a cracker so as not to look her in the eyes. "I killed Coombs."

Adelia leaned forward and spoke in a hush. "Please do not misunderstand me. I am very glad you survived. It must have been horrible. And I know that, under extreme circumstances, people can find the capacity to perform feats they might not be capable of otherwise."

Now I looked directly at her. "You do not believe that I could defeat Coombs."

The Gentleman leaned in as well. "And you did *not*, if you recall, dear boy. Not without my help."

Adelia reached for my hand, thought better of it, and leaned back. "I believe that you did, since you are alive, and he is not." She took a breath. "But I met him. I saw how he moves. *Moved.* And knowing what he did as Silas Lee, and…"

"Knowing *me*," I finished for her, with sharpness in my voice.

The Gentleman tsked. "You aren't going to tell her about me, are you? Oh, perfidy!"

"Please know that I'm not trying to diminish or belittle you," Adelia said. "Even putting that question aside, since clearly you *were* the victor, there are so many questions regarding your activities leading up to that day. You spent all that time with Coombs, who, we come to find out, was in some sort of cult with all of those others. There are those who believe you were doing more than gathering information."

"Adelia. You *know* me." It was as much a plea as a statement. I *hoped* she knew me, for I barely knew myself.

"I believe I do, yes. I have a sense of you. That perhaps you are caught up in larger things. Things beyond your control. That you are largely innocent."

"'Largely'?" My heart sank. She could sense something was wrong, but the truth was too deep a chasm.

"*Tell your story,*" Adelia said. "Tell it all. Tell it to *me*. I will corroborate everything you tell me. Your case will be unassailable." It seemed she wanted the measure of the chasm, but only because she knew not what lay at the bottom. I would not be the one to tell her.

"My case …"

"You are a logical man. Take a step back. Look at the situation from the outside, so to speak. Surely you can see that any reasonable person would have questions."

I stared at my tea for a time. She was right, of course. But how could I possibly answer such questions? Any explanation involving the truth would be seen as madness and, lacking said truth, inadequate. Adelia waited for my response.

"These have been … trying times," I said. "Confusing, to put it mildly. Give me time. A day, perhaps, to gather my thoughts. Put things in order."

"Concoct a fiction?" asked the Gentleman, seemingly reading my thoughts.

Adelia nodded. "As I said, I will corroborate everything I possibly can."

"Of course. I would expect nothing less."

"Thank you." Adelia stood. "I will take my leave now, Mr. Burkett," she announced.

Burkett, hovering at the door, made a grand gesture for her exit.

"You know," said the Gentleman, "*she* would make a grand feast."

"*No.*"

Burkett and Adelia stopped and turned to me. Even the young men turned my way.

"No," I stammered, "Miss Clavijo should *not* leave. Not like that. I should escort her to her carriage."

"Fine," said Burkett. "Go ahead."

The Gentleman moved to my side as I approached Adelia. "Oh, you don't want to feed her to me, do you?"

"Escort me?" said Adelia. "Not necessary, but welcome."

"You *like* this one. And what of Mary? You can't make up your mind, can you?"

I shook my head as we moved into the small lobby.

"Is something wrong, Dr. Johnson?" she asked.

"No, Miss Clavijo. I am shaking my head at Mr. Burkett's scowling. I find it amusing."

Arms crossed, Burkett's scowl deepened as he leaned back against the counter.

"I see." She put her arm in mine. "You are very tense."

"Apologies, Miss Clavijo," I said. "It has been a trying day."

At the door, she paused. "Are you sure you're all right? Is there something you want to tell me?"

"Tell her she's doomed," said the Gentleman. "Tell her she's *mine.*"

"*No.*"

She recoiled from my sharpness.

"Pardon. I am just ... this gossip business is perhaps bothering me more than I care to admit."

"Perhaps it is," Adelia said. "When you are ready to talk, send for me."

"I will. I promise."

"Yes," said the Gentleman. "Send for her. That way you can watch me take her."

I clenched my jaw and covered it with a smile until we passed under the arch at the alley's entrance, and I saw her into her carriage.

Back in the alley, there were smokers lingering about the Langford's entrance and coachmen at the end. I marched back into the street. "You *must* stop doing that," I hissed at the Gentleman when we were free of witnesses.

"I will," said the Gentleman, "when you give me her soul."

"Never." The idea of sacrificing Adelia tore through my mind. Was that the only path before me? To save myself and Mary, I would have to send Adelia to Hell?

"Hmm ... I sense a power struggle coming on. I cannot afford to let you think you have any. No, I'm afraid I'm going to have to insist on you giving me the lovely Miss Clavijo's soul."

"Under no circum –" I stopped speaking when I nearly collided with an older couple. After apologies, I continued down the street.

"You see, the more you resist, the more I feel I must assert myself."

I moved to the edge of the sidewalk and put out a hand to a lamppost to remain upright. An omnibus filled with labourers and bootblacks hanging off the side pulled to a stop before me. A few desultory passengers piled in, pushed past me, shoving themselves between those already clinging there. A street urchin asked me if I needed help, his hand out. I shook my head. He uttered an oath that no child should know and jumped back onto the bus. The driver whipped his horses, shouted at them, and they strained to pull the overloaded bus to the next stop.

"Is it class that gives you pause?" asked the Gentleman. "Status? I could settle for an earthy stew such as they would make."

Hands pressed to my head, I begged him to stop.

"Did you not see the despair in those people? The emptiness? You would be doing any one of them a great service, ending their miserable lives."

"By sending them to *actual* Hell?"

"A minor detail."

"I will not give you Adelia's soul, not in exchange for my own life."

"Not even Mary's?"

I fell back against the lamppost. "I cannot make that choice."

"Oh, this is *delicious.* I was skeptical at first, thinking she would be a distraction. But the way you torment yourself over her is truly precious."

I continued walking, without regard for my destination, unable to focus. The Gentleman would find a way to force me to make an impossible choice. He was uncharacteristically quiet, but his constant presence at the edge of my vision was even more unnerving, for it forced me to turn the conflict over in my mind. Sacrificing Adelia for Mary was an impossible choice, and yet, by doing nothing, was I not making a choice?

"I must say, however, that I do not understand all this angst," said the Gentleman. "If, as you have previously stated, Hell does not exist, then what horrors are you unleashing? You'd be tarnishing her reputation, but once she's dead, that would hardly matter to her."

I walked onto a bridge where I could lean on the rail and talk to the Thames. Or perhaps let it take me.

"You do not receive a soul until the person dies, is that correct?" I asked.

By all appearances, the Gentleman casually leaned back against the railing, propping his elbows on it. "If I tell you, will you get to work, or will you use the information against me?"

"If you do not, I will leap over this railing," I said, staring at him.

He held my gaze for a moment. "There are degrees. When a victim believes the new reality, such as when your friend Batleigh believed what you said about him and saw his own hands – quite clever, by the way."

"Continue with the explanation, please."

"Certainly. A moment like that is, shall we say, an *hors d'ouerves.* When said victim dies, that is the meal, the sustenance. That is the work."

"I cannot undo what I did to him, can I?"

"No, dear boy, you cannot."

"And yet, Coombs' work was reversed."

"When he died, yes."

"Then if I were to jump this rail, my words would be reversed?"

"That is correct. But I still haven't made up my mind if I would make you torture Mary, or vice versa." He snapped his fingers. "You could take turns!" he said excitedly.

I sagged against the railing, my will to merely stay upright escaping me. What if there was no Hell after all? What if his threats of Mary's and my fates amounted to nothing? Was I willing to risk an eternity of torture on that notion? I was not.

"Wait," I said. "You claim that if I die, you will return to Hell with me."

"And take out my frustrations with you until the end of time, yes."

"Then why did you not return to Hell with Coombs?"

"Because, in case you've forgotten, dear boy, I had already been burdened with *you*. Otherwise, he would have survived, and I would be happily feasting on innocent souls."

Was that the triggering event that had reversed Coombs' work? Rather than his death, had it been the Gentleman's transfer to me?

"Come, come, come," said the Gentleman. "Enough of this wallowing."

"Back to the work," I finished for him.

There were degrees, he had said. Getting someone to believe the fiction created for them would give him life, and thus, to Mary and me. Recalling the weakness I had suffered earlier, could I stave off his demand for Adelia's soul by merely getting her to believe?

I pounded the railing with my fists, causing it to ring and my hands to throb. How could I even entertain such thoughts?

I marched off the bridge, with no direction or destination, trying to shut out the Gentleman's voice.

CHAPTER FORTY-FIVE

MISGUIDED OVERTURE

I FOUND MYSELF IN THE ALLEY behind the Langford. One of Burkett's sons stepped out and dumped a bucket of grey water, nearly soaking my feet.

"So sorry, sir. My apologies, sir."

"Not to worry. There was no reason to expect someone would be wandering back here. You are Mr. Burkett's son, yes?"

"Yes, sir, I am. Dennis, by name, sir." He tipped his cap. "And you're ..."

"Dr. Johnson."

He was ready to go back in but hesitated out of politeness.

"Young Miss Woodmore," I said. "Is she still working in the kitchen? How is she doing?"

"Young Miss ... oh, *Mary.* Yes sir, she is working. Well, I must return to my own work, sir." He opened the door.

"Is she doing well? Fitting in?"

"See for yourself." He pulled the door open fully and stepped aside.

"Oh, dear boy, stop wasting time," said the Gentleman.

I ignored the Gentleman and stepped into the kitchen. Mrs. Burkett oversaw a flurry of activity. She barked at Dennis for having taken so long, then turned to me. "And what may I help you with, Doctor?"

Mary was completely focused on the carcass on the butcher's table before her. Joanna, at the opposite corner of the table, deftly sliced thick carrots. They laughed as they worked, but about what I could not tell.

"Doctor?" Mrs. Burkett's increased volume drew the attention of everyone in the kitchen.

"Just wondering how Miss Woodmore's doing."

Mary looked at me and waved, smiling.

"As you can see, Doctor, she is doing fine. We all are. And we'd like to continue to do so if you don't mind."

"Of course, of course. Sorry to disturb you." It warmed my heart to see Mary so comfortable. "Miss Woodmore, say hello to Nigel for me, would you?" I felt a rare smile.

Mary went still, ashen. She looked at the cleaver in her hand, then set it down carefully. She held the edge of the butcher's table.

"Mary?" asked Joanna. "Are you all right?"

Mary drew herself up. "Mrs. Burkett, I need to step away." With that, Mary walked around a screen and out of sight. Joanna followed her.

Mrs. Burkett let out a heavy sigh. "Unless you'd like to take over for her, Doctor, I'd appreciate it if you would leave my kitchen."

I apologized and scurried back out into the alley.

When I sat down for dinner, Joanna came to take my order. I asked after Mary, and she hurried back into the kitchen. A moment later, Mary came out, her expression hard. Burkett's daughter lingered just behind her. Mary's expression hit me as if I lay on the butcher's block. I regretted asking for her, yet I longed to see her.

"May I take your order, sir?" Mary asked impatiently. Her eyes would not come to rest on me.

"No, Mary. I do not want you to take my order, I want you to have dinner with me." I gestured to the chair opposite me.

"Dinner? With you? Are you courting me?" She took a step back.

"Courting?" My face felt hot. "No, I am merely concerned about you. I should like to talk with you, see how you are faring."

"I'm faring fine." There was a finality to her tone, as if she wished to end the conversation. Had I lost her?

"Please, Mary. Sit. Have dinner." I was practically begging. It was embarrassing, but I could not help myself.

"It wouldn't be appropriate, would it? I should get back to work."

Mary turned away, but Joanna stopped her. They whispered a conversation, with gestures and glances in my direction. Joanna told Mary something to which she reluctantly agreed.

"I'll speak to Mother, and she'll speak to Father," Joanna said to us both before hurrying into the kitchen.

"I see you have become friends with Mr. Burkett's daughter," I said as Joanna hurried to the kitchen. I stood to pull out Mary's chair, but she held out a hand to stop me.

"Yes. We get along quite well."

"That is wonderful. Glad to hear it."

Mary gave a slight nod.

Joanna stuck her head out the door. "Mother said you can have one minute."

With casual conversation out of the question, I went directly to the question on my mind. "Are you angry with me?"

She considered that for a moment. "I didn't like what you said."

"About …" Seeing her tense, I did not repeat the name of the sheep's head. "I apologize. That was not my intention. It warmed my heart to see you so happy today."

Her eyes shot up to meet mine briefly. Her expression lightened. "Thank you."

Mary then told me a little about her duties in the kitchen. When Joanna came to the kitchen door and whispered her name, Mary thanked me, and we said our goodnights.

⊰══◐ ◑══⊱

Returning from a walk the next day, I found two of Burkett's sons carrying a trunk into the lobby. I followed them in, and Burkett approached me. "It's yours," he said. "This came with it," said Burkett as he handed me a note from the Tavistock Police. "Woodmore's personal belongings," was all it said.

The Gentleman recoiled from the trunk, as if from an open sewer. "Get rid of it."

"This trunk is not mine," I said. "It belongs to Mary."

Burkett summoned her from the kitchen.

"Your belongings, Miss Woodmore," I said with a grand gesture.

She reached down to the trunk and touched it gently. Realizing that all eyes were on her, she straightened up. "Can someone help me take it to my room?"

"Go ahead, girl, but hurry, or the Missus will tan us both. Boys, give her a hand."

Mary pulled out a key that was tied around her neck and hurried to the stairs.

As the Burkett boys lifted the trunk, the elder one muttered a comment about finally getting into Mary's room.

"You hush, there, Dennis," said Burkett. "Her beau's right here. Don't pay him no mind, sir. *Doctor.* He's just a boy headed for the mills, he doesn't watch his mouth," Burkett called after his son.

"Mr. Burkett," I said, flustered, my face hot. "I am not Miss Woodmore's 'beau'."

He looked at me quizzically. "Why not?" he asked, then moved off to help a patron.

I stood there for a moment, pondering the question.

"You might as well," said the Gentleman. "Perhaps you'll focus on the work more if you're not pining after her like a schoolboy at a burlesque."

The work. I listened to Mary and the Burkett boys' footsteps reach the top of the switchback staircase and continue down the hall to the women's section. How could I possibly consider courting that young woman, knowing what my future held? But knowing how intertwined our futures were, how could I not? I retreated to my room for another fitful night attempting to ignore the Gentleman and sleep.

CHAPTER FORTY-SIX

LASHING OUT

POUNDING. HAMMER BLOWS. CRUSHING ME. "DOCTOR." A prison guard's cudgel, Keat's foot, driving me down. "Doctor." The arc of a cleaver wielded by Coombs, rending me. *Dr. Johnson!*

Bursting from my dreams, I wrestled free of my blankets. Early morning light limned the curtains. A bedpost held me upright. A healthy dose of laudanum the night before had resulted in a sleep akin to unconsciousness.

"Miss me?" asked the Gentleman in what had become his usual place in my room, sitting in the chair by the windows.

"No."

Again, the pounding, and I realized it was on my door. "Dr. Johnson? Are you all right?"

"Mary?"

"It's Joanna, sir. Mary's being arrested."

"A moment, please." I pushed away from the bedpost, fumbled on my robe and pulled open the door.

Joanna stood there, wringing her hands, her wet eyes pleading. "You must come, sir."

I hurried along behind her. "Mary arrested? Whatever for?"

"Fightin'," said Joanna as we took the stairs. "She's been off since that trunk come in. Then Dennis went and did something stupid."

At the kitchen, she held the door open and let me enter first.

Burkett's eldest was in the corner and held a piece of raw meat to his eye and cheek. Mrs. Burkett hovered near him. A constable and a bobby stood on either side of Mary. She sat on a stool with her arms folded. Their conversation stopped as I entered, and they all turned to me.

"Mary," I said, "what happened?"

The constable started to respond but I politely stopped him so I could hear Mary tell it.

"Me and Joanna went to market. People said things."

"*Mean* things," said Joanna, moving to Mary's side.

Mrs. Burkett hushed her.

"When we got back," Mary continued, "Dennis made a face."

"With his fingers for horns," Joanna added. "And waggled his tongue."

"So I hit him," said Mary.

"I was *funnin'*," Dennis interjected.

Mrs. Burkett slapped him.

"Ma!"

"Get another piece of meat for it," she told him. She moved closer to Mary. "Girl, I'm sorry he did that. I thought I taught him better, but I guess he's got a lesson or two comin'."

Dennis groaned.

"Officers," Mrs. Burkett continued. "There's no need for gaol. The young miss been through a lot and my boy deserved what he got. I'll talk to Mr. Burkett. There won't be no charges."

"Why would you *do* that?" I barked at Dennis. Could he also sense the Gentleman? Could everyone?

"I was funnin'." His cockiness was gone.

"But why devil horns?" I demanded.

He looked at the floor, contrite. Everyone else held still.

"I don't know," he said with a shameful shrug. "The stuff in the papers, I guess."

"When did this idea come to you?"

"Dr. Johnson," said the constable, "the matter is settled."

"No," I told him. "I need to know." Was it the Gentleman's doing? I turned to Dennis. "When did you decide to do this?"

He seemed genuinely frightened. Mrs. Burkett's anger shifted to me, but propriety held her tongue.

"Just there, then. Right when people were saying stuff."

"What people? What 'stuff'?"

"*Doctor.*" The constable stepped in front of me. "That's enough. This isn't a case for you to solve. People can be cruel and boys can be stupid. Be done with it."

I stepped back and took a long, calming breath. "My apologies. I feel responsible for Mary's – Miss Woodmore's – situation." I apologized profusely and went to my room.

"I can see you are conflicted," said the Gentleman. "Let me make this simple for you. Lose the young lady and get on with the work."

"I will do no such thing," I said as I sat at my desk.

"Do not forget your place." The Gentleman came to stand over me. "Nor your job. Speaking of which, what is the plan, hm? More covens? Effective, but I admit no small amount of offense that all the evils of the world are put upon us."

"'All the evils … '? Upon whom else *would* we put evil?"

He gestured expansively. "Yourselves, of course. As I've explained, I have never made anyone do anything they did not already *want* to do. I merely help them overcome their fears, their inhibitions."

"The more you speak, the less I am inclined to do your bidding." I turned away and opened my ledger, futilely attempting to end the conversation.

"Are you growing tired, dear boy?" The Gentleman moved beside me and put his hands together, an expression of mock pity on his face. "A shame, but irrelevant. The work must be *done*." He moved to gaze out the window.

Frustrated, I pushed away from the desk and stood. "Must it? Oh, yes, I recall what you have said, that Mary and I will be dragged to Hell and tortured for eternity. But death is inevitable, is it not? The longer I live, the more misery I sow in the world. Is there no other way forward? Must it always be you at my ear, nagging at me, forcing me to make the world a darker place?"

"Yes." He turned to me with a smile. "It must."

"*Why?*" I demanded, taking a step toward him.

"Because I do not wish to return to Hell!" The Gentleman turned his face away. "There is no other recourse for me, dear boy. I send souls to the Underworld, or I am sent."

Stunned, I searched for a response. "Have you actually told me a truth?"

"Yes, and I already regret it."

"Let me understand this."

"I doubt that you can."

"It sounds simple enough." I began to pace, to let my mind work. "You are tasked with the duty of creating misery, of condemning souls and causing their deaths so that they are sent to Hell. If you fail in that task, you become condemned. Is that the gist of it?"

"I remind you that you do not believe in Hell."

I waved his response away. "Irrelevant. *You* believe in it, and it seems clear that you prefer your current situation to it. Is that correct?"

"Are you interrogating me?"

"I am trying to understand the true nature of 'the work'. What is the frequency at which you must send souls to Hell? Is it related to the weakness we all experienced at the inquest? Before I – Is that the process of being pulled from this plane to the one referred to as Hell?"

The Gentleman gave me an amused look. "Planes, is it?"

"The terminology matters not," I said with a wave of my hand. "Only that your motive for coercing me is entirely self-serving. Which further suggests that I should resist you and let come what may."

"And what of Mary? Have you forgotten that your attempt to save her has condemned her to Hell?"

I sat on the bed, unable to deny the Gentleman's accusation. "She is a good-hearted person. She would not want to continue living – to keep *you* alive – knowing it was at the expense of other people's misery. Their souls."

"Ah. I seem to have missed that conversation when she accepted damnation even though she committed no wrong. When did you discuss that?"

I looked up at him. "Pardon?"

"When did you ask her if she was willing to die and be dragged to Hell?"

"I have not asked because –"

The Gentleman leaned down to me. "Because you know her *so* well after all this time, yes?"

"I … admit I do not actually know."

He straightened up. "Then you must ask her. Tell her everything. Let her make the choice for herself. She deserves no less."

"Why are you suddenly so concerned for Mary? Is it because you realized if not for her, I would have given up 'the work' immediately?"

"Oh, such brave and noble sentiments when you know you can hang it all on Mary. Keep telling yourself that *she* is the reason without ever having to face what you would do to save your own life. But none of that matters. You know you have to give her the choice."

I was trapped. It was pure torture to admit, but the demon was right. Mary had no choice in any of this. She was not even aware there *was* a choice. My choice, made in weakness and fear, the last of a string of fear-driven choices, had taken away hers. I had to fix this.

"You are right, of course," I told the Gentleman. "I must tell her everything. And then I must let her choose." I turned to look at him. "And I will abide by her choice, whatever it may be."

CHAPTER FORTY-SEVEN

TRUTH REVEALED

Both Mrs. Burkett and Mary resisted allowing us to take the air without a chaperone. My insistence that we would go no further than the gazebo less than a block away was little help. It was only when I suggested that I might take my business elsewhere that Mr. Burkett stepped in and helped to quiet his wife. Still, not until Mary said she trusted me were we able to leave.

"What is this about, William?" Mary asked as we walked.

Though the evening was cold and damp, the alley in front of the Langford was busy with tourists and boys looking to earn pennies.

"Best we wait until we are alone."

Mary stopped. "What do you mean, 'alone'?"

"There is something I must tell you and it is best done without any listeners. We will be in public, so you will be safe. You said you trust me, yes?"

She nodded. "But this is … unusual."

"She has no idea," said the Gentleman.

"Unusual, but necessary," I said. "Please, continue to trust me."

"All right."

We walked in silence the rest of the way to the courtyard where the gazebo stood. Mary sat, huddled, shivering, and not a little impatient.

"Is this about my situation?" she asked. "I've been sacked from the kitchen, haven't I? This isn't necessary. I said I wouldn't hit Dennis again."

I sat on the bench beside her. "Mary. I have much to tell you. About how I came to be in Meavy Prior. Of the true nature of what occurred there. I believe you are prepared to hear it. More importantly, you *need* to hear it. May I tell you my story?"

"It was warm inside. Can't you tell me there?"

"I apologize, but this telling requires privacy."

She gave a long sigh. "Go ahead."

"Excellent. I must ask you, however, to just listen. Please say nothing until I am done."

Her brow furrowed, her mouth twisted, but she nodded.

"Well," said the Gentleman, "This is already tedious. Ta ta." He moved towards the road, then disappeared. My relief at his absence was quickly overtaken by fear of what he might be doing.

"What are you looking at?" asked Mary.

"Nothing. Sorry, just thinking." I struggled to find words, feeling as if I was about to expose a festering wound.

I began my telling with the Marylebone and Battersea cases. Her agreement to remain quiet was short-lived.

"Wait, how could the bodies *change*?"

"I will come to that, and it will be much easier to accept in context."

"Very well."

I neglected to tell her of my beating at the hands of Keat, or of Coombs' response. Instead, I moved on to Coombs' failure in Newington. I told her of my findings in Angel Meadow and my trip to Meavy Prior.

"I *knew* that man was evil the moment I met him. And he brought a … *demon* to my *home*?"

I wondered how she would react when I told her that I now carried that demon and that it was keeping her alive. "Coombs was testing his powers. When he … accused your father. All that Satanic business, birth certificates, he was pushing the boundaries of it."

"And *murdering* Father? Was that part of the test?"

"Yes, I believe so. That was why he suggested your father be kept in the chapel. He was confirming whether his power worked in a church."

"For *that* he … ?"

"Yes."

She stood and paced angrily. "I wish he was here so I could stab him again."

"Indeed. If you could sit, I will continue."

"I can listen while I pace. Keep talking."

"Very well. He accused that young bobby, Murrish, of murdering your father. He invented evidence to support it, but nothing appeared."

"Like in that church in Newington."

"Yes, exactly. Apparently, the demon cannot enter a church. And he needs to hear the words to make them manifest."

"'Cannot'? 'Needs'? You're speaking of the present."

I stifled a gasp at my faux pas. "Mary, *please*. Let me continue."

Her pacing slowed and her eyes narrowed on me. "Go on."

"After returning to the vicarage, Coombs accused *me* of killing your father. His invented evidence appeared in my pocket."

"Another one of those damn contracts?"

"Precisely. I confronted him about his past and he seemed ready to be taken in."

"I know what happened next …"

"Not all of it, perhaps." I raised my eyes to meet hers. "You should sit for this."

She lowered herself onto the bench.

"After he impaled me with the saber –"

"Is *that* what happened to you?"

"Impaled, yes, with Sheasby's saber. Did you not see me?"

"No."

I laughed. "I thought you attacked him to save me."

"I saw him raise the saber, but I didn't know at who. I just wanted to kill him."

"I do understand that sentiment," I said, turning away. She had not been thinking of me. Rather than saving me, she was lashing out at Coombs. Her statement shed a harsh light on my innermost thoughts. I had tried to convince myself that I had asked the Gentleman to save her because she saved me, and the pain I suddenly felt revealed the truth that I had done this because I had feelings for her. But it seemed she had none for me. Still, I did not regret my decision.

I turned to face her again. "As it happens, I was, in fact, impaled through the stomach against a wall with Sheasby's saber. And I saw your fight with Coombs. How he gutted you. Do you recall that?"

Mary's face went pale. She looked down and touched her stomach.

"He opened your belly and you fell. Dead."

"Dead? But …"

It was my turn to pace. "I watched you die, knowing it was my fault. Then Sister Ellen attempted to stop him with some kind of poison sack. I watched him beat her to death. And I hated him as I had never hated anyone before." I sat next to her and set my arm on the bench back. "I wanted nothing more than to bring you back and kill him. A voice came out of the darkness offering help. I accepted the offer and asked for the strength to kill Coombs and for you to return to life. I found myself on the floor, healed and alive. I ended Coombs. Then you coughed and breathed again."

"And what of my father? Sister Ellen? You didn't think to save any of them?"

Words failed me. I shook my head. I could not tell her that I saved her due to some adolescent, romantic dreams. "You see, I thought *you* had saved *me*. But, even if that was not your intent, the result was the same. If you had not drawn Coombs' attention, he would have killed me straight away."

Mary withdrew into herself. I could see her processing my words, memories coming back to her. Then her eyes shot up to meet mine, and horror took her expression. She pulled back and jumped up from the bench.

"Then you …"

"Yes. The demon is with me now."

She spun and staggered, hands to her head. I moved towards her, but she extended her hand to keep me at bay. "Why should I believe you? Believe *any* of what you told me?"

"Why on Earth would I make up such a thing?"

"Haven't the foggiest. I don't know you that well."

"You do not know me? After all that happened?"

"But I still don't *know* you. Just because something terrible happened to both of us, that doesn't mean I know anything *about* you. Maybe you think I'll be beholden to you."

"There are better ways to go about *that*. But think back, Mary. About all that has happened. You were sliced open with a cleaver. Do you remember that?" My voice quivered as I said it. "Is your belly open now? Your organs falling out?"

She sat hard on the bench. "That was not a dream, then."

"No. Would that it were. One more thing …"

"One. *More*. Thing?"

"Yes. The demon's life is tied to yours. When he weakens, you weaken. If he dies, if he leaves this Earthly plane, you die. To stay alive, he requires souls. All that you heard about Governor Thornsbury and Superintendent Batleigh? I invented that to satisfy the demon, and, in turn, keep you, and me, alive."

"Now you're just toying with me."

"In hospital, what did you feel?"

She considered her answer. "That I was dying. No, beyond that, I felt I was … leaving."

"Then you know I am not lying. And I will not lie now. If we are to remain alive, the Gentleman – the demon – must be fed. He must be fed *souls*. That means sacrificing other human beings in order to maintain our own lives."

Horror, revulsion, and rage all played on her face until she broke down and buried her face in her hands. Without raising her head, she opened her hands enough to say, "How can you expect me to live that way?"

"I have no such expectations. I am merely telling you the truth of our existence."

Her tears had stopped. She wiped her face but remained bent over with her elbows on her knees. "So matter of fact," she muttered.

"I know of no other way to be. And let me be clear, I prefer to remain alive."

Mary straightened and turned to me angrily, but I spoke over her response.

"Please do not mistake that for callousness. I –" My throat tightened, and I had to force the next words out. "I *hate* what I did to Superintendent Batleigh. But I cannot …" I paused to look for the Gentleman, but he was nowhere in sight. "I cannot solve the problem if I am not alive to do so."

She held her words, though the anger remained in her eyes. "So. This is a problem to be solved, is it?"

"Yes. That is exactly what it is."

"And what if you *can't* solve it?"

That gave me pause. "I honestly had not considered that. I have never encountered a problem I could not solve. I grant you, I have never been faced with such a problem. I will say that I will not go on forever. However, I do suspect that I could live with this longer than you. Therefore, I leave the choice up to you, Mary. If you are willing to go on, I – we – will work out how to live with our fates. But, if you wish to end this, I will abide by that decision."

Mary balled her fists. Her entire body tensed and she let out a long, piercing scream. She stood, the fury in her eyes burning through her welling tears. I thought she would attack me and, having seen her battle Coombs, I feared for my life. Instead, she ran past me towards the Langford. I followed as closely as I dared.

Mrs. Burkett met Mary at the door. They exchanged a few words I could not hear, and Mary pushed past her.

Mrs. Burkett confronted me. "What did you do to that young lady, Dr. Johnson?"

"I am afraid I had to pass along some very bad news."

"And why on God's green Earth would you burden a lovely young thing such as her?"

"I assure you I had no choice."

I continued on to my room, only to find the Gentleman in his favourite chair. I collapsed on the bed.

"And how has our little drama played out?" he asked.

"She experienced all of the emotions one would expect. Shock, horror, rage, betrayal."

"And our collective fate?"

"I cannot tell you. I would not be surprised if she decided to simply kill me."

"There is potential for entertainment there. Should that be our fate, I think I will incorporate your inability to choose your own fate into your tortures. For instance, if you can't choose between, say, fire or acid, then I will have Mary use both on you. How does that sound?"

I struggled to keep these images from forming in my mind.

"No answer? Well, you needn't worry. You have a capacity for self-preservation that I believe will supersede any decision Mary makes."

Self-preservation? Was the Gentleman correct? If Mary chose to end this, through violent means or not, would I resist her?

⋯⟫─◉ ◉─⟪⋯

I awoke with the feeling that my muscles were made of lead. Mr. Burkett met me in the lobby.

"Young Miss Woodmore has asked me to convey a message." He seemed about to give a sermon. "She will be taking holiday for some time, the number of days unspecified. You are to cover her expenses and wait here until she returns, should she decide to, and do nothing at all as you wait. She was quite clear on that. You should do nothing. Also, you should keep her room available. She said you would know if she decided not to return, and you would know what it meant if she did return. I don't quite understand that last part, but nevertheless, that is the message. Mrs. Burkett would like me to add that she hopes Mary returns soon and that if you hear from her, tell her she won't have to do dishes anymore."

I thanked Mr. Burkett and, after agreeing to his insistence on paying a week in advance, returned to my room.

"Oh, this is not a good turn, dear boy," said the Gentleman. "Not a good turn at all."

"There is nothing to be done for it but to wait. I have put my fate – all three of our fates – in Mary's hands, and that is where they will remain."

I had to catch myself on a bed post. My head spun.

"Ah, you begin to feel it," said the Gentleman. "I know that I am growing weaker." His form had become blurred.

"How long do we – does she – have?"

"An hour, perhaps."

"An *hour*?"

"Or days. I have no way of knowing, as this situation is new to me."

"Or you find it more entertaining to torture me."

"If you think this is torture, our time in Hell may be quite fun after all."

The Gentleman's high-pitched laugh felt as if shards of glass were being pressed into my brain. A dose of laudanum was no help. I wandered the inn, and the streets surrounding it.

My wanderings provided no relief, therefore I took myself to the tearoom and snatched up a newspaper. I scoured it for stories of young women meeting untimely ends. In one moment, I imagined Mary in mortal danger, in the next believed her to *be* the danger.

Soon, I found myself drawn to stories of criminals in general. A murderer here, a burglar there. Surely, such criminals would not be missed were I to satiate the Gentleman. London would be all the better without them, I told myself. I could do the Gentleman's bidding, but rather than sowing misery, I could do good by ridding the world of its worst elements.

But then I would still be doing the bidding of an entity with evil intent.

No, I would wait for Mary to return. An increased dose of opium allowed me to shut out the turmoil, as well as the Gentleman, and sleep.

The next day, I was grateful to be informed that a wire had arrived for me, until I read the name of the sender: Dr. Walker, the coroner involved in the Marylebone case. Did he still hold resentment towards me for not corroborating him? The wire said nothing of this. It only claimed urgency regarding a case in which he required my assistance and gave the address of St. George's Hospital in Marylebone.

CHAPTER FORTY-EIGHT

A MURDER OF FAITH

A BEARDED, PUDGY CONSTABLE WAVED MY cab to a halt. "Fallen horse," he said. "You'll need to go around." We were at the corner of the block St. George's occupied.

I told the cab driver I could walk from there. He expressed doubt as I held onto the cab for a moment to steady myself, but I threw him a half crown in answer.

"I have business with the coroner," I said to the constable.

He waved me on. Prone across the sidewalk was a horse, its panting rapid and shallow. A young man wearing the clothes and mud of a farmer tended to the animal, pleading with it to rise. A pair of attendants lifted a stretcher out of the tilted wagon. An unconscious girl lay on the stretcher, covered with a blood-stained blanket. The young man stood, watching the stretcher. The cab driver told the man to go inside and that he would tend to the horse. The young man followed the attendants through the pair of doors held open by nurses.

"That's a promising scenario," said the Gentleman, suddenly beside me. "You could tell the police he tried to murder the child."

"*Stop it*," I said through gritted teeth. My head spun and I put out a steadying hand to the wrought iron railing next to the basement stairs. As the dizziness subsided, I vowed to exert better control over my responses to the Gentleman's prodding, lest I end up in an asylum.

"Dr. Johnson." It was Walker, standing halfway up the steps that led to a basement entrance. "Are you quite all right?"

Had he heard me? I straightened up and brushed my hands. "Just a bit tired, thank you."

"This way." He gestured and turned down the stairs. "Pity about the horse."

I followed him into the musty basement corridor.

"Glad to see your working conditions have improved," I said.

"Indeed." He led me to a large open room at the end of the corridor. The air was laced with charcoal. On one side there were three coffins, and on the other a table with a sheet-covered body. Immediately I could tell it was that of a male, slight of build. A teen, or a small man.

"May I ask why you have invited me here?" I hoped Walker would ask me to assist in his duties, as I longed to keep busy while awaiting Mary's decision. Performing autopsies would be just the thing.

"As I said in my wire," Walker said, "I am in need of your assistance. I should like to employ your … skills."

"Your hesitation suggests something other than admiration. What do you believe my skills to be?"

Walker addressed me directly. "An eye for details, primarily. I recall that you discerned aspects of wounds that I had missed."

"And yet you failed to mention that in your inquest and claimed them as your own findings."

Now he withdrew. "Let us not speak of the past and only of the case at hand." He pulled the sheet down to the chest of the corpse, an emaciated teen. "The body was found in an alley. The man who found him is a known criminal who has been in and out of gaol. He claimed he found the boy dead. The police believe otherwise. Well, they don't so much as 'believe' as insist that this man was responsible, despite the lack of violence in his record. While I do not wish to prejudice your findings, there is evidence of, shall we say, occult activities. They tasked me to provide the evidence for the conclusion they have already drawn. I am not able to do that."

"I do believe he's onto you, dear boy," said the Gentleman.

Walker's insinuation rankled me more than the Gentleman's voice. "And you believe I am?"

"That was not intended as a slight. I cannot abide injustice, but I simply haven't the time to investigate this. I have many other cases," he said, sweeping his hand towards the coffins. "Not to mention my work in hospital. I believe you have more time than I. If I read the papers correctly, you do not currently have a situation and have taken up residence at an inn?"

"That is true."

"Combine that with your apparent penchant for such cases …"

"'Penchant'? What do you mean, precisely?"

He considered his answer. "I would rather not prejudice your findings, but I believe you will understand when you examine the body."

I was tempted to challenge Walker to tell me exactly what he was thinking, but thought it better to conduct an actual investigation. This time, I knew that nothing about what I discovered would change, unless I willed it.

"I will do my best to find the truth," I said. "Do you have any preliminary findings or information for me?"

"Here is the police report," he said, handing me a sheaf of papers. "The inspector in charge wants my proclamation by tomorrow end of day. I'll leave you to it."

"Understood."

The police report stated that a known criminal by the name of Wilhelm Luftig had found the boy, identified as John Pliny. Luftig had stated that the boy was sixteen, though no actual birth record was available. My initial reaction was to question why Luftig would go to the police if he had killed the boy. There was no mention of this in the report, only that Luftig had been held for questioning. Though his record showed a history of selling stolen goods, falsifying bank cheques, and even dabbling in prostitution, there was, as Walker had stated, no indication of violent behaviour.

The victim, John Pliny, was a young man, a teenager. His body was so emaciated, he looked like a skeleton wrapped in parchment. There were scars on his back and legs. Some scars appeared to be symbols I did not recognize, carved into the flesh. The wounds were cauterized, therefore a hot blade was likely used. Other scars were lashes from a whip. His wrists and ankles showed signs of bondage. That his left hand was broken suggested how he may have escaped his captor. The bottoms of his feet were shredded, and I found bits of broken glass in the flesh. But what had caused the extinction of life? The accumulation of injuries and starvation? Walker had left an array of surgical tools and a wash basin. I dipped my hands in the cool water, dried them, and selected a scalpel.

"You are in your element now." The Gentleman's voice was surprisingly soothing. "Cutting flesh, sawing bone. We are very much alike."

I knew better than to respond aloud but rather shook my head at him, then bent to the boy's chest.

Having parted the dry flesh from the collarbones to the base of the sternum, I shrugged a silent question at the Gentleman.

"Don't you see, dear boy? I dissect *souls*. Open them up, look inside. I seek out maladies and injuries, abuses and the like to root out their causes, reveal their effects."

With the slices across the collarbones and belly complete and the abdomen open, I set down the scalpel and took up a bone saw. "The key difference," I whispered, "is that corpses feel nothing."

"You know that how, exactly? Simply because there's no audible screaming?"

I stopped and stared at him as my heart pounded, my hands trembled.

"Perhaps death is akin to anesthesia," the Gentleman said as he circled around me. "The body no longer moves, but the soul remains for a time. Are there not cases where anesthesia did not render a patient fully unconscious? Though they cannot respond, they feel everything. Perhaps this boy felt each cut of your knife."

Every beat of my heart was an increasing tremor, a spasm of electricity through my body. The saw fell from my hands and clattered on the floor.

"Are you quite all right, Doctor?" Walker called as he came to the door.

A firm grip on the table held me steady against the raging falls of my mind that threatened to bring me down. "I must admit that I am not."

Walker picked up the saw and set it aside. "Can you continue?"

Slow, steady breaths allowed me to straighten. "Perhaps just some tests for poisons and the like? I see no sign of fatal wounds or other violence beyond those observed on the epidermis, therefore further cutting is not necessary. The victim likely died from starvation and exposure, coupled with the trauma caused by flagellation."

"What of the cuttings? The symbols, or whatever they are? Do you make anything of them?"

"Some form of ritual torture, it appears. All were made prior to death."

"You don't recognize them? All this occultism you've been in – or, rather, around – and there's nothing familiar about them?"

"*No*. If there was, I would have said as such."

"All right, Doctor. If that's all you can manage ..."

"No, I would like to continue the investigation. I do wish to be of service." Before the Gentleman's interruption, I had been fascinated by what I had seen.

"Very well. I have people to handle the tests. But if you'd like to interview the accused, that would be of benefit to me."

"Thank you, I will do so right away." I took my leave.

Waiting for a cab, I said to the Gentleman, "Why must you plague me so?"

"Because I am *bored*! Keep me happy and I will allow you some happiness of your own. Not a great deal, mind you, but some."

⊰══◉ ◉══⊱

Wilhelm Luftig was being held at a small, local gaol. His responses to my questions were terse and his thick German accent forced frequent repeats, pushing him into a state of aggravation. I was able to draw from him that he had not seen the Pliny boy for months. He knew it had been that long because of a dip in income. When he had last seen him, the boy had no scars on his body. However, he let slip that the smoothness of the boy's skin was what had made him valuable. As I left the gaol, I felt a wave of hatred for this man who would sell someone who was barely more than a child, and whose only reaction to the boy's death was concern over a loss of revenue.

"This has great potential, you realize," said the Gentleman. His voice was faint, his shape vague in the afternoon fog. "Such despicable circumstances. Pin them on an innocent and oh ..." He kissed his fingers. "Delicious. You will feel *much* better, as will Mary."

I kept my silence, as much to spare what little breath I had as to simply avoid yet another pointless argument. I wanted to give Luftig to the police. I wanted to see him hanged. I understood the police wanting to use this to convict him. But I believed his statement, and convicting the wrong man would only mean that the killer would remain free. I pondered my own freedom then and wondered at the injustice of it, considering all I had done.

Another wave of dizziness struck me. My breathing became laboured.

"Fine. If you must give me the bad man, then do so. It will be a sour meal, but a meal nonetheless."

"I have no intention of naming him, but not because you would be displeased with the *flavour*. I believe he did not kill the boy and –"

"You are waiting for Mary." The Gentleman sighed deeply. "Your devotion disgusts me. This is no drawing room mystery, you realize. This is an ugly death on an ugly street. There will be no clues leading to the killer. You are unlikely to find the killer, even given a great deal of time. Which, I might remind you, you do not have."

"I am content with leaving my fate in Mary's hands. If she chooses to accept our situation, I hope to be able to name the true killer. If not, well, at least I will have occupied my time with a worthwhile endeavour."

"You are becoming quite boring."

Through my weakness, I smiled.

CHAPTER FORTY-NINE

THE ALLURE
OF THE CRUCIFIX

THE LOCATION WHERE THE BODY HAD been found was an alley in a rundown section of London. There were various shops – most of them closed – along with a Catholic Church. I inquired at each of the shops, but none of the proprietors had anything to offer, and some refused to even answer questions. The church, St. Martin's, I saved for last.

This church looked older than its architecture indicated. It had seen difficult times and was not well kept. It looked abandoned, forgotten. The stained-glass windows, their colours obscured by years of soot, still managed to show a flicker of lamps behind. Would I find clergy inside? A huddled congregation? Or perhaps the denizens of the streets, their refuge invaded by a well-dressed stranger? Whatever I found, it would include peace from the Gentleman.

The heavy oak door was scratched here, cracked there and the squeal of the hinges made me grind my teeth. Once inside, I leaned back against the door and breathed in the incense and silence for a moment. My limited experience with Catholic churches told me there would be racks of votive candles on either side of the altar, with most, if not all, lit. Here, only one was lit. The others were burnt down to their bases. The red glass holders resembled scabs.

I chose a pew in the middle and sat. The tortured, crucified Christ loomed above me. The crown of thorns dug into his head, the painted blood ran down into his eyes. His drained, emaciated body bore a deep gash in one side. More of the expertly painted blood emphasized the depth of the wound. He was nearly naked, exposed to the world for all but a wrapped loincloth. Crude, heavy nails tore through the palms of his stretched hands and crossed feet. His expression bore every injury, physical and spiritual, every decision and choice, that had led him to be in that place, in that time, in that pain. I wondered how the sculptor who had made this had known how to depict so much pain so accurately.

For the first time I understood why some people wanted such a brutal depiction of their saviour hanging before them. They could look at each one of those wounds and feel their own. They could feel that someone shared them, some-one had suffered much worse than they, all for their salvation. Rather than accept their own failings, they let another take them, and they reveled in it. This I could not abide.

A door in the wall behind the altar creaked open and a priest emerged. It was Malvagna, the priest from Newington. I leapt to my feet.

"Why are you here?" I demanded.

Malvagna smiled ruefully. "Isn't it you who is more out of place?" He looked tired, sad. "But to answer your question, I was relocated." A defeated bitterness coloured his tone.

"Why?" I recalled Batleigh making a remark about Malvagna having been previously transferred.

"Because the Lord, through the infallible church, willed it so. Would you like to sit?" He took a seat in a pew across from me. "Please. Tell me about your adventures. About how you exposed Coombs and Batleigh and saved us all from Satan's power."

I could leave and face the Gentleman, or I could spend more time here, away from him. I sat. "It is not quite so dramatic as that."

"The papers, they make it all so apocalyptic."

"They do, indeed. With many things."

"When I saw you in Newington, when I spoke to you of an evil presence, did you not yet know of it, or did you choose to lie to me?"

"I did not know the full nature of Coombs. I thought he might be a trickster of some kind."

"A trickster." He seemed amused by the idea.

"I knew nothing of Batleigh's involvement then." Because I had not created it yet. "I, too, was heartbroken by it." As truthful a statement as any I had made of late.

"Still, you came through the lion's den, as it were, and are all the stronger for it, I hope?"

"May I ask why you were transferred?"

"After the revelations regarding Batleigh, I may have become overzealous in defending him. You see, I had witnessed how the harm had come to his hands and why they were in need of covering. For them to be anything else, then a thing, an evil thing, must have happened." He levelled a hard stare at me.

I forced myself to hold his gaze. "Yes, something did happen. As I stated during the inquest."

"Yes. The inquest." Still, his eyes did not move, and I believe he did not blink.

Recalling his reaction to being around Coombs, I wondered if he was yet another person who could sense the presence of the Gentleman. Could he be a help to me? In his mad eyes I saw no room for sympathy, only judgement.

"Enough of the past," I said. "On to the present. I am here because a young man, a boy, really, was found dead in an alley nearby. And I am assisting in the investigation."

"Because the police, they do not wish to investigate?"

"That is exactly correct. Did you know the victim?"

"Yes. A troubled young man. So sad."

"What can you tell me about him?"

Malvagna turned to face the crucifix. His eyes tightly closed, he crossed himself and whispered prayers in Latin. He bowed his head to his praying hands, now pressed against the back of the pew before him. When he showed no sign of letting up, I steeled myself and said something I had promised myself I would never say. "'Father' Malvagna?"

He turned sharply to me, a smile beneath his tear-filled eyes. "Thank you for saying 'Father'." He wiped his face and stepped out of the pew. "I have something to show you." He moved down the aisle. "Come."

Confused more than anything else, I remained seated. Not one moment of our interactions had been something I had expected. Still, I was intrigued. Malvagna was upset by the mention of the Pliny boy and had been transferred to an empty church due to his defense of Batleigh. Perhaps there was more to him than what I had seen in Newington.

I got up from the pew and followed him to the door. He held it open and stepped out into the grey afternoon and continued down the steps.

As expected, the Gentleman was on me when I reached the bottom, but what he said was *not* expected.

"Get away from that papist!" he shouted.

I recoiled from the force of his words and stumbled.

Malvagna took me by the elbow and guided me across the street. "Quickly. We must hurry."

He pulled me into a three-story brick building. The vague sunlight revealed its decay. The first-floor windows were boarded up, the others broken. The place reminded me of the safehouse in Angel Meadow. I felt a similar dread as we mounted the loose-stone stairs.

At the rotting wooden door, Malvagna paused to scan the street. His gaze fell on the base of the stairs. The Gentleman stood just beyond them. Could Malvagna see him? The priest said nothing. He pushed the door open, picked up a nearby lantern and lit it, then ushered me inside. He pushed the door tightly closed, then stepped back and waited a moment.

"This way," he said, seemingly satisfied. He led me to a room with a missing door, where only hinges remained.

Crosses hung about the room, interspersed with strings of garlic and leaves I did not recognize. A mattress lay to one side and at its four corners were straps chained to the floor. Beside it was a stool and a table with knives, a basin and towels. A commode sat in the corner. The room smelled of incense and human waste.

"I did not wish you to see this," said Malvagna, "because you misunderstand, yes? Without understanding, it looks horrible. Like a prison. It was, but not for the body, for the demon inside the body."

This was where the Pliny boy had spent his last days. Months, if it had begun when he went missing. The thought of what he had gone through made me sicker than the smell.

"I have a confession of my own to make," said Malvagna. "Perhaps that is why all this has remained in place. I wanted to be found out. I wanted to confess. I knew the boy, yes. He came to me in pain. He wished to change his life. To get away from the man who sold him. But getting away from the man was not the answer. No. He needed to get the demon out, to be exorcised. I tried to help him." Malvagna choked on a sob.

In my feet, I felt the urge to run. The room was horrifying, the man before me a clear danger. But the Gentleman feared this man, and now he spoke of exorcisms. I stepped into the corridor, then held myself still. The Gentleman's vague form wavered just inside the front door. Not so his eyes, which flared as a forge well-bellowed.

Malvagna followed and looked at me with wet eyes. "There is no understanding." He turned his gaze to the room. "John Pliny, he was *possessed*. The straps, they were *necessary*. They were. The demon? It wanted to take the boy away." Sadness overtook him. "The process was taxing, yes. It weakened his body. The carvings, the lashings, all meant to drive out the demon. We were close to freeing his soul, but the demon was strong. It took him from me, and he did not last long without my help." He wiped his eyes again, then turned to me. "You know something of demons, yes?"

I stepped back and bumped against the wall behind me. "Pardon?"

"There is a darkness that follows you. I felt it in the street. It is nearby. Do you know this darkness follows you?"

My heart pounded. Words failed me utterly. Not so the Gentleman.

"Get away from that papist." His voice was strong, though his form had become tendrils of fetid, decaying flesh. Fingers and claws reached for me.

"It speaks to you maybe? A voice, or perhaps just a *bzz-bzz-bzz*."

"You're not thinking of confessing, are you, dear boy?" His voice was a worm sliding in my ear.

"I really do not know what you are saying," I told them both.

"Sorry." Malvagna said. "Let me say clearly: evil follows you here." He thrust a finger at me. "No denials. This I *know*. So, I ask again: do *you* know evil follows you? It is the darkness that followed Coombs, yes?"

Malvagna's amber eyes held me as Coombs' had, as my father's had. I wanted to confess, to please him, to placate his anger. I wanted him to take away the darkness, to pull me from the abyss. I wanted the darkness of the past months to flow out of me in a torrent of words. But fear was a dam I could not break.

The Gentleman's necrotic tendrils stretched towards me, a single claw mere inches from my eye. "It is time to be done with this papist trash." The words slithered through my mind.

Malvagna set down the lantern and held out his cross. "*Princeps gloriosissime caelestis militia,*" he said, deep in his throat. "*Sancte Michael Archangele, defende nos in proelio et colluctatione.*"

Though I knew nothing of Catholic rituals, I knew enough Latin to know he was calling down the forces of Heaven to drive out the demon before him.

The tendrils snapped back, and the Gentleman returned to his usual form.

On his back foot, the Gentleman crossed his arms in front of his chest, each hand on the opposite shoulder. "*Matoutii bentiom ana ru.*" The strange words split the very air, a thunderclap mere inches away. The words were from no language I recognized.

Malvagna blocked his ears and shouted, "*Virus nequitiae suae, tamquam flumen immundissimum, draco maleficus transfundit in homines depravatos mente et corruptos corde!*"

The Gentleman's form wavered as a reflection upon troubled waters. His voice was weaker now. "*Iecuru gobejontu uru aioxt tu!*" He spat his last words at the priest.

Malvagna cried out, fell back, then reached into a pocket and took out a crystal vial. He thumbed off the vial's cap and swung it in the Gentleman's direction in great, saber-like arcs, holding out the cross at arm's length. The holy water slashed through the Gentleman's form and burned it away as if he was made of dead leaves. His shriek was hot nails in my ears.

"*Adesto itaque,*" Malvagna continued. "*Dux invictissime, populo Dei contra irrumpentes spirituales nequitias, et fac victoriam!*"

Then the Gentleman was gone.

Father Malvagna pulled me back into the room. "It is gone now, yes?"

I covered my nose with the back of my hand as the stench became a burning sensation. I nodded.

Malvagna looked at me closely. "You do know it follows you, then. Do you hear it? I think that you do. Perhaps you hear its words and answer it?"

Where would I even begin? Should I tell him of the voice I believed to have been my brother's? What of the savagery at the vicarage that resulted in me accepting the help of a demon? I reached out to the nearest wall to steady myself.

"I think maybe that is a yes." Malvagna took my face in his hands. "I think you are not a bad man. I look in you, the darkness I see is a mote. Only a mote.

It is not your eye. Not yet." He released me. "I can remove this mote. Before it becomes your eye. It is quiet now, in this room, is it not? No *bzz-bzz-bzzz*? You can say. Say to me. *Chiedi di essere libero.* Ask to be free."

"Free?" The word escaped as a whisper. Were I to be freed, what of Mary? Was there time to tell him all? Could Malvagna help us both?

His words came faster. "It has you. Yes. But you can be freed! Say to me now, *per favore.* Say you wish to be free. You must wish it for it to be so. *Dillo a me.* Say it now, *figlio.* Say it to me now!"

I pushed away from him. My eyes fell upon the filthy mattress, the chains, the commode and I realized the absurdity, the danger, of turning to this man for help. "I have nothing to say to you."

"It has you. I see that." Malvagna's grip on my arms was powerful. He pulled me toward the mattress. "I will not fail this one!" He muttered in Latin as he tried to drag me down.

I kicked him between the legs.

Malvagna cried out and doubled over, collapsing onto the filthy mattress. He spoke incoherently through his pain.

I stumbled into the hall, then ran to the door. Frantically, I pulled on the knob until it opened. I heard Malvagna crawling and saw a hand emerge from the room.

All but falling down the steps, I ran as fast as I could. The Gentleman was on me immediately. "Name him. Go to the police now. Tell them what he has done." He stayed beside me no matter how fast I ran. I continued glancing back, watching for Malvagna. I was nearly run over by a ratcatcher's cart.

"Why the hesitation? You can name the actual killer this time. That is what you want, yes?"

I stopped, fell against a building, and peeked around the corner. "But is that truly 'the work'?" I asked between heaving breaths. "Am I not expected to name innocents? To break their will, shatter their hope like a chocolate so you can have the treat inside?"

"I can make an exception."

Satisfied I was not being pursued, I continued walking, but with haste. "You fear this priest, and that is a joy to witness."

"I believe I am beginning to understand you," said the Gentleman. "Anyone is allowed to make decisions, so long as it is not *you.* You put our fate in Mary's hands and seem more than happy to let the papist have a say. You saw what he did to that boy. Do want the same to happen to you? To Mary?"

Part of me knew he was right. This priest was a danger, and not just to the Gentleman. Still, he was able to repel the Gentleman. Was there not a way I could use this to my advantage?

"You do realize," said the Gentleman, "that if he is successful in banishing me, then you –"

"Will follow, tortured forever, et cetera, et cetera."

"Is that what you want? Eternal damnation because you're so afraid to make the *wrong* choice, you prefer to make none at all?"

Continuing my rapid pace, I had to admit that, once again, the demon was right. Malvagna was clearly a danger to me, but he was also a danger to the Gentleman. Could the priest be an effective weapon against him? Dynamite could be an effective weapon against an enemy, but could be deadly if one knew not how to use it.

CHAPTER FIFTY
JUSTICE AVERTED

When I came to both a busy street and a decision, I hailed a cab. I gave
the driver the address of Walker's office. As we pulled away, the Gentleman
remained on the sidewalk, arms folded impatiently. Another piece of the puzzle regarding his existence: Why did he sometimes travel with me and sometimes not? No, it was a distraction to ponder such things. What did it matter?
He would eventually reappear. But it seemed I would have a few moments to
think in peace.

All of this brought me back to the question of whether or not to condemn
Malvagna. He had caused the Pliny boy's death and deserved to be punished
for it. But he could harm the Gentleman to the point that the Gentleman actually feared him. Could Malvagna be the solution?

There was no scenario I could imagine in which Malvagna would cooperate
with me. While it was possible that he could extricate the Gentleman from me,
it would be accomplished with extended, life-threatening torture. Either the
successful excision of the Gentleman or the torture itself could result in my
death. And what would happen to Mary? I could not answer that question, nor
could I see a safe path to using Malvagna himself. Perhaps I could find some
way to learn from him? Unlikely, but I was reluctant to throw away the one and
only weapon I had against the Gentleman.

The cab driver had to nudge me to break me out of my spell. I climbed out,
paid him, and cast my eyes about the sidewalk. The street was busy but calm,
unlike when last I came here, and a horse lay dying in the street. I wondered
what had happened to it. I shook myself out of such pointless reverie. I was
waiting for the Gentleman to reappear and realized that he would do so of his
own accord. I took the stairs down to Walker's office.

"Have a good think, dear boy?"

Gasping, I stumbled down the remaining steps. "You could have killed me,"
I said to the Gentleman, who stood a few steps above me with his amused
smirk.

"Oh, don't be so dramatic. Besides, I might be less inclined to seek my own
form of entertainment if you would do the work. I would be ever so grateful."

"Now you sound like a teenage girl. Please stop that." I pushed through the door and made my way down the hall to find Walker finishing the autopsy on the Pliny boy.

Though I had made the decision, I found the words would not come. Walker had closed the chest cavity, and I could plainly see how emaciated the boy had been, along with the many scars inflicted by Malvagna.

"Well?" said Walker.

"Tell the police to let Mr. Luftig go," I said. I would find some other way to fight the Gentleman. "A priest named Malvagna captured the boy and held him captive for months. The priest confessed this to me. The boy escaped and died shortly thereafter, a direct result of his starvation and wounds."

Walker sent for a constable while I wrote out every detail of my encounter with Malvagna. When I handed it over, I added one. "Malvagna also told me that he wrote out his confession and left it in a closet in the back room."

"Excellent touch, dear boy," said the Gentleman as he gestured.

I asked the constable to wire me at the Langford as soon as Malvagna was arrested. I would be only too glad to provide any further testimony, including at the inquest.

⊷⊶⊙⊶⊷

Back at the Langford, Burkett informed me that there had been no word from Mary. My growing headache kept me bent over and holding onto whatever was nearest. I dismissed Burkett's concerns and sent his eldest boy to the apothecary with a list and orders to bring it directly to me posthaste.

Before long the boy had returned with my medicine, and I was in bed with a dose of opium. It relieved the pain but left me in a fog.

The Gentleman came to stand beside me, looking down at me like a kindly caregiver. "You realize he lied to you, yes? 'Possession'. Ridiculous. It is merely an excuse to blame us for your own horrible behaviours, even those caused by damaged minds. Do you have any idea how many people have been accused of being possessed merely because a disease or an injury manifested as inexplicable behaviours? Talk about evil."

I longed for sleep, but the Gentleman's statements nagged at me. "Are you telling me there is no such thing as demonic possession?"

"Do *you* believe in it?"

"Answer my question."

"Would you attempt to wear a fur coat while the animal still lived? Of course not."

There came a knock at my door.

"Dr. Johnson? It's Dr. Walker. I have some news."

I sat on the edge of the bed. "Be right there," I said, letting my spinning head settle.

The Gentleman stood by the door. "It looks as though your hopes for a weapon against me have been crushed. He wouldn't have helped you, you know, especially not now that you've sent him to jail, likely to hang."

Had he read my mind?

"Are you all right, Doctor?" Walker asked from the other side of the door.

"Yes, coming." I pushed off the bed and went to the door. "Dr. Walker," I said, opening it. "What brings you here?"

"May I come in?"

"Of course."

The Gentleman made a playful show of letting Walker have the chair by the window and stood to the side. I sat on the bed.

"You said you have news?" I asked.

Walker stared at me intently. "I also wanted to check on you. It seems you are not well."

"I am not, but I am being treated."

"By your own hand, I assume?"

"Yes. What is this news, please?"

Walker shook his head ruefully. "Very well. The priest, Malvagna, seems to have fled. The police found no one at the church, and the room you described had been cleared out. They did find the confession, so no one doubts your claims, but it seems the good father has vacated the premises."

"Oh, dear," said the Gentleman. He looked genuinely concerned.

My heart began to pound, making my headache worse. I futilely rubbed my forehead. Did this mean Malvagna would be hunting me? "At least they have the confession," I muttered.

"Yes. However, since the church will not provide us with samples, we can't prove that the note is written in Malvagna's hand. And it is strange that he would take everything else but leave that." He leaned forward, peering at me.

"Yes. Strange. What about the church, do they know his whereabouts?" Sweat formed on my forehead and neck.

"If they do, they're not willing to share them with the police. They claim he was transferred out of Newington some time ago and that the church where you met him has been closed for years."

"Closed? Well, that would explain its condition."

"Indeed." Walker stood. "And speaking of condition…" He moved towards me.

I put up my hands. "Please, Doctor. I appreciate your concern, but I have treated myself and am on the mend."

"You don't look it. In fact, you look worse."

"I thank you for that, but I think we can both agree that I need rest more than anything else."

He spread his hands. "Very well. Do get some rest, and if you would like to be treated by someone other than yourself, get in touch."

I thanked him, we said our farewells and I closed the door behind him.

The Gentleman was back in his chair, elbows on the arms, hands clasped before him, deep in thought.

"It seems the weapon is still in play," I told him, returning to sit on the bed.

The Gentleman turned his gaze on me, his eyes a smouldering fire. "The papist is not a weapon you can aim at me."

"I realize that. He is more akin to a stick of dynamite than a rifle." My head felt liquid, and I feared that laying down would roil it.

"If dynamite caused eternal suffering, then yes. And bear in mind," he said, sitting forward and raising a finger. "First your body will be tortured here in this world until you are dead, which will likely *feel* like an eternity. But that will be a minor discomfort and a blink compared to what will follow."

"The more you make those threats the more mundane they seem."

The Gentleman's eyebrows shot up in surprise.

"If Malvagna finds me and takes me, you will lose something yourself, yes?"

He gave me a lopsided frown. "Yes. I will lose my playtime privileges. And I, too, will be tortured."

"Truly? I thought you would be torturing Mary and me."

"An eternity of that is its own form of torture."

I found myself laughing. "Then what are we to do? I have sent the police after him to no avail. The church protects him. And if it comes to another fight, I doubt he will allow me the opportunity to kick him between the legs again."

"Indeed. I have … let's call them 'allies'. Men who only need the merest whisper to act upon their darkest urges."

"Like Hughes with his hammer? Garret and his blemishes?"

The Gentleman smiled. "You give me too much credit."

"You did not answer the questions."

His smile broadened. "No, I did not. At any rate, I'm quite sure I can send some allies the papist's way."

"How will you find him?"

"He is not the only one who senses things." With that, he disappeared.

⊷═◉ ◉═⊶

I drifted in and out of a state akin to sleep, with dreams both disturbing and too fleeting to recall. Slowly, I became aware that the Gentleman had returned.

"Is it done?" I uttered.

"You mean is the papist still alive? Yes. He is … difficult, which only empha-sizes the danger." He sat forward, another surprisingly human action. "Let me teach you some words. Please, dear boy."

The change in the Gentleman's tone was so startling, I sat up and pushed myself back to lean against the headboard. The sleep had done some small measure of good as the fog had lifted somewhat. "Words? What words?"

"Ones that will help you against the papist. Help *us*."

"You speak as if we are a team."

"We are, of a kind. We have the same goal: remain here, out of Hell, yes? If the papist kills you, then we all go there. You, me, Mary."

I rubbed my temples. "Explain it to me."

"Freedom, dear boy. I have freedom here."

I considered that as I lay back down. It seemed as though this demon was being honest with me. "These words you wish to teach me. Why can you not say them?"

"I can. I *did*. But aside from my weakened state due to your refusal to do the work, I am not in this realm, not in the way you and he are. When he said his words, they nearly ended me. When I said mine, they were but wind. An ill wind, but a wind, nonetheless. If you say them, they will be a cannon."

"What language is it?"

"An ancient one. Much older than the filth that spills from the papist's mouth."

"Why do you hate Malvagna so?"

"His kind brought death to my people. Murdered our gods and any of us who would not accept theirs." He shook his head. "It is enough for you to know that the words will hurt him. You will use any further details against me, and I will give you no ammunition for that."

"Yet you expect me to say these words."

"If you wish to survive your next encounter with the papist, then yes."

"Either way, it appears Mary and I will end up in Hell. Soon, it seems, unless Mary returns, having agreed to do the work."

"Then you want the papist to decide our collective fates. Very well." The Gentleman went silent.

I studied him, the translucent image of a man that represented a demon. How accurate were his expressions and mannerisms? They seemed as real as any man's. Could I trust that his face showed me his thoughts? If so, he seemed weakened, helpless even.

Weakened. As I had been. As Coombs had been. "Answer a question for me, as truthfully as you are able."

"Will you then let me teach you the words?"

"Perhaps."

"What is this all-important question?"

"Why do you come to those who beg for help?"

"Because they are at their weakest. They seek to be caught, like a fish seeking bait. When they have opened themselves in that way, they are easiest to hook. And ..." For the first time, I saw the Gentleman struggle for words. "My people begged them for mercy, them with their chests of shining metal and gleaming swords." His body moved as if he breathed deeply, stoking his rage. "But I did not beg. As I burned on their stake, as they chanted their condemnation of my spirit, I vowed to put out their light. And I, like you, like Coombs, was offered a hand not by the One they brought, but by the Other, who could give me what I wanted. I gladly accepted."

"But, like me, like Coombs, the bargain you made was different than what you expected."

"And I am forever trapped in their Hell."

"'Their' Hell?"

"There are worlds, dear boy, and there are beings and gods, Hells as well as Heavens."

I tried to imagine this, tried to hold it all in my dulled mind. Then I recalled with whom I was conversing. "Is any of that true?"

His laugh was bitter. "Perhaps. Perhaps not. What matters is that you do not let that papist bastard win. Let me teach you the words."

I pictured the room in which the boy had been held. I recalled the state of his body. Emaciated, wrapped in carved and flagellated flesh.

"Teach me the words."

CHAPTER FIFTY-ONE

DAMNED SALVATION

BURKETT'S FACE BLANCHED WHEN HE SAW me staggering into the dining hall. My breaths were shallow, my vision shaded. My head was an anvil hammered.

"What time is it?" I asked him.

"We're just finishing dinner," Burkett said, worry on his face.

"I see. Would it be possible to get a bowl of soup?"

"Of course. Let me help you to a table."

Through blurred vision I saw what appeared to be a cloudy sunset outside. I rubbed my eyes for clarity and suddenly flames licked the windows. "Fire!" I shouted and stumbled past Burkett.

"It's just the sunset, Dr. Johnson," Burkett insisted.

"No, no!" I grasped the curtains, collapsed and took them down with me. "Look!"

Burkett rushed to my side and tried to help me up. "Where, sir? Where?"

"There!" My outstretched finger wavered and shook in fear. "Just outside!" It was a roaring, angry fire, spewing black, fetid smoke.

On the floor, as I was, tangled in curtains, I must have looked comical as laughter arose from the stunned patrons.

"But sir, there is nothing." Burkett raised the window. The cold evening air flowed in. There was no fire, no smoke.

"I ... I was sure ..." I tried to stand but immediately fell.

Burkett and Dennis helped me on to a chair, but sitting upright was too much for me.

Joanna brought me a glass of water while Burkett's son Dennis fanned me with a menu. Burkett calmed the other patrons, assuring everyone that there was nothing wrong with the food.

The Gentleman, a figure made of smoke, floated nearby. "If you're going to die, at least you're doing it with style."

I struggled to focus my vision. Dennis stood to my right, frantically waving the menu up and down. Joanna, to my left, looked worried and wrung her hands. Through the Gentleman's vapourous form, I could see the patrons staring at me while Burkett tried desperately to draw their attention away.

"Not here," I told Dennis. "Help me up, please."

He tossed aside the menu and helped me up.

"I should like to go back to my room," I said.

"As you wish sir," he said.

Burkett watched us, exchanging a nod with his son, then used my exit to assure everyone that everything was fine and there would be no more disturbances. In the lobby, when I saw my reflection in the glass of the grandfather clock, I screamed.

My face was covered in boils. One of them burst, oozing a viscous yellow discharge. A long insect with bloody mandibles emerged from the wound. Behind me in the reflection stood the Gentleman, now with bone-white horns protruding from just above his crimson face. He reached a clawed hand around my head. A talon touched my cheek and opened the rotting flesh. I fell to the floor, my throat raw from screams.

I heard Dennis and his father talking about getting a doctor. Despite the hoarseness of my throat, I kept telling them to take me to my room until I could say it loud enough for them to hear me.

The Gentleman's vapourous form hovered nearby.

"I *am* a doctor," I reminded them. "I can assure you that there is nothing to be done for my condition."

"There is *something*." The Gentleman's voice floated to me like fumes from a sewer.

The end was near if Mary did not return soon. "Just help me to my room."

Dennis all but carried me up the stairs, whereupon I collapsed onto the bed and told the boy to leave me be.

"Do us all a favor and don't die," Dennis said before closing the door.

Moonlight filled the room. The dresser mirror became a window overlooking a field of great mouths full of rotting fangs and teeth gnawing at frantic, naked people desperate to escape their biting and snapping. Tongues laced with fire curled around their legs and drew them down into the gaping maws. Sounds of crunching, chewing, and swallowing underlay the victims' screams. Brimstone and bile wafted over me.

"Is that what awaits me?" I asked the Gentleman. "Or is this more madness?"

The Gentleman's furious face burned before me, a cauldron with eyes. "You think something so pleasant as gnashing teeth and tongues of fire awaits you?" His laughter came as a wave of fetid air. "You will *wish* you could join them."

"This seems quite the show for someone who claims to be in a weakened state."

He bellowed his rage at me. "I could have kept Coombs going for *years*, but now I sink to the depths of Hell because your pathetic story caught his eye."

A pulse of pain struck my side where Coombs had impaled me with the saber. It felt worse than at the inquest. "That feels very real," I said through gritted teeth. A hand to the wound came back with blood. More spread into my shirt. The wound had opened. "It seems we are done." A whisper was all I could manage.

"As long as you have voice, you can save us." The Gentleman, barely more than a column of smoke, moved to the chair by the window. "Put something horrible in Burkett's room, along with a confession in Walker's desk drawer. Simple enough."

"I see what you mean about my words carrying more force here. You can say these things, and nothing happens. All you can do is whisper and hope you are obeyed. That must be eternally frustrating."

"Damn you."

It was my turn to laugh, but only for a moment as I bit my tongue when more pain seared through me.

So, this was to be my end, lying alone in a hotel bed, awaiting the eternal punishments of an elegant demon. Was Mary already gone? Would she arrive in Hell moments before me, or would eons have passed for her?

Mary. I saw her as she was when she held Nigel's head, a mischievous smile on her face, a light in her eyes. I even imagined hearing her voice. It seemed to be mixed with another, a male voice.

There was commotion at the door. Mr. Burkett seemed to be in a tither. A knock came, but I could not raise an answer. The door opened and a wavering shaft of light from the hall lantern showed two silhouettes.

"Dr. Johnson?" called Burkett.

Mary pushed past him, one hand on a cane, the other holding her stomach tight.

"This is most unorthodox," complained Burkett.

Mary came to my bedside. Burkett's lantern lit one side of her ashen, sallow face.

I had not the strength to gasp at what had become of her. Was this a ghoul? Had Mary died and this was her spirit come to take its revenge?

Mary waved Burkett away and stood in rigid silence until he left.

She stifled a cry and doubled over. Then she showed me her hand, covered in blood made black by the moonlight. Would her organs spill out of her here, in my room? Was that why she had returned, so that I could watch her die?

"What you have done to me." Her voice was hoarse, ragged.

To myself, I wanted to retort. To Batleigh, Thornsbury. And more yet to come, it would seem. "I saved your life."

Her eyes burned, but her voice was quiet. "You condemned my soul. You should have let my body die."

I struggled to speak.

"Save your breath," she said and pressed a folded paper to my chest. "For this. Read that aloud when I am gone."

"But I will be gone, too."

"Gone from the *room*. Read it aloud when I have left the *room*."

"Oh, yes. I see."

She shuffled out the door.

Moving as if deep underwater, I sat up, found a match and lit the lantern beside my bed. Each breath was an effort. I struggled to unfold the paper with stiff, weakened hands. The parchment had the weight of iron. The handwriting, with my blurred and dimmed vision, was unreadable. I pulled the lantern close and held the paper next to it until I could make out the words in their jagged, unsteady script. I willed breath into my lungs and began to read aloud.

"Taylor Brown was jealous. He wanted Helen Swendson to himself, but she was in love with Edwin McTernan. Mr. Brown wrote love letters to Miss Swendson, but they came back to him unopened. When he learned that Miss Swendson and Mr. McTernan had married, he took a pistol and shot them. He filled their pockets with stones and threw their bodies into River Rother. Then he took all the letters he had written to Miss Swendson, and his confession to their murders, and tied them together."

Wisps of smoke in the corner of the room, I realized, was what still remained of the Gentleman, gesturing. I continued reading.

"Mr. Brown thought he threw them away, but another resident of his boarding house found them and left them in the shadow of the front stairs of the Rotherton police station."

I recognized the names Mary had used from the local papers. A man and a woman had been found in a river, shot dead with their pockets full of stones. In another story, Taylor Brown had been arrested for stalking a woman and beating her fiancé. Mary had combined the stories and provided a way for the police to find the evidence.

The reading of the note took the last of my strength. I collapsed onto the bed. "Am I still dying?"

"Yes, until the police find that confession and arrest the culprit, Mr. Brown. She is quite brilliant, though," said the Gentleman. "She should be commended if we all survive until the confession is found."

I pondered what Mary had done. She had let it be known to me that she intended to remain alive, choosing the name of a criminal and writing a story. She had caused no direct harm, and merely signaled her intentions. She had also put the choice back in my hands. I could have chosen to read the story aloud or not.

"She is indeed. Now, be quiet." I sat up to douse the lamp, then lay back on the bed and closed my eyes, feeling both comfort and horror in knowing that should I awaken, it would be at the cost of someone's soul.

⸻○⸻

"You're looking much better, Doctor," said Burkett as I rounded the last turn of stairs behind the counter. I felt healthy and strong. I hated it.

"I am feeling much better, thank you. I apologize for the commotion yesterday. Bit of a fever, I suspect. And I also must apologize for the state of my bed. Had a bit of bleeding last night. Perhaps that was what I needed, to get out some ill humours, so to speak. At any rate, I will need some new bedding. And here are a few quid to replace them." I gave him some coins. "Any sign of Miss Woodmore?"

"None, sir. After that bit of inappropriateness, she went to her room and ain't come out since."

"I see. Well, I will take some breakfast, and if you would be so kind as to inform me when she emerges, it would be much appreciated."

The morning papers carried the news of the arrest of Taylor Brown, the man in Mary's story. It described in detail his resistance and death at the scene by pistol wound. His reported vows to "kill them all" as he died pleased the Gentleman.

"An unexpected bonus," said the Gentleman. "His soul was a bit sour, but acceptable."

I felt both physically invigorated and mentally drained.

Well after tea I received a message from Burkett that Mary wished to take the air with me.

CHAPTER FIFTY-TWO

RECONCILIATION

MARY AWAITED ME JUST OUTSIDE THE inn's door wearing a fur-trimmed, black wool coat and leather boots. I dismissed the thought of the bill I would be receiving and greeted her warmly. She, in turn, only slightly less so.

It was cold for March, and a wet snow had fallen. Boys in ragged clothes pushed the slush to the sides of the alley with fireplace spades and tipped their caps as we passed. One held his cap out and I tossed him a ha'penny. Mary did not stop or even slow as she led the way beyond the cleared walkway and continued to the street. When I came along beside her, she kept her eyes forward.

We walked in silence for some time until we came to Southwark Bridge. She slowed her pace and came to a stop at the midpoint, then looked out over the Thames. We appeared as any other unchaperoned couple strolling the bridge, though not as affectionate as some. Ripples and eddies reflecting the setting sun appeared as flames.

"Push her over."

I winced at the Gentleman's voice, but thankfully Mary did not see it.

"I should thank you," I said as I approached.

She turned a surprised look to me. "For … ?"

"Your story. It was an elegant solution to the immediate problem. It was also informative, in that it made clear how you feel about continuing in this manner."

"I have no clear feelings about it."

"I understand. Neither do I. It at least told me that you wanted to live. But know this: you should not have to do that again. I brought this … curse, whatever it is, upon us and it is my responsibility to maintain it for as long as we both choose to live."

She nodded and watched the river again. "I left it in God's hands," she said after a time. "When I had no strength of my own left, I started to make my way back to you. I told God that if I made it back here, if I *survived*, that meant He wanted me to continue. To find a way to redemption."

"I am glad you did." That was all I could think to say.

"There is always hope, you know. Redemption. Forgiveness."

Never having ascribed to the notion that one's transgression can be wiped clean because one asks nicely, I had no response.

"We are bound together, it seems," Mary said. "A situation I'm not pleased with at the moment, but one I can't change."

Absurdly, I had held the expectation of gratitude. Instead, she aimed a hard look my way. "I don't want to die. Do you understand that?"

"Yes. I do. But does that mean –"

"I don't know what it means! What you have *done* to me!" She turned away, fighting tears. "Saved me? You have doomed me."

"I am sorry. I only wanted –"

Her hand shot up to silence me. "It's done. Behind us. The question isn't what *was* done, but what to *do*."

"And what is that?"

She took a long, deep breath. "Dinner. Dinner is a thing we can do now that isn't likely to have anything to do with Hell."

"Depends on where you go," said the Gentleman.

"Then dinner it is," I said to Mary. "We will dine. Feast, if we so wish."

"I hate watching humans eat," said the Gentleman. "Have your fun," he added and disappeared.

We walked in silence to the other side of the Thames. I let her lead the way through the bustling streets. She stopped at each restaurant that displayed a menu.

"This one," said Mary, indicating a restaurant with an Italian name. "It looks exotic."

To me, it looked like any other brick-faced establishment in this section of London, but the sign and windows sported bright reds and greens, and I supposed that seemed exotic to someone from the moors.

The restaurant was crowded with boisterous patrons and was well-lit with electric lights. This utterly fascinated Mary and she questioned the staff – who assumed we were married – extensively about it. The potatoes and cabbage were served without sauce and the beef could have greased a railroad track, yet Mary ate ravenously. She would not allow me to send back the chicken and plucked the pinfeathers herself. Only the curried whitebait proved too much for her. Two servings of Vienna pudding eventually cooled her tongue.

Upon exiting the place, I raised the collar of my coat and tightened my scarf against the cold. Mary donned leather gloves. I found myself glad to see her enjoying her recent purchases. As we crossed back across the Southwark, we talked as any couple might after an evening out: the food, the weather, the sights around us. It was exquisitely banal.

The Gentleman appeared at my side as if he was just another companion. The streets were quieter now.

With the Langford arch in sight, Mary stopped. "What if it doesn't work?" she asked. "This business with the demon. It's with us now, I assume? What does it say about that?"

"As long as you do your job, dear boy, you both will remain alive."

I looked about us to ensure we would not be overheard. A lamplighter worked a distant part of the street. "He assures me that it will."

"And you trust it? A demon from Hell. You take it at its word?"

"Do you, dear boy?" Standing beside Mary, the Gentleman wore a pleasant smile beneath his burning eyes.

"Yes and no. I trust nothing he says, but I have no way to verify it."

The Gentleman laughed.

"So," Mary said, "we don't know from day to day – moment to moment, really – if the demon might decide to end the arrangement."

"He has said previously that he prefers this to being in Hell himself. Which, if I do not meet his quota, is a fate destined for all three of us."

"Ah. He has an incentive to maintain the status quo. Assuming, of course, that he is being truthful. About anything."

"Why would I lie about that?" asked the Gentleman.

"I cannot fathom why you would do anything. That was directed at the Gentleman."

"I gathered." She brushed her chin as she pondered something unspoken, then led the way back to the Langford.

The lobby was empty even of Mr. Burkett. A bell with a "Ring for service" sign adorned the counter. We said awkward good nights and took the stairs to our separate sides of the inn.

⇥═◉═⇤

A thud startled me out of restless dozing. Then came a rustling sound and the closet door slowly opened. A white figure emerged from the shadows and whispered, "William?"

"Mary?"

Suddenly she was on my bed, the white of her night gown distinct in the darkness.

"How did you … ?" I asked.

"There are back halls and doors. Joanna showed me."

I only had a moment to ponder this before Mary's lips were on mine.

"Mary, I –"

She shushed me. "Is it, this 'Gentleman', always with us?"

Only his burning eyes showed among the shadows. "He is here now, yes."

"Can it leave us alone?"

"Absolutely not," said the Gentleman.

"He says no."

"I hope it is entertained." She kissed me again. "I want to live. For tonight."

"But Mary –"

She held my head in her hands. "Listen to me. I. Want. To. *Live.*"

She pressed her open mouth to mine, using her tongue in a way polite society ladies do not. None I had met, at any rate.

Aroused, I pulled her in tightly. "So do I," I whispered in her ear.

The Gentleman made some comments about being disgusted, but I paid him little attention. Mary was enthusiastic, hungry, even. Her hands were rough, but elsewhere she was not. And she was considerably more experienced than I.

"We must be careful," I whispered.

"Joanna also gave me a sponge."

"Remind me to thank her." We laughed into each other's necks and continued unabated.

Later, as we lay in each other's arms, Mary whispered, "I want to go to church."

"Certainly, we can. Though we should probably wait until they are open, and we are dressed."

She laughed and it was a wonderful sound. "I'll take you to church. I assume you've never prayed? I'll teach you to pray, to ask forgiveness. If we are truly repentant, whatever our fate, we'll be redeemed."

Perhaps she had found the answer. Not in begging to be absolved of our chosen actions, but in allowing our Earthly fates to be what they will. If there was any truth to Mary's beliefs or what the Gentleman had told me, perhaps we would both end up where we belonged.

⊷➤◉◆⊶

When I awoke, Mary was gone, but her scent lingered in the sheets, her warmth on my body. I kept my eyes closed so I could hold the image of her smile. There was a peacefulness, a simple comfort, that I felt with her that was lacking in my few previous encounters. I felt a connection to more than her body that I believed went beyond our shared experience. I wanted to stay in that for as long as possible.

"Have you had your fun, dear boy?" As usual, the Gentleman sat in the chair as if invited.

I threw off the blankets and stood, letting him see my full nakedness.

"Yes, yes, now *that's* been taken care of," he said with a dismissive gesture, "you can thank me by getting on with the work."

I paused as I pulled on my underclothes. "Wait. Are you saying you *made* Mary do that?"

The Gentleman sighed. "I have told you this before. It is not within my power to *make* anyone do anything. If it were, where would the fun be? Does Punch feel remorse for beating Judy? Is he to rend his clothes, having squashed the baby?"

"Of course not. He's a puppet."

"Precisely. And does the punchman torture his puppet? No, that would be silly, would it not? How tedious it would be to punish them for following the script he gave them. He may as well slap his own hands."

I sat on the edge of the bed, buttoning my shirt, recalling the night before, picturing what I saw in Mary's eyes. I recalled the look in Garret's eyes while I was in his room. I knew now that the Gentleman had been whispering to him then. His gaze had turned inward, much like I imagined mine did when I listened to my brother's voice. Mary's eyes had been piercing, probing mine as her hands had explored my body. "I do not believe you," I said and went to the dining room.

CHAPTER FIFTY-THREE

COURTSHIP IN ADVERSITY

MY MORNING SCONE CAME WITH A note. Joanna stood by my table, bouncing on her feet and sporting a devilish grin. As I suspected, the note was from Mary.

The note said, in clear, precise script. "You should start courting me now. Aside from appearances, it will give us some measure of joy as we navigate this life of ours."

My breath quickened and my heart raced. I asked Joanna for a pen and she had one at the ready. I wrote, "And so the courting shall commence."

Joanna took the note and pen, gave a delighted squeal and dashed back to the kitchen.

I leaned back smiling, and breathed as if the air was new.

"Oh, we're smiling now, are we?" asked the Gentleman as he sat.

"I am." With my foot, I pushed the other chair out so that the table would not cut through him. I found it disturbing for some reason.

The Gentleman leaned forward. "Then you've fully embraced the work you must do?"

With a toss of my napkin, I got up from the table. I should have known better than to think I could express happiness. I took the air and pushed the Gentleman's nagging from my mind. I had a new puzzle to work out: how to court Mary. The joy I had felt earlier returned, but I strove not to show it.

We would need a chaperone. We had gotten away with a few private conversations, each of which had raised the eyebrows of many a passerby. But, if we were to begin courting, it would have to be done properly. Though I had dreaded the idea of courting while still in the thralls of my family's expectations, I looked forward to proudly escorting Mary around London town.

Mrs. Burkett would not be able to spare the time from her duties, and I suspected her social skills would be inadequate to the task. Joanna was too young. Short of hiring a chaperone, I could think of no one else but Adelia.

After returning to the Langford, I dictated a wire to Adelia, requesting her services as a chaperone so that I may properly court Mary. I waited anxiously in the lobby for her response, which came quickly. She was inclined to agree, but only after meeting with Mary privately.

"More distractions," snarled the Gentleman, his voice hot coals pressed into my ear.

I rushed out of the lobby to hide my reaction.

"We are getting further afield, dear boy."

The Gentleman appeared in front of me. I changed my direction and again, he was before me. "I can't let you continue like this."

Walking through him, I was nearly struck by a young lady on a bicycle. I called my apologies after her as she pedaled and swerved away. I continued to the gazebo where I had revealed the truth to Mary.

"Was Mr. Brown's soul not enough?" I hissed at the Gentleman.

He threw his head back and laughed. "Of course not. There will never be enough. But it is amusing that you could ever think so."

"I meant enough for *now*. A day, perhaps? You could grant us one day of peace."

"You're right, dear boy. I *could*," he said and continued laughing.

A laugh nearly burst from me, bitter though it would have been when I realized the futility of arguing for peace with a demon. "You will have your souls in due time," I said and marched back to the Langford.

⊷══◉ ◉══⊶

A tea was arranged for Adelia to meet Mary. Burkett allowed Mary and I to be seated together, having received a wire from Adelia stating that she would be late, but would arrive on the nonce.

"My apologies for shocking you with my note," Mary said.

"The note was considerably less shocking than your visit," I said with a grin.

Mary blushed. "You must think me so forward. But it is the proper thing to do. Courting, I mean. The other was … well, after recovering, I had so much energy." A sly grin spread on her face. "It had to go somewhere."

"No apologies necessary," I said, blushing as deeply as her I suspected. "Courting seems prudent, given our circumstances."

"We are already bound, in a certain way. A way that would make courting others … difficult at best. What would I say to a husband? 'Sorry I'm late with dinner, dear, but I had to feed a demon first.'" There was bitterness in her laugh.

"I agree we are bound. And yes, such matters would be problematic, but I believe we could work them out, if so desired. But …"

My heart began to race. I feared that if I revealed my feelings, she would assume all I had done had been simply to entrap her.

"You have wanted it, haven't you?"

My face grew hot.

"Why else would you have done all that you've done if you weren't interested in me?"

"Please know that my actions have not been predatory. You have always been free to choose another … path."

She pulled her head back in surprise. "Free? Have I?"

"I believe you know what I mean."

After a moment's thought, she relaxed. "I suppose I do. I think you've proven yourself. You have been a gentle –" She stopped, cleared her throat, then continued. "You have been a kind man. Considerate."

"Thank you. I do admit a strong attraction to you upon meeting."

Now it was her turn to blush. "Really?"

"Yes, of course."

She contemplated her tea. "I … I'm surprised. I mean, all the elegant, high-class women you must meet …"

I reached out and touched her hand. She wrapped her fingers around mine. I held her hand until she looked into my eyes. "Do you not know how beautiful you are?"

She gave a tiny gasp, then pulled her hand back to cover her mouth. "I'm not …"

"You *are*. Truly."

"Thank you," she whispered. "Perhaps courting will be more than just a duty resulting from our situation." She beamed a smile at me.

"While the circumstances that brought us here are not ideal, the result is precisely what I hoped for. Let me add that rarely have I felt such a strong, immediate attraction to someone."

She took a sip of her tea. "I can't deny something similar, but I have learned to be wary of men and my feelings towards them. I have … made mistakes."

"So have we all." I raised my cup. "To mistakes!"

Mary laughed and joined my toast. "To mistakes!"

Those patrons who were not already eyeing us now turned and cast their frowns our way. I cared not, and Mary seemed to be unaware.

Adelia arrived soon after and introductions were made. To placate Burkett, it was agreed they would take their conversation to the ladies' tearoom.

"I did say I wanted to meet with her privately," said Adelia. "Woman to woman, as it were."

"Certainly," I said, bowing.

"Here's a deal for you," said the Gentleman. "Give me both of them and I'll give you peace for a week."

I tensed in an attempt to hide my reaction.

"William," Mary said quickly, "it's all right." Likely, she realized what had happened. "We won't say *too* many awful things about you."

I forced a laugh with them and took my leave.

"*Two* weeks?" the Gentleman asked. "One for each soul. You can go on holiday!"

"Stop it," I said, feigning a cough.

In the lobby, I sat in the chair by the fire, then on the bench by the door.

"I could go in and listen," said the Gentleman.

"No, thank you," I said as I stepped out into the alley. "I would not be able to believe anything you told me. And, it goes without saying that I want to respect Mary's privacy," I added.

"Yet you said it."

"Be quiet, please."

Later, I went back to the chair, trying to steal glimpses of their conversation. Were they relaxed? Tense? Enjoying each other's company? A fear brewed in my mind of how much Mary might tell Adelia. My glimpses were few and far between as patrons and servants often blocked my view.

Finally, they finished their tea and came to the lobby.

"Dr. Johnson," said Adelia. "I would be only too happy to serve as chaperone to you and Miss Woodmore. However," she added to stop my response, "Miss Woodmore will no longer reside here at the Langford. She will continue to work in the kitchen, of course, because that is her desire. But living here is not appropriate. There are stories of secret passageways in old buildings such as this, and that can lead to untoward situations."

Mary, just behind Adelia, gave a shy smile and a shrug.

"Therefore," Adelia continued, "Miss Woodmore will reside with me. My father engages a jobmaster, and thus Miss Woodmore will be provided transportation. As for courting, a schedule will be sent to you shortly. Is this acceptable to you, Dr. Johnson?" There was an amused glint in Adelia's eyes.

"Yes, Miss Clavijo. Of course." I wondered if Burkett would reimburse me for Mary's room for the remainder of the week. "I look forward to receiving the schedule."

"Excellent." She turned away. "Mary, gather your things, I'll explain the situation to the Burketts."

Mary thanked her, started a hug, retracted it, bowed, and hurried off.

Adelia stepped closer to me. "She is a remarkable young woman. In need of guidance, but she has excellent instincts and was brought up well. Listen to her. And treat her kindly, or you will hear from me." That she said without humour.

"Of course. And thank you."

"You will have to change your living arrangements," Adelia said with a chuckle.

I laughed with her and, as Mary returned with a single bag, I promised to make changes should the need arise. However, I had no desire to purchase property and engage household staff, which would only provide fodder for the Gentleman's demands. Should Mary and I survive long enough to require a house, I would deal with the problem then.

Just after dinner, the courting schedule arrived in a lavender-scented envelope with a hand-written card. Two evenings hence, I was to bring Mary to her favorite restaurant. I held the note close, breathing in the perfume while I grit my teeth against the Gentleman's voice.

⊷═◉ ◉═⊷

Adelia and I together chose the evening's fare: oysters and lemon, Julienne soup, soles with mussel sauce, prawns in aspic, pigeon, mutton, vegetable and Russian salad, with chocolate pudding for dessert.

I watched helplessly as the Gentleman hovered around Adelia and occasionally whispered in her ear. I could not hear what he said, but his grin was as mischievous and evil as ever.

Adelia struggled to maintain her composure, but I could see her expression darken as she cast her eyes downward.

Mary seemed to recognize the dip in Adelia's mood, but I had no way of knowing if she understood why. She kept trying to engage Adelia in conversation, as did I, but Adelia kept reminding us that her job as chaperone was to merely observe and let us have our time together.

Despite this, Mary's excitement was both undeniable and infectious. We primarily discussed what we would do while courting, other places we would go, sights we would see. Her wide-eyed wonder and bubbling laughter thrilled me and sometimes even drew in Adelia, until the Gentleman would bend to her ear again and the light would drain from her eyes.

Was the Gentleman preparing Adelia for sacrifice? He had said he required his victims to forsake hope and light. Could this be the first shadows of a looming darkness? Perhaps he was beginning to loosen her hold on her own mind, to make it that much easier to eventually let go.

There was no opportunity for me to speak privately with Adelia through the rest of the evening, nor the carriage ride back to the Clavijo estate.

When the three of us retired to the sitting room, Adelia said, "I must check with my maid-of-all-work. I will return shortly." Her wink and smile suggested that our time alone would be anything but short.

"Did she seem sad to you?" Mary asked me the moment Adelia was gone.

"Yes, I did sense that." I decided not to tell her about the Gentleman's manipulations. There was nothing either of us could do about it. It seemed to me that it would be yet another burden Mary was forced to carry.

"Maybe we could help her find someone?" Mary said. "We could go courting together. It would do me good to see people who are actually happy and not playacting."

"Are you not happy?" I asked, taking her hand.

"How could I possibly be *happy*? I suppose I'm as happy as can be expected. I do enjoy your company. Very much so." She gave me a lengthy kiss. "But the circumstances …" She took her hand back and dabbed her eyes again. "Do we have any idea how long it will be before we need … another story?"

Putting my arm around her, I held her close. "The Gentleman prefers not to tell me such things. I think he finds it more entertaining to keep us in the dark. And I would not be able to believe anything he tells me. Still, he does grow impatient. His appetite for souls far surpasses our need for survival."

Mary touched my cheek. "Is he terrible to you?"

I smiled and put my hand on hers. "So far, he has only been a pest," I said. "But I suspect he will use more drastic measures if we wait too long."

"You *will* tell me if it becomes unbearable."

I kissed her hand. "Of course," I said, knowing I would not burden her with such things.

She took my head in her hands, turned me to face her and stared deeply into my eyes. "You will tell me." She smiled, but it was a demand. "Since I returned, we share this burden now."

"I will tell you," I said, accepting the truth of her words.

We kissed and continued to do so for some unmeasured and wonderful time until there came a soft knock on the door.

"It's Adelia," she said through a tiny opening.

Mary and I separated.

"It's all right," Mary said. "Come in."

"It's getting late," Adelia said with a sheepish grin.

I said my goodnights to them both and found the butler waiting at the end of the hall. I followed him through the quiet mansion. He was a tall, fit fellow with a confident stride.

"Downes, is it?" I asked.

"Yes, sir," he said with barely a turn back to me.

"I appreciate you staying up so late."

"Wouldn't want you getting lost, sir," he said as we entered the foyer at the main entrance. "McKenna will take you home, sir."

He opened the front door for me and there stood the Gentleman. "He's here," the Gentleman hissed. "The papist is nearby."

Downes tried to close the door, but I held it open.

"Sir?" Downes said.

Malvagna had easily bested Coombs, so I knew I would need help. Perhaps the mere presence of another would be enough to put Malvagna off whatever he had planned.

"Did you hear something?" I asked.

"Such as, sir?" Downes peered into the darkness beyond the door.

"I am not sure. But in my work, I have made enemies. Step out here with me and perhaps I can locate the sound." I said the last to the Gentleman, hoping he could give me some direction.

"I'm not sure," said the Gentleman. "But his presence is very strong. Perhaps the stables."

"I think it was by the stables," I told Downes, pointing. I knew they were off to our left.

Downes stepped out and peered in that direction.

A silent moment passed, as tense as a compressed spring. A horse whinnied.

"McKenna?" called Downes. "Have you readied the carriage?"

Silence followed.

Downes stepped back inside. "Wait here, sir, while I –"

"No, Downes. We go together."

He gave a flash of surprise, then a grim nod. "Take a walking stick, sir," he said, indicating the stand next to the door. "I'll get a lantern."

I chose the heaviest one, with a brass ram's head.

Downes had turned a corner. I heard him whisper names. Grumbling voices and footsteps followed. Downes hushed them. "Possible trouble in the stables," I heard him say. "Bring weapons."

Soon, he emerged with a lantern and two young footmen, only half dressed, just behind. One carried a pickaxe, the other, a hammer.

The Gentleman awaited us outside. "Fine young men," he said as he examined them. "Perhaps when this is done –"

"*Quiet*," I hissed.

Downes shot a glare at me. "Yes," he said to the footmen, "as he says."

He led us across the yard, with only the lantern to guide us in the moonless night. At the stables, he stopped us.

"McKenna!" he barked. "Are you there?"

One of the footmen moved to the stable door. There came a shout from inside. A startled horse squealed and burst out, trampling the footman.

Downes and I charged into the stable while the other footman tended to his fallen comrade. We came to a carriage and heard footsteps at the back, followed by the crash and clatter of crates and equipment falling. We ran to the back door, but our path was blocked.

In the distance, I could just make out a figure running across the yard and disappearing into the hedges beyond. It was a stocky figure, dressed in black.

"It was *him*," said the Gentleman, beside me.

As Downes summoned Mr. Clavijo, I examined the scene. The driver, McKenna, had been in a brutal fight, as evidenced by the damage to the area where I found him and the wounds on his face and head. He was still unconscious when servants came to carry him away.

Malvagna's plan seemed clear: subdue the driver, then take his place so that when I thought I was being driven home, I would be whisked off to his torture chamber in the closed church. If not for the Gentleman having sensed him, it would likely have worked.

Mr. Clavijo praised me for my alertness. It was decided that, since the women had not been awakened, they would not be told of the events.

Downes himself drove the carriage that returned me to the Langford.

I stood at the opening of the alley. The street was dark and quiet. As much as I hated to, I quietly thanked the Gentleman.

He was not appreciative. "This only emphasizes the need to practice the words."

CHAPTER FIFTY-FOUR

HARD LESSON

Two evenings later, Mary, sitting next to me, peered out the carriage window as it rumbled to a stop. We had come to a village square on the outskirts of London.

"Is this more to your liking?" asked Adelia, across from us.

We had started the evening at Piccadilly Circus, but Mary had been overwhelmed by the sheer number of people milling about. The chaos and noise had made her uncomfortable, though she had been reluctant to say so. As soon as Adelia suggested a quieter place, Mary had leapt at the chance.

"Yes," she said quietly. She set her hand on mine. "I'm sorry, I know you had the whole evening planned."

I kissed her hand. "The plan was to spend the evening with you."

Downes, whose new duty was to remain by Adelia's side, held up a hand, then opened the door.

"I still don't understand why you're here, Downes," said Adelia.

"Master Clavijo's order, my lady," he said with a practiced smile.

"Yes, but I don't know *why* he gave such orders."

Downes glanced at me then said, "He chose not to explain why, my lady, and it is not my place to question."

He opened the door, looked to both sides, then stepped out. After another check of the sidewalk, he held out his hand for Adelia.

Mary gave me a questioning glance as she stepped out, but I had no answer for her at the time. I felt it was not my place to inform either Mary or Adelia of what Mr. Clavijo chose to keep from them.

Afternoon drizzle had left the roads muddy, the sidewalks slick. The square was lined with shops and restaurants. They were busy, but nothing compared to Piccadilly. Mary and I walked arm in arm. She was fascinated by the number of shops and people.

A dress shop caught her eye. She and Adelia began to talk about Mary's wardrobe and how to expand it.

"Perhaps," I suggested, "you ladies should continue without me while I take the air."

Adelia and Mary expressed mock reluctance to leave me on my own, then hurried into the shop. Downes lingered at the door.

"Look at all the colorful souls around me," said the Gentleman.

"Do be quiet," I grumbled.

The Gentleman's eyes flared, and his voice burned in my ear. "You are not doing the work, and I will not be put off any longer."

Across the road I found a stone bench, dried it as best I could, and sat. The square bustled with happy people. A pair of cart drivers argued over who should pass while their horses whickered at each other.

"Do *not* ignore me," said the Gentleman. "This could end at any moment. The papist hunts you. Mary could suddenly be infected with her 'conscience' and all she would need do is jiggle her flesh and you would follow her into oblivion. I demand souls and I am tired of your games."

I chose not to tell him that I was tired of his threats. Constant fear had exhausted me.

"Would you mind?"

I turned to see a bearded man in tweed and a bowler hat. With a newspaper, he gestured towards what was, to him, the empty end of the bench. The Gentleman, sitting there, peered at him.

"Quite all right with me," I said to the man. "But my friend would prefer it if you did not sit on him."

The man huffed, puffed, and stormed off.

"Or would it be *in* you?" I asked.

"I see you still do not take me seriously. Adelia's soul. I will have it." An idea came to him. "Perhaps Mary could write another story. Yes, the added weight of such an act on Mary's soul when she eventually comes to me will be quite delicious."

Through a shop window I saw Mary and Adelia share a bit of gossip, perhaps, then simultaneously burst into laughter, leaning back, and throwing their joy to the ceiling. I had never made Mary laugh in that way.

"I will not give you her soul, and neither will Mary. No Hell you can conjure would be worse than the one we would be living in."

"Then it seems a lesson is in order." The Gentleman dissolved like powder dropped in water.

My entire body clenched. Would lightning strike? Perhaps creatures breathing brimstone would burst from the ground to devour us.

The man in the bowler hat had found a perch on a low stone wall. The Gentleman was at his ear. The man turned to me, his face twisted by anger. Then he shook his head and turned away. The Gentleman kept at him. Finally, the man pushed off the wall and stormed towards me.

"That's a public bench!" he shouted.

Jumping to my feet, I apologized and told him to take the whole bench. It was not enough to quiet him.

"Who do you think you are?" His gestures were sharp and threatening, his face nearly purple with rage.

"And so it begins," said the Gentleman.

"I can call for a constable," I told them both, but the Gentleman was gone.

I moved away from the angry man and let a hansom separate us.

A gangly teen boy rushed up to me. "*You're* the one what's got my thruppence?"

Behind him, the Gentleman held his arms high and waggled his fingers as if operating a marionette.

"I beg your pardon?" I asked as I tried to move past the young man.

He stepped in front of me and pushed me by the shoulders. "You pick my pocket, ya thief?"

He ignored my denials and even my offers of money, as this only served to convince him that I was guilty.

The angry man in the bowler caught up to me. When I tried to evade one, the other intercepted me.

The Gentleman danced and capered joyfully.

Mary and Adelia emerged from the shop. They strolled along the street, arm in arm, with the air of lifelong friends. Out from an alley nearby stepped a tall, brutish man. The Gentleman, now as tall as the man, stood behind him, whispering in his ear.

Shoving the two men away and sending them tumbling, I ran towards Mary and Adelia, calling their names. The noise of an approaching omnibus, its horses whinnying under the shouts and whips of the driver, obscured my voice. I ran around the back of the bus.

Mary and Adelia stood at a linen shop window, unaware of the approaching thug.

The Gentleman was at Downes' ear, keeping him distracted.

My calls to them were too late. The thug clubbed Downes on the head, then shoved Mary into the shop window. She cried out fell to the sidewalk. He struck Adelia across the face, lifted her over his shoulder and lumbered away quickly to the next alley. People nearby shouted, some followed.

A passerby helped Mary to her feet. She saw me approach. "Adelia!" Mary cried, pointing.

I ran at full speed in the direction the thug had gone and caught a glimpse of Adelia's flailing feet as he turned down another alley. I charged around the corner and shouted at the thug to halt. He did, and my racing heart nearly stopped.

Adelia, still on his shoulder, pounded her fists at him, though her face dripped blood. He dropped her on the alley floor. She cried out and writhed in pain.

A constable's whistle pierced the din from the street.

Spittle dripped from the thug's mouth as he charged at me. I curled into a ball, rolling into his legs. He went down face first into the stones. His legs felt like trees on me. He kicked as I tried to pull away, then scrambled to his knees and turned around. He spat out a bloody tooth as he lunged at me. My attempt to escape failed as he pulled me to the ground. I tried to bat him away but soon his hands were on my neck. He shook me as he choked me, my shoulders and head striking the alley floor. A darkness tinged with sparkling lights threatened to take me until the thug let me go to fight off a constable with a truncheon.

Gasping and coughing, I was vaguely aware of their battle and of more bobbies coming to join the fight. As they took him down, I dragged myself over to Adelia, who was unconscious but breathing.

The Gentleman came to my ear. "There are many more like him. I only need encourage them to give in to their urges. I want this woman's soul."

"Then why involve me at all?"

"Why should *I* do all the work?"

I pressed my handkerchief to Adelia's head wound. "You believe this will make me give you Adelia's soul?"

"If you don't give it to me, I will *take* it." The Gentleman's eyes burned. "I will send such misery her way that when one of my acquaintances finishes her, she will have abandoned all hope and will be in Hell, waiting to join us."

Mary found us then. I wondered if I should have told the truth in Governor Thornsbury's office and let the hangman's noose take me.

CHAPTER FIFTY-FIVE

BALANCE TO BE FOUND

AFTER BEING BANDAGED AND GIVEN PILLS for my headache, I checked on Downes. He was conscious but still in a weakened state. I left the men's ward of Westminster Hospital and waited in the lobby, where I found Adelia's father. I had met him briefly the day Mary moved into the Clavijo estate. He was darker than Adelia by a fair sight, and his hair of pitch-black waves was slicked down tight to his scalp in a vain attempt to hide its recession. Where he had been cold and aloof in our previous meeting, now he was effusive in his praise of me for saving his daughter. I let false humility mask the disgust I felt for myself for having put her in danger in the first place.

A nurse brought word from the women's wing that Mary wished to stay by Adelia's side and that I should not wait for her. Adelia's father insisted that he would provide protection and transportation for her. I let his driver take me back to the Langford, as the hour was late, my neck still pained me, and my head still rang.

The Langford was quiet, the lobby empty. I made my way to my room and lay down, but sleep was impossible.

The Gentleman, in his chair, became alarmed. He sat up, tensed. "Something is coming."

I had only ever seen the Gentleman afraid of one person. "Is it Malvagna?"

A part of me hoped it was the priest. Perhaps we would finally have an end to all this. Still, I pushed myself up, grunting with pain, and looked about the room for a weapon.

Footsteps sounded in the passage approaching the closet. "I believe it is Mary," I said.

"No, there's something else," said the Gentleman. He took the same stance he had at the abandoned building, with his arms crossed, his hands on his shoulders.

The closet door rattled, Mary stepped through, then closed it.

"You see?" I said, breathing my relief. "It is only Mary."

"I don't have long," she said. "The driver is waiting to take me to the Clavijo estate. Adelia will be staying the night at hospital. I wanted to let you know."

"Thank you for that," I said.

But the Gentleman did not relax. "What are you doing, Mary?"

Mary turned from the door as she closed it, and I saw that she wore a cross around her neck. She held it between her fingers. "This was my father's," she said, her voice full of quiet menace.

"Mary?" I said as I moved along the bed.

She took out a small glass vial and I recognized it instantly: holy water.

"Be very, very careful, child," said the Gentleman.

"You said it doesn't like churches," said Mary to me. "Is it the building? What about the holy objects within it? Perhaps it's both. Let's find out, shall we?" When she pulled out the stopper, it made a small, almost comical, pop. She put some on her fingertips, then dabbed it on her neck as if it were perfume.

"Oh, this will not end well for you," the Gentleman said.

I was equal parts thrilled and terrified.

"Where is it?" Mary asked. "Your 'Gentleman'?"

"He is standing before the chair in front of the window," I told her, pointing.

"That was your work today, wasn't it?" she asked in his general direction.

"Yes," I said. "It was him. He coerced that man into attacking you, Adelia, and Downes. He thinks that will convince me to give him Adelia's soul."

"Ah," said Mary. "I see. And what was your response?"

"I refused, of course."

"Good." She sprinkled some of the holy water on the floor in front of the chair.

The Gentleman recoiled and disappeared, reappearing next to me. "Control your woman, dear boy."

"Did I get it?" Mary asked.

"No, he moved. He is beside me now." I pointed at the spot.

"Traitor," the Gentleman said. "If it's revenge she's after, it will be a short-lived victory."

"He says that if you want revenge –"

"That's not what I want," said Mary, facing us. "Not today. I want it to know how very, very serious I am right now. What I came here for is compromise. Balance." She looked at the space I had indicated, but not quite at the Gentleman. "We can give you souls, but only of our choosing. If you try to force us again, I will drown you in this." Having capped the vial of holy water again, she held it up, turning and examining it. "It seems to have an aversion to holy things, yes? Churches, crosses, and the like."

The Gentleman gave no answer.

"I believe so," I said. "I have seen these things cause him harm."

"Harm, yes," said Mary. "But not from ordinary things. Any two pieces of wood nailed together, a bit of water, these wouldn't do anything, I'm sure. But when they're blessed, imbued with prayers and faith, they become deadly to him."

"Take that thing from her and pour it in a sewer," the Gentleman growled at me.

"So it would seem," I said and immediately began devising methods by which to test this theory. Would the prayers of any devout Christian work? And what of Buddhists?

"Those are objects," said the Gentleman. "And objects can be taken away."

"Is it talking to you?" Mary said. "Does it think it can take this from me by sending more thugs? It should know that my father left me *many* things I'm sure are equally dangerous to it."

The Gentleman's eyes flared. "If she thinks she can dictate terms to *me* –"

"But," I interrupted, "it appears she *can* dictate terms to you. She has in her hands the means to send you to Hell. And I believe she has in her heart the resolve to do so."

"Yes, I do," said Mary, beaming at me. "The only reason I can continue with this is that I can see a path to redemption. If you – by which I mean the Gentleman, of course – block that path, then there is no way forward for me."

The Gentleman's eyes smouldered.

"He seems to be considering it," I said.

"Very well," the Gentleman said. "I recall watching her recklessly attack Coombs, despite the fact that he could easily kill her. It seems her rage is sufficient to overcome her self-preservation. So go ahead, feed me the dregs, the flotsam and jetsam of humanity. Destroy my palette."

"He has agreed," I told Mary, and we embraced.

"Yes," said the Gentleman. "Celebrate. Tell her this or I will give you such nightmares that you will never sleep again: her path to redemption is a gilded road in a graveyard. All you are doing is denying the downtrodden their own chance at redemption. Cutting them off from the forgiveness she seeks."

The turmoil in Mary's eyes was obvious. I kissed her gently and sent her on her way. When the closet door was closed, I turned to the Gentleman. "Give me your nightmares. None will be so bad as it would be to diminish the light in her eyes."

Sitting at the desk, I could not sleep. There had to be a way to end this, short of giving up and letting the Gentleman drag us to Hell. Perhaps there was something in the items Mary had received from her father. Was there a holy object of some kind, a ritual or prayer that could excise him?

"I would ask you what you're thinking," said the Gentleman from his chair, "but I believe I can guess. And let me assure you, there is nothing you can do."

"You realize the more you say that, the more it makes me want to prove you wrong?"

"Oh, yes. And the more it makes your defeats all the sweeter."

The desire to scream at him was powerful, but I would not give him the satisfaction. There had to be a solution, but how could I research it and make any plans with him constantly at my side?

CHAPTER FIFTY-SIX

ACCIDENTAL SACRIFICE

I AWOKE IN PAIN. I STRUGGLED to dress and to convince myself that this pain and weakness was due to the fight with the thug, but I knew there was more, that I was weakening as I had previously. My vision was dimmed, my breathing was shallow. It would soon be time for another decision.

"Are you punishing us?" I asked the Gentleman. "Making us weaker, forcing us into another sacrifice because of what Mary said last night?"

"Punish you? Force you?" The Gentleman shook his head. "You speak as if all of this is *my* fault. As if *I* were the one to put us in this situation. You, dear boy, *you* created these circumstances. I have never been bound to two people, therefore I know very little about what will or will not happen."

"None of which answers my question."

The Gentleman's only response was to smile and shrug.

I had no appetite, and so after coffee I took a cab to the Clavijo estate. Downes, sporting a bandage on his head, answered the door.

"I'm on the mend," he said in response to my query, though he looked subdued.

He summoned the maid-of-all-work, who informed me that Adelia was much better but that Mary had taken ill. She told me the ladies apologized for not being able to take visitors. Then, while barely hiding a puzzled expression behind her mask of service, gave me a sealed envelope with the words, "Read aloud" written on it.

I accepted the envelope with gratitude that I did not feel. I knew it would be another story, another sacrifice.

The Gentleman walked beside me as I returned to the cab. "At least one of you has some sense."

I did not open the letter until I was in my room. I held it in my trembling hands without looking at it. This was Mary's choice, but was it mine, still? I weighed the thought of some stranger's eternal suffering against that of Mary's, first here and then in Hell, and began to read.

"Miss Bertie Deneau was a wicked woman. She sold stolen goods, false papers, and even her own body, all to support a penchant for gambling. When her debt became too great, she offered herself as payment. But in the heat of passion, she sliced the throat of her debtor and ran off."

Once again, Mary had found a way to combine stories in the papers: a woman arrested for prostitution and a loan shark found murdered. As I read the story aloud, I could feel the shadows forming the confession connecting this woman to the murder.

"In her rush to escape, Bertie left behind, in the pool of her debtor's blood, the note she had written to gain the debtor's access, promising herself to him. That blood-stained note had been left by persons unknown in a constable's desk drawer."

When the Gentleman finished his gestures, he frowned.

"What is it now?" I asked, not really wanting to know.

"Mary left this Bertie person alive. Being a woman, she's not likely to hang."

"True, but you said the misery a victim experiences gives you sustenance."

"Chocolate pudding gives you sustenance, but would you make a steady diet of it?"

A sad laugh rolled out of me. "Perhaps there is no balance to be found." I used the lamp to burn the letter, then staggered back to bed, wondering how long before the misery of others would restore my life and health.

The following morning, I expected to read about the unfortunate Miss Deneau over breakfast, but the kitchen was closed and only Mr. Burkett seemed to be about. He was near to tears and wore a black armband.

"I apologize for the lack of service today," he said, "but I'm afraid there's been a death in the family. My wife's sister, Bertie, was found dead last night. Murdered, it seems."

"Bertie? Do you mean Bertie Deneau? She was murdered?"

"Yes, but how do you know her name?"

I stammered. "I saw it. In the paper. I was down earlier," I said in response to his questioning look. "Then I went back up."

He nodded, puzzled, but it seemed he had more important matters on his mind. He shook his head sadly. "She was a troubled woman, she was. Never married. In and out of jail. My wife, she hardly talked to her. Wouldn't let us even mention her name. But then ol' Bertie would show up for a holiday here or a birthday there. And the children, oh how they loved her. She didn't come 'round often, but when she did, it was always a party."

My heart sank. "I am so sorry, Mr. Burkett." I fought tears as I spoke. He undoubtedly took them as sympathy for him, but they were for Mary and the pain I knew she would feel. "If there is anything at all I can do to help, please let me know."

"Thank you, Doctor." He turned away, then back. "I know Joanna could use a friend right now. If you could fetch Miss Mary, bring her here. She's always a bit of brightness in the kitchen."

"Of course, Mr. Burkett."

"Yes," said the Gentleman. "Send the person who caused the misery to comfort one suffering from it. Delightful!"

Clenching my fists, I took a long, slow breath to fight off the urge to rage at the Gentleman.

I took a newspaper from the lobby, then went out to look for a cab. I fought against the wind to read the newspaper but was determined to know what had happened. Bertie Deneau was supposed to have been arrested, not killed. Her story was indeed in the paper, but there was more than what Mary had envisioned. It seemed the man whom Bertie had killed according to Mary's story had a vengeful acquaintance. When the police, acting on the confession Mary's words had created, came to arrest Bertie, they found her dead. They believed it to be an act of revenge.

"This was you again, was it not?" I asked the Gentleman.

"Why would you assume that?"

"Because Bertie Deneau and the murdered man were unrelated until I read Mary's story. There was nothing to connect them until we created that confession. And no way for the person who killed Bertie to know about it. Unless you told someone with a penchant for violence."

The Gentleman smiled. "You did not truly expect me to take Mary's threats lying down, did you? A whisper in the ear of the right person and vengeance is carried out. It makes for a much better story, don't you think?"

A quick cab ride to the Clavijo estate and I found myself standing before Downes once again. I asked him to inform Mary that there had been a death in the Burkett family and that her friend Joanna would very much appreciate her company.

Mary came running, and Downes summoned a driver for us. During the ride back, I explained what had happened.

"We killed Joanna's *aunt*?" Mary wailed. "I should have known this wouldn't work. To think that *I* could judge who should die and who shouldn't. First the attack on Adelia. Now *this*. I don't know if I can continue." She cried in my arms all the way back to the Langford. Once there, she ran to Joanna.

I returned to my room.

"Did you know that was Joanna's aunt?" I asked the Gentleman.

"Of course, dear boy. Why do you think I whispered her name to Mary?

Bertie Deneau's soul was quite delicious, and she just keeps on giving. Joanna has cursed God and vowed to never step foot in a church again. Thank Mary for me, would you?"

"Our little game may be coming to an end," I told the Gentleman. "I suspect Mary will not wish to continue in this way. And if she does not, I expect I will not have the will."

As the evening turned to night, I lit no lamps and instead welcomed the dark. I lay on the bed in my clothes and watched the clouds slither over the waning moon.

"Are you so afraid of your own choices?" asked the Gentleman. "You keep putting this in Mary's hands. It's easy to say you accept the consequences of your own choices when you don't make them yourself."

My first response was to deny his accusation. Instead, I took it in. "Perhaps," I said when a cloud revealed the moon again. "If it was only my choice, I would have made it months ago."

"You say that to justify yourself."

I laughed. "Have you been reading my psychology books over my shoulder? Did you not recognize that I am not the leader? I am the assistant, the helper, not the one who stands at the front and points. Even as a child, I let my fantasies about my brother lead me. The very fantasies upon which you preyed. The open mouth for your hook, to use your analogy. So do not feign surprise that I am willing – eager, even – to let another make decisions."

"That is the key to your ability to accept consequences, I think. You can tell yourself you did not make the big decisions and are thus blameless."

"Is this analysis a preview of the torture I will receive?"

Now it was the Gentleman's turn to laugh.

CHAPTER FIFTY-SEVEN

AN UNWELCOME GUEST

THE NEXT DAYS WERE DIFFICULT AS the Burketts dealt with the death of Bertie Deneau. They still had a hotel to run and did the best they could. Mary stayed with Joanna the entire time. Adelia even took time to be with both of them. A wake was held in the dining room. Stories were told of Bertie's life and what she meant to everyone, and I believe Mary wept as much as Joanna.

In the morning I sat on the edge of the bed for a time. I had no desire to dress and face the world. Even Mary, ever hopeful, faithful Mary, seemed to have lost her will to go on. What was there left for me? Nothing but the mechanics of daily living. If Mary was done, who was I to convince her otherwise? But was I ready to leave the world behind? Regardless of where I might end up, in nothingness or Hell, I did not want to let the Gentleman win. I made myself presentable and left the room.

One of my fellow residents who had a few years and a few inches on me came out of his room across the hall and gave me a polite nod. We made small talk on our way downstairs, about how pleasant March had been thus far and how we both hoped there would be sausages. I made all the polite, socially expected sounds as we walked, but I could not help but wonder if Mary and I might find his name in the paper, if he had committed some crime that might put him on our list.

When we reached the stairs, I let him go ahead as an even more disturbing thought struck me: what if he was a murderer, as yet uncaught? He would enjoy his breakfast while some other person who had made an unfortunate choice and had the ill luck to be arrested for it would be condemned for eternity should his name catch our eye. I recalled that I myself had once appeared in the papers and would have been a likely target for one of Mary's stories. I held the rail and took the stairs slowly as I found myself shaking.

"Do you smell that?" asked the Gentleman, waiting for me at the bottom of the stairs.

"Bacon?" I asked, grateful for the distraction.

"No. It is *him* again."

Through the tiny lobby, I saw in the dining room a sight that nearly brought me to the floor: Malvagna. He sat at a table, across from Mary. She turned and gave a friendly wave while patrons stared at them, aghast that a young woman was sitting with an older man – let alone a priest – unaccompanied by a chaperone.

"Ah, good morning, Doctor," called Malvagna, waving me over. "Perhaps you could look at this?" He showed me a bruise and a cut on his cheek. "As I told the *bella donna*, Miss Woodmore, the work I do can be dangerous," he said with a knowing grin.

I moved to the table as quickly as I could without causing alarm.

"Mary, are you all right?" I asked.

"Of course," she said with a polite but empty smile. "Why wouldn't I be?"

"We have been having a lively discussion about redemption and the value of confession," Malvagna said. "How could that be harmful?"

"Because I have seen what redemption means to you," I said. "Mary, there are things you should know about this man."

She stood. "I think I know all I need to. I should get back to work." She hurried into the kitchen.

"What do you think you are doing?" I demanded.

Malvagna sipped his coffee. "Learning. The newspapers, they do not tell you everything, do they?"

I waited while Joanna brought my usual coffee and biscuits. "And what have you learned?"

"That you have bespoiled that young woman," he said with a pleasant smile, though he spoke in a menacing tone. "The evil Coombs carried. He gave it to you, and you have stained her with it. You both must be cleansed."

"Cleansed? Like the Pliny boy?"

Malvagna reeled as if I had struck him, then regathered his strength. "I will not fail you as I did him." He stood, set his hands on the table and leaned down close to me. "You will not escape while the Beast still has you," he said, then strode out of the room.

Burkett shook his head at the priest's back. "Catholics. He said he had business with you and Miss Mary. Should've known better than to trust one of them. My apologies, Dr. Johnson. No charge for breakfast."

I needed to tell Mary as soon as possible the truth about Malvagna. When I went into the kitchen, Mrs. Burkett stopped her work at the stove to look at me. Her eyes were red, her expression one of confusion and anger. Her daughters glanced my way with equally sad eyes and the occasional sniffle. Mary looked over from the large sink where she scrubbed pots.

"Can I help you, Doctor?" asked Mrs. Burkett.

I could not burden them by taking Mary out of the kitchen. "I just wanted to see how everyone was doing."

"We are doing our work," Mrs. Burkett said. "Is there anything else?"

"No," I said and returned to my table.

When Joanna next waited on me, I asked her to tell Mary to "use the passage" at her earliest convenience.

⊷━◉ ◉━⊷

I remained in my room through dinner and into the night, then finally heard footsteps in the passage behind the closet. The door cracked open.

"It's me, Joanna." She stepped into the room.

"Where is Mary?"

Joanna was in tears. She struggled for words. "Gone, sir." She held out an envelope.

"*Gone?*"

She nodded. "Her things, too."

I took the note, then she dashed back into the closet and back down the passage.

On the envelope, Mary had printed: "Read aloud." It was not in her usual flowing script, but rather in somewhat shaky block printing. She was gone and had taken her things. I knew how heartbroken she had been after the death of Joanna's aunt Bertie, but something was different. Something was wrong.

"Read it aloud," whispered the Gentleman. "It's what she wants. That more than anything is what you've been striving for, dear boy – to let Mary decide. Things will be so much easier for us both."

I turned to the Gentleman. "You look like a dog who has smelled a plate of meat."

"I only want what's best for all of us."

I decided to read the note silently first. It told her own story, that of a young woman who had made many mistakes and had come to the point where every action she took, brought the lives of those around her to chaos and darkness. This woman's folly had caused the death of Bertie Deneau. Further, she claimed to have paid a thug to attack Adelia Clavijo because she was jealous of her beauty and wisdom. But with her written confession, sent to the man who had rescued her, she hoped to free him of his bond, his obligation to her, so he could find happiness. She hoped that all would understand as she took this final step to be cleansed of her sins before paying the ultimate price for what she had done.

On the back Mary had written, "Be happy. Be with Adelia."

I could barely read the words through my tears.

"There, you see?" said the Gentleman. He sat beside me on the bed, as if he were a friend offering comfort. "This is her desire."

"Did you whisper in her ear?"

"I have been here, with you. No, dear boy, you must accept that this is her choice."

I raised the note to read it aloud. The paper shook in my trembling hands. The letters blurred as tears filled my eyes. I would not see Mary again. I tried to picture her, to find an image by which to remember her. That last time I had seen her had been …

"Malvagna," I said. "She had met with Malvagna just before writing this."

"Does that matter? She has made her choice."

"No. Not like this." I held the letter over the flame of the lamp and let it burn. "I will give her one more choice. If she still wants to end this way, I will grant her that wish. That is, after I end Malvagna."

CHAPTER FIFTY-EIGHT

CLEANSED

THE DARK ROAD BETWEEN THE ABANDONED church and the empty building was silent. There was no light in either place.

"You said you can sense him?" I asked the Gentleman.

His gaze darted about like a fox who picked up the scent of a wolf. "He has been here. But all I sense now are the two gaping maws. One is of that room where he kept the boy, and the larger one, the *church*."

"The room where he kept the boy? That had been emptied."

"Well, it seems he has filled it with his vulgar toys again." The Gentleman reached a hand towards the abandoned building. "It is as if there is a giant cauldron beyond those walls."

I slowly mounted the building stairs and lit the lantern I had brought. Then I drew the knife I had taken from the kitchen.

"If you go in that room," said the Gentleman, "I will not be able to help you. I hope you remember the words."

I tightened my grip on the knife. In times past, I would have fled from such a fight. But this was not the time for hesitation. It was time to make a choice.

"Malvagna!" I called as I entered the building. "I am here. Your prize." I stopped in the hall and listened but heard nothing. I moved further down the hall and came to the room where Pliny had been held. There were thick, white candles with gold crosses and brass basins of what had to be holy water. Crucifixes hung on the walls. In the far corner, on a crate turned sideways, was the Woodmore Family Bible.

"Know one thing," I called out "If you have hurt Mary, your faith will not shield you from me." I could feel the violence in my hands, in my heart. My hatred had burned away all fear. I wanted him to come out, to face me.

"You were right about me," I said as I moved past the torture room. "I have sided with the Beast. At least I admit it. You kill young boys in your saviour's name. He would be the first to condemn you." I stopped again, listening. I readied my knife, hoping he would charge at me so that it could find a home in his throat.

I heard movement in the next room along to my right. I moved slowly to its doorless entry, looking to each side. No sign of Malvagna. Then at the edge of the light of my lamp, I saw Mary on the floor. She was bound and gagged but breathing.

I circled her, looking for Malvagna before I knelt beside her and set down the lamp. I whispered to her as I started to cut her bonds, but she did not respond.

Then came a flash of light and pain. The world spun as I fell. In and out of consciousness, my hands were tied behind my back and I was dragged along the floor. Malvagna's Latin mutterings fell upon my ears. Soon, through the throbbing and spinning of my mind, I felt the quiet that came when separated from the Gentleman, the quiet of a church. That could only mean I was in Malvagna's torture room.

Forcing stillness in my mind, I caught a glimpse of Malvagna at the iron stove. He made the sign of the cross as he heated a knife.

I struggled to speak.

Malvagna turned to me. "Your Beast cannot help you in here. You should beg, plead for redemption."

Finally, I forced out a few quiet words.

Malvagna leaned down close to me. I could feel the heat of the red, glowing knife. "What did you say?"

"I tried begging once before. Look where it got me."

He smiled ruefully. "Because your heart was impure, your pleas were answered by the devil."

"What will answer you?"

Malvagna's expression turned to confusion, then sadness. "*Sancte Michael Archangele, defende nos in proelio et colluctatione.*"

My mind slowed in its spinning. Malvagna's words reminded me that I had some of my own. "*Iecuru gobejontu uru aioxt tu!*"

Malvagna staggered back as if struck and spilled one of the basins of holy water. "What … what have you done?" He took a crucifix in one hand and raised his knife with the other.

"*Iecuru gobejontu uru aioxt tu!*" I shouted.

He stumbled wildly and crashed to the floor, knocking over candles. I squirmed and rolled until I felt flames by my hands behind me.

Malvagna pushed himself to his knees.

"*Iecuru gobejontu uru aioxt tu!*"

I held a scream in my throat as the fire burned my hands and the rope until I could break free of my bonds. Cradling my blistered hands, I scrambled to my feet and kicked over more of Malvagna's protections.

Malvagna started to rise again. I kicked him backwards into another basin of holy water. As he struggled to move away and stand, I pulled down the crucifixes.

"Yes, dear boy." The Gentleman's voice came to my ears, but I could not see him. "Destroy it all. Let me in."

Malvagna was nearly on his feet. I took Mary's family Bible in both hands and struck him across the face with it, sending him reeling.

I moved to the stove.

"The last piece, yes," whispered the Gentleman. "Burn that vile tome."

"No!" Malvagna pushed himself up with one hand and reached for me with the other. "Look at what you're doing! What the Beast makes you do!"

Though I held it upside down, the words, "Woodmore Family Bible" in gold script, reflected the firelight at me.

"This I do of my own accord." I threw it in the fire.

Malvagna roared his horror and pushed himself upright.

The Gentleman formed fully in the room. "Thank you, dear boy."

"Do not thank me yet."

I kicked Malvagna down again, then picked up his knife. Cringing with pain from the burns, I stabbed him in the shoulder, cutting the tendons, then did the same on his other shoulder. Then more slashes and stabs to immobilize him, causing pain and bleeding, but not so much that he would bleed to death.

"He's harmless, dear boy," said the Gentleman. "You can get the police now."

"No," I said. "I have something else in mind."

I knelt on his back and pulled his head back by his hair, pressing the knife to his face just under his eye.

"Beg your God for help," I whispered in his ear, "for he is the only thing that can save you now." My blood dripped on him as the blade pierced his cheek.

"Dear boy," said the Gentleman, "what are you doing?"

"Testing the truth of what you've told me."

Malvagna's mouth moved with raspy whispers.

A fire ignited inside me. It seared my very being, my every pore. I screamed and fell backwards, away from Malvagna. I could no longer see the Gentleman as I writhed in pain.

A perfect circle of brimstone fire had formed around Malvagna.

The priest got to his knees. He gazed up, clasping his hands in prayer. "Father, into your hands I commend my spirit."

"Do you think that is your God before you?" I rasped, struggling to sit upright against the wall.

Malvagna slowly rose to his feet. "The blasphemer?" He turned his gaze on me. His eyes were wild, and he trembled with rage. "Yes, the blasphemer must die." He stepped from the ring of fading brimstone, his mouth spread in a predator's smile.

Using the wall to pull myself upright, I saw the knife I had held beside Malvagna on the floor. I tried to rush for it but fell from weakness. "That is the Beast," I shouted.

The priest turned his head as if listening. He nodded and his eyes alighted on the knife. He turned back to me. "All that comes from your mouth is a lie. I stand at the right hand of the Archangel Azrael to dispense justice and I begin with you."

Still weakened by having the Gentleman torn from me, I scrambled across the room on my hands and knees. He was gone, there was no doubt. But had he answered Malvagna's call? Or had the priest's prayers come true?

"*I must thank you, dear boy.*" The Gentleman's voice rang in my head, but it was no longer part of me. "*The papist will gladly torture and kill whomever I point him towards. The day will come when he will know the truth, and that will be a feast beyond even my imagining. I had no idea he could be so much fun!*"

I crawled towards the door, but Malvagna grabbed my foot and pulled me back. "Your evil burns you," he growled, standing over me.

Hot coals formed under my skin. I screamed as boils bubbled and burst. "It is the Beast!" I cried. "I *gave* it to you!" Would the realization paralyze him?

"Your lies harden your tongue," he said as he knelt over my chest.

My tongue became a stone lodged in my mouth, causing me to gag.

"The light of the Lord blinds you."

Darkness swallowed me. I awaited my death.

"With the righteous glory of God at my hand, I strike thee down!"

There were footsteps, then the unmistakable sound of a blade rending flesh and bone, yet I felt no pain.

After a moment of silence, a great weight fell on me. Light slowly returned to me, and in the greyness I could see Malvagna lying across my legs with a cleaver buried in his skull. Behind him stood Mary with tattered rope on her wrists, spitting out stray strands.

"William? Are you ... ?"

I reached for her as I pushed Malvagna off my legs. She helped me to my feet.

My tongue began to soften. We stood there as if we expected Malvagna to rise. I waited to hear the Gentleman's voice bragging that he was still there, that he was still with me and would be for eternity, but nothing came.

Mary and I turned to each other and embraced.

CHAPTER FIFTY-NINE

RECOVERY

MARY AND I STAGGERED OUT INTO the street shouting for help until we heard a constable's whistle. Before long the street was swarming with them.

Mary was given a blanket and helped into a police wagon while I led the constables to Malvagna's body. There was talk of arresting me for murder, but I convinced them to send for Dr. Walker. He arrived soon after, bleary and disheveled, but quickly vouchsafed for me. He insisted that Mary and I be taken to hospital.

While a doctor treated the burns on my hands, Mary wired Adelia. Upon our release, we were taken to the Clavijo estate to rest and heal. There were no secret passages here, but Adelia was kind enough to keep the staff busy so no one would know when Mary came to visit me.

"Your note," I said. "You gave me a choice, yes?"

She nodded. "It did seem a way out. I know that much of what you've done is because of the obligation you feel towards me. If that obligation was gone ..."

"Do you believe I would prefer Adelia over you?"

"There is an affection between you two, isn't there?"

"Yes, she is important to me, but not nearly as important as you. Would you prefer it if I courted someone else? Freed you from *your* obligation, so to speak?"

Mary blushed. "No, but at least now we can court only because we both want it."

"That is true," I said, and reached out a bandaged hand to her.

For a moment I expected to hear a remark from the Gentleman. Mary read my reaction and her face went ashen, her mouth agape. "He's still here?"

I looked about first, then closed my eyes. Even when he was not visible to me, I could feel his presence. I felt no such thing now.

"No, I have no sense of him," I said, looking at Mary. "I believe he died with Malvagna. My understanding was that the Gentleman was cursed to offer his help to anyone who begged for it while near death, then become attached to that person upon acceptance. He had no choice. Even though I felt the Gentleman leave me and saw the results of the changes, I still fear that …" I could not say it aloud, as if the words might be as a pin to a balloon. "If he is truly gone, I do not know how you are alive."

The realization darkened her expression. "Then that was all a lie? The things we did? The souls … ?"

"That may have been the case. All part of his manipulation. Or perhaps because of the transfer to Malvagna …" I shook my head. "It was a rash decision. I had no way of knowing whether it would work."

"But it did. And for that I will thank God every day for the rest of my life. I hope you'll do the same someday."

"I apologize for burning your family Bible, but I needed to be sure the Gentleman could come fully into the room. That was the last of the items that repelled him, and it seemed the most powerful."

Mary nodded. "I understand."

There was a knock at the door, and Adelia came in. After pleasantries, she told us what she had found.

"Malvagna had been trained in performing exorcisms, but according to a priest at one of his previous parishes, the idea of demons living inside people became a driving force in his life. It seemed he came to believe that virtually anyone could be so afflicted. While the priest to whom I spoke agreed that anyone *could* be possessed, Malvagna had come to think that virtually everyone actually *was*. He had a history of increasingly violent behaviour and was moved from parish to parish. Each time they believed they could pray it out of him."

I looked at Mary, but before I could say anything, she held up a hand to stop me.

"Because the prayers of those priests failed, that does not mean prayer doesn't work."

"I think that is perhaps what has kept you alive. Your prayers, your essential goodness somehow saved you from the fate described by the Gentleman. I know so little about how it all works, that seems as plausible as any other explanation. The most plausible is, of course, that he simply lied and manipulated us. Still, that doesn't seem wholly satisfying."

Mary threw herself on me then, shedding joyful tears and laughing with me at how much her sudden embrace hurt me, and how much I wanted it to continue. I needed it to continue. I needed something to distract my mind from the nagging feeling that this was not over, not completely.

The Gentleman had been quite emphatic that there was no escape. Still, I felt only Mary's kisses, not the deep chill that had accompanied the Gentleman.

And what of Malvagna's reaction to the words I had spoken, the ones given to me by the Gentleman? It seemed there was more to them than just a weapon against the priest. Had the Gentleman lied to me about their purpose? Perhaps the true lie was the one I told myself: that the Gentleman had truly been banished to Hell upon Malvagna's death.

THE END